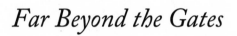

Far Beyond the Gates

Books by
PHILIP LEE WILLIAMS

NOVELS
Far Beyond the Gates
Emerson's Brother
The Divine Comics
The Campfire Boys
A Distant Flame
The True and Authentic History of Jenny Dorset
Blue Crystal
Final Heat
Perfect Timing
Slow Dance in Autumn
The Song of Daniel
All the Western Stars
The Heart of a Distant Forest

POETRY
The Color of All Things: 99 Love Poems
The Flower Seeker: An Epic Poem of William Bartram
Elegies for the Water

NONFICTION
It is Written: An Autobiography
In the Morning: Reflections from First Light
Crossing Wildcat Ridge: A Memoir of Nature and Healing
The Silent Stars Go By

CHAPBOOK
A Gift from Boonie, Seymour, and Dog

Far Beyond the Gates

A novel by

PHILIP LEE WILLIAMS

MERCER UNIVERSITY PRESS
Macon, Georgia
2020

MUP/ H982

© 2020 by Mercer University Press
Published by Mercer University Press
1501 Mercer University Drive
Macon, Georgia 31207
9 8 7 6 5 4 3 2 1

Books published by Mercer University Press are printed on acid-free
paper that meets the requirements of the American National Standard for
Information Sciences—Permanence of Paper for Printed Library
Materials.

Printed and bound in the United States.

This book is set in Adobe Caslon Pro.

Cover/jacket design by Burt&Burt

ISBN   978-0-88146-736-9

          978-0-88146-745-1 (eBook)

Cataloging-in-Publication Data is available from the Library of Congress

For *The Athens Observer*
And all my friends there
From 1978-1985

MERCER UNIVERSITY PRESS

Endowed by

TOM WATSON BROWN
and
THE WATSON-BROWN FOUNDATION, INC.

If there be one righteous person, the rain falls for his sake.

—Attributed to Gautama Buddha

Far Beyond the Gates

1. Lucy

And so I have returned to this life-long love, to his presence, up there in the grand house overlooking green valleys and feathered waterfalls. I have been a woman of small ambitions on a small scale, one of life's placid miniaturists, painting the world with tiny exact strokes. He has washed across history like a strong tide, up there with his Pulitzer plaque on a trivet, with his medallions and photographs, with his framed letters from Susan Sontag and Hannah Arendt, the wallpaper photographs of him and the famous. My father and Günter Grass. My father and Andrew Young. My father and Norman Mailer. I sit here on the long twisting trail below his house and dream myself into another life.

He is much worse than I feared when I got here from Oxford last night. The MS, just diagnosed six months ago, has left him sometimes numbed and worried. The latest medicines haven't helped. He is a wildly waving creature, sixty years old, and his fear fuels the MS like coal to a flame. He has had and has ignored symptoms for three years. The collapse came at a conference in Vancouver. He has now seen five doctors in Asheville and in the Research Triangle, and the diagnosis is the same: progressive, relentless, non-responsive.

We are consumed by what we fear most. As I have feared attachment, so solitude consumes me like a ravenous beast. James, back there almost in the shadow of Rowan Oak writing his endless novel, comes to see me, to ask me back, and I cringe and withdraw from his touch. But he comes less and less. He cannot finish his book for the same reason I cannot begin mine. Nor can I seem to end this gentle quarrel with Pratt McKay—when was the last time I called him Father? He has been Pratt almost since I remember.

I bought this journal at Square Books in Oxford just before I left. So I could tell him I was "doing my writing." So I could flee the sickroom and his scarecrow poses. And yet he begs me for affection with his eyes. His voice flutes and softens, though his words won't quite shape the vowels of love. His loving professional assistant, Victor Ullman, hovers and shields, hovers and shields, and so I can scarcely ask my father if we are bound by more than blood.

This place is beyond imagining. The sprawling mansion, Biltmore in miniature, decks cantilevered out over hundred-foot plunges—daring and dramatic. The landscaping alone would take three years' worth of my high school English teacher's salary. The house appears to have filled itself. There are souvenirs from Paris—a poster of Sylvia Beach and the young Hemingway in front of Shakespeare & Co.; a framed front page of a newspaper announcing the murder of Viola Liuzzo, one of the subjects of his prize-winning history of women of the Civil Rights Movement; a poster from the 1997 MLA meeting announcing his "sold-out" keynote speech called "Gender and Darkness: The Price They Paid"; a knuckle bone from the cemetery at Stratford-upon-Avon. A life's worth of prizes and cultural debris, the flotsam of academia.

In my apartment, I have nothing on the walls. I stupidly believe that such decoration is presumption. My Teacher of the Year Certificate lies moldering in my bedroom closet. I collect nothing. The place says: "Don't look for Lucy McKay here; you won't find her."

I did not want the grim certainty of my deliberate wreckage to follow me to this mountain. I am here for him, for my father. I want to believe in souls and their ability to suture the wounds of history. I want to walk through this magnificent gorge with a woman's brightened eyes. I want to lie with him, to curl against his breaking body. I want to stroke his hair as he once did mine.

I want to dare myself to love him again.

June 2

Spent all morning trying to get Pratt to work with his therapist, who refuses to be discouraged no matter what words break their silence.

"I would move my arm that way if I could, goddamnit," Pratt said, but his voice has weakened, and he can't make it sound angry enough. That frustrates him, and so he growled and then stopped by force of will. "Again."

"Dr. McKay, we need for you to push back against this thing," said the therapist, whose name is Ginger Dumont, ripe and not yet thirty, with a pale constellation of freckles across her pretty cheeks and nose. "Can you do that, Sweetie?"

"Don't fucking call me *Sweetie*," Pratt said, his voice breaking and broken. Then he smiled to show that we must think of this as *family* anger, shared and thus dispersed. Ginger stroked her arm and said something I could not hear.

I came outside on to the grounds and saw a tall bearded man directing three Mexicans who were clearing a corner for a new perennial bed. I walked over to him, and he turned, shearing me with aqua eyes and a slight smile.

"You must be Lucy," he said, his voice theatrical and testosterone-poisoned, deep. For a moment, I thought he was making fun of me, then I knew he wasn't.

"That's me," I said. "And you are?"

"Avoiding my dissertation, I'm afraid," he said. "Sean Crayton." He extended his huge hand and shook mine, and his skin was dry and rough and yet somehow damp and soft. "In landscape design. At Chapel Hill. Where your father's a professor. I know you must be proud of him."

"I must be," I said stupidly.

"I thought I wanted to teach this stuff in the classroom, but apparently I don't. Seems as if what I really want is a low-paying job running my own design and maintenance company. It leaves me time

3

to do the really high-paying things like reading and someday sculpting wood. I'm giving you my résumé, and you didn't even ask."

"Yes, I'm Lucy. What are you going to do then, Sean?"

"This, I guess. I had been thinking of wandering the Earth or going to law school, but neither of those pays well." I hated myself at that moment because I liked him so much. I run away from people who want me to like them. Pratt smothered me in high school, trying to get me into Harvard, where I didn't want to go. Instead, I went to Carton, modeled on the old Black Mountain School, a place where you can sit on a bench and call it an independent study. I did it to piss him off, and in the end he was too busy to fight me. So I transferred to FSU. My stupidities are legion.

"Maybe you could be a lawyer who wanders the Earth," I said.

"I'm so sorry about your father, Lucy," he said, suddenly serious. "I don't get to campus much—I've finished everything, as I said, but the dissertation. But he's famous, and people really admire him. Which I'm sure you know better than I do."

"Actually, I haven't been around much since I grew up. I teach high school English in Oxford, Mississippi."

"Been there," he nodded. He turned and spoke for almost a minute in fluent Spanish to the workers, who went to the truck for something. "Did the Faulkner thing. Went to his gravesite and threw pennies on it. Stood in his house gazing at his outline for *A Fable* on the wall of his study. Imbibed the milieu. Well, I've got to get back to work. How long will you be here?"

For the rest of my life. No. For the rest of the summer.

June 4

I say I do not understand men. I say I do not need a man. Then I see one, and my resolve is broken like a cheap vessel on the concrete floor of a pottery barn. Tried to talk with Pratt and did, a little.

4

This town, Haycombe, North Carolina: a lymph node in a mountain pass, with gated communities high on the mountains around it. Several other small towns nearby so that it seems like one blight, one long uncuttable knot where the metastasizing can be clearly diagnosed.

June 5

My mother called my cell phone today, the Thomas and Morene Schantz Professor of Art History at Duke University. Blah, blah, and blah. But I don't mean that. We talk once or twice a month, and she instructs me and speaks to me as if she's cornered a recalcitrant colleague at an international seminar. I love her desperately.

"He's not responding to anything," I say. "The demyelination seems to be increasing geometrically. Onset of the primary progressive variety is not uncommon in someone his age, they say. The CSF tests show oligoclonal bands. His hearing is worse. They're fitting him for hearing aids, and he's just outraged. No, that's the right word. *Outraged*. He still can't believe it happened to him. As if it has some nerve. So to speak."

"I can't find any cases of primary-progressive changing to relapsing-remitting," she lectures, ignoring my lame joke. "Seems pretty clear that T-cells are involved, but I don't think they know how yet. I found all this online. Amazing. Lot to learn. How's your high school job?" I bristle at her locution and choose not to respond. She has always acted as if this is something I am doing until I come to my senses.

"How are *you*?" I ask. "Are you happy?"

"Gerald and I have a new book coming from Oxford next year," she says excitedly. "Number four. Yep. Four books with Oxford. Very satisfying, as you know."

No, Mother, I do not know that. I am starting to forget your face. And I can still remember how you smelled right after shaving your legs when I was seven and believed nothing ever changed.

I hear Pratt mumbling in his room at night, through the wall. So sad.

June 6

Pratt had a visitor, someone who moved into this fairyland, gated-community world two years ago: Ella Seitz. She resembles a Bauhaus practice-model of plastic surgery; her flesh is not of flesh. The only things that move on her face are the eyes, wild purple irises (in both senses) that appear to be plotting an escape. She suffers from acute echolalia, blows her nose every thirty seconds, and swings a clattering drapery of gold jewelry with each motion of hand or leg.

"So you moved here two years ago?" I ask.

"...years ago. Yes. Is it hot in here? Pratt, you look good, you really do. Maybe Jerry Lewis will find a cure soon."

"That's MD, not MS, and they're nothing alike," says Pratt, whipping all over the chair where he cannot rest. "And Jerry Lewis is dead."

"...nothing alike," agrees Ella. "I send money every year to Jerry Lewis. But I always wait until he cries. I don't send a *penny* until he cries. That's when I know he means it."

"How is Golo?" asks Pratt, each word carved from sheer mad effort.

"...is Golo," nods Ella. "Well. *Well.* He and his research *ahem* assistant are in Colorado working *ahem* on the book about about about. Her name is *Barbara*. That Barbara." Ella nods fiercely with meaning. I can't stand it and drift off.

I walked to the back deck, which makes Hitler's Eagle's Nest in Bavaria look like a trailer park in Arkansas. Across the valley is Angel Hair Falls, and that white strand, shimmering with froth and gravity, catches sun and won't let it go. My cell phone began to play "My Woman Done Gone," a Leadbelly tune. Lona Belle.

"Hey, woman, how are the Great Smokies?" she asked. She talks too loud, almost braying when excited. My friend and fellow teacher of senior English, though we usually do only *The Sound and the Fury*.

"It's hard, Lona Belle," I said honestly. "I don't like it. I don't. The whole damned thing."

"Oh. Look, remember Janie Lucas being sick all spring?" Janie, our favorite student, wildly creative, plain as a shovel, quiet as a tree. I go *um*. "Well, what she came down with was pregnancy."

"Oh, God. No. What's she going to do?"

"Have it. She won't say who the father is, and I can't even guess. She's never dated. Some boy told her he loved her, at least for half an hour in the back seat of a car, and she must have felt like a Disney princess. I'm not telling this good. Faulkner tells it better."

We spoke for fifteen minutes about the webs of our life: the petty scandals, the weather, not politics, our bodies and the bodies of others. Our friends' hair. Gardening and cooking. Faye Larson, who has had cancer for twenty years.

"What can you see from that deck?" she asked.

"…see from that deck," I said.

June 7

Victor Ullman, who is living here for the summer, handles bills, phone calls, workers, academia, and invitations for Pratt to speak, meals, home health. He is probably thirty, his hair pre-professorial-gray, and he stays in motion, always. He takes dictation from Pratt, a new book about two southern sisters who moved to the North and became Abolitionists in the mid-Nineteenth Century. Pratt's narrative is filled with side trips and *culs de sac*, interpolations about his academic enemies and former students, most of whom have published little past the cleaned-up versions of their dissertations. Victor writes down every word and tape records them, too, and Pratt is all over the chair, stopping to curse about his numbness and thickening speech.

"Pratt, can I get you anything?" I ask.

"*I'm* here," says Victor. He looks at me like a wildcat whose kitten has been threatened.

"So you are," I say.

I take a walk down the street and am hailed by a clearly retired couple in their pre-sickness years, twin tans gleaming in the mountain light. They're the Beardens, they say, Betty and Hunt.

"Hunt was chief historian at the Gettysburg National Battlefield for ten years," Betty says, using well-educated consonants. Their house seems modest from the street, but then I notice that if it has little breadth, it has insane depth. "You're Pratt's daughter from Mississippi, aren't you? We have a daughter in Memphis." I wait to hear that she's cancer researcher or a corporate lawyer.

"What does she do in Memphis?"

"She's a singer-songwriter," says Hunt. "We're so proud of her. She has a CD. Doesn't she, Mother, a CD?"

"She sounds a little like Judy Collins but with a vibrato," says Betty. "You're here for the summer? Poor Pratt, he's had such a hard time, and it came on so quickly." I realize suddenly that Betty Comes From Money. You tell that Breeding instantly.

"You teach high school in Oxford," says Hunt. He's not tall but so lean and warm-eyed that he has an enormous presence. Betty adores him hopelessly. "I taught high school history for 10 years before I got my master's and went with the Park Service. I was at Shiloh and then at Antietam, and I ended up at Gettysburg."

"We say he fought most of the war, and the only weapon he had was his mouth," says Betty. "We would like it so much if you could come visit when you want to get away from it. We know what it's like to be around illness like that."

"Lost a son," says Hunt. "Had lymphoma. He was nine. Hardest thing I've ever faced in my life. He passed in 1965, and he's still the first thing I think of every morning when I wake up. We tell stories, don't we? We turn the world into narrative. You come down here and visit us when you feel like it's more than you can stand."

"For us, it was Howard and Lou Smithing. They took us in when Jimmy died. I cried for a year. Not that it's the same thing. *Smithing*. Strange name, wasn't it, honey?"

"Strange name," said Hunt Bearden. "You come down here when you need to talk it out. I'm serious. We need rain. Lord we need rain."

He looked at the sky as if the clouds would take pity on us all and weep.

June 8

On the deck, I watched for rain myself and read Julia Glass. I can't read with sunglasses, so I squinted my eyes from word to word, like someone free-climbing slowly up El Capitàn. I heard a throat-clearing and turned to see, oh my God, Sean Crayton, standing there in cutoffs and work boots, his white socks slid down his sun-stroked legs and flopped over like a little boy's. He wore sunglasses, attached to a thick cord that draped up and around his neck. His beard glistened with sweat. Closer, I could smell him, pheromones and madly marvelous sweat. I tried not to look there, but I did, and he saw me, caught me. Shit.

Victor came swooping through the French doors like a gleeful predator. He literally intercepted Sean before he could get closer.

"You'd be wanting to settle up," Victor said feyly. He tilted the plane of his face up like a dare. He believes wholly in his superiority. One eyebrow arched up as if to say: *I control everything here, and do not think you can take my place.*

"I would *not* be wanting to settle up," said Sean. I wanted to hug him. "I would be wanting to speak with Ms. McKay here on a matter not directly related to landscaping or to business. Even, yea, to academia."

"Meaning what?" bristled Victor.

"Meaning I would be wanting to speak with Ms. McKay here on a matter not directly related to landscaping or to business. Even, yea, to academia." He turned his whole body in the middle of the sentence toward Victor, who shrank backward and turned and slipped back inside.

"*Even yea to academia?*" I said. I burst into laughter. "Landscapers sure do have odd speech in these parts."

"I could caulk a sidewalk with that man's demeanor," said Sean, and I laughed again. He didn't take off his black shades, just stood there grinning at me.

"You'd be wanting to settle up," I said.

"Actually, I was hoping you'd let me pick you up around five-thirtyish tomorrow to go get a beer and engage in deep conversation about Gabriel García Marquez or under which conditions of general relativity waterfalls would start to go backwards."

"They then wouldn't be water*falls*," I said.

"They'd be water*sucks*," he said. "The little burg of Harwich, which is seven miles south, has a brew pub that makes something called Communion Pilsner. It's a little heavy, but it sings on the tongue. Am I getting anywhere at all?"

"Maybe you can finish your dissertation over Communion Pilsner," I said.

"I'm busted. You have a mean memory, Lucy. Would mind going on my bike?"

"Your bike?"

"Motorcycle. Don't worry, it's the most unsafe vehicle on the highway, and you'd probably want a double Communion Pilsner when you got there. Plus, I'm a terrible driver."

"Maybe a car, then."

"A cranberry Prius. Save the whales, hug a redwood, sing Woody Guthrie songs. Or we can just glower and emote."

He grinned, this huge, happy beardy grin, and, oh my God. Lucy McKay, what in the *hell?*

Victor, bless the gods, has gone back to Chapel Hill to get Pratt's mail and do whatever sycophants do in their off hours. That gave Pratt and me a chance to talk this morning. I rolled him on to the cool deck and wrapped him snugly in a blanket against the mountain chill, holding a cup of tea to his lips for sipping occasionally. He *can* still hold a cup without spilling it, but I wanted to help. His arms and legs thrashed constantly beneath the cover so that he looked like a butterfly trying to escape from its cocoon.

"I want to...go to...Mmmayo Clinic," he said. His voice patterns are odd, like a Dizzy Gillespie riff. Then: "No, don't want...goooo...to to Mmmayo Clinic." Then he pounded the chair arm with his fist. I won't try to recreate his speech beyond this—I can't bear it. Then, Pratt, turning to me: "I have something to tell you."

"What?"

"I was so young. So young. A girl and I...she became...pregnant." A huge crow, laughable omen, landed on the deck rail and coughed and muttered for five seconds while I pondered how to respond. Another landed alongside it, and they quacked softly, like confidential ducks, before lifting off. He looked devastated, as if he had meant to tell it in a better way and had blurted it out badly.

"Excuse me?"

"Rachel Moates. Had my daughter."

"My God." I felt my blood kin extending across America, silent sister, adopted siblings, on and on. I tried to say anything else, failed.

"Rachel. In college. I knew better. I wasn't drinking or anything. I just thought: It doesn't matter. Nothing matters. I was wrong. Everything matters."

"My God."

"You're the atheist," he said. "I'm the Episcopalian. I've wasted my life. I don't mean professionally, of course. I'm stable about my professional life. But the personal thing—not so good. Not so good."

He had never spoken to me like that, and I warmed to him, scooted my chair close, lay my hand on his arm.

"I'm in shock, Pratt. What was she like? Rachel, I mean."

"I don't want to talk about it."

"You just did. You can't tell me something like that and then re-treat."

"God*damn* crows," he said, using the second part of *goddamn* as a verb. Then he took off on a long, confused explanation of his new research, of vindictive colleagues, of the surface along which academic men skid in this life, pleasing and pleasing and pleasing others, then dying alone and lost. I refused to listen anymore and put him to bed, and he thrashed and just before dropping off to sleep called Victor's name. His home health nurse, Mary Lou Wadely, arrived just as I got Pratt into bed. She's tall and strong, lovely and with intelligent eyes. She spoke as if she were teasing me, as if she already knew the an-swers to her questions. She seemed familiar and warm.

"Your father with all these people," she said, pointing to the gal-lery on the hall wall. "Who is that one?" She spoke softly and know-ingly. Was this a question or a gentle test?

"That's Pratt and Susan Sontag and Harold Bloom."

"Are they friends of his? That Susan should do something about that skunk stripe in her hair. Wouldn't take five minutes."

"That was her signature. She's dead now."

"I declare. To leave that on purpose. People surprise you all the time, don't they?" She said it like a joke—was it? She sounds more educated than she lets on and must be. The cant of her head, the gen-tleness of her voice. She is trying to soothe me.

It's just before five, and I'm not yet ready for Sean Crayton. I'm *so* ready for Sean Crayton. And my god, what do I do now?

June 10

Father Tanner here too early, arriving just as the hovering Victor does. Hard to believe there's a parish just for the gated communities in this lair of the wealthy, but he is tennis-trim and pleasantly unpretentious. Victor arrives with a double-arm-load of mail and papers for Pratt, coming in the door with a ring of keys in his teeth, as if he's been hunting in the topiary and just caught it.

James calls from Oxford early—before ten—and says he got two more letters from agents reporting that his unfinished manuscript doesn't sound like something they'd want to represent. He luxuriates in artistic depression for four minutes before I tell him I have to go, that he's my ex, and I don't want to sound angry, but I don't really care, not today. Which is what he wanted to hear, of course, his permission to start drinking before noon, Faulkner except without the talent. I lived with drafts of his first novel for years, four hundred pages of increasingly nebulous throat-clearing and faux *Light in August* imitations. It was as if he'd read Faulkner in a bad translation and mistook it for Art.

So here I am, halfway down the mountainside, having walked along the community's community trails, sitting on an expensive, recently shellacked park bench with a view of a small fountain of a stream that gushes, manly, toward the bottom of the V. Here I am, trying to think of what to say about *him*.

The brew pub was nouveau Black Forest, with heavy steins and wallpaper of Mad King Ludwig's Wagnerian castle. I loved it. We took a snug, high-backed booth, and Sean ordered a pitcher of Communion Pilsner, and god*damn*. It was dark *and* light, and he let it foam in his beard, then he licked it off and raised one assessing eyebrow.

"Holy shit," I said after a long gulp. "This *is* good."

"Not the best blessing over Communion Pilsner, I'd say. The Church hasn't sanctioned the use of *Holy Shit* since the Council at Nicæa."

"I meant to say *Holy Fuck*," I whispered, leaning over the table, wearing my own beer mustache and leaving it there.

"That one's good," he nodded. "It was out for awhile, but it snuck back in during Vatican II."

I tried madly to find a chink in the conversation to tell him about Pratt's bombshell, to use the story to plug a hole in this conversational dam. The time never came. I felt myself melting beneath his exuberance and smart-assedness, and for awhile we became Dorothy Parker and Robert Benchley, with one-ups and bon mots enough to wear us both out. And yet I wasn't worn. I felt myself getting drunk after time and told him.

"Ah, the point of luxuriance," he said, toasting the moment. "One of the main differences between men and women. A man will drive right off that cliff into drooling drunkenness, but a woman will get right to the edge and drive straight along it for two hours without going over. Most women. Well, some don't. When I was an undergraduate, I knew a girl named Heather Ann Nelfman. *Nelfman.* When she introduced herself, it sounded like she was about to sneeze." I was laughing helplessly. "Heather Ann always said she didn't want anything if she couldn't have too much of it. Some of the more-Royal minded guys started calling her Heather Ann Nelfman, OBM." I looked blank. "Out before midnight. If this were a cautionary tale, I'd explain how she was killed in a wreck or got liver cancer. Life isn't a cautionary tale, Ms. McKay. She's now assistant vice president of a bank in Raleigh and has one point five children. I swear."

I can't believe I remember all of what he said. I can't believe I am writing it in this journal. Nothing else. No hug, no goodnight kiss. Just back here to Pratt's and: "See you around, Lucy McKay." Which was enough.

June 11

Communities aren't gated to keep anyone in. They're gated to keep the Unlike out. You can be crazy like Ella Seitz as long as you are wealthy. In my apartment building back in Oxford are: Rico, the Cuban who dresses like a pimp and works as a shift supervisor at a poultry plant; Luna Marcovic, transplanted Eastern European of vague lineage who is a cutter at Hair Today, a mall-hugging style salon; Bobby Vunal, who is idly poor; and Dwight Peale, a woman—I'm not kidding—whose father was a faithful Republican and saddled his girl with the name Dwight—she's a substitute rural postal carrier. There is Doreen, my fellow high school teacher. She plays the Eagles and corrects algebra papers all night. And, of course, there are the Ole Miss students, dozens of them, black and white, who drink and plot getting laid all hours of the day and night.

Who are you, Lucy McKay? Should you be locked in here or locked out?

Pratt's nighttime mumbling getting worse. Is he praying? Does he speak to God?

June 12

This morning, I provoked A Scene with Victor. He was taking dictation from Pratt, and I went in and said I wanted to be alone with my father.

"He's *dictating*," said Victor, as if I were trying to drown out an Oracle. "Come back when he's not doing work."

"Get your ass out of here right now," I said coldly. Pratt smiled and thrashed and didn't try to stop the unfolding scene. He always loved being fought over. When I was a little girl, and Mother knew he had been seeing another woman—which one I can't recall right now—he taunted and provoked her constantly. Once he even said,

"Honey, for God's sake, if you love me, fight for me!" She told him to go to hell, and he said, "Good. Good start."

So V. went storming out, muttering about what is lost and what is saved. He dropped his notebook, and I picked it up and said, "Don't forget the Holy Writ." He tried to give me a withering look, but it fell flat. Pratt was uncharacteristically quiet, even smug. His waving sorrow seemed to control itself.

"That wasn't like you," he said. "Wasn't like you. No. Not like you."

"Pratt, why did you tell me that story about you fathering a baby as a college student? Was that true, or did you just say that to see how I would react?"

"We believe what is true is good," he said, warming up. "And what is good is true. We are all taught that. But everything in life is built on fabrication. And we call these lies narrative. You have your narrative, and I have mine. You have a story about why your marriage failed, and so do I. You have a reason why you have settled for so little, and I have a story about why I have needed so much. Narratives."

It was the longest speech he'd given since I had arrived and made me think of his long-winded lectures when I was a teenager, filled with homilies and aphorisms culled from whatever he was researching at the time. I got the same thing from Mother, the art historian, who, when asked what I should wear to a prom, would launch into a lecture on the clothing of subjects in Hans Holbein or something.

"Bullshit. It's bullshit, and you don't know the difference. Did you or did you not father a baby when you were in college? I want to know the truth."

"The truth?" cried Pratt McKay. "And where did you ever get the idea that such a thing even exists?"

June 13

Sweet, sad Timothy Sain—where are you now? Student in my senior honors English class, who came to me that rainy January afternoon wanting to talk about Andrew Marvell. Where have you gone? You were willowy—headed for the certainty you did not yet know. You were bullied and mocked, and you had a finer heart than any of them.

You came to me after school that day—I was grading papers and planning for the next day. James and I were breaking down but not yet breaking up. He believed that the more he drank the more artistic he became. He simply got drunker. And I had no girlfriend-confidante in those days, and of course neither Pratt nor the Thomas and Morene Schantz Professor of Art History at Duke were there for me. So you came, Timothy Sain.

"Ms. McKay?" Your small thin voice in the doorway. I said, "What?" You said, "There is this poem in our book, and I can't stop reading it. I'm afraid something is wrong that I can't stop reading it." Too shy to speak in class, too kind not to suffer, Timothy Sain. I told you to come in and tell me. You did, and your shoes did not make a sound on that industrial and mud-stained tile.

"Which poem is it?" And I heard my own voice soften as my sentence came out, word by word. You read it. One I knew so so so well. And in the last stanza, your halting voice broke:

> *Let us roll all our strength and all*
> *Our sweetness into one ball,*
> * And tear our pleasures with rough strife*
> *Through the iron gates of life:*
> *Thus, though we cannot make our sun*
> *Stand still, yet we make him run.*

And you said, "I don't know what it means, but I *feel* that I do. How could I know what something means without knowing what it means?" And I sat there in the gloom of a quiet high school class-room, trying not to start falling apart again, fighting it wildly, in all directions. And I must have said silly academic things to you rather than saying "Love before it's too late, and love even if it makes no sense and does not last, even if you only wind up with a hatful of rain."

Now, on another rainy day when I am here, bound by my fa-ther's illness and wondering if Sean Crayton will call again, or if I want him to, I think of you, Timothy Sain. And I remember that I said nothing of value and that when you left, looking as if you loved me, the voice of your eyes was deeper than all roses.

June 14

Victor and I took Father to the neurologist in Asheville, and I gave up and let V. wheel him up the handicapped ramp, speaking all the while about problems with his dissertation, which is on women of the Un-derground Railroad. Pratt is directing it of course—for seven years he has been directing it. I understand that V. plans never to graduate and that Pratt likes it that way.

The office is filled with pastel prints of scenes without people. A courtyard overflowing with new growth and life. A seashore with huge waves that break like a whisper on smooth stones. A tree-lined small-town street in perfect order, permanent and dreamed. All to say: *You are not here. You are not suffering. You will live forever.*

Pratt is eight minutes late getting in, and he keeps looking at his Rolex and muttering in disbelief, and V. takes up a mantra against the AMA, the United States of America, and traffic. I don't even try to fight Victor when they called Pratt's name—all three of us go back.

A beautiful nurse—gorgeous really—named Nikki comes in and takes Pratt's vitals. Nikki moves in her body with such grace and as-surance that I should dislike her, but I can't. I am a stranger in my own body these days, and my face isn't mine anymore—I have no idea who looks back when I'm washing in the morning. We help Pratt from the wheelchair on to the examining table, and his slacks slide up his ankles, and V. touches him just above the foot.

"Need to shave your legs," jokes V. My father gives a single violent shake of his head, not to say no, but to argue that nothing in his situation can feel good. It takes twenty minutes more for Dr. Hugh Retherston to come alpha-maleing into the examination room, draped with a red-tubed stethoscope. He has graying temples and a waist he can't quite control. Victor launches himself into a hovering speech, and Dr. Retherston waves him off with his hands and eyes. I want to kiss him.

"I'm the daughter, Lucy," I explain, and I hate my tone, ingratiating, seeking approval. He looks blank. "I live in Mississippi." He nods blankly. "I teach high school."

"I always say public school teachers should get combat pay," he says, eyes brightening to remember something appropriate. "What do you teach?"

"English literature."

"Good for you," he says, turning to Pratt. V. clears his throat loudly and meaningfully. The examination takes less than fifteen minutes, and it is clear he thinks Pratt is worse. He says it this way: "We certainly face increasing challenges. We will do the best we can, of course. We want to make sure your discomfort stays in a range you can handle as the months pass. So let us know about the efficacy of your palliatives." I swear to God he says that. *The efficacy of your palliatives.* Pratt laughs bitterly. Victor hovers.

I say almost nothing on the way back to the community. I am weak.

June 15

Idiot. I drove through every street in Cedar Acres, the name of our fenced-in sanctuary, looking for Sean Crayton at work. Me, in my twelve-year-old Honda with a dented fender and untossed fast-food trash and jumper cables in the back seat. I saw four different land-scaping companies at work, or rather I saw their Mexicans, in constant motion, wasting neither effort nor time. An unsmiling woman waved me down.

"Dear, are you lost?" she asked unpleasantly.

"Yes," I said. "Completely." Then, without waiting for directions, I rolled away from her as she stood, arms akimbo, at the edge of a perfect lawn leading to perfect shrubbery and then a perfect house.

Idiot. Sunday?

June 16

Colleagues from the U, mostly women, here to plan a fundraiser for Save Our Mountains, a left-wingish, Green Party plan to stop the cutting of trees for development in the Smokies. *Here!* In the Community, behind its gates, where thirty acres must have been slashed and burned to insert mcmansions! Victor gave the gatehouse nine names, and a tenth came, and it took everything but a Congressional order to get her in. Not one of them saw the irony. The house absolutely floated on aggrieved estrogen, and I fled.

The golden Beardens waved at me, puttering in their perfect yard. Father Tanner in mufti, in his own yard, tending roses or giving them rites. I drove through the gates and waved at the guard, a six-tyish man with iron-gray hair and a spare tire; a sidearm, even. I moved on a few miles to a rare-book store my father has repeatedly asked me to visit. It is called (like many) Dogear and is filled with dangerously high shelves and the close, wonderful warmth I always feel in the Strand when I go to Manhattan.

I remember James's epiphany in NY not long after we met there. We spent a rainy afternoon in the Strand, and I bought Aldous Huxley's letters, and he bought Carlos Baker's biography of Hemingway. Later, back at his awful apartment, where we were inevitably heading,

James stood looking into the alleyway from his bedroom window and said, "I am going to be a writer, Lucy. I *know* I can be a great writer. Will you let me try and be a great writer?" *Let* him? I'd just *met* him. But he was gorgeous, I was besotted, and fool that I was, etc.

In truth, *I* was the great writer who never matured, who discovered that teaching is more important. And it is. I will believe it until death and past it. But poor James. Dreams drain us finally, send us back to the mirror, where we see ourselves horribly in focus. And then we drove back to Athens, where I was finishing my master's in education, and James's "Oh, my God, Lucy—Oxford!" And us piling our few belongings in the U-Haul trailer and lugging it across the South, him reading and marking Baker, and me driving, miserable Alabama hours.

In Dogear. A guttering AC whose outside unit had a clattery fan blade. But, oh, my God what a place—maps, rare and used, sheet music, impossible to find much-loved old volumes. The inexpensive (an old New Directions copy of *The Wall* by Sartre: three bucks) and the priceless (signed first edition of *Ulysses*: thousands and thousands). The owner, a dusty old man named Olaf Knussen (I'm not kidding), who sat in an ancient glass-walled office reading and licking his finger for page-turns. On his desk was a photograph of a woman about my age with a little boy, her son I guessed.

"I don't think you've had the pleasure of meeting me before," said a deep male voice. I nearly jumped through a tall bookshelf of biography. I was trapped in one of the many cul-de-sac neighborhoods of Dogear. He stood leaning on Albert Camus, a multiply shaved (or so it looked) Fifties Playboy, complete with a flowing blue silk shirt and an ascot! His shoes (I always look at shoes) were out-of-the-box tassel loafers. Crisply pleated black wool trousers. Perfectly manicured fingernails. I wanted to laugh so badly it hurt.

"Excuse me," I said, hoping he would let me pass. He folded his arms over his chest.

"I'm the ridiculous Howard Reuther," he said. "I have a red Jaguar convertible." My blank face. "You're supposed to find me repulsive at this point and flee but then think about me later." Now I did laugh. He *was* ridiculous.

"If this is your come-on line, I can't imagine many women have come on," I said.

"Besides, you're married," he said. "That's what you're supposed to say. Go ahead and tell me you're married."

"I'm married."

"You see, *everyone* is ridiculous. I just decided to come out of the *ridiculous* closet. I don't really have a Jaguar. And you're probably not married."

"I am married."

"Actually, I really do have a Jaguar. Want to see it?"

"Sure. But I'm married." Olaf Knussen paid no attention to us. We went out the front door, on which a jingly entrance bell had been mounted. Indeed, Howard Reuther did have a Jaguar, an antique, cherry red, a two-seat convertible from the Sixties.

"I'm very good at accents," he explained. "Say the following sentence, and I'll tell you within thirty miles where you are from." He babbled something, and I repeated it. "You're from around Manchester, New Hampshire. Am I right?"

"Nailed me," I said.

"Okay, I can't tell where people are from by their accents. Lied. I'm a liar. Part of being ridiculous. Actually, I'm a professional loser. Would you like a ride?"

"Of course not. I have to tell you, the ascot is embarrassing."

"It is, isn't it?" he crowed. "I'd have a cigarette holder, too, except that it interferes, so they tell me [rolling his eyes in a fey way here] with my chemo. Pancreatic cancer. I'm on my farewell tour."

"You're a liar," I said. "You already told me that."

"Not about *th-at*," he sang, getting into the Jaguar. Suddenly a profound, shocking change came over him. His face turned sheet-white, and diamonds of sweat appeared all over his cheeks. He folded and groaned, and then threw himself back in the seat. His eyes rolled.

His hands trembled on the wheel. It wasn't an act. Sickness roared off him, feral and flailing.

"My God, are you all right?"

"No," he whispered. He started the car and put it into gear. His voice was a husk. "Just ridiculous." And he was gone in a poof of dust. Maybe it was cirrhosis. Maybe it was an audition. But I don't think so. It shook me.

When I got home, the group was arguing, with some heat, over whether only old-growth forests should be protected or, as one woman said, "Every tree! Every goddamn tree in the goddamn forest!" I went to my room and had a headache.

June 17

Today I argued with Victor over grocery shopping. In a fury, I told him I would do it, that this wasn't his house, and Pratt was *my* father. V. said there were twenty-three kinds of yogurt, and how would I know which one to get? How would I know? I gave in, and he went shopping.

I called Sean's cell phone in the afternoon and got voice mail, hung up. I feel itchy with desire. I know my cycle better than Lance Armstrong ever did his. Sean hasn't called me because I'm older than he is, practically *old*.

Pratt lectured me bitterly on what a fool Simone de Beauvoir was to stick with Jean Paul Sartre all those years. "You know what he was?" he asked. "He was nothing!" His laughter at the joke was like a rake on a rusted drum.

Mary Lou Wadely, his lovely nurse, came into Pratt's study where I was surfing the Internet. My dad was taking his nap.

"What's it like in Mississippi?" she asked. "I've never been there."

"You've never been to Mississippi?"

"I've traveled, but I've managed to miss Mississippi. So to speak. Of course I know about what happened there. Your father wrote about it."

"It *was* a very terrible place for a very long time," I said. "It's not much like that now. But even when it was a wilderness, it had art. I can't explain that. Have you ever read Faulkner?"

"I've read *The Sound and the Fury*. You want to protect Benjy, don't you? To keep him from having to go out into this world alone?" Her tone surprised me, warm and close and meaning more than I understood.

"I guess I do. I don't know. When I read Faulkner I'm not in this world anymore. I'm in his, and it's a dark place sometimes, but it's also very beautiful in its way. It's a mystery. Nothing is what it seems. Everyone thinks they know what's going on, and they're usually wrong."

"I guess that's what life is," she said softly. "Trying to tell yourself a story your whole life, as if that might make it come true. But it never does, sweetie. Never does."

Her close comfort and gentle wisdom shook me. But I suppose that's what a nurse must be—guardian of body and soul if she is to have any chance at helping a patient heal. I like her more than I can say, and I love the ease with which she navigates her aging but still lovely body.

I hate my body. I can't *stand* looking at it in the mirror. My boobs droop. That's the only word for it. My nipples are taking dead aim on gravity. Soon they will be pointing, like Jules Verne, toward the center of the Earth. My labia have always been a mess, like an overripe, about-to-wither flower. The inner lips half an inch too long and hanging down, like a clown pooching out his mouth for a laugh. As if they're about to emit a Bronx cheer. Remember how, on the fifth date with James, when it was clear we'd do the deed, you spent an hour folding them up inside in case he got a look? And he did, and they were like tropical petals, rouged with autonomic anticipation, hanging like a for-sale item in a hot-house?

My ass is getting saggy, too, I think. But maybe we overrate how much men need. Maybe they don't need perfection. Maybe they are as worried as we are. But they never show it, damn it. And it's not fair, the roaming Alpha Males of the world, exuding confidence and bonhomie while we fire off estrogen in every direction like pollen blown from a field of daisies.

The betrayal of my body is small next to Pratt's. He should be in his Glory Days, enjoying the fruits of Pulitzer and incipient Golden Years. But he is having some trouble controlling his arms and legs, though he still has good days when he can move around quite well without crutch or wheelchair. And his bathroom functions have begun to trouble him—my God, I can't imagine the humiliation. There is more than Victor between us. But how do I break it down?

June 18

Ella Seitz over with a Bundt cake, its thin white icing looking glial, metastatic.

"Thank you so much for that, Ella," struggled Pratt.

"…for that, Ella," said Ella.

June 19

I took a long walk through the Community in the early morning air, hoping it would shred the ennui. I desperately want out of here. I want to drive my little blue Honda with the fast-food trash and the jumper cables back to Oxford and not think about Pratt. I want to walk to Square Books and buy a paperback and go read it in the cemetery, hanging out with Billy Faulkner and Estelle. I passed Betty and Hunt Bearden, who were up in their matching walking suits, holding hands as they walked. They saw my pensiveness, I suppose, and waved as they passed. I hated them. I didn't hate them. I just hated their happiness.

I had on white short-shorts and a teal shell top, and the shorts weren't tight, so I had my cell phone in my pocket, and it went off, buzzing right down near my crotch. Not a day too late, either. I almost didn't answer it because it felt so good. Then I did.

"I've been waiting for you to call me," the smiling voice said. Sean Crayton. I could hear him grinning through his beard. "I thought the woman always called the man now. Or didn't we almost make it after all?" He was referencing a Whitney Houston song, for God's sake. I felt as if I'd left my voice in another set of clothes. He waited two beats. "Or maybe I've misread the tenets of mainline feminism again. Not impossible. I'm coming by to get you around five this afternoon so we can celebrate."

"Celebrate what?" My thin voice came back like the Prodigal Daughter.

"*Thursday*, ma chère," he said in a Pepé Le Pew accent. Then, in his own rough and laughing tone: "Don't Mississippi women celebrate Thursday? It's practically a holiday in the great state of North Carolina."

"What are we going to do? Dinner and dancing?"

"Flying to the top of Marlow Bald," he soothed. "On my I-promise-to-drive-like-a little-old-lady motorcycle. Safe, I promise. It's not a well-visited place. But it is a clean, well-lighted place. Just not well-visited." He was flirting with me in the street at 8:30 in the morning. My hand, my goddamn adolescent hand, was shaking.

"I'm afraid of those things," I said.

"You *will* have to hold on to me, but I can demonstrate how it can be done in a brotherly way, rather than the standard clutch-and-grab method, if the one seems too familiar." Does anyone else in the world talk like that? I heard an odd, hiccupping sound, and I realized it was my giggly laughter. Oh, my God.

Dear diary: It is four-thirty, and I'm already showered and dressed and waiting for him. *Dear diary?* More in the afterlife.

Oh, Jesus. What in the hell are you doing, Lucy McKay, thirty-something high school English teacher? Tell! Tell *whom*? My phantom sister? I have tried not to think of that since Pratt told me. He won't tell me anymore. Maybe he is not a liar. Maybe he suffers with his truth.

I *did* hold on to Sean on his motorcycle, and I was not prepared for the roaring vibrations between my legs. By the time we had ascended three thousand feet to an old and little-used Ranger lookout, I felt as if I'd been straddling a vibrator for half an hour. I kept shifting to arrive but it was too strange—never got there. When we stopped I was so shaky I could barely walk for two or three minutes. He wore work clothes but smelled of soap and shampoo, and I wanted to gnaw the clothes off his back.

"Behold the world, which I will give you, if you but fall down and worship me," he said, extending his arm toward a plunging overlook. Breathtaking. "Okay, I'm not really the devil. Don't believe the word on the street. But it *is* beauty, isn't it?"

I was struck that he said "beauty" instead of "beautiful," since the former is general and the latter specific. I didn't answer. We walked to an old creosoted rail, and one step over would have dashed us down the steep rocky mountainside.

"I wanted you to call me," I said. I couldn't believe the words came from me. I flushed and stepped over the rail and straddled it, girl or whore I couldn't say. I rode it like a still stallion, looking to Sean on the parking lot side, and to the fall-away mountain on the other. "I have thought about you, you know. But I couldn't tell what you thought of me." He sighed and sat against the rail a couple of feet past me.

"Thing is, Lucy, see, thing is, I'm married. Sort of." I froze astraddle and then slowly swung my leg back over to the parking lot so that I was sitting in the same orientation as Sean. I wanted to push him off the cliff. Not the first time for me. I wasn't a virgin for having a crush on a married man. Maybe I knew, I thought. Maybe his inaccessibility was his attraction. My creed: Never love anyone you might really have. The only time I did that was James, the drunken poet of a would-be artist.

"Take me back to my father's house," I said.

"I haven't even talked to her in more than a year or seen her in nearly two." He was nearly whispering by then, and the familiar electrical buzzing began down there, and it shocked me. Then the flood of me, petals unabashed and opening. Almost, almost, and almost, and I didn't believe it, held my hands in front of my shorts as if to ward it off, like chasing spirits. The biology of it, the mental construct of it, made no sense. "She left me and went off with a carpenter I'd hired. I got one postcard from Seattle about eight weeks ago saying that she wasn't coming back. I've hired a lawyer and keep canceling meetings with him. Turns out I'm indecisive and stubborn. I wake up every morning hoping she will be there in bed beside me. Never is. Never will be. I didn't mean to lie to you, Lucy."

He touched my arm, reaching out, and I looked down into the sun's last brazen rays that lit the dark suntanned skin of his arm, from which blond hairs grew in fertile profusion. I wanted to fall down and worship him, whether he gave me the riches of the world or not. I did not think, *Get thee behind me, Satan*. I did think, *Get behind me*. My God, this diary makes me sound like an unbrained starlet. Then he did something odd. He pushed himself off the rail without taking his hand off my arm. Instinctively, I looked around the lot to see if anyone else was coming or there, but we were alone with the run-down wreck of the old unused Ranger station. He slid his hand up my forearm and rested on my biceps, and I vaulted on to him.

I traffic in narrative as a teacher. I explain how we make stories of the simplest incidents and give them beginnings, middles, and ends. There was no story for that moment. My mouth folded over and over his, and I blurted out my orgasm at the pressure of his cutoffs against me. I snuck one hand away and plunged it down to rub hard once and make the spillway open completely. We kissed for maybe thirty seconds in all, and I roared in his mouth, clamped my right leg hard behind his left. Then, as if Roger Corman had finished directing a scene in a C-movie from 1960, we stopped, and he stepped back, turned away from me, and faced the gorge. When his back turned, I rubbed quickly for the genie, but she was gone, vanished into mythic smoke.

It began to get dark, and I was suddenly afraid and disgusted with myself. This was more like seventeen than thirty-five. He hung his head like a saint in shame. We both started to say something at the same time and then stopped.

"I brought you here for the view," he said hoarsely. "Just the view. I've wasted my life. Can't finish my dissertation because I want to fail. I want to fail because I'm afraid. I'm afraid because of my father. Jesus, let me take you home."

"Sean, don't. It's all right." I felt like I was in an episode of *Days of Our Lives*. My whole body glowed like a firefly—it felt that way. But he drove me home, and I held on to his shirt but not his body, and when I got off, I felt nothing. And so I am here, furious, unchanged.

June 20

Pratt: So you came back a little grumpy from your date last night. Did it not go well? (*V. sitting in the corner by the window doing the* Times *crossword puzzle, dramatically and audibly knowing clue after clue.*)

Me: It was good. (*Nurse Mary Lou Wadely comes in, checking pulse and temperature, saying Pratt is stable. She, Mary Lou, will be back on Monday. "Call if you need me, darling." She actually said "darling," and she said it to me, gently, sweetly.*)

Pratt: You strive for more than "good" in everything you do, Luce. Settling for "good" is what most people do. Don't be like most people.

Victor: Seven letters for "lighthouse keeper's brother."

Me: (*No hesitation*): Leonard. (*Blank look from Victor.*) As in Leonard Woolf. (*Victor huffing softly, like a filling sail.*)

Pratt: Besides, you can do better than a yard boy.

Me: Yeah, you married the Thomas and Morene Schantz Professor of Art History at Duke and look how good that turned out. (*Ginger Dumont, the physical therapist, freckles into the room, all sunshine and humming.*)

Pratt: She wasn't a professor when I married her, God knows. She was a girl with fifteen thousand dollars of tuition debt and a willingness to be educated.

Me: By you, you mean. Educated by you.

Victor: Prattster, you need anything? (*Prattster! I almost spit up. Pratt holding up his trembly hand to say no. Victor sets his folded puzzle and yellow pencil on the coverlet and leaves the room.*)

Me: He's not a yard boy, goddamnit, Pratt. He owns his own landscaping business.

Pratt: His father was a famous banker in Asheville. Then the Feds descended. Killed himself. Did you know that?

Me: (*shocked but silent*) Why do you always try to ruin everything for me?

Ginger: I can come back if this is a bad time.

Me: I was just leaving.

Pratt: It's worse today, Ginger. Everything is worse today.

Ginger: Poor baby. (*The close sound of a toilet flushing.*)

Exit Lucy.

June 21

Things stay the same when we want them to change, and they change when we want them to say the same. Pastors say the world makes sense, but the world says it doesn't. One of them is lying.

My father speaking to demons in his room, deep into the night

June 22

V. and I took Pratt to St. Michael's for services this morning. I always say that I started losing religion the day I was born, but it's not true. I don't believe in a white man with a white beard sitting on a white cloud and pointing the fickle finger of fate at pathetic sinners. But I cannot escape the mystery. And I am a sucker for ritual. So the kneeling and the crossing secretly got to me, though of course I showed nothing.

Pratt could no longer cross or kneel, and we sat in the very back pew so he could thrash at will, and I hated it. Pratt managed to drop his large check in the offering plate, and Victor put in a five-dollar bill, which for some reason I found touching. What do I know of him? Nothing, really. One of my problems is that for a woman, I'm a miserably poor gossip. All my friends watercooler me to death at school and after, reporting breakups and divorces, dust-ups and trysts. I say, "You're trying to make a narrative out of a world without stories." They stare at me.

Pratt began to cry during the Lord's Prayer, and I held his hand, and in his trembling I felt True Suffering. He doesn't want this martyrdom any more than Christ did, but this is the tip of it. The progress of the disease from here will be terrible, until he is wasted and worn. Before church this morning, he wanted to tell me the life story of Jacqueline du Pré, and I said, "Pratt, come on." I'd seen the film *Hillary and Jackie*, and I knew he was imagining the drama of his own demise. But my father told it anyway, the first intimations of numbness, the strange symptoms that doctors misdiagnosed at first. I sat staring at him as he told the story, inventing feelings of despair he attributed to du Pré, even though he was just guessing. He didn't make it to the cellist's death, but he didn't need to.

We escaped before the last Amen of the service so Pratt would not have to clog the arteries of the Church Triumphant. I am a miserable bitch for writing this.

I have risen each day with a plan to ask Pratt to tell me more about the baby he says he fathered in college. And each day I navigate around it. Today I googled Pratt and got 324,592 hits, and I read through the list for nearly an hour. The Pulitzer, constant speeches, journal articles, four honorary doctorates, his books on Amazon and B&N.com, his *used* books on abebooks.com—the hits stretched on for miles. And yet I was struck how impersonal it was, as if he were a two-dimensional historical figure, not my father.

What did I expect? "Long-lost daughter seeking dad?" Pratt knows I always wanted a confidante-brother, that I despised our academic move-around from salary to salary for him and Mother, the Package Deal that finally broke apart under the strain of competition and rancor. When Duke offered the chair to Mother, Pratt said he'd be goddamned if *he*'d be a spousal hire. I was gone by then, of course, having fled after high school.

I gave up on the googling and took my honors English textbook to the back deck to try and think of innovative lesson plans for this fall. Fog erased Angel Hair Falls from the view, Alzheimer's of the landscape, and I began to think of the first time I met James. I was still in New York working my way nowhere as a sub-sub-sub editor at Taylor-Caughton, mostly dealing with the third-tier representatives of celebrity authors who hadn't written a word of the upcoming books with their names on them. James came over with his then-agent Serena Berman, a powerhouse hatchet of a woman, to see Selwyn Catman, the British editor we'd hired away from Simon & Schuster earlier that year and promised his own line, which was called simply Catman and bore a black-cat colophon.

Selwyn was, as they say, the kind of man who can strut while seated. His Oxbridge English, his three-thousand-dollar suits, his impeccable manners, and above all his instincts for bestsellers made him hot for a while. James didn't know until much later that the Catman imprint was already shaky, that Selwyn had bought nine books giving lavish advances, and that sales of them had been abysmal. Poor James—he thought it was all about art, having read too much about Maxwell Perkins and Scott Fitzgerald.

He got left in an outer office after meeting Selwyn and after Serena beelined into Selwyn's office for what she knew must be a hopeless pitch. I felt so sorry for James, wretched and still hopeful on the leather sofa, that even though I was from another office, I sat and talked with him. He was almost gorgeous and had a rough sheen, and when he talked, the heavens opened. Oh, God, the words that came out of his mouth. Beautiful, sequential, as if he had ordered the world and pitied it. I could smell alcohol on his breath, and that made me pity him more.

I never made it any further up on the editorial food chain, but he managed to get my phone number and called me three days later. Selwyn had, of course, turned down the manuscript, and Serena let James go as a client. Not long after that, the Catman imprint folded, and Selwyn retired to Scotland. Serena became a vice president at the William Morris Agency. Three weeks later I was living with James. That was nine years ago, but it might as well be a scene from *The Song of Roland.*

Now, still trying, still slipping, poor drunken James in the shadow of William Faulkner, drowning in bourbon and failure. We choose different roads to failure, but we're always arriving at the same place. Just then, Angel Hair Falls came out. A shimmering harp-string far across the valley.

June 24

It's almost midnight. I called him earlier and said to come get me and let's go for a ride. He was in a pickup truck so high off the ground I thought I might need a Sherpa to summit.

"Where are we going?" he asked. He was apologetic but less than what I wanted.

"How the hell should I know? I don't live here."

"It depends on what you want to do. If you want to smoke cigarettes and shoot pool and drink beer, we could go to Shady Stan's. If you want to talk, we could go to my place, which is strictly for celibates and madmen, in case you're worrying about my intentions."

"All men have bad intentions," I said. "Is your place presentable?"

"Of course not. No self-respecting man would have a presentable house. But anticipating possible company, I removed the main debris in the living room with a front-end-loader and buried the unwashed laundry in a pit. So you are unlikely to be stung, bit, or chased. I'm making it sound like a penthouse on Park Avenue, aren't I?"

"Do you have this giant truck in compensation for something?"

"Yes. It's because my ambitions are so small. Never talk to a man about the size of his ambitions. He'll always lie." He had me laughing again, and with our good humor restored, we roared up the mountain to his house, which astonished me.

(Am I changing? Can I change? Does God believe in me or pity me? When my students see me again, will they see me or see through me? Is what I feel for Sean different from what my father feels for me? Am I changing?)

His house was a lodge—glacée logs (or so they looked), a stone chimney, broad front porch with rustic furniture and tools, all nestled in the woods without a yard. The steep steps surprised me, and from the porch there was no view at all, only more woods slanting away at a fairly non-scenic angle. He lit some sandalwood incense, which I liked, and got us each a cold Moosehead, which I loved. His furniture is deeply worn red leather, huddled protectively around a gorgeous glass-topped coffee table on which lay great humps of nature and outdoor magazines.

"...summer of 2004," he was saying. I realized I hadn't been listening. His house was rustic but stunning, walls covered with black-and-white Ansel Adams prints and floors a high-gloss heart pine.

"I'm sorry, I wandered off there looking at your house."

"I was saying I lost my interest in doing more than sitting around this place when I hiked the Appalachian Trail in 2002."

"The whole thing?" Shocked, but believing it.

"From here to Maine." I couldn't think of anything to say and tried not to look him over, but he was beautiful to me, as I knew I was not. I lust most after what I know I cannot have or should not. Maybe that's the cheap trick life plays on us. It gives us the chemistry to mate like wild animals but then wags a finger and says, "But of course that's just theoretical." I wanted to do something insane. I felt it coming off me like a sheen of sweat.

"I'm afraid of getting what my father has," I blurted. It came out like a lid being steam-popped from a boiling saucepan. "There's a genetic component. Not that I don't love him. I love him. I just. You know, I was, I mean the other day, I." Then I clamped silent. My face glowed red, I'm sure. "I don't know why I kissed you. You...I think I'm losing it, see." I shook my head and took a gulp of beer. That was pretty insane, but it gave me no release. I want to be shattered by release, to have my religion changed, to come out gasping and changed on the other side.

"I know it," Sean said. "My father embezzled nearly a million dollars, and when he got caught, he shot himself in his office in Asheville. It was on TV for three days. My mother was already sick with cancer when he did it. It was the...Lucy I'm...." He fell silent.

"God. I'm so sorry. Jesus."

"Your dad *owns* Chapel Hill," he said. "And I don't mean that in a literal or a bad way. We all thought he had the perfect life. Every award in the world. Then when the crash comes, some people start saying, *well*. Well. That explains *that*. After my father, I finally just left school because everybody knew, and I wanted to go somewhere I could do something small and hard. So. My confessions. I can't imagine how bored you must be. Would you like to go see my waterfall?" He wasn't telling me the whole truth.

I did, and the evening lingered, and we walked through a well-trod path in a close-shouldered forest of firs and white pines. That single beer made me tipsy. He took my hand, and I let him. I felt as if I were about to break out bawling. We walked for about fifteen minutes, and suddenly we came to a simple, gorgeous, but tiny waterfall—perhaps twenty feet high and two feet wide, sparkling over cracked granite and plunging into a pool and then streaming onward through a crowd of green rocks and sunshafts. There was a beautiful hand-crafted bench with a back before the falls, and we sat, and he let go of my hand as we settled.

"I come here to ponder," he said. "Do you believe in God?" The question was an assault. I felt slapped, insulted, adored, and needed. Any answer could be fatal, and I realized just then how very much I liked him.

"I believe in a narrative mystery behind things," I said, halting. My voice was as shaky as Pratt's, a connection I did not miss.

"That's right," he said, nodding. "That's right." Then: "I come here when I'm afraid."

"I'm always afraid," I said.

"Don't be afraid."

"Well, I am."

"Don't be afraid."

I waited for the Harlequin Romance Moment, and it never came. We walked back to his house, drank another beer, talked baseball and politics (I'm left of him, but I'm left of almost everyone), and then he brought me back to Pratt's, and I felt confused and satisfied at the same time. If he had led me to the bedroom, I would have let him, in less than a heartbeat. Something holds him back from reaching for the happiness he needs desperately.

And now, strung between religion and delicious sin, between heredity and the here and now, I sit here. I wait for a sign.

Actual screaming fight with Victor. Pratt gets vocally between us, and soon all three of us are screaming at the same time. I want to kill V., and I tell him that, and Pratt calls me Cricket, my childhood nickname, three times, as if it might open-sesame a cave of riches.

I go to my room and pack everything I have and then sit there, stony. My cell phone rings, and it's my teacher friend Laurie Teagarten, and she's spilling out news before I finish saying hello. Our idiot principal, Raleigh Richards, has been caught having an affair with Heather Mirabelle, who teaches eleventh-grade science and has been in heat since the moment she arrived fresh out of Ole Miss. She flirts with everyone of every age and both sexes, oozing availability. But *Principal Richards?* Good God. He is a fat fifty, goggle-eyed, married to a famous local harridan, with two sons of equally unbelievable stupidity. A former baseball coach, whose team won state and that qualified him to be principal of the school. I try to laugh, but I'm too furious, and I keep hitting on one-syllable words, which makes Laurie talk more.

"Caught them actually doing the dirty deed in his office," she says. "Rolanna wonders why he's late getting home, and she has a front door key and finds them butt naked on the sofa in his office and takes three pictures of them on her cell phone. She marches herself straight to the board office and shows the pix to the superintendent, and Old Raleigh's out on his ass the next morning. Fired Heather, too. It's all over town. Nan Bright is acting principal, not what you'd call a huge improvement, but better. Jesus!"

Oh, how we love our petty larcenies and idiotic crimes. We keep dashing our hands through the flame because we know it burns.

I unpack and take Julia Glass to the deck and sit there and steam away my rage. Later, V. creeps up behind me and touches me on the shoulder when I don't hear him. I jump and turn, ready to fight, but his eyes have gone soft.

"What's wrong?" I find myself asking.

"My dad died on me when I was a baby," he whispers. "That's why. I wanted you to know."

I stare at him as if looking at a friend from many years ago, one I never thought I'd see again.

Later, Mary Lou Wadely, Pratt's home health nurse, came to my room and sat on the bed where I was reading. She seems so familiar, and yet I'm not sure why. There is a calm purpose about her that is almost addictive—part of her job, I guess.

"Honey, I know it seems like your Dad is having a hard time with all this, but he's struggling with a lot of things," she said. I could not believe she called me *honey*, but it felt marvelous, and I wore it like silk. "Sometimes sickness makes men go on a very long journey back over their lives, and it's hard for them to navigate that distance. Very hard. He's trying to reach out—you can see that. But it's like pushing a rock up hill and having it roll back over him before he can reach the top."

"Sisyphus."

"Exactly. Be kind and patient. I know it's not my place to give you that kind of advice, but I *am* old enough to be your mother."

"Just barely," I said, laughing. "Okay, I will. And I don't mind you saying it at all. I do feel like you really care. It means a lot to me."

"I do really care, honey," she said. And she put her hand on my leg and squeezed it. Her gentleness poured over me like a warm waterfall.

June 26

J. called from Oxford on my cell phone when I was out buying groceries for Pratt. He was drunk at 10:37 in the morning (I looked at my watch), and said he was giving up on being a writer and had decided to kill himself. I told him to stop being dramatic, and that I was looking for frozen broccoli. (Did Susan Sontag ever go shopping for broccoli? I'll need to ask Pratt, who would know.)

"I'm serious this time, Luce," he self-pitied. "I went out to four stores and bought up all the over-the-counter sleeping pills in town. I'm going to crush them and mix them with bourbon and then drink it all. It's over. I'm not a writer. Coming here hasn't made me a writer. I was kidding myself."

"Everybody kids himself," I said. "You're being pathetic."

"You never kidded *your*self."

"Every hour of every day of my life," I said, stopping in paper goods and warning a tubby young woman away with a glance. "I thought that coming here for the summer my dad and I would have some kind of epiphany, that he would say for once in his life that he needs me, that he needs anybody but sycophants and certificates. I was kidding myself, James."

"This isn't about *you*," he whined. "I could see my picture on the dust jacket. With a baseball cap and a dog and an old pickup truck and the starred review from *Publishers Weekly*. `A new voice in American literature.' Turns out I'm an old voice in the mirror, a shout in the street."

"You're not getting any sympathy from me quoting Joyce. I have to find broccoli. Now are you really going to kill yourself? Do you want me to go ahead and call the morgue in Oxford and tell them to stand by?"

"Broccoli's in produce or frozen foods," he slurred. "I don't know how you do it."

"Do what, James?" Sighing heavily here, passing luncheon meats and cheese.

"Just go on," he said hoarsely. "How do we just go on? We're all going to die. I wanted to be a famous writer. *Famous*. Nobel Prize famous."

"Here's broccoli," I said with a penultimate tone.

"Have some pity, miss."

"That's from *The African Queen*. After Hepburn pours out all of Bogey's gin. You're not even original in your clichés." He hung up on me.

We go on. We watch our world shape itself like the Taj Mahal and then burn to ashes. We go on.

June 27

Ella Seitz came thrashing in during Pratt's physical therapy with Ginger Dumont this morning, her I-don't-need-to-work tan glowing orange in the recessed lighting of my father's mansion. Why do the wealthy always pretend they are just scraping by? Ella launched into manic and fluent echolalia, and I fled and went online and looked up Sean Crayton's father.

Jesus. *The Asheville Citizen* was filled with it for days. All the background, and Sean was only nineteen, a sophomore in college. I thought of Kayley Calhoun, my student from five years past, whose mother was arrested for, good grief, robbing a liquor store in broad daylight wearing a clown mask. About meth. Desperate for cash. And Kayley, a flat-chested, thin-haired sixteen, too ashamed to take her eyes from her book. Her small hands seemed to shrink, and when she did look up, she looked away. That day after school when she showed up.

"Ms. McKay?" she said. Her mouse's vowels, wren's consonants. "Would you talk to me? I need somebody to talk to me?" The inflection of that second sentence, turning a statement into a soft question, tore at my heart. I surprised myself, standing and coming to her and wrapped her in a snug embrace, and she began to cry, and we both walked to the door, attached, and I closed it quietly, and she cried and cried. I rubbed her hair, I kissed her hair.

She said, "I'm tired of hurting. I'm just tired of hurting."

"So am I," I didn't say. What I did say was: "I'll hurt with you. We will cut the hurt in half, okay?"

"Okay." I had no idea what I really meant, and she couldn't have.

So I started looking up Sean's father, began to think of Kayley Calhoun, and wound up considering Pratt McKay, my own father. Maybe that's why I came here—to have him fall into my arms and ask for my help and my love. To say, "I'm tired of hurting. I'm just tired of hurting."

Instead, last night, he spent an hour sputtering about Foucault and Derrida and a term he's lately invented, Postfeminist Literalism. V. urged him on, as if self-flagellating before a hoary Oracle. I stood in the doorway watching them, thinking of myself (what else?), Sean, James, Pratt, and Victor, thinking, "I'm tired of hurting."

I got an e-mail from the Thomas & Morene Schantz Professor of Art History, announcing that I might watch for a paper she has coming out next week in some famous journal.

June 28

Earlier this evening, in a what-the-hell mood, I drove up the mountain to Sean's lodge and saw him, through the window, standing by the fieldstone fireplace embracing a leggy woman in short-shorts. I slowed but did not stop, and they turned to the sound of tires in the dirt driveway. I fishtailed getting out and back down into the valley, sick and stupid.

I am a teacher. I am master of my room, but I see a stranger in the mirror these days, a vaguely familiar woman breaking down from age and serial disappointment. I want to take her to a county fair and win her a sawdust teddy bear, to buy her something as lovely and insubstantial as cotton candy. I want to pretend and have the pretense come true. I want every student I've ever taught to come back and serenade me as I watch Angel Hair Falls thread down the distant side of the valley.

Drove to a juke joint called Bo's Cantina and flopped my ass right on a barstool and ordered a Sam Adams. TEACHER KID-

NAPPED FROM DIVE; BODY DISCOVERED FLYING OFF ANGEL HAIR FALLS. Nah—too long. Tourist found dead. More like it. I googled my own name once and found an obituary for a Lucy McKay in Tampa, who was killed by a hit-and-run driver. My run-down doppelganger.

A foul, pustular redneck settled on the stool next to me.

"Leave me alone," I would have hissed if the sentence had any S sounds. But I said it with pit-viper venom. I meant the world, not him personally.

"I ain't said a word to you," he said. He ordered a beer. "Besides I don't have the house-jack it would take to pry your legs apart. I'm just tired."

"What's your name?"

"Odell Perclar. If you want to know the truth, I don't see no point in nothing."

"Perclar? Is that French?"

"Probly. I'm stupid enough to be French."

"What have you got against the French?"

"I thought you wanted to be left alone. You're chatty for somebody who ain't looking for compny."

I left. He didn't even watch me leave. *Chatty*. That wasn't his word. We pick up our personalities from TV or movies, on the side or the road, in a bar. Stir vigorously and pour. Nothing comes out. I cannot stand being here. I cannot stand being in Oxford.

And I hate Sean, and were I God, I would strike him, strike him down.

June 29

My June 29 Resolution (since it's far too late for New Year's): Stop Being Pathetic. So I will. I shouldn't even be keeping a journal, because they're an invitation to whiny navel-gazing, but who else can I talk to? Betty and Hunt Bearden? The Reverend Tanner?

V. went to the dentist to have his fangs cleaned, so I forced myself to sit down with Pratt and have a father-daughter talk. I sense that he is struggling with more than the MS. He still can't quite believe the temerity of it to have attacked him, but maybe he's innocent as a lamb. Did I come here to extract Dramatic Revenge for my misloved childhood? I must have spent two years at Tonya Webb's house, my best friend during the five years we lived in Princeton. Pratt would go to Chicago for five days, while Mom lit out for Brussels. They'd cross paths after that just long enough to have screaming arguments about infidelities and dropped responsibilities. I sat in my room with rock music turned up to tympanum-shattering levels, but you can still hear a dish break over it. I pretended they were boarders, a cross-matched couple called Mr. and Mrs. Stinky. Ergo, when they fought: The Stinkys are at it again. Tonya had a D cup at fourteen, and boys chased her relentlessly, and yet she floated above it all, magisterial in her diffidence, which of course made the boys want her even more. I loved her, and I know she loved me, sisters under the covers, able to whisper the darkest secrets. I got dropped off there for two days, three days, a week. And her parents adored me. He sold refrigerators, and she was the office manager of a well-drilling company. They had a son much older than Tonya, who was in the Navy. Tonya and I read books—ate them, really—and then talked about the characters as if they were real. She went to a junior college, got married after a year, and settled down to making babies, five of them at last count. We swapped a couple of e-mails, and she said her husband was a good man. She didn't even say what he did for a living. She said she didn't have a chance to read much anymore.

"I kn-kn-kn-know that you are miserable here," Pratt began. I asked softly if he'd taken his medicine, and he nodded, head pivoting and wobbling as if it would fall off momentarily.

"I'm just miserable," I admitted, caught. "But it's a choice, Pratt. You learn to need it. I don't want to need it. I wanted to come up for the summer and help, but I see I can't do that very well."

"I'm all Victor has, and I've gotten used to him," said my father. (I cannot force myself to reproduce his struggles with his own body; I will make him speak here as if he were whole.) "He helps me, and I'm with him. He's almost thirty years old and is never going to finish his dissertation. He says he isn't cut out to be a professor, just a grad assistant. If the university weren't so desperate for teachers, he'd be out of a job."

"Or teaching in a high school," I said, and I instantly regretted it.

"You do more good in one year than I've done in my whole career," he said. I felt he was being patronizing, and I flinched and even, *God*, balled my fists. "I don't change lives, not any more, if I ever did. I'm playing to the grandstands, trying to be world-famous. But if I won the Nobel Prize for history, which they don't even have, do you think I'd be satisfied? It would kill me. I'm diseased, Cricket. And now this hideous *thing* has me, and it's eating me alive. Ask Lenora. She knows."

Lenora Shingler, his second wife, a Brit musicologist who made her name by discovering a Bach cantata at a castle in Bavaria, for God's sake. His wife for four years. Then he married Alessandra Marchese, an Italian geologist who left him for the landscape in the Kamchatka Peninsula. She had only two years of servitude with Pratt. She still fights with my dad on the phone—the only match with real passion she ever had. Lenora announced she was lesbian in 2002 and took a position at Oberlin along with the real love of her life, the pianist Ellen Sigmatich. The poetry of it all. I write to remind myself of the lineage. Jesus.

"I just don't know how to talk to you anymore. I can talk all day to my students like the Oracle at Delphi, but I come here, and I'm still Cricket, the kid shuffled off to the neighbors while her parents wander off to be coddled at conferences."

"Oh, for God's sake." I began to get angry and couldn't stop.

"Are you talking to yourself at night? I hear you through the wall. You could talk to me, you know. Have you seen a therapist?"

44

The words soured in my mouth before they were fully out. Victor came into the house with his right hand holding his jaw.

"I'll do letters now," said Pratt, turning away, dismissing me.

"I got butchered at the goddamned dentist," said V. I got up and went out into the world and took a walk. Enough with you, Mr. Stinky.

Sunday, even.

June 30

I'm leaving next week. I want to spend the rest of the summer in Oxford, dodging James and working on lesson plans. Sipping piña coladas poolside and reading Bad Fiction. (Students, don't look.) Trolling for a man who will tell me he loves me and then start cheating on me two weeks later. Ah, life!

B. & H. Bearden to lunch, with Pratt hosting and V. making delicious Cobb salads and homemade dressing, fresh-baked bread, and sweet butter. Considerable faux conversation. I catch Victor's glance, and I see in his eyes something unexpected, a plea for forgiveness, which I almost give back.

Around four, with me dozing on the deck, my finger in a book by E.L. Doctorow, I blink awake, and there is Sean, wearing khaki trousers and a blue dress shirt and mirror gloss black tassel loafers. I barely recognize him.

"That was you, wasn't it? You came to see me the other night and saw me with Junie."

"Junie, is it? My, you like them with cute names, don't you? Junie? Lucy? Is there a Betsy in the closet?"

"She's my first cousin," he said. "We grew up together. My mother's sister's daughter. We went outside when we heard the car, but nobody was there. It was you, wasn't it?"

"Shit," I said. "That was your cousin? Why are you dressed? Where have you been?"

"My aunt's funeral in Asheville. That's why June was here. She's an assistant professor at the University of Florida. Genetics. We were reliving old times. My aunt was healthy, only seventy-five, and she just dropped dead in her kitchen. Come on and let's go driving. I'm feeling a little raw."

"Give me five minutes. I feel like a complete bitch idiot. I'm so sorry."

"It's okay." A different voice from Sean, soft, asking solace. He was in his Prius, not the huge work pickup truck, and an Earl Kluge CD was playing.

"Sean, I want to formally apologize. I must like you. I was so jealous I couldn't stand it. I wanted to kill you. I feel like hell giving you an `unlucky in love' speech when you're just been to a funeral, but that's what happened. Where are we going?"

"To the top of Mount Mitchell, highest point in the eastern U.S., ma'am, where you can see from here to eternity or other novel titles. Not the tourist center but down a trail a few hundred yards."

"Sean?"

"Mnn?"

"Are you seeing other women? I mean, it's none of my business, I know. None at all. I just—I want to know where I stand before we, I mean, if there was…crap."

"Not now, no. Not in a long time. I've had a hard time caring for others since the thing with my father. Then losing Kay but not divorcing her. I've been angry and sick with sadness. I have dates and turn on my inherent smartass charm, and then I'm right back where I was, refusing to finish my dissertation or grow up. And here I am with a suit, just like my father wore, and I realize I'm going nowhere fast. I just coined that cliché. It's copyrighted, so don't even think of stealing it."

"Let's go to your house, not Mount Mitchell. Please?"

"Yes."

That one word killed me. He could have said *okay* or *sure* or demurred, but he just said *yes*, and I knew at that moment I would. I tried to remember if I'd missed any birth control pills, and I was pretty sure I hadn't, but I felt dozy and close to him. I knew that I would anyway. We got to his "lodge" and went inside and had a large, lovely glass of a glorious Madeira, then half of another one before we were kissing on the couch, fumbling, touching, touching.

I have never wanted any *thing* more in this life. His body was muscled and beautiful in the late-day light of his bedroom. His bed was homemade, massive and motionless, unsqueaky, meant to hold two. Our eyes stayed open, and I felt every part of him enter me, sex, mouth, face, eyes, tongue, legs, hips, fingers. It had been long—so long—and I made hideous noises, which he echoed, and I thrashed around, I realized to my shock, in the same motions of my father's sickened body. For a moment, sorrow and shame poured through me like drugs at an execution. Then I forgot, and we loved wholly, and we went through the complete cycle three times, and he could not believe the second crest or the third—I believed him and felt it, saw his bright crimson face, felt his rough-wired chest on my breasts.

We completely soaked the sheets, and finally, as he held me, I felt peace. God, we have such small times of joy in this life. Before our rough breathing had subsided, I was staying for all of July, hell, maybe forever. I sat up on the edge of the bed, and he ran his rough landscaper's finger down the length of my back, shoulder to cleft, and it started again. Now, emptied, still in flood tide despite a shower and a sandwich, I watch the words I make on this lovely page. And in his room, my father prays aloud, speaks to ghosts.

2. Pratt

Dear Lucy, dearest Lucy.

I speak to you on this tape in my room here in the night just as my strength begins to wane, a man with infinite love for you and infinite ways to avoid saying it. My love is mute, and that is my curse, and I cannot form the words, and I know why.

Forgive me. I think often of the words of Bianco da Siena: "Come down, O Love divine, Seek thou this soul of mine, And visit it with your own ardor glowing; O Comforter draw near, Within my heart appear, And kindle it, thy holy flame bestowing." May that comfort also be yours.

I have in my memory the strangest things. I am told that my memory may well remain intact even when my body is broken, and I am frozen and mute. And so I shall learn to be a prisoner of silence in my own body, and I rail against it and you, and there is more that you must know, things I cannot yet speak aloud even now but must before the summer ends and you leave.

You were a glowing and strange little girl, sweet and sweeter Lucy, and your mother and I knew you were perfect. We trotted you out at graduate student parties, and we could hear the cascade of young girls' praise—*Lucy's here, she's here!* And you, precocious, adorable, would give lectures, sing on command, lecture and recite while the future-unemployed still held the shine of grad school in the palms of their hands. As you know, I was in history and your mother in *art* history, and you sat enthroned while we drank cheap wine and others puffed joints in bedrooms or even made love there.

Yet, as our careers grew and you matured, I lost sight of you, could not remember the sole vision of my early life—to love and be

48

loved. Meaning that I was a very good father of a very small child and a very bad father after you hit thirteen. But you must understand that I had looked as a boy of thirteen into the darkness too many times, and it seared shut my lips to say things that teemed and aimed to pour. I strangled them then and strangle them now.

God grant me the strength to get through this. I love you so dearly, Lucy, and I am so tired.

June 2

I see the tension between you and Victor, and it tears me apart in a way that I cannot yet explain. For two years now, he has been my ears and my voice, a man who himself has no goals other than to assist me. And I have demanded much so that my name will glitter and glow, and it is pathetic to me. I have lectured my life away in universities, written my love into others' narratives, and *still* it is not enough. I must be burnished like a Greek urn each day, told I am beautiful when I feel ugly, told I am brilliant when my stupidities would fill libraries.

Do you remember that you turned your face away from me when I came back to the table after accepting the Pulitzer? That you would not look at me? The award turned to ashes in my mouth. Now, none of the medicines in their military rows can stave off this hideous enemy, and I cannot hug you for fear of hurting you, cutting your cheek with a nail.

"So what do you think, Lucy?" I asked, showing you the framed certificate.

"I have a headache, Pratt," you said distantly, and that was the first time you called me in public by my name—that middle name I thought sounded more professional when I began to publish: Robert Pratt McKay.

You spent this morning cheerleading me in my therapy with the ever-sunshiny Ginger. I chewed Ginger out for calling me *Sweetie*, and I'm sure I was the nasty bastard you expected, Lucy. You went outside and talked to Sean, the landscaper. I saw you through the window, bouncing girlishly on your toes, and I wanted to start over when we were both young, to change everything I did, every word I said. I wanted us to be the best of friends, intimates, and buddies. Because I have so much to tell you, darling.

But you must believe it does not come from selfishness but from fear. I cannot get past it, having tried for a lifetime. You do not know the story of my life, not the hundredth part of it. That is what I will try to tell you on this recorder, the story I will hand you as you leave. That you can listen to on your long drive back to Mississippi. (I know your car is so old it has a cassette tape deck—I *did* do that much homework.) So that you can hear the voice of one who loved nothing in his life as much as he loved you but was too broken apart to say it. To say any of it.

June 3

I knew she was sick from my first memories of her. I was born when she was forty-four, a shock from which she could never recover. My father was a drunk and a roamer, a man who once left for three years without a word, and then casually drifted back into Mama's life with a wink and a sawdust-filled teddy bear. He was a small man with a slanted toothpick always dangling from his mouth. He had a child's teeth, small and perfect, and did coin tricks and sang sentimental songs in a wobbly Irish tenor. The one time you saw him, he was a shriveled old man bunked up in a rest home, voiceless and bitter. And yet even with his wastrel waywardness, he was the better of them.

Why she let him into her bed that night, I know only too well. When you've suffered a lack of love for too many years, you accept offers that even in dreams you could not bear to consider. I am certain that my attachment to the women of the Civil Rights movement can be traced to their isolation and suffering, knowing their husbands were chased endlessly by women from demonstration to demonstration. So he wandered back through town, rural Odysseus to suburban Penelope, and it was Leda and the Swan, and he struck her, and I grew in the soft folds of her shocked belly.

When she found out she was pregnant, she tried to induce a miscarriage. Oh, God. To be that unwanted. She leaped off a chair a hundred times. She drank foul toxins. She opened a wire coat hanger and slid it inward, failing only because she had little idea what was inside her own body. I know all this because she told me, with increasingly lurid details after her mind began to go. He left the morning after their midnight mating and my conception, and he didn't return until I was two. I don't recall that visit, but he came again when I was six, and I can recall Mama's flat voice, rigid with anger:

"Robert Pratt, this man is your father." She said it as one admits a political defeat.

"Hello," I said. He took me on his knee and removed his cigarette and kissed me on the cheek. His breath smelled like a fireplace two days after the last flames have gone. He smoked with a toothpick in his mouth, out of the same side, and he took big theatrical puffs and winked at me and bounced me. I had no idea what *father* meant, but I presumed it meant we were related somehow.

"Put him down, you goddamn son of a bitch," Mama screamed. That is my clearest first memory, of that phrase, and her disorder in shouting it. Then the fight began, and they broke things, and he hit her and then he started to cry and said he was sorry, and I ran back to my room and closed the door and got under the bed with my doll, Binnie.

I have never told anyone any of this, not any of my wives and certainly not you. And no, I have never told Victor. And now I have begun it with a machine, and no doubt I will end it with a machine. Dear Lucy, forgive me. Forgive your father.

June 4

You and I talked today, and I asked about your job teaching English in Oxford, and about James. I didn't ask why you divorced, because I know, though you have never really told me. The simplicity of it chokes me to death: I never taught my own daughter to love because I did not know how. But she learned beautifully anyway.

Can you imagine what the women went through in Jamestown? Daily death, the hopelessness of hell? Their men dropping dead from fever or hunger? When I first read about Jamestown, I must have been twelve, and I dreamed every night for weeks that I was a little boy there, and that I was kidnapped by the Indians and raised in the woods, taught fire-craft and plant-lore. I hated waking up. I had a best friend named Gregory, who had shiny black hair and perfect teeth. (What a horror they would be to us through our twenty-first-century eyes: bad teeth, stinking, infested—white *and* Indian.) Gregory was strong, though, and every night in my dreams he came back and taught me about the circumscribed pre-contact world. He was my muse and guide.

I speak of Jamestown now to say that what we never saw with our own eyes we must re-imagine. I must re-imagine that evening on the balcony of the Lorraine Motel. Just so, I must imagine your life in Oxford, what led to the divorce, how dearly you love your students, and what great things you have accomplished. I, too, have known the paradise of the lector's stage, the special students and their star-struck eyes. But it is best in high school or even better, middle school, when a teacher can shape another's life. I was too busy with the mirror to be, on my best day, the kind of teacher you must be on your worst.

Let me believe this, darling, true or false. These words are all I have left for you.

June 5

So your mother called you today. You did not tell me—Victor over-heard you and surmised, which no doubt will enrage you. But hear me out slowly on Victor, for it is not what you must suspect.

Your mother and I have become prisoners from each other, you see. I am house-bound in the Smokies, and she is tenure-bound at Duke. I am on trial for my sins while she basks in her gray-temple years and believes that her small scratch on the world's breakable pane will make her name endure forever. But neither of us is bound for glory in the end. For each of us, it is the enduring shriek of pain that we must leave it all. And yet without knowing that, we should have done nothing at all.

Lucy, forgive her. Forgive me. And I speak now because the doctors say I will not be able to in perhaps only a few months. Beauty may be about to come back into our lives. Did you know? How could you?

Did you speak with your mother about my condition? Surely she must have asked, though for her it must be like asking about the Par-thenon—so long ago has it been. And yet I remember her from our first meeting, in an American history class when we were undergradu-ates at Vanderbilt. She looked almost exactly like Carole King did in her *Tapestry* years—beautiful, thoughtful, quiet, like a minor second turning into a major third.

She always felt "plain history" was beneath me. This history of *art*—now *that* was something to believe in. But we never got far in talking philosophically in those days.

Our first date was to a football game, and we lost, as we always did in those days. I think we played Alabama and got beat by some-thing like 59-0. And even at the end, she cheered as if we were the 1962 Yankees. Crazy. And admirable in her way. She took me to a party with her friends, and I drank until I was dizzy.

"Well," I said to her in the lobby, "I got this for you as a bribe to see me again." I took from the hip pocket of my bell-bottoms a slim paperback copy of *The Narrative of the Life of Frederick Douglass*. In the front I had written this: *For Hannah, as the journey begins*. And I signed it, *Love, Robert*. She opened it and read those words in the empty lobby, and she fell—oh God, did she fall, Lucy. I grew beyond the assault of my childhood. She said later that she felt an unfamiliar sting behind her eyes, and when I looked up, one of her eyebrows was cocked, Mephistophelian and waiting for an answer. I wanted to throw myself into her arms, but I couldn't. She said thank you, but her voice was the husk of winter fields. I said, "So, did it work or what?" She whispered, "It worked." I said, "I want to kiss you good night, and then I want to see you again and again and again and again." I said it four times. And at each syllable, she told me later, she felt her bones dissolve. And she said, "Oh, Robert." And I leaned down to kiss her, and it took weeks, *months*, and that kiss changed my life. She was too ripe, I know now, but we are only too ripe once in this life.

That was your mother, receiving my only perfect gift at the end of our only perfect day. So forgive her, Lucy. She saved my life.

June 6

I saw the merriment behind your eyes today when you met Ella Seitz and her forty thousand dollars' worth of botched plastic surgery. Ella thinks she looks exactly like she did at twenty-five, which I find terribly sad. She looks like a doll that someone pulled out of a house fire just before the walls collapsed.

My speaking voice was exceptionally bad today because I didn't take my pills. I refused when Victor brought them to me.

"I want to die!" I cried. "Just let me goddamn die in peace!"

"Why are you tormenting me?" said Victor, and he turned pale, and I was unmoved, Jovian, patriarch of the mountains. So by the time Ella came, I was swinging my arms like Beowulf and his club, and anyone in my path was my own Grendel. I asked nastily about her husband Golo Seitz, a research professor of genetics at Duke who doesn't live with her most of the year. I knew he had been living with a graduate student half his age; he made no secret of it. In fact, he brought her back to our community several times, ostensibly to finish work on papers, and I can imagine Ella's humiliation, but she settled, long ago, *settled.* You know what I mean by settled, Lucy. We settle. We all settle.

June 7

You quarreled with Victor today, and I'm sure I appeared to enjoy it. But I want to scream.

I invited you for the summer with a distinct purpose in mind, Lucy. It was not to nurse me or to receive my wrath, but to hear this confession—many confessions, in fact. Now, though, I believe it can be much more. I am trying to work it out. Can I? After you and Victor became nothing but your clashing voices, I had him take me outside on to the eyrie deck, from which I could look over the world of these green and folded mountains. And there, across the valley, the white waterfall, whose name I always forget, shimmered in the late-morning light, and I wanted absolution. I sent Victor away so I could sit there enfolded in my blanket, not quite believing that the world will go on after I die.

June 8

Victor is enraged at you and comes to me with his liturgical complaints. It's about settling up with the landscaper, Mr. Crayton, and Victor says a person who can't separate business from pleasure is doomed to enjoy neither.

"If you believe that, then I am sorry for you," I say. Victor crumbles, his face a blotchy mess. "Just stop it. I saw them talking on the deck through the French doors. He's flirtatious with her, as men will be. But she will find out about him, and that will be that. I know all about our Mr. Crayton and his family trials. But they are nothing, Victor. Nothing."

"What are you talking about?" he asks. He is confused, and in that moment his expression shocks me with its familiarity.

"Put on that CD with *The Lark Ascending* by Vaughan Williams," I say, and Victor sighs and does it, and then I dictate notes for an hour for a book I shall never write. I see your summer glow of health and youth on the deck, and the dance of your conversation with Sean Crayton, and I think of that Nashville night and a woman with Frederick Douglass's life in her pocket.

Someone has been here for several years now, and memories unsteady me.

June 9

Victor has gone back to Chapel Hill today, and me left with my therapist and nurse, and my daughter, my love, you. *Nurse?* My God.

I could see your relief that Victor was gone, and I knew why, and at first, after you took me outside on to the deck, I felt as if the time had come, that we could speak words we had been meaning to say all our lives. But then I began to feel ill, and I asked you to make some Lapsang Souchong—the tea of graduate school—and you held it up for me to sip, tenderly, lovingly. The disease chose today to dance upon me, Old Testament demons without a Galilean Jew to cast them out. I told you I wanted to go to the Mayo Clinic, but the truth is that I know nothing about the Mayo Clinic except its reputation.

Then it began to come up out of me, like birth, except it was my soul which began to open. I felt a desperate need, like a battle that everyone knows is hopeless but cannot be stopped. (As white Southerners must have known, Jim Crow was morally bankrupt, but they held it like a security blanket anyway, long enough for eternal disgrace.)

I said, "I have something I need to say to you." You asked what, as if I needed groceries or medicine. "I fathered a baby when I was in college with a girl named Rachel Moates." You said, "My God."

I told you I'd wasted my life, but that is hardly all of it. It isn't even the *beginning* of it. I don't remember what happened next— crows coming up like a Van Gogh painting, our shock, and the arrival of my gentle nurse. I wanted to tell you the secret right then but I couldn't, Cricket. Thank God for that sweet and gentle nurse.

So I told you what I could, but I told you poorly, of course, as I was bound to, blurting out what I have held secret from you for all our lives as father and daughter. If you knew what it cost me to speak of it at all, what grave madness it brought forth, I believe you would feel compassion for me instead of the disgust that comes so easily.

Because as I say there is more, and I shall tell it in time if my voice remains to me.

June 10

Father Tanner came today to talk with me and offer prayers I do not believe. A summer ago, I played tennis with him and tormented him as agnostics tease believers. He is too fit to understand real suffering, and I challenged him this morning.

"If Jesus lived thirty-three years, how could he understand the suffering of the aging?" I asked.

"He was the Son of God and understood everything perfectly," he said. "That he lived in bodily form for thirty-three years is of no consequence. That he lived at all is the miracle given to us and for our salvation."

"Shit, Parnell, you're sounding like fucking Pat Robertson," I said. "If you want to convince me of that, bring me a miracle next time you come. Unwind me from this hideous disease. Stop my windmill arms." He didn't flinch. I'm sure he's heard worse, though probably not here in Tastefulville, a Gated Community.

Lucy, I can't remember how I wound up here. I never thought of myself as part of the financial elite. In fact, I have always argued for a life of the mind. But the money came in, and I took what it gave me, and it gave me plenty. I know you disdain it, live in an apartment there in Oxford, that you must loathe this house.

But that is not why I asked you here this summer, not real estate, and not God. It was something far greater, a new knitting, the prerogatives of a ruined family that I might yet save. I am so tired. And I have surely sinned. Does this mean I have begun to believe? Perhaps it does.

June 11

You seemed restless and lost in thought today, sitting at the breakfast nook table and writing in your journal. What are you saying in there, Lucy? How much you hated your girlhood—your parents always jetting away to conferences and collecting awards, one-upping each other or trying to? I followed your mother's election to some learned society with my Pulitzer, and do you know the first word I said to her? I said, "Checkmate." And she showed no reaction at all, which she knew would savage me, as I was trying to savage her, and it worked.

A voice-operated recorder. I don't even have to press on or off. What will they think of next? So each evening I come in here and begin to speak to you, and my voice, my not-quite-dying voice, is saved for you.

I have not been able to tell you more about Rachel. I have not tried, to be honest. I have suffered in silence these decades, and now words equal pain for me. I always thought that I'd fade away at ninety, going to sleep a little more each day, full of years and victories, reaping more and awards until I might sink from them. I could not imagine this sudden sickness, and so I must see it as my earned punishment and forced penance.

And yet I have my joys, Lucy. You are the main joy of my life, and I ruined our life together as I ruined my marriages. Is there time still? Can we come to each other and salve the wounds? There is a Christ because we need him, whether he was true or not. We invent and re-invent the narratives of passage and salvation in each generation. I have read the slave narratives and thousands of pages of journals from women in the Civil Rights Movement, and I have read Shelby Foote's American *Iliad*, and we say and do the same things over and over, Luce. My serial marriages are the same story as serial wars—filled with dazzling stupidities and a willful lack of insight. I did it because I knew better. That's why, darling. Like touching a hot stove or wet paint—to prove that we can disobey. Parents raise their young to believe in rules or to believe in breaking them. The former get "good girls" who marry young, stay faithful, have 1.75 children, and show up at Rev. Tanner's little cottage of an Episcopal church each Sunday morning. The latter get girls with tattoos and piercings, cigarettes and wanderlust, who drink and love, even when they are not loving or loved. Each of those children, the good and the bad, winds up paying for those twin sins. Both writhe with regret.

Parents say, "I did the best I could for her." I will speak the unspoken, then: "I did *not* do the best I could for you, Lucy McKay. I could have done so much more. I am trying to do what I can in this Last Chance Saloon, but so far I can do nothing. I am held captive by more than disease. I try each day to break away from it. I want to feel myself coming toward you in the dark, to save you."

June 12

So you came in and started a fight with Victor today, and I gave you a classroom lecture. I think I said something like "We believe what is true is good." Oh, my God. But Victor wanted to fight you as well, and I am not so naïve as to believe that you fight over me.

You fight over the past. I know it.

The parts of my body that do not hurt are growing number by the day, but it's a slow-growing garden, Lucy, and I can't bear your anger. (How odd that "number" means "with less feeling" and "an integer.") This anger that I created in you for your eternity. It accuses me, and I am guilty.

I wish that I could have made love with a woman once more. Men of my age still do and can, you know. The young always believe that those who grow old do so without physical love, but that's not true. Men much older than I am still make passionate love with their life mates, filled and fulfilled in the world. If you have the chance, do you take it? A divorced man in a college town with several thousand horny young women? Do *you*? I hope so. Not your own students—don't want you to get fired. But a few women always throw them-selves at their male professors, because they want the intellect inside of them. Natural selection drives them together. Almost always, it is a disaster for both, but for some, it is beautiful.

I want the beautiful again, Lucy. I want something almost true in my life. I need for us to love each other this summer. Please love me. Please love me. Please. Oh Lucy, please love me.

June 13

Rain came today, and I stayed inside and looked out the glass wall toward the mountains and daydreamed of health. You were pensive all day, Lucy, remembering something you would not share.

You looked the same way when we visited Edisto Island that year you turned seven. The day we got there, you made a friend named Maria, dark-haired and fizzing with life, while I watched your mother cozy up to Maria's father, who looked like Montgomery Clift. Her flirtation infuriated me, and I finally dragged you back to the room—a small one with a clattery air conditioner, which was all we could afford in those days.

"Please bring me back to Maria," you moaned an hour later. Not *take* me back but *bring* me back. I felt as if I would die. Your mother had not yet returned, and I stood on the balcony and saw her talking with Monty Clift, and I hated them both with a rage I can't quite describe.

"Not now," I said. "We are busy."

"We're not doing *anything*, and she's still down there!" you said. "I can see her! Please bring me back to Maria, Daddy, *please!*" I refused to budge, and you sat on the foot of the bed and cried while bright and charming Maria made another friend and played her heart away.

Years later I asked you if you remembered it, and you looked at me as if I were a professional storyteller, a *griot* from Africa with fanciful family histories. I have suffered for that moment all my life. And when your mother, with her beery breath and innocent conquest came back to the room, I savaged her with my silence, and she knew.

I still do it. I hate your interest in the Crayton man, whose father killed himself rather than face the truth of his justice. But I fear this disease is killing me so that I can atone as well. Do saints also suffer, Lucy? Are they saints because of their bad consciences? Are they saints because they are afraid?

June 14

Oh, my God, I am tired tonight, Lucy. You and Victor took me to that clinical moron Dr. Retherston in Asheville today, and I fought with my body all the way there and back.

Victor went on and on about the dissertation we both pretend he will one day finish. He can't, of course, at least not until I am dead. He is the student I recruited to the department and now won't release, and both of us are happy with the idea. It sickens me that you see through it all.

But you can't see through it all. No one can see through my opaque life, and each day I feel farther and farther from the truth. Victor has probably read every book, every paper—everything—ever written on the Underground Railroad. This makes him an expert on Victor.

We were late getting in for my appointment, and I wanted to slay armies! I could never abide waiting, and once I had achieved my fame, I always had the phrase in my contract "Events shall run on time," which frightened some of my university hosts. Once, I swear, we were half an hour late getting from a classroom to a dinner, and I walked out on my escort, roared back to the hotel, checked out, and flew home, still demanding full payment.

Then that goddamn idiot of a doctor saying "let us know about the efficacy of your palliatives"! Your face turned red—did you know that?

So Dr. Retherston's stupid phrase assaulted us for its deliberate obfuscation, its attempt to make suffering sound like a day in the country. I started laughing, quite hideously, I am sure. Then, on the way back here, Victor jabbered like a spring blue jay, and you were silent as a midnight cemetery.

I love you so madly. I am ruined and destroyed. I cannot love at all what I love nearly alone in my dark passion. God help and forgive me. I am so tired.

June 15

I felt rather good today, Lucy, but you weren't around much. I always took Sundays as a challenge—if this was a day on which everyone rested, I'd work twice as hard. Remember? I'd drag you to the office with me, and I'd sit there for hours while you colored or read or did beadwork. Maybe that's what you did with your long walk today.

You tell me you've met some of the neighbors, especially Betty and Hunt Bearden, who lost a son to leukemia, I think, years and years ago. I want to hate them for their obvious happiness, for their sharp retirement planning, for the obvious affection that binds them in the sunset years. They glow, don't they? They have passed the dread of their own parents' deaths—Betty's mother was the last, and she died a year ago. But I can't hate them for being what I cannot.

I had Victor read me from Psalms today, but all that tearing of clothes and watering their couches with tears annoyed me. I made him read from the Song of Solomon, and he hated it so much that he read through his teeth like Kirk Douglas. I sent him away and came to my room and listened to the early Beatles, which usually makes me happy.

I *do* want to be happy, Lucy, I want to find an angle on joy that has nothing to do with my honors or my books. I want to feel the pleasure a child must when she sees it will be a sunny summer day, and she can play outside for hours. I want to believe in a future for all of us. But no one has an imagination that rich. So I must face down the inevitable and make my peace with it. And with you.

I had to beg you to come this summer, remember? And tomorrow is the fund-raiser for Save Our Mountains, and Victor has planned the whole thing, and I am to be the paperweight at which the supplicants worship. Hideous.

What do we save and how can we save it? None of the wealthies who will be here tomorrow will see the irony of it all—this gated community where they mowed down so many acres, and we men and women, saying we should protect our trees. You will see it immediately, no doubt.

I am going to try to be happy, Lucy. Already, I have wasted half a month being myself. But I have always courted fame and misery in equal measures. Each was permission to drink and make terrible mistakes—I have made them since infancy, it seems. When my life began to feel too middle class, I would sleep with my host at UCLA or Brown. God, what you must think of me.

But I am not the horror of a man you probably imagine. So I will say it again: Forgive me, and if you can, maybe I can forgive myself.

June 16

You fled before the first woman arrived, and I don't blame you.

"Where are you going?" I asked. Victor was in the kitchen arguing with the caterer.

"Out," you said.

"Out where?"

"I don't know, Pratt," you sighed. "Shopping. Doing tourist crap. I don't know. I just don't want to be around while your friends from the University come to help plot." I started laughing, because that's precisely what academics do, don't we? We *plot*.

So I watched you drive away just as Victor came into the room saying, "Carrots! She brought carrots instead of broccoli for the veggie plate!" You would have thought Barbarians were at the gate.

Barbara Lully, from comparative literature, is our eco-firebrand, and she came to rail, and she did. The passion of the healthy is turning odd to me, Luce. The more I age, the more I am ravaged, the more I believe that everything we do in life is dithering. We are simply taking our mind off what will happen to us. I'm thinking of geniuses again—are they simply the ones who fear death the most? Einstein was twenty-six and living inside his own head when he came up with Special Relativity. It isn't the work of a normal man, thank God. Barbara, no genius, delivered herself of a speech that was prepared to a T, but which she pretended was impromptu. She was perfect, meaning mildly ridiculous, and Victor looked at me and raised one chevron eyebrow, and I started to laugh and cough—hideous, I admit. But Barbara only paused and glared at the interruption and then launched right back into it.

When you got home, they were fighting about new-growth versus old-growth forests, and we hadn't raised a penny or made any plans to. We were just dithering, as you were.

June 17

I apologize, Lucy. I am the greatest fool in the world's history. I know it. Last night I dreamed that I was at a sort of run-down movie theatre with my mother, and we were both young, and the bathroom was like something from the Spanish Inquisition as designed by Aubrey Beardsley. There were all kinds of plumbing devices that I couldn't understand—rusted tin tubs filled with reddish brown water; urinals with huge fluted lips; lead pipes routed endlessly around the room over which one had to step. And I needed to go, and I didn't know where or quite how. So I simply stared at the structures, and then men and women came in, and they moved as though one sex couldn't see the other, and both sexes seemed to pee against a wall standing up.

I awoke thrashing and soaked and humiliated. Victor came and cleaned me up.

"Don't tell Lucy about this," I said.

"I won't," said Victor. "Pratt, I'm trying to be good. I don't want her to hate me. This is so complicated."

He has no idea how complicated it is.

Then, after I was up, you and Victor started fighting yet again, this time over the grocery list, for God's sake, and I lost my goddamn mind when you mentioned the Crayton man, and I, fool and bastard, began to lecture you on Sartre and de Beauvoir! As if you didn't know all about them. I remember when I first fell in love with both and the idea of existentialism, that nothing really mattered, that we are circumscribed in this world by no rules but the ones we create.

That was when I began to cheat on your mother. At first, it was rather like the usual drunken flings we have after seven years of marriage, but then it became a weapon. I was a pure shit, as my father would say. I wanted to know the limits of suffering. You saw it, and that was when you pulled your heart from your mother and me and began to retreat, to grow silent. You all but quit talking, like some medieval nun who has taken a vow. You became a connoisseur of silence. And so I lectured you this morning and said that Sartre was "nothing," my idea of a joke. Jesus.

I am ruining this summer, and it was to be the season of our epiphany.

June 18

I am too drugged to dream these days. I rarely sleep. I nap. At first, when I awaken, I have forgotten what has happened to me, and then I remember, and I want to cry, but I can't. I am trying to shape a new narrative for us, Cricket, one that you will remember when you are my age, and I am long dust. I watched Westerns on TV today, and I loved the distance they brought me. James Arness, John Wayne, Roy Rogers. They make me forget, and I love things that make me forget.

Then Ella Seitz came over with, in the name of God, a Bundt cake. After Victor took it into the kitchen, Ella sat with me and rubbed my arms and legs and talked about her late grandson, Isaiah, and then she showed me pictures and as always said the last three words of every sentence I spoke. She endowed a chair in Russian history at UNC in his memory—that's how we first met.

She must seem like yet another crazy neighbor to you, Lucy, but she's mostly alone and she needs to hear the words of others spoken twice—perhaps to make them last. Not all echoes are unmeaning repetitions in this world.

June 19

I can't sleep. So here I am talking into this thing at 8:30 at night, and you're still out with Sean Crayton, and I hope you are doing what I would be doing. I hope you are accepting the love I never gave you.

We fear death but we love sleep. And the latter is just the little sister of the former, isn't it? Is that why I can't sleep?

I did nothing today but rip away a calendar leaf. I really thought I would narrate the story of my life into this machine, as I said a long time ago, but that hasn't happened because I cannot face the eventual end of the story. So here I am, speaking of me me me me me.

I need to sail beyond this self-absorption, Cricket. I want to giggle again and feel a woman's caress on my neck. I want to swim in the Danube, scale the Matterhorn. I want to be the King of the National Archives. And the whole truth is so close to both of us. Closer than you could ever dream.

I hear you coming in, so perhaps it wasn't a night of new romance. It takes a while to learn love, doesn't it? I fall out of love easier than I fall into it.

If I traffic among academics, it is because they were my salvation, Lucy. If I have been unable to trust the real world, it is because it betrayed me first. But this is still the half of it. I want to tell you the whole truth, but I can't. This isn't the whole truth. This isn't any of the truth.

June 20

Oh, God. *God.* I am so sorry for today. I tortured you today, Cricket, about your date with Sean Crayton, and it was jealousy. I can't imagine that you didn't see through this, but I am as usual ruining our summer, destroying what is left of my attempt to love you and show you my life.

Victor sat like Buddha working on the *Times* crossword puzzle while I fought my body, and my mind fought me. I decided to wound, or rather the wound asked me to unleash it, so I called Crayton a *yard boy*, and you bristled, even though the date couldn't have gone well since you were so unhappy. Then I told you about his father, and I did it with cold calculation, with lancing effect. Like the bastard I am. Then my physical therapist, Sunshine Ginger shows up, and I whine and complain, and you flee, Lucy.

This is nothing new for me, since I have always tried to win victories and destroy others at the same time like a scrap fighter, a club-level pug. I am capable of blind revenge, like a mythic monster mother, and I once single-handedly set back the career of a young assistant professor named Ron Milsen, a scholar of the Italian Renaissance. His book got delayed at some university press, and I held him to the rules, and we voted against giving him tenure. He wound up working in an archives in Arizona. At the time, I thought of myself as some Kraken rising from the sea in revenge, because he had ruined the marriage of one grad couple in the department and compromised another, while shaming his sweet wife. But I was no better. No one is any better.

So I think of Ron Milsen now as I sit in this goddamned room with its goddamned view and regret every angry word I have ever spoken to you. And I am ashamed for telling you of Sean Crayton's father.

My elbows are getting numb, but slowly, slowly, like lichen growing in a cold climate.

June 21

We were distant from each other today. Lucy, you must know. Each victory in my life, each ambition fulfilled, was like a silver stake in the heart of my childhood. I have been saying, "You cannot destroy me.

You tried and you failed. I almost died but I did not break down. Lie there and roar yourself into eternal rage."

This is my voice, Pratt McKay, for his daughter Lucy, the one to whom I cannot speak, whom I adore and cannot say it out loud. I am a fool.

June 22

Yet more serial stupidities. Before church, I tried to tell you about Jacqueline du Pré, but you knew already—*of course* you knew. As if that chance connection somehow made me like her. You rightly ignored me and turned away.

Faith is the great mystery. We sophisticated people deride it, laugh at it, find ways to deny it all, and then we genuflect in the night. I believe it must serve some genetic need—some biological imperative, and I tried to talk to your mother about it once when our marriage had begun to crumble, but she laughed at me and said I must be going soft in the brain. That hurt me terribly. Now, I begin to cling because I fear. There is no more elegant explanation.

So you and Victor took me to church, and while tan and trim Parnell preached, I felt myself being thrown around the pew by demons. Others watched me with sympathy and horror, and with their eyes they screamed, "Leper!" and with their hellos, they stoned me. I can no longer make the sign of the cross, though I tried and my right arm flailed all over the bruised air before me. Nor could I kneel in supplication to a loving and naturally violent God. (I have already told you I am not a believer. Oh, what a small liar I am.)

But the most terrible moment was during the Lord's Prayer when I began to cry. It wasn't what you probably thought, darling—it was the memory of my boyhood, of the screaming and drunken fights on those hideous Saturday nights between my mother and father, and how on Sundays I hid in the Word. I have always, it seems, hidden in words. I believe in their talismanic effect, their ability to shield and engage. So when we came to "on Earth, as it is in Heaven," I broke apart, rotten as a mud clot in an arroyo. You took my hand, and I sought a grip, and I watched my own palm as if it were someone else's—a starving woman in Bangladesh, a Jewish boy headed for the terminal shower, a man bearing bloody nails for the salvation of this world.

So, I am not Jackie du Pré. I do not have within my hands the music that makes others tremble. Do I still have the music of our lives? Are we growing, finally, closer together?

I wanted to stay until everyone was gone from the sanctuary, to have you bear me altarwise so that I could whisper the tatters of my ending prayers toward God, toward the power and the glory. Instead, you and Victor gave me the bum's rush just before the sending hymn, hustled me out the back door beneath the spare symbols of our cottage church. I did manage at least to pitch mammon into the offering plate with my club of a left hand, but that was a sad gesture, I know.

Oh, God, look down upon us all with your magnificent pity. Let me speak the words to my beloved daughter I must speak before I am struck mute and lie down and turn into stone.

June 23

You were pensive today, Lucy. Are you thinking of Sean Crayton? Do you want to believe something? I have believed in Saint Pratt for most of my life, a laughable proposition. I wanted honors—more and more of them. I made sure I was in a position to earn them. I was not so much pensive as acquisitive.

Oh fool. Oh dear stupid fool and waste of a man—so I am.

I love you. Can you, now driving back across the South toward hot Mississippi, love me again? If not, please work to forgive me. I am lost in geology among these green folds, these fir-haired labia. I am waiting to be born again.

June 24

Another day in prison. I am in Chillon, my own Romantic cage, but unlike Byron I can't scratch my name on anything. As I speak to-night, you are out again with Sean Crayton, and I hope he takes you to bed. I do. I have read that the presence of semen in a vagina releas-es endorphins for the woman—the sheer presence of that tablespoon of fluid.

Hearing this from your father probably nauseates you. Sorry. Isn't this the kind of thing that fathers and daughters should be able to share, Lucy?

You are not too old to be abandoned, but we need seducing from time to time. I pray that tonight you are involved with sweet seduc-tions—done to you or by you, it doesn't matter which.

June 25

It's the middle of the afternoon, and calm has shakily been restored around here. It began over orange juice. Victor saw you getting it for me.

"I'll take that to him," he said, and he tried to pry it from your fingers.

"Goddamn, Victor, take your fucking hands off me," you shout-ed. I was impressed. Victor clamped like a pit bull, and the two of you threw the juice glass halfway across the room, turning a streak of my white carpet orange. I wanted to break you up immediately, but I liked being fought over, God help me. You went nose to nose, each of you claiming me as conquered territory.

"Lucy, look at the mess you made," said Victor, malicious and snarly.

"Just—stop—you two idiots!" I screamed. Your hands were drip-ping and sticky, both of you, and we all posed like a statue of family disorder.

"I'm going to tear his goddamn eyes out!" you screamed.

"Cricket, Cricket, Cricket!" I cried. I don't know where it came from, Lucy, but it came, and I felt myself trying to cry, but nothing came up, my emotions stuck in the dry heaves. You ran to your room, and I could hear you shouting aloud and throwing things around, but the noise finally slowed.

"Pratt, I was just …." Victor began, but I cut him off.

"I want it stopped now," I said, each word weighing tons. "Go to her and make it up or I will ask both of you to leave."

He fumed, and I suppose he thought I would forgive him, but I didn't. I managed to fold my arms and watch him with Olympian disdain. He apologized and cleaned up the juice and sprayed out the stain. He couldn't go at first, but as I speak, I can see him through the doors of my room speaking to you on the back porch. He is telling you something untrue, a lie he believes.

It is my lie and my sorrow.

June 26

You went grocery shopping for me this morning after I gave Victor a warning glance not to argue with you. Soon, I will no longer need anything to sustain me but memory. I am terrified, Lucy, absolutely *terrified*.

I went into my bathroom this afternoon, and managed to strip myself and climb into a hot tub. Could it be possible that I might be restored by love? I had to get Victor to test the temperature because I can't tell hot from cold on my hands very well anymore. That, I believe, is how evil begins, when people can no longer make distinctions between the night and the nightmare. After the tub was full, I asked Victor to leave, and I sat naked on the stool in front of my full-length mirror.

Oh, that mirror. Just two years ago an assistant professor of comp lit and I made love in front of it, me admiring her taut young body a little and my strong lithe middle-aged one more. I wanted to howl against every person who had done me ill, at every real or perceived injustice. I can't remember her name. Fran. No, *Franny*. Who tried to explain *Faust* to me! I brought Franny for the weekend, and that was it, a saccharine tryst, what in my youth was called a "fling." I told no one about it, but Franny did, so much that a colleague in the department, two weeks later, asked if I "and the Faustian" were going to the mountains that weekend.

I called her up and argued. But it was ridiculous, Lucy, because I thought she was *my* conquest, and she thought I was *hers*. I never saw her again, but I remember our standing dance in front of that narcissistic mirror. So today, when I saw my immemorial body, I felt shocked and horrified.

Death is putting me on like a Sunday suit. He numbs my elbows and knees, turns my once-strong hands to stone. He is familiar and terrible, the man sitting with his knees apart in that mirror. His skin is lemon and unshiny, and his wrinkles gather to gossip. The belly is shrunken up, a *National Geographic* photograph from the Thirties. He can't control some of his muscles, and so his bones go jumpy beneath the stretching skin. He and his tics tack from one side of the stool to the other.

And yet he felt sexual sitting there, too, that much memory stored away. You may want to fast-forward beyond what I will tell you now, Lucy. But if you want to know me, listen, darling. I will still speak in the third person to unmanage the focus.

He sat there and could not stop looking between his legs, remembered sex and lusty bed-sheet nights. He recalled conferences with Jack Daniel's and the common thrust of strangers. He told himself stories of vindictive sex, getting-even sex, enraged sex, bored sex, surprising failures, and wanton slick successes.

So I thought of Angela. I was dating your mother but had not yet succumbed to the monotheism she demanded of me. Angela was a graduate student in history with me, and she wore the sheen of the doomed, the acceptance of early crisis and wrong decisions. Angela

Hammer—odd name but perhaps one naming an occupation, like Smith. Angela was unexceptional in almost every way—washed out blue eyes that never seemed to land on anything, pale skin, and slender wrists. She had one passion: The Civil War. So I let her take me to the Gettysburg battlefield for the weekend, and during our walk, she was trembling, explaining. When she held out a pointing finger, the sorrow overwhelmed her. She spoke of Meade and Lee, of feints and fishhooks. That night, in a slat-board motel with eavesdropping walls, I pounced on her, and halfway through, she became cold and unable.

I gave her the standard face-saving speech, the one that must appear theoretical, since she probably believed I was a virgin. We lay in the dark, and she began to sob—really sob—and it frightened me, Lucy. Then she said, "Oh, the boys. That terrible day. That *terrible day.*" And I did something unconscionable, though I've done worse. I said, "Angela, the battle took three days, not one." I said it to wound, sniper of the heart. She turned into a monument. I apologized, but it was too late. She had been seeing herself as a sacrifice, as a heroic girl—this weak young woman who could never have been any kind of Clara Barton, even. And I had killed that image for her forever.

So as I sat before the mirror, I thought of Angela and how I had squandered her affection, and then I remembered that after I won the Pulitzer she sent me an e-mail, congratulating me, asking me if I remembered her, and telling me that for two decades she had owned a model-train store in St. Louis. She had three daughters. Her husband was an oncologist. She sounded very happy. All of this came to me as the water in the tub cooled, and my arm flopped between my legs, and I left it there, and closed my legs on it—odd that I could barely feel my arm and exquisitely felt my crotch. And I looked at the man in the mirror and then closed my eyes and thought of Angela, and within a minute, it happened, and it wasn't the sparkler and fizz version but something Mahleresque, like the panorama of a Napoleonic battle or a Tolstoy novel.

I nearly fell off the stool, and I frightened Victor, who knocked and asked if I was all right. I don't know where you were—reading on the deck? I had to speak rationally to Victor and I didn't want to. The sensation began to spread all over me, too, and the nerve endings from toes to scalp rejoiced, and I was a man again, perhaps one last time. I managed to slip into the water, which was still warm, and I closed my eyes, and I was back in that cracker-hard bed, just off the field of battle, a young man with a young girl, neither of us understanding what love requires of us.

And then, in the glow of climax and a bath, I launched into an after-dinner speech about Foucault and my idiotic invention, Postfeminist Literalism. I think I was trying to impress you with how smart I am. I have always thought that to be a perfectly acceptable substitute for love. Oh, fool, oh, fool that I am. Are you sorry, yet, for me?

Do not hate me for sharing this intimacy. I want to love you, and I am learning how. Be patient with what is left of me.

June 27

We are not speaking. You have your orange juice and coffee mornings, your paperback afternoons, your out-for-a-drive evenings. I narrate, first to Victor, and then to you.

I must begin to tell you. We have held too many secrets between us, Lucy. Will you forgive me when you know? When you realize how close the truth is to both of us and has been all summer?

I wish it would rain.

June 28

I was so afraid today that I could not bear it. I could not bear it.

June 29

You and I talked today, finally, a month after you came to spend the summer with me, and it was cathartic, at least a little.

"You should make sure you don't miss a dose of your medicine," you said. I replied that I knew it. I said I understood that you had come to spend time with me in my illness but that you were miserable around me. You admitted that you were always miserable, and I wanted to die for it. I tried to defend Victor a little, but of course it isn't what it appears.

We argued about which of us had the real influence through our work, each of us on the side of the other. You brought up Lenora, whom I married for her accent. I had this vision of me taking her to parties in my honor and then launching into her Queen's English; it would make me more international. Then there was Alessandra. She loved to shop and chat, and in the end I wanted someone with whom I could fight. I wanted someone I could make hate me. Nothing I did outraged her. When I spent the night at a conference with a lovely young wonder from Yale, I confessed immediately. She was giddy for details. I should have left her then. I should have suspected.

You asked me if I was talking to myself in my room at night. How could I tell you about this oral history? How could I say that I speak to you in your absence because I cannot speak to you in your presence? What mad grandeur is that?

Am I still alive or have I died, Lucy? Are you still in the mountains or are you almost home to Oxford? Or am I a bucket of ashes on the seat next to you? And is this the same thing as always, pride, bombast, and appalling self-interest? If I am gone, I cannot know. If I am still here, I cannot know.

June 30

You were gone all day. Victor said you left with Sean Crayton, and I sent you to his bed with my failing powers of concentration. I wanted to say: *Make a mistake. Do not have a life without mistakes. Do not design your days to avoid suffering.*

When I was fifteen, I used to sit in my room and wish I'd never been born. But it was never true. We dramatize our lives for narrative's sake. And so I say to you now: Stay, Lucy McKay, stay with me for July and let me make right what I never have before in this life. Give me another chance. Give me another month. Forgive me.

I want to be a father once more.

3. Lucy

July 1

I cannot leave next week, not after last night. Pratt's soft bedroom mumbling, his incantory sibilance drives me mad in the night, but it cannot take me from Sean. I think of him all the time, always.

J. called from Oxford at 10, manic but apparently sober, to tell me he knows what he's been doing wrong as a writer. He's given me this speech a hundred times since our New York days, since he had an agent and made it as far as the cusp. J. has listened over and over to the recordings of Faulkner and now sounds like him, that patrician softening, that belief that mankind (if not J.) will prevail.

"It's a mattuh of moah cayhfully renderin' mah characters, Luce-eh," he says in his summer-morning-on-the-porch syllables.

"For God's sake, James, you're from New Hampshire," I say. "Stop with the old-folks-at-home accent before I barf. I really don't want to talk about your book. We're not married anymore, remember?"

"To make othuhs believe, you fust haf to believe youself," he Faulkners. I can almost hear him whittling. He, who has never believed in me or much of anything else more than a day.

But that's unfair. He believes in the *image* of the writer. If he had the tiniest seed of talent and a million years, he might write a book through sheer evolutionary chance. He has neither. I can't write about J. more or again.

And how in these pages have I rendered Sean Crayton? Or my father? The former has green cat eyes that glow in a bedroom nightlight. The latter whispers to ghosts in his room. I want to weave them together into a single story, but they cannot fit yet. I do not see beyond their differences. We are born judges. We can't avoid it. We sit lordly on our imperial thrones and watch for weakness and then attack it; we cull friends from the herd if they show weakness or have the poor grace to age.

And so when I awoke this morning, Sean sat Indian-style, naked on the bed looking at me as one might a rare dream. His flat tan stomach and his sharp clavicles, standing out like spokes of a marimba, ready to be played. His outdoor beard and his sandy hair curled from love's exertions. His big hands resting on his knees, Asian, a perfect poise. I followed the landscape of his body with my eyes, and he followed mine as I sat up and let the covering sheet fall away.

"What are you doing?" I asked hoarsely. "What time is it?"

"Watching the sun rise," he said. I started to laugh. No. Accept the compliment and wallow in its unaffected juvenilia. I am nothing to study anymore, and his eyes loved me anyway. Then bathroom and then bedroom again, and for an hour we curved our lines, one inside another. Toothpaste kisses and the rough skin of his hairy chest along my breasts.

I've felt him on me all day. His deep impression, his shape on the aging mattress of my body. I can't subside or think, even if J. does try to trickle back into my life.

Late at night

Pratt did something I thought impossible: he walked with me in the warm evening down the street. He is weak as a hatchling, and he took my arm, and I was his escort, debutante and date, strolling down the safe and guarded streets of homogenous America. Victor danced with fear.

"But if he falls," said Victor, all but wringing his hands. "If he *falls!*"

"For God's sake, I won't fall," Pratt said. "I'll hold on to Lucy. We're just going to the corner and back, Victor."

"We were going to continue dictation," V. said, petulant, all but sticking his lower lip out like a mad little boy. Pratt can't bother with a response.

From the first steps outside the house—our last walk together?—I knew it was a mistake, for my father can hardly bear his own weight anymore. The perfect lawns blossomed perfect couples. The threatless street threatens me. I want to hear Rico, the poultry plant shift supervisor who lives in my apartment complex, screaming at his girlfriend and calling her a whore because she smiled at a man when they were eating out. I want to run into Timothy Sain in Square Books and buy him the complete Marvell and tell him love is a brief salve he can't count on. Even poor James, brigand for Southern ghosts and crumbling mansions, would be a relief here. But I could only think of my father and bear his weight against me.

"The thing is, it came on so fast, Luce," he said. "One day I was getting ready to fly to Boston, and the next I couldn't feel my left hand. I thought it was a stroke. I told everybody I'd had a stroke. I felt like a hero. Then to find out it's MS, that slow monster. Not as much glory. Not."

It took him half a minute to say that much, his sentences broken apart by the disease in ways I cannot reproduce. It was *agony*. I waited for his confession. He smelled like the coming dead—stale and old-mannish, though lilting with a bit of cologne.

And how have I rendered his character? In this journal and in my life? I do not understand fathers and daughters, never have. My parents are both academics, and yet I feel their jealousy when they speak of my high-school-teacher's life. How can that be? It can be because it is true.

My father did not fall. James will not write his great novel. I cannot see beyond this summer with Sean Crayton. I do not know what matters. I will try not to fear what I cannot see beyond.

July 2

I drove to Dogear Books today, an impossibly steamy day, still and cloudless. The owner, Olaf Knussen, seemed not to have moved. He sat in his office smoking his pipe and reading, waiting for any annoying purchasers to bring their loot to him.

"Do you happen to have any signed Faulkner?" I asked. He raised his right eyebrow and marked his page with a long paper bookmark. He is shaggy and slow. "Not that I could afford it, I have to tell you ahead of time."

"I got a signed *Sound and the Fury* for Mr. Aalens over in Blowing Rock," he said, dithering. "He's a completist."

"A completist?"

"Trying to obtain the entire signed corpus. Ah. Eh. Was an executive with ah Eli Lilly. You have to be a, ah, wealthy man to be a completist. What is your interest in Faulkner?"

"Actually, I live in Oxford. I teach high school English. Faulkner's the town's number-one tourist attraction."

"Glad you're not one trying to *be* Faulkner," he said, gesturing to the empty bookshop with his pipe, which had gone out. "Lot a them, too. People don't like who they are, pick out somebody else to try *be*."

Bizarre and unbelievable. He brought out *A Fable*, my least favorite Faulkner, and there in the front was Faulkner's famous cramped and disappearing signature, his creeping need for near-invisibility. The price was insane. Mr. Knussen hovered, and I held it only a moment and then gave it back to him, and he locked it back up.

"So *you* wouldn't want to be Faulkner?" I asked on my way out.

"No, ma'am," he said. "He was an alcoholic. Didn't you know that?" As he spoke, he picked up the photograph of the woman and her little boy and buffed it with gentle love on his shirttail.

Would I not trade my Lucy-hood for such talent? Would I trade my health for a Pulitzer? My stability for a summer love? And how important is it, really, that we complete anything in this life? Or that we make a point in making a point?

July 3

Disappointed that it took him two days to call me again after our night together, but he came by at morning coffee time, when Pratt was struggling to dictate and failing. Victor kept trying to finish my father's sentences for him, eliciting howls of protest.

"No, no, no, no, no!" cried Pratt, his arms flailing air like Bernstein. Victor's shoulders slumped just as Ginger Dumont, chirpy therapist, came freckling into the room to Pratt's obvious disgust.

I had been on the deck for only fifteen minutes when I saw Sean standing not twenty feet away, arms folded over his chest, a Cheshire cat grin peeking out from the hedge of his beard.

"I'm here to explain the pitfalls of asceticism," he said, stepping on to the deck in his work jeans and a snug green T-shirt. My eyes went straight for his mark, and he saw me. "Sometimes Jains stand with one arm over their heads for years or refuse to use a foot as a means of showing they do not need it. Fasts of a month are not uncommon, even among Christian ascetics. Some of them have a special broom they carry to sweep away insects that might be on the ground, lest they tread upon them fatally. Howdy. Want to go to Independence Day in Carver tomorrow?"

I giggled like a girl, finger-bookmark snug in one of Julia Glass's plots.

"What's with asceticism?" I asked.

He flopped down beside me in one of Pratt's sturdy wooden Adirondack deck chairs.

"Self-denial is our victory over self. Where better to practice it than here, in a gated community, where nothing is denied or admitted? Where nothing tacky or tasteless is allowed? How's your father, Lucy?"

"God, Sean. Your mind works like a colander sifting the ashes of the Earth."

"Good non-sequitur. I was serious."

"About Pratt or fireworks?"

"We're putting in boxwoods on the next block. A woman wanting boxwoods and an arbor and two magnolias. I almost offered to throw in a couple of happy servants for free. I meant your dad."

I told him about the evening before, our walk and Pratt's wobbly struggle, and during that brief time, I saw him struggle with fathers and sons, with betrayals and the need for a hermitage. He ran his finger along the back of my hand.

"We can't reclaim what we never had in the first place," he said quietly. "Maybe that's not you and your father. It was me and mine. I think I never finished my dissertation because I didn't want to be a professional."

"There's nothing wrong with what you do, boy. A good business."

"You've heard the phrase `small businessman'? I'm a *midget* businessman. A micro-businessman. My net worth is too small to be netted."

"Ergo the explanation for asceticism."

"Ipso facto, Q.E.D," he said, leaping up. "And *ergo*, if we have to use all the Latin we know. Let's dance." He jerked me up by my hand, and we weren't Fred and Ginger. He didn't lead, and I didn't follow, but somehow we managed to glide around the deck, and I molded myself into him, and once I saw, glaring from the deck-window, Victor, holding a sheaf of unfinished dictation.

Yes, Sean Crayton, I will go with you to the Fourth of July. And I want to reclaim what I never had in the first place, a primacy among mother and father, to be the history he studied, the art she revealed. Is this why I have come?

Late in the day, Father Tanner came to pray with Pratt, and afterward, I walked him outside into the perfect street with its sheen of perfect manicure and mannered dogs clearing their throats at the setting sun.

"He's getting worse and worse," I heard myself say. "I want to think he's getting better. He's still a young man, and this disease is stalking and taking him, like some medieval monster that's crept from its lair."

"I don't think it's so fast as you think," Father Tanner said. "You've only been here a month. You have to see the sick over a long time to know the progress of their suffering."

"Nobody's supposed to suffer in Cedar Acres, though. Wasn't it gated to keep bad things like Death outside? Speaking of Medieval. Gated communities are liked walled cities, except the barbarians are black and Hispanic and work with their hands for a living. I guess that sounds pretty crass."

"That doesn't offend me. It's true." He nodded three times. "Actually, Pratt's the exception. There aren't that many academics here, particularly ones still working. He always wanted a place in the mountains, he said. When he was a little boy, he thought Mount Sinai was in North Carolina. I guess he told you that."

No, Father, he didn't tell me that. The idea that God would choose this place to live made me snort. Then, suddenly, I felt a sharp chill of recognition and memory: *streets of gold; perfect order; no suffering; no need, no want; a place where you never fear again.* The idea of it felt shattering: the recreation of heaven or at least its childhood narrative. The entranceway with its guardhouse: *pearly gates.* I wanted to scream, but the streets were silent.

"He told me about it," I lied.

"Then you know that how haunted he's been all his life about the South and about the Civil Rights Movement, especially the suffering its women came to know so well. You understand that his need for heaven confused itself with the South's need for redemption. That's why he is here. On these streets. Maybe we imagine it all, Lucy. Maybe. But we tell the same old stories, and the stories aren't important. It's the voice that matters. His voice matters."

"Faulkner's voice."

"Absolutely. The voices of the family falling apart over generations. That story's been told since the Greeks. But they never told it the way he did. Of the stranger coming into someone's life and changing it utterly. That's in the Bible. But Faulkner made it all new. I'll tell you something if you promise you won't tattle."

"Cross my heart."

"I love *The Sound and the Fury* better than eighty percent of the Bible." He tented his hands with just-suppressed glee as he laughed, and in that position, someone down the street might have though he was praying for me.

July 4

It's cricket time by now, really July 5. I arose early yesterday morning, and V. was pacing in the kitchen with a glass of OJ and a look of sleepless horror.

"What's wrong?" I asked.

"Lucy," he said. "Lucy." I felt my arm hair bristle, and I knew Pratt was dead, and I saw myself tottering into his bedroom, friable ruin that I am, bursting into unfelt tears. "I've wasted my life." I felt murderous.

"Victor, take a pill or something. It's the fucking Fourth of July. America the Beautiful and all that crap."

"Would you let me hug you?" I felt assaulted and put on the kettle for coffee.

"No, of course not. Call Father Tanner."

"I don't feel *anything*. That's the problem Lucy. I don't feel anything. I'm just like your father." He could see my anger, which was turning into rage. "Sorry, sorry. This is going all wrong. Please, forgive me. I'm so sorry. It's just that you seem to feel everything, and I feel nothing. I kill every feeling I have before it can surface. Something's wrong with me."

"Let me make coffee first. Then tell me. Okay?" Human warmth crept into my voice, and he almost wept for it. I felt ashamed of myself. We sat on the deck in the warmth of a perfect mountain morning. His tale was long and barely punctuated, filled with verbal cul-de-sacs, misplaced modifiers, and long bouts of personal history, which might have been written by Will Durant.

"The truth is that I don't want to be like Dr. McKay," he said finally. He had wet himself with flop-sweat. Songbirds had awakened, wild for arias and for morning. "I always wanted to teach high school history. That's what I really wanted to do. I had Mr. Tuttle. People made merciless fun of him. They splattered the board with spitballs. But he made American history come alive for me. I hated the *now*. I wanted to live in the *then*. I'm not cut out for writing books, and I'm not even sure about teaching college. I never was going to be famous at anything. I just made myself try and then I got addicted to failure. I never told this to a living soul."

I was almost too shocked to react, and my first thought was he was manipulating me; if he had been a woman, I would have known it to be true. We're smart that way and proud of the strength of our deviousness. So I looked hard at him, and I knew he was falling apart. So I came to him, and I held him—the man I'd loathed for the past month—and I held him close until control came back to him. The songbirds never missed a note. His grasp was not sexual or even adult. His disease retreated, and in that mastery, gratitude came out like sunrise. I was stunned at how much I liked him at that moment.

"Probably not good to be sentimental about teaching high school," I warned him. "Most of my students sleep. Yours would sleep during the French and Indian War and wake up during Prohibition."

He laughed and nodded, and that was it. Our bonding, his confession. I still find him intrusive and distasteful, wish he weren't here. I understand Pratt's need for an assistant and graduate student; the desire for sycophants is always strange, though.

Sean picked me up late morning, and we drove to his house for the lazy day, and I kissed my father goodbye and apologized for leaving, and he flailed around me and shooed me off, and I wanted to die. He tried to speak to me then, my father did, and perhaps it was the story of his own history or the wandering of love, but no narrative appeared. I held his hand for a long time, and Sean faded from the room, and then Victor, and we sat alone.

"I'll be late coming home tonight," I said. "He's taking me to the fireworks." My father gathered himself enough to laugh. He closed his eyes and laughed merrily and nodded against the grip of his disease.

"I bet."

"Literally, I mean."

"I bet."

"This is getting worse and worse."

"Be happy each day," he struggled. "It may not come back. May not."

His body trembled around the still center of his mind, and I could do nothing for him and hated myself for leaving. If I came into his room at night, would he stop his ceaseless mumbling? I am frightened by the sound, but I cannot say so. I wanted to point out that he'd had a great life, that he'd been crowned with all glories, that he was a man admired worldwide, that his students still crowed about studying at Chapel Hill with Pratt McKay.

"I'll make it come back for you," I said. "I promise you an epiphany. Hang on Pratt. I'll find one for you."

"Will you, now, Miss Lucy McKay?"

"Or die trying." On the way out, his nurse, Mary Lou Wadely, was coming in, and her smile warmed me and felt so familiar, so deeply comforting that for a moment she seemed like someone I had met years before. We talked for a while, and I did not want her to leave, though finally she had to. I presume Pratt and Victor hired her. I don't know and am too embarrassed to ask. But I like her so much.

Die trying. I hated saying that. I wanted to say what I said as a girl, what he taught me to say when we sweetly agreed: *Right as rain.* I loved the sound of it, the feeling that a gentle summer rain held us close and together. He would say, *Aren't we having a fine time today, Miss Lucy McKay?* And I'd hug him close and say, *Right as rain.* But I hadn't said it to him since I was twelve and had witnessed a shrieking fight between my parents, the beginning of their end. If I said it, I'd be erasing more than years. I couldn't do it. I just couldn't. I had said it often to James in our early years, but I quit saying it with him, too, After the Fall.

I was too silent for Sean as we drove, and he reached over and tickled me in the cool cabin of his truck, and I flinched and told him to quit. He sensed my unhappy hesitation and apologized.

"Do you ever start feeling closed in up in the mountains?" I asked. "Oxford is in the Piedmont, and it's right at the Delta. The West isn't far away."

"Well, I grew up in Asheville, which really isn't a mountain town, but I got out when I had to," he said slowly and softly. I knew: his father. "Closed in was what I wanted, Lucy. I wanted to be alone and to work with plants. I could come back to my house and hide. Probably why my wife ran off and left me. Marriages don't last when the partners are half hermit and half whore."

He made me laugh, something James never did, and I just adored the man. Still, in my heart, I felt sick about Pratt. A month into my stay, I'd accomplished absolutely nothing in knowing my father better, and he was slowly growing worse by the day. My own love life had been ridiculous, too. After the usual serial blunderings, I'd attached myself to James, attracted by the power of his dreams, not wanting to remember that empty dreams bring down dreamers in the end. They promise transcendence and then they torture and kill. In turn, James had wanted to be Thomas Pynchon, Ernest Hemingway, Sylvia Plath (!), and finally Faulkner. I, his proposed muse, finally told him Art was exhausted and needed greener pastures.

We got solemnly to Sean's house, and immediately I felt the fires of our earlier tryst ignite me, and by the time we'd walked up the rough-hewn steps, I was wrapping myself into him and apologizing, running my right hand beneath his T-shirt and over the topographic map of his back. I shamed myself with teenage kisses, but they transported me away from the narrative I faced. I would have gone straight to bed, but he is slower, and first we drank a frothy cold beer in his airy den.

"So, tell me, in twenty words or less, why you like landscaping," I said. He sipped his Molson Pale Ale and nodded.

"I knew it would get around to this sooner or later. The source of my serial philandering. When I was a boy, and I wanted to run away, I ran away to my mother's garden. I'd lie on my stomach and look at the flowers and vegetables and look at the colors and the textures, inhale their perfumes. Vegetables all smell different. Kale smells nothing like broccoli. We always had two rows of corn, and the day we picked it, when we stripped open those ripe ears and that aroma washed over me, I felt like Parsifal kneeling before the Grail."

"I'd rather hear the more-exuberant version."

"There *is* a more-exuberant version, Miss Smarty Pants, I'll have you know. You haven't even begun to know an exub from me yet." He raised a lecturing finger. "All through high school I'd grow these insane gardens. Dad bought me an acre outside town, and I worked and made the money to hire plowing and planting. I tended it all, grew strange cultivars. It started out as a farm, but by the time I graduated it was a herbarium and a nursery. I was selling plants to the locals and installing landscapes and making so much money I stuffed it in socks and so forth. Turns out I was a chip off the old block."

I wasn't ready for that sharp turn in his narrative. I don't think Sean was, either.

"How did your father get trapped into that? You don't have to talk about it if you don't want to?"

"It's hard for me to talk about." He was suddenly in near-collapse, and I felt ashamed to have mentioned it at all. "My mom was already sick then with what eventually killed her, too. Hard. A dark time. Dark."

"Sorry—let's talk about something else. Say the first thing that comes to your mind."

"My darling, you look wonderful tonight."

"It's early afternoon."

"Eric Clapton weeps. It takes a real Snopes to ruin a moment like this, missy. I'm on to you."

Fathers. A thousand images spun in cotton candy webs through my mind as Sean finished his beer and came to sit beside me on the sofa. A hundred facts. Men do *not* smell like women. Each of us is our own variety. All of us are mutants. We want to see ourselves as smart lads and lasses in our red sports cars, but we are diseased. I want to transcend my father's MS, to tell him who I am before he no longer is who he was.

Sean and I shared a cold beery kiss. After a few moments, it warmed up, and we were half-undressed before we had the presence of mind to make it to the bedroom.

Later, safe beneath his arm, filled with a dinner of barbecued ribs and a conversation about the most overrated writers in America (we both agreed on Salinger), we went to the small-town fireworks. A brassy band blatted out its labial march rhythms. Sean delivered himself of a lecture on the Chinese people and the origins of what he called "firewifery." He slipped from there into a talk on Zen landscaping and minimalism. He was quoting from James Dickey's poem "Kudzu" when the first huge shells exploded to the delight of the crowd.

I did not think of America, not once.

Now, back home, filled and filled and filled, all I can think of is Victor's collapse and his desire for a human touch, even from one whose presence he fought for a full month.

July 5

In shock, utter disbelief, I look below me at the summer world of the South. The call came just after seven this morning when I was still asleep. At first, I couldn't unscramble the message or the messenger, but it was my teacher friend Laurie with the new, the terrible, inevitable news.

"Lucy, it's horrible, *horrible*," she said hoarsely. "They found him in the woods out behind Rowan Oak." I knew instantly, and my flesh flushed and then turned icy.

"Oh, my God."

"Looks like maybe liquor and pills. Not a gun. No violence. Within *sight* of Faulkner's house."

I started laughing and then fell apart crying, sobbing and remembering. Faulkner died in July, and this was the only part of his life James could claim. Summer death in Mississippi. When I told Pratt, he held up his arms to hold me, but I couldn't, *couldn't*. It wasn't right as rain, wasn't my time to fall in with him. The best I could do was to say I would fly home and then come right back after the funeral for the rest of the summer.

"I'd understand if you didn't," he said.

"*I* wouldn't." I don't understand anything, though. James could not bear to be who he was. Maybe none of us can. I tried to call Sean, but his phone was busy, and I gave up. Victor drove me to the airport in Asheville for the flight to Memphis, and we said nothing the whole way. His collapse from yesterday "never happened." Our edited world.

Oh, how I loved James when we first loved in New York, though. He was thin and handsome and ambitious, so sure of his talent that I believed, too, becoming needy as a sinner at an altar call. I came home from work and listened to his endless typing, his battle to the death with the muse. But the first draft of his first book was his best effort, and after that, he bled out, like a battlefield casualty.

With each new identity came a new style, and every time he showed me pages I wanted to cry, but for a long time I gave only praise. He *became* Hemingway, even going duck hunting with a friend on Long Island. I have no idea why I went along with his sequential identities or why I agreed to use our last savings to move to Oxford. We arrived to find he was one of several dozen pathetic wannabes, all with corduroy minds, corncob pipes, and a crock of liquor at their elbows.

I bring my journal because it has become my best friend this summer, my days of sweet confusion. Of beginnings and endings. Oh, James, you have failed me as I have failed you. We could have done so much better.

Late night

I'm home in Oxford, back in my apartment. It's quieter in the summer, of course, since most of the students are gone. Luna Marcovic saw me opening my door and came to me, palms up in supplication and shared grief.

"Oh, Lucy, this is to be terrible for you," she said in her charming fractured English. "The girls at the parlor, we took up this for you." She handed me eighteen dollars, and I sat down on my suitcase and cried. My apartment was still as a tomb, broiling hot. I had tried to sublet it without luck for the eight weeks. I don't have a cat. I don't even have a fish or a plant. I left nothing perishable in the fridge. I could vanish without any planning.

It has been a year since I left "our" house, the one James kept after our divorce, the one in which he couldn't face his death. But I still have my key. I drove by and picked up Lona Belle at her house, and we went to the funeral home.

"Some boys on a nature walk found him," she said. "They knew who he was immediately at Rowan Oak, since he spent so much free time around anything to do with Faulkner. He was sitting up against a tree. Not gone too long. Not too long, Lucy."

"Jesus God, I can't believe he really did it. He'd been talking about suicide for years. In the end, I guess it was the only thing he could do like famous writers. He was so beautiful nine years ago. You wouldn't believe how *beautiful* he was. When he was twenty-five, he had a literary agent and a full novel manuscript. I thought I would be his muse. He could write, and I could inspire. Turned out we couldn't do either."

"Go on and cry your heart out, hon," she said. I started laughing. She just shook her head. "That's the Lucy McKay we all know and love. Never made sense in your life, girl."

"I know."

The coffin was closed, but I told the funeral home director I wanted to see my ex-husband's body, and he opened the hood. James was dressed in a blue cotton shirt and khaki trousers, unmarked, too thin, and *not* James. He was like a photograph of my old lover taken from some odd angle that rendered him unknowable. Lona Belle wandered off. No other mourner was about.

Suddenly, I couldn't feel my life anymore. I thought of all the people I knew in Oxford, but the only ones who crawled through my imagination lived in the mountains of North Carolina, and my sick father was their gatekeeper, the memory-master of my summer and my life. My cell phone rang in my purse, and I fished it out, and it was Sean, and I didn't answer. The distance was too vast.

I leaned down over James.

"You prick," I said gently. "You son of a bitch."

The room suddenly filled with my friends, and I knew Lona Belle had betrayed me, had loved me, and had done what small-town friends always do. Former students and their parents, teachers and administrators, Rico, the Cuban who dresses like a pimp and works as a shift supervisor at the poultry plant—the room swelled out with my hugging friends.

I stayed two hours at the impromptu wake, and found out only when all had left but Lona Belle that James had bought a lot in the city cemetery within sight—distant but visible—of the Faulkner plot. There would be no service at James's request. There would be a summer-tide planting. I was invited to read "a favorite passage."

I am more tired than I have ever been. I do not believe in my life anymore. I have not called Sean or my father. I have not tried to repair the breakage of my days.

July 6

Black-and-white memories of Faulkner's funeral, the photographs from *Life* magazine, from Blotner's magisterial biography. The heat today will be hideous—101—but right now, at morning coffee, I sit at my own breakfast nook with Folger's and toast I can't swallow, disbelief my solitude. Today, when I still have not talked to Sean or Pratt, I wait to shower and dress, to drive the three miles through Oxford for the 11 a.m. burial. No preacher, no prayers, no invocations to send the soul toward its heaven. James, atheist that he was, would disapprove any such late sentimentality.

But I know what he would want, and I don't have to read it. It's written in my heart and mind from years of teaching it and knowing it. I've been a sucker for Housman since girlhood, and so was James. I can't see this page for the tears.

On the plane back to Asheville

James's drinking friends carried him, other writers-in-waiting, and I sat as if I were his wife beneath the hot canopy of a green tent at graveside. His parents dead, sister in London unable to appear, no one else there—just forty assorted Oxford citizens, many my teacher-friends and former students. I sat trying not to smile, because I knew James's ghost stood tiptoe, trying to see if Billy and Estelle sat on the veranda of their grave to watch the show.

The funeral director, oily Mr. Creighton, raised an eyebrow at me. This would be the shortest funeral in history. No eulogy. Just the poem read over thousands and thousands of graves for a century, a poem skirting sentiment and yet plowing straight into the heart, chestnut from films, and set-piece for English schoolboys. I offered no introduction and no apology. I simply stood and faced them in my simple dark dress—not widow's weeds, but respectful brown, which I was staining with sweat before I said a word.

The time you won your town the race
We chaired you through the market-place;
Man and boy stood cheering by,
And home we brought you shoulder-high.
To-day, the road all runners come,
Shoulder high-high we bring you home,
And set you at your threshold down,
Townsman of a stiller town.
Smart lad, to slip betimes away
From fields where glory does not stay
And early though the laurel grows
It withers quicker than the rose.
Eyes the shady night has shut
Cannot see the record cut,
And silence sounds no worse than cheers
After earth has stopped the ears:
Now you will not swell the rout
of lads that wore their honours out,
Runners whom renown outran
And the name died before the man.
So set, before its echoes fade,
The fleet foot on the sill of shade,
And hold to the low lintel up
The still-defended challenge-cup.
And round that early-laurelled head
Will flock to gaze the strengthless dead,
And find unwithered on its curls
The garland briefer than a girl's.

It wasn't Faulkner, but it was right, and I knew that James would approve. When I finished, everyone stood waiting for the funeral to begin, and I had to look at them with my thin smile and say, "That's it. That's all he wanted." Someone in the crowd said *Amen*, and I felt faint.

I wasn't the widow. I wasn't anything. His friends came up one by one and laid pennies on James's coffin and patted it and wandered off to their cars, pulling out flasks, laughter beginning before the doors opened. My girlfriends hugged me, and Laurie invited me back to her house for coffeecake, but I said I wanted to be alone, and they nodded, and I did something strange: I began to walk.

Always, when I was small and my parents would fight, I would walk around the neighborhoods, endless crisscrosses with a book in my dress pocket. And I wouldn't go home until the last light had been squeezed from the sky, or I couldn't stand the cold anymore. I did it when James and I were breaking up, too, and I knew all of Oxford intimately on foot just as the Faulkners must have. So I walked.

Sweat drenched me. My dress dripped. My panties felt sticky and soggy. No one followed me, but I knew that only by the sound. Some distance away, an old man was cutting grass, and that sound broke my heart. I couldn't breathe, and suddenly I thought of the mountains and of Sean and of my father, and I wanted to be away from Oxford—a violent need. I loved the town and my students. But love had broken it for me.

I came to shade trees and sat on a wall and realized I was looking right at William Faulkner's grave, and I laughed, had to. I'd been there dozens of times, but now it seemed new. He'd lived into his sixties and never wore his honors out. James never even tried any honors on, but he searched his soul for them.

My honors come from my students, from the gentle and bound-to-be-broken such as Timothy Sain. It is enough. Now, above the clouds on this brief flight from a place that is not my home to a place that is not my home, I beg for final leave from my James, townsman of a stiller town.

July 8

Yesterday, useless all day, I slept late and wandered ghostly through the house. Mother called and consoled, Pratt was considerate and sweet, and the MS seems to have oddly receded—a good day, as they say. He dictated all day to Victor, worked on a new manuscript, and they both glowed from the effort. I called Sean in the middle of the afternoon to apologize.

"Please don't do that," he said.

"Why?"

"You're suffering. My heart's been with you." Nothing any human could have said could have rivaled it. I wanted to profess mad love, to write his name a thousand times in loopy schoolgirl letters. To drive straight to his house on the mountaintop and make love.

"Can I see you tomorrow?" I asked softly.

"I'm flying to Seattle," he said. I sat straight up on the bed and almost dropped the phone. My voice broken into shards. "It's just for one day. Business. I'll be right back."

"Sean."

"Lucy? I think about you a lot. I think about you all the time."

I cannot repair the broken ends of my relationships, it seems, father, lover, late husband, world. I want to make things right. I want to start over.

"Are you going to see *her*? Your wife?"

"We're going to talk out the divorce. She's no longer with the guy. She says she's sorry. But that she's not coming back. I need to see her alive so I can know it's over. I've imagined her dead, I think, and I haven't quite been willing to let her go. I want to see her and tell her goodbye, and that's it."

"What if you don't tell her goodbye?" I hated myself for speaking the words. "Sorry, sorry. None of my business."

"I want it to be your business, Lucy."

But is it? I did not come for him. I came for Pratt, and now I have lost the last shreds of James, and I am losing my father, and I hold on to the ledge of my life with gnawed nails.

S. gone west. I think of him in midair, suspended over sunstruck America, and I know he will reconcile, see it, can almost taste their forgiving kisses. He will bring her home. He will finish the dissertation. I will fade to a sliver of memory.

Once in NY, I saw a man bearing a small sack of groceries, a dinner's worth, and a modest bottle of nice wine nosed out the top. I was about ten feet from him when I realized it was John Ashbery, my favorite poet, and I felt buckly, starstruck, as giddy as a teenager. Seeing the famous in Manhattan isn't such an accomplishment. I once saw John Updike, Salman Rushdie, and Anne Beattie on the same day. But that Ashbery day imprinted me like one of Konrad Lorenz's geese. He was trim and handsome and wore tan slacks and a pale blue shirt. He'd worn a mustache in his dust jacket photos, but it was shaved off that day. He looked down the street past me at nothing. Even before I reached him, I wondered if he thought of the old days, of lost friends. I wanted, at least, to make eye contact. I did nothing. I turned and passed on the hot sidewalk, gone forever. I have never forgotten what he never even knew.

How will Sean recall me? Indelible? Or will I be the face whose name he can't quite reassemble on some fireplace evening twenty years from now?

I heard the sound of quarreling from the den and when it didn't stop, I went it to find Victor in tears and Pratt in a foaming rage. My father, his hands like clubs, scattered papers from the coffee table all over the floor. His face was blade-magenta with rage. Victor was almost incoherent, and he began to kick at the scattered pages, missing most of them, a little boy dancing with fury.

"...fucking finish *nothing* because I fucking said I said I *said*." Pratt, clearly, had had enough, and Victor was goading him to keep working, and I saw it all at a moment's scan: If Pratt quit, Victor had no life. If Victor quit goading him, Pratt had no life. And neither wanted the work, not really. They simply wanted the motion.

I'm not this insightful. I work hard to understand the world. But in a lightbulb-flash I knew all that.

"Stop it, both of you!" I shouted.

"Burn it!" cried Victor. "Why not just burn the whole goddamn thing, then? What's the use? What—is—the—god*damn*—use?" He screamed each word. I took two steps and slapped him across the left cheek, hard. My hand stung, went numb. A welt lifted out of his flesh and announced itself. They both stopped. For a moment, I could feel nothing below my elbow, and then pain came.

Victor's hand rose to his face, not to ward me away but in shock to cool the assault. He wanted to kill me. His eyes bore absolute menace, and for a moment, fear spread through me. Instead, he broke. Everything in him broke, and he must have remembered what he told me on the deck, and of this betrayal of his own need. His eyes became liquid saucers. He took his hand down, and on his cheek was a huge raised welt, topo map of my rage. Pratt's body crawled against his will back and forth in a small space on the sofa.

"Lucy, what have you done?" said my father.

"Oh, my God," said Victor.

I did not wait for denouement, for the rotting mansion to collapse and burn, for the revelation of identities, for lost love to be assuaged. I did not imagine the end, the funerals and the mourning, the college boy shouting that he doesn't hate the South. I ran from the room, from the house, outside off the deck, and down the communal nature trail, on which not a soul hiked.

I hated the pine-bark path, the nursery-tended landscaping, the blueprint trees, and the five-thousand-dollar benches, each with its own gilded memorial plaque. I despised this cave of wealth, with its barriers to all the people I'd ever known. Yet this is what my summer lover did for a living. He created an unnatural world, an imaginary place for those bruised by time far past the gates.

I collapsed on to a bench, utterly out of breath, thinking of John Ashbery, of James with his scenic view of the Faulkners, of Sean and his father's deceptions. I sat there for a long time, and I tried to weep, but nothing came, and so I walked shakily back to Pratt's house and sneaked in to my room like a thief. My cell phone was ringing.

Sean had landed in Seattle and was calling me from the terminal.

"I sat next to a guy whose mother was a hair stylist in Memphis and once did Elvis," he said. "The King sang her the first verse of 'Love Me Tender' and gave her a twenty-dollar bill. He still has it. His mother framed it. It's raining here. I miss you."

"In that order?" I sounded mousy, masking my Bad Day.

"Of course. What comes before Elvis?"

I am not a sliver of his memory. I am not his amanuensis. He will be back, and I will be here with ferns and conifers, with rain and roses.

July 10

I apologized to V. for slapping him, and he quietly said *he* was the sick one, not Pratt, and I told him that he was maudlin, and he agreed, laughing.

"I'm maudlin, and you're violent," he said. "And Pratt is trapped in the nightmare of his own body. Among the three of us, we make one sorry human being."

I liked him then. After a dinner I cooked—pork chops, green beans, baked potatoes, and blackberry cobbler—I suggested we sit in the den and listen to some Bach and take turns reading aloud. Pratt began to thrash and say he couldn't hold a book, but I shut him off with an offer to be his personal lectern.

"What shall we read?" asked Victor.

"Anything. This is what people used to do instead of watching TV or getting into slap-fights."

Pratt warmed to the idiocy immediately and, with Victor's help, chose the most wildly improbable selection imaginable: a nutty narrative poem by Browning called "Mr. Sludge, 'The Medium.'" I'd never heard of it. Pratt had us prop him in the corner of the sofa, and V. and I held the book on either side just below his face so he could peer down through his glasses:

> *Now, don't, sir! Don't expose me! Just this once!*
> *This was the first and only time, I'll swear,—*
> *Look at me—see, I kneel—the only time,*
> *I swear, I ever cheated—yes, by the soul*
> *Of Her who hears—(your sainted mother, sir!)*
> *All, except this last accident, was the truth—*
> *This little kind of slip—and even this,*
> *It was your own wine, sir, the good champagne,*
> *(I took it for Catawba—you're so kind)*
> *Which put the folly in my head!*

It took Pratt nearly a minute to read this much, but we were all laughing so hard it mattered not, as Browning might have said. By the end of that first stanza, each of us delivered an encomium on the death of narrative poetry, the deserved obscurity of Browning, and nominations for a Mr. Sludge in our own time. Pratt's body swam the English Channel in his corner while we dallied.

"Fear of exposure—the great fear of our lives," said Victor.

"The dream of walking down the street naked," I said. "The loss of pretense, the shield gone, the nerve-endings bared for the world to see."

"Death," said Pratt, croaking like Poe's Raven.

"No, just being exposed for the fakers we are," said Victor.

"*Fakirs*," I corrected.

"No! No! No!" Pratt was maddened beyond bearing, and he clubbed the book from our hands, and Browning, all thousand pages of him, hit the floor with a hollow thud. "Don't expose me just this once!" He was wild, not looking at either of us but praying to Death, and we both knew instantly. Fear braised me. Whatever impulse of knowledge and rage made him do that dissolved like sugar in hot coffee, though, and within ten seconds, a lopsided grin lit his face, and he tried to shrug, though his shoulders canted up and different times, with different angles. He said, stuttering. "Sorry."

Victor read from Pratt's award-winning book on women from the Civil Rights movement, and I was sure it would provoke scorn, but my father's delight lit the room. I have always been shocked by how rarely the accomplished can enjoy their accomplishments. They fear losing the gift more than what the gift has given. Victor read for a full half hour on the death of Viola Liuzzo, and the story touched me again in Pratt's quiet and substantial retelling.

What would I read? Not from *Three Junes*, the lovely Julia Glass novel I was reading for the summer. Not from *War and Peace*, through which I was slogging as part of a New Year's Day resolution. Instead, I prowled Pratt's well-stocked library and plucked out *Bunny Brown and His Sister Sue at the Summer Carnival* by Laura Lee Hope, a children's book in a 1931 reprint by Grosset & Dunlap. The cover attracted me, a doll-like little boy and his doll-like sister, holding hands at the beach, all innocence and clean clothes, dressed by loving parents for a happy day in the sun.

I opened the book to the inside cover and read the inscription from its long-forgotten first owners as if it were part of the text: *To Ginny from Mommy and Daddy.* I turned back to the cover and looked at the girl in her pink dress, tiny lace petticoat showing, pale blue socks slipping down toward her strap shoes. In her right hand she held a sailor dolly, and at her foot was a starfish. With her brown hair and brown eyes, she might have been any child. She might have been me in another, happier family.

I burst into tears. Once, in a fit of unstable need, James had announced he would be a children's author, that he could write something as good as *The Secret Garden*. I did the most foolish thing imaginable for a would-be muse: I turned sharply and said, "*Nobody* can write anything as good as *The Secret Garden*, James." I said it to wither, with the most blistering and biblical scorn I could summon. I didn't say it to wound; I meant it. To me, that book is sacred text. James deflated, like a let-go balloon sputtering around a summer backyard. He went out drinking and never wrote even a sentence of a children's book.

To my horror, Pratt stood, with Victor's help, and came stumbling toward me, his face tortured with unspoken confessions. I wanted to push both of them away, to run down the streets of Cedar Acres beneath the *sh-sh-sh* of summer lawn sprinklers. Instead I stood to take my father into my arms, and when I did, Bunny Brown and his sister Sue hit the floor with a sharp whack. We held each other for two full minutes while I managed to control my tears. I wondered if Ginny was still alive somewhere, if she told her grandchildren about the books she owned as a little girl, about happy summers at the seashore, about starfish and waves. I thought of Viola Liuzzo and of Mr. Sludge, and I wanted Sean back home. I found myself thinking of Pratt's nurse, Mary Lou Wadely. Why? I had no idea.

I wanted to be five again and to have someone break the world to me gently so that I could take it when it came.

July 11

Pratt back to Asheville and Dr. Retherston's office for his checkup. The doctor's nurse Nikki was more gorgeous than ever, impossibly beautiful, and too lovely even to be a starlet playing a nurse in a soap opera. The waiting room was filled with the sick and sicker. Their eyes give up hope first. I sat next to a young woman in her thirties who was there with her mother. The daughter was the sick one, and I smiled at her, and she shifted in her seat, muscles mostly frozen or freezing. She asked what I did. I told her I taught high school English in Mississippi.

"What does your husband do?" she asked. Her mountain accent revealed her.

"I'm not married," I said.

"Me neither. Was. Was married. He was a painter 'n' he felt oft a scaffolt and broke his neck." She paused from the effort. "That was a good day."

"Ida Mae," said her mother.

"He beat me up l-like this," she said. She turned her palms over, a model displaying a game-show prize. Slowly, she lifted her hands to the sides of her head, and her eyebrows went up to ask if I understood.

"I'm so sorry," I whispered.

"He toted this post into the trailer and beat me to a pulp with it," the woman said. Nurse Nikki came out and called her name. "We was waiting the trial when he fell. God pushed him down."

"He did," said the mother. They struggled inside, and I glanced at Pratt. One of his professor's eyebrows was raised in chevron delight.

"How shall I love thee, let me count the ways," he whispered.

After the examination, Nikki helped Pratt redress, and he seemed dazzled, while Dr. Retherston nodded me into the hallway. I knew what was coming.

"He's had some noticeable erosion of motor skills in the past month," he said. "The disease is progressing apace, I'm afraid." I bristled, and he saw it instantly. "Sorry, I know that wasn't helpful. I'm sorry to say that even with adjusting his medicines and with the excellent therapy, his condition seems to be going downhill. It's hard to know what can happen from here, Ms. McKay. I've offered to refer him to a large center somewhere, and he says he's not interested. I have to tell you his chances are much better somewhere else. But I can't make him go. Is there some reason he might not want to go on?"

"Go on?"

"Living, I mean."

"God, is it *that* advanced?"

"I'm afraid so. He needs care we can't give here."

Victor and I helped get him back into the car, and Pratt is somber all the way home. At night, he's back muttering in his room. Prayer? I have not asked, and I am not sure he would tell me if I did. I feel sick to my soul.

Sean tomorrow.

July 12

He stayed two extra days in Seattle, and I felt my life shrivel inside me. Lona Belle called from Oxford and said our lawyer friend Will Wilson, probating James's estate, found he'd left what little he had to me. (I will be getting the formal call in a day or two.) So when I go back I'll have to clean out what is once again my own house or move back to it. Too sad to consider.

Sean picked me up at five, looking tired and harried, and we drove to an Italian restaurant for dinner. All the way, I knew what was coming, his reconciliation, a new hope for his fractured marriage, a way out of the labyrinth left by his father's death.

But I was wrong.

"I didn't recognize her, I swear," he said, slurping off a beer mustache. "She's lost weight and looks hard and distant and vague, like a dream of someone I once knew. She missed two appointments, so finally I went to her house, and it was a trailer, and it was filthy and sad. She signed the papers while yawning and chewing on a handful of pills like they were a kid's cereal."

"Signed the papers?"

"Divorce papers. That's why I went out there, Luce." I sit here writing in my journal from Square Books, trying to tell myself that I knew—*of course* I knew all along—but I didn't. I felt like toasting myself, celebrating, but I could see in his eyes the wreckage of his life, and I simply nodded and looked into my spaghetti marinara. "Nothing in my life's turned out like I thought it would. My father, my wife, my degree. The only thing that feels right is my house. A place I can hide from the rich and the poor alike. It's probably up there burning down as we speak."

"Don't you dare tempt fate," I said.

"Fate's just a lack of estate planning," he said bitterly. He leaned back. "I'm sorry. Sorry. When I was a little boy, I had an Uncle Cale—my mother's younger brother. He was this golden *god*. Played football at Tennessee, was going to law school, had a girlfriend more beautiful than sunrise. I swear. And a week before he graduated, he drove to a scenic overlook up near Boone and shot himself. It hit me like a two-by-four in the back of the head. It hit everybody that way. Then my father. Even though they weren't even related by blood, people started to say suicide must run in the family. Then your James. God, I didn't know what to think."

"Sean, it's been a long time since he was *my* James."

"Point taken. But you know what I mean."

"Not really." I was furious. I wanted the evening to be about us, and I saw a man wallowing in his misery over garlic bread. I felt shallow and jealous and stupid. His lips curled and twitched, and he ate his salad, and for the next five minutes, neither of us spoke a word.

"How's your father?" he asked finally.

"Slowly failing," I said. "I want to touch him and let him touch me, but I don't know how. I don't. All I can think about is getting back to Oxford and starting school. I wanted to do a different Faulkner book this year. Something we've never done before. Maybe *The Reivers* or *The Unvanquished*. Or maybe I want to leave Oxford and never think of Faulkner again. He killed himself, too, you know. Not with a gun but with grief and liquor."

"I was just asking about your father," said Sean. I pushed myself back from the table, and the chair legs made a feral screech.

"Take me home."

His face hardened, then softened, went solid again, and he threw down a tip, and in twenty sullen minutes I was back here in my bedroom, as miserable as I wanted to be, planning revenge on myself for believing in fathers or lovers. Forty minutes later, I looked up to see Sean standing in the yard outside my window, half in shadow, holding a single fern blade up like a prom flower. When he saw that I saw him, he reached in his back pocket and took out a stick and then he thumbed a lighter and the stick burst into fire: a child's sparkler. He stood there, fern leaf in one hand and sparkler in the other, and then he began to walk toward my window.

Pratt's voice rose through the wall. He, too, could see. Did he understand? Did he know? Had he ever courted my mother so beautifully when they had little money but a great deal of love? I met Sean on the broad back deck. Moonlight looked phosphorescent on the falls across the valley.

"The sparkler's part of an old Cherokee ritual," he said. His voice was casual and soft. "I doubt they used landscape plants, though. Maybe it's the other way around. I forget. The idea is to wash away the enmity between warring towns through ritual instead of through cutting off an adversary's privates and sticking them in his mouth."

"Fern is native to these parts, buster," I said. "Even if it is a landscape plant. Sparklers grow further west, in Alabama, I think."

"They would." By then, the sparkler had sputtered out, and he laid the wizened rod and the fern leaf on top of the grill. "I'm so sorry. I hadn't been able to be mad out loud since I got back. I guess I needed to hear myself say those things to a friend. It was a stupid thing to do. Would you accept my apology?"

I would have thrown myself off a precipice if he'd asked. He was leaning against the deck rail, and I folded myself into him and put my head on his chest, and I could hear the slow gathering drum of his heart. He kissed the top of my head and then held me snug. For a time, I thought I heard my father's phantom voice, but I was wrong, for there was no deep, resonant note to the night, just the high-decibel joy of crickets and tree frogs, the songs of night birds carving out the melodies for which time and descent designed them, families together in darkness.

And that was all that happened. We stood like that, leaning against the deck in each other's arms for probably half an hour, and I loved his warmth, and I never wanted to move, and I didn't want more. It's nearly midnight now, and Pratt is silent in his room. His prayers have ceased.

But have mine begun? Is there any difference in the beauty Sean makes and what Faulkner did, beyond its reach? If we are to change others by our love, we must first know the art of forgiving the face in the mirror. I learn, Lord. I am learning.

July 13

My summer is growing toward its end so fast I can hardly believe it. I think back on what has happened and who I have met, and I, the woman who traffics in narrative, can barely keep the threads untangled. It's midmorning as I write, and already today, I've seen an odd edge of something new in my father—a brassy will to fight against the monster within.

He was up very early with Ginger Dumont, his perky freckled therapist and walked—walked!—all over the deck thrashing some but aiming his steps into bravura grace by will alone. Betty and Hunt Bearden came by with a pecan pie and a copy of their daughter's latest CD. Their love filled the room like perfumed roses, and I accepted the gifts with gratitude. I hugged them both and held Betty a little too long. She patted my back and hummed in my ear as mothers will.

Not even midmorning, with Victor gone for groceries and me alone with Pratt, he patted the sofa seat beside him for me to sit, and I did. I snuggled up, and I took his hand, and his gripping strength surprised me. He looked at me in a clear-eyed way I have not seen in a long time. Then he changed my life. I want to set it down as well as I can, for he spoke a long time, slowly and evenly, without hurry, not letting his sentences fly apart. A John Field Piano Concerto played in the background. I will meet Sean tonight. I felt grief letting me go.

"Honey, I need to tell you things. Important things. When you first came in June, I told you about Rachel Motes and the daughter she bore me in college. That was as close as I could get to the truth then, but having you here these weeks, I've begun to see what I must fear and what I don't have to.

"Rachel was an undergraduate student with your mother and me at Vanderbilt." He stopped to see how I would react, and I tried not to show what I felt, but I'm sure I did. "I don't quite know how it happened. I loved your mother more than air. But she was off in the art school, and I was in history, and that's where Rachel was. She was tall and mysterious and beautiful and she also had an interest in the Civil Rights era, even though she was in those days mostly interested in the Civil War. One November afternoon, we were sitting alone on a bench, and she started talking about her childhood. Terrible things. Terrible. And I was moved beyond bearing. And I slid over and I held her hand, and she leaned against my shoulder and wept.

"That is how it began. The betrayal left me sick with revulsion and hatred, but I couldn't stop it. I fell in love with her. When she became pregnant, I wanted to die. Finally, I did what I had to do as a man. I confessed to your mother."

"You *what?*" I said. "You told her?" Suddenly I understood a thousand things about them both—their failed marriage, her coldness and career mania. "That must have taken courage."

"No, that wasn't the courage. *Her* courage came after that. Her courage came when Rachel put the baby up for adoption." He stopped at that point, and I waited for him to go on, and I realized suddenly what he was telling me and why I had been summoned to the mountains for the summer. A surge of icewater adrenalin pumped through me, and I stood and walked to the French doors that looked over the deck.

Who are we? Where are we going? What shall we become? I'd asked those rhetorical questions to my students a hundred times, to the gentle Timothy Sains and the snide quarterbacks, sure that I knew at least part of the answers for myself. Now, I saw, I knew nothing at all. *I was not my mother's daughter.* And yet she was in some ways more beautiful and more courageous than I could ever have imagined. It was too much to dream.

I came and sat back down beside him, this time closer, and I took his hand.

"It was me," I said. "The baby you had with Rachel Motes. It was me."

"Yes, honey. I died a thousand deaths for that betrayal. Your mother was magnificent, too. She was the real hero. She said she wouldn't let my child go to another family."

"What happened to Rachel?"

My father sighed and shook his head. He cut his eyes oddly, looked up and down.

"She dropped out of school. I tried to keep up with her for a while, and I know she moved out West, to Wyoming, I think. She married. I don't know what she told her husband. I wrote down her married name on a piece of paper that I lost, and now I can't even remember it. It was Telfair or Selfair or something like that. But that doesn't seem right. I don't know."

He played with his hands, and I knew immediately that he was not telling me the truth, and I did not hate him for it. The truth was closer and maybe right before my eyes. He wrestled with whatever lies he told me now.

"This is so unfair to you, Lucy. I've dreaded telling you about this my whole life. For a long time, I wasn't going to. Your mother said there was no reason to. She didn't want me to. But she wasn't going to have children with me after we had you. She made that clear enough. There were affairs for both of us. For years. It was tawdry, soap-operaish.

"I guess what I want to tell you, sweetheart, is that you have nothing to live up to in me. It's me who can't live up to you. I haven't come close to changing a tenth of the lives you have. I've gotten the glory, but you did the hard work. And now the suffering has come to you, too, and it makes me sick for you. I felt bad for you after the divorce. I had no idea James would take his life. I may not have time for proper atonement, Lucy. But I'll do what I can. I am trying."

By then, I was in his arms, and we were both crying as I am crying now all over my journal, crying too hard to see these words.

❧

I want to tell anyone, but whom? Lona Belle or Laurie, my teacher friends back in Oxford? I could have told James years ago when he wasn't drinking. Then, he could be a good listener, but when he tried to become Faulkner or Hemingway, when the obsession stormed him, he looked at me like a distant, annoying relative. Out of any faith, I can't confess to Father Parnell, this artificial town's artificial priest. (That is unfair; he seems like a decent man, and faith is the Mystery we cannot unravel as we can skeins of DNA.) I want to drive over to Duke and weep in my mother's arms and thank her for that sacrifice, for heroically taking me in. And yet we are also estranged, a mother and daughter who have been drifting like icebergs from sea to sea and season to season. Now I wish I could tell my girlhood friend Tonya Webb, my best bud for five years and whom I haven't seen for so long.

No. There is only one person to whom I can speak, and it terrifies me that I care for him so much. When I look at Sean, I see the same fractured, hurt creature I saw in James. And yet they are so different. Sean is younger and sunnier, filled with summer light, and he isn't paralyzed by what he can't create. He draws gorgeous landscaping blueprints, kneels in the rich loam, picks perfect plants, and inhales the rich variety of that loveliness. I need a new girlfriend here. But where can I find one?

I try to imagine her, the Rachel in whose womb I grew. Tall and beautiful, he said. Sad, a terrible childhood. He repeated that word, *terrible*. Has he really forgotten her last name, or is he trying to steer me away from that mythical journey toward the birth-mother so

III

many orphans make? Will this journal entry ever end? I'm writing so fast that I can barely keep up with my pen.

There's something Faulknerian to all this, isn't there? Mistaken identities, southern families breaking apart, fractured narratives, and wayward loves. I find myself missing James as I first knew him, full of hope and as much talent as he'd ever know. He was sweet and kind. He was learning to juggle from a book. He took me to an Italian restaurant in the Village where the waiters already treated him like a celebrity since he had a literary agent. He radiated bonhomie, but the fire was already banking. I found him and married him just past the crest of his confidence and joy, and I suffered his decline and fall and was made his prop, his crucifer. As his desperation grew, his identity shifted. He grew a Hemingway beard and took up fishing in New Jersey ponds. He rewrote his novel, minimalist and then maximalist, but he wouldn't start anything new. I begged him.

"A writer can't move on until the project he's working on is really finished," he said. Oh, James. You really believed that. My heart breaks for you. Even your wife wasn't who you thought she was.

Sorrow, be gone! Hence, away! It is afternoon now, and I am an hour away from seeing Sean. I am taking my journal with me, because I will try to spend the night with him if he will let me, and I do not want to be far away from these words. I came back in to see Pratt a few minutes ago, and the change in him is startling. He seems relaxed and happier than he's been since I arrived.

"Where's Victor?" I asked.

"He's gone back to Chapel Hill for the day," he said. "I told him I needed to be alone for a time. He said to give you this." And he handed me a note. This is what is said:

Dear Lucy,

I never meant to cause you sorrow or come between you and your father. Forgive me. Perhaps we are all looking for our fathers and our mothers in some way. And it's a search that never ends. It is an honor to know and work with this good and great man. Your presence has healed him more than medicine or miracles. Thank you for allowing me to see your love.

Warmly,
Victor

"Was he nice?" asked my father.

"He was nice," I said, no longer able to see the single sheet of white paper through my blurry eyes. "He is a nice man."

❧

July 14

I sit here in Sean Crayton's den beneath the light of one lamp, wearing only my panties and one of his old T-shirts, balancing this journal in my lap and listening to the crickets through the open window. It's almost midnight. I want to write it, but it scares me half to death: I love this man. And I know he loves me.

We live in fear and die in sorrow. It must not be. We love, we pray, we laugh, we drink, we write, we sing, we dance, we hike, we kiss, we hold hands beneath the spray of an ancient waterfall, we cry for joy, we bring forth the young, we eat fine meals, we grieve our dead, we salve the wounded, we write and rewrite our histories, we spill into the knowable mysteries of science, we watch our shadows grow briefer, and yet we still reach for joy.

I want to have one perfect day, to hear my father say, "Right as rain, Luce." Was today that perfect today? It has come close, and I cannot stop writing it.

Sean picked me up at 4:30, and he drove me to a secret place we hadn't been before, a hidden glen with a small waterfall, filled with fern and rhododendron and mountain laurel. It did not have a view. There was nothing grand about it. And yet I never in my life saw anything more perfect.

"Dazzling," I said.

"See, I can't reproduce this, Lucy," he said, teaching me. "There's no way a landscaper can do better what nature already does best."

"I heard my father's confession," I whispered, holding on to him in the fern-light. Then I told Sean, and he kissed the top of my head.

"You were loved," he said. "That's what it meant. You were wanted."

"But my birth-mother didn't want me, and I'm not sure that Pratt did," I said. "It was my Mom, the one I've always felt least close to, who wanted me. *She* was the one who took me in. I don't know how to feel about that."

"Grateful," he said. "You were brought here for revelations, Lucy. For the narrative of a great mystery."

"I think somehow it's why he focused on certain women of the Civil Rights Movement—the ones out of the limelight who were the foundation of it all," I said.

"May be."

We stayed there for more than an hour after that, talking little, walking on lovely small trails in the summer shade of fragrant oaks and cedars. At his house, he grilled tuna steaks, and we talked quietly and listened to wonderful soft music, and I thought of my father and of James and of my students, and of the wanted and unwanted in this world.

Sean talked out the sorrow of his father's death, the divorce he'd gone to Seattle to achieve, and his failure to finish his dissertation. I tried to stretch out the time like some pliable child's toy, to make this girl's summer last. I want to believe I'm at camp, and Sean Crayton is my beau because I am smitten utterly. Because I know it is hopeless, it is more desperate than bearing, but is it love?

We began on the sofa what we finished in his big bed, barely making it there. The act was frantic, built on the melting sand of a slipping season, and it went on for nearly two hours, went on until it hurt. Now I am sore and filled with joyous epiphanies. It is the next day, and still I will not let yesterday go. And yet the knowledge does not quite set me free as it has Pratt. How will I face the new day's light? Like Howard Reuther, with his red Jaguar, the man dying of cancer? Like my father's second wife, Lenora, scouring European castles for scraps of ancient musical scores? Like Pratt's number-three, Alessandra, the Italian geologist?

I want to be like the only mother I've ever known. I want to have that much courage. I want to walk in the house I shared with James back in Oxford and clean it out, to find in its nooks reminders of a love once whole, photographs of us skating at the Rockefeller Center ice rink or playing in Central Park.

I want to be the woman who would take in a little girl, who could not bear to dream of the child in another family's heart.

July 15

Longest journal entries in history. I'm feeling hung over from them. I call the house first thing, and Victor's voice is filled with soft regret, and I wonder if perhaps he's jealous, if all along he's wanted me. Love this morning is careful because we're both raw from last night, but it doesn't matter—we want each other so bad that friction is a myth. It doesn't exist. He brings me fresh strawberries and coffee in bed.

He leaves for three hours to get his crews started on the day's projects, but it's raining out there—steady and dark, winter-covers-over-the-head dark. I rifle his CD collection, and it's amazing, and I pick out the *Irish Rhapsody Number Three for Cello and Orchestra* by Charles Villiers Stanford. Lovely and perfect for this sodden day.

I want to move here. I could find a teaching job. Then I would be near Pratt and Sean. And yet I can't quite bear the thought of leaving my students in Oxford or my friends there. Some people's bonds are built with elastic; mine are steel. Even coming here for the summer has been hard. All I want to do is make love with Sean. I feel insatiable. I can't bear his absence even for this long.

Sean says to leave my birth mystery alone, but I can't. I know I won't. So after he leaves, I spend two hours of frantic googling, trying to uncover any clues to who my birth mother might be, but, of course, it's hopeless. That doesn't stop me from identifying a dozen possible candidates—but I'm almost delusional, and I know it. I shouldn't be here. I should be with my father. That's why I came to this mountain. And yet I am hidden here, sanctified in this slow rain, waiting for my lover to return, Penelope of the Mists, unweaving her past and trying to create a new image from which to steer.

I want to be one of those women meant for happiness. Is that too much to ask? Just before I left Oxford, I asked Lona Belle if she loved her father, and she laughed—so hard she showed me her perfect teeth.

"He's called me Princess since I was a baby," she said. "He calls me Princess now, in front of my husband and kids. He came to my class here one time, and when I told him I was glad to have him visit, he said, `It's a pleasure to be here, Princess.' Everybody giggled, and he didn't even notice. He sends me Valentines and Halloween cards. He sends me *Hallmark Halloween cards*, Lucy. The man's hopeless for me. And I just adore him."

And she shrugged like a Fifties movie queen revealing a schoolgirl crush. I was jealous and didn't quite believe her, but Lona Belle is anything but duplicitous. She isn't capable of that kind of lie. Fathers and daughters—how do we craft that love beyond girlhood if it isn't natural as the light from stars? And what am I doing here, making love with a man I don't know very well, desperate for the warmth of his long skin and the contour of his muscles?

No, I am wrong. I am not hung over from love but rather centered from it. I am liquefied from our passion, a wash that, from James, made me feel the need to bathe. From Sean, I want to lie back and float in our liquid love, arms across my chest like an Egyptian princess, bound to live forever and ever.

&

Sean came back, mud-cuffed, stepping out of boots, and I knew immediately that something was wrong. The rain came harder, and his features crowded together in the center of his face, as if trying to hide. I asked him what was wrong.

"My ex called from Seattle on my cell phone," he said. "She's been arrested and wants me to come back and bail her out. Jesus H. Christ is this ever going to end?"

"Arrested for what?"

"Selling goddamn meth," he said. "Of all the things in the world. Fucking trailer-park heroin."

"You're divorced now. You don't have any legal reason to help her." The words came out of me like venom from some spitting cobra hidden on a path in Pakistan. I wanted to apologize, to take it back like a five-year-old, but the hatred I felt for her paralyzed me.

"Jesus, Lucy, it's not about what's legal," he said softly. "Don't you know that?" I was too ashamed to speak and too angry to look at him." So I went to Baltimore. That's what Pratt called it when I was a little girl, and I'd stubbornly go into my silent act: "Don't even try to talk to Lucy McKay: she's gone to Baltimore." Sean stormed into the bedroom and then back out, went into the kitchen and then on to the porch. He seemed to be veering around his home from one nook to another cranny, hoping the problem wouldn't follow him. But it did.

I dressed and asked him to take me back to Pratt's. The bright glow of my perfect evening had vanished utterly, and I arrived back here to find Pratt napping and Victor actually working on his dissertation. He smiled at me wistfully—as if he'd looked up the word *wistfully* in Webster's and decided to embody it. I felt suddenly sorry for him but not enough to have a conversation.

I napped myself—a long, dreaming sleep—and when I woke, I could hear my father speaking to himself through the wall again, dear God, his soft drumming voice coming syllable by syllable through the rain.

July 16

I had my cell phone in hand to call my principal this morning and resign. I spent an hour rehearsing in my head what I'd say. Every word would be a lie. My father needed me. James's death had left me with severe emotional problems that required therapy, which I was receiving in Asheville, courtesy of my mother and father. I had decided to go back to graduate school. I was writing a novel. The last one made me giggle, because it was James's conversational icebreaker for the nine years we were together. Soon after he said that, he'd mention his New York literary agent, neglecting to say that had been years in the past, and he no longer had an agent at all.

Then the phone itself rang, and I threw it across the bed like a rattlesnake. When I retrieved it to answer, the caller was a robot selling insurance. When it paused and asked me if I'd like to speak to a representative, I said, "What do you think was really wrong with Benjy Compson?" There was a pause from the addled robot, which then said, "Sorry, I didn't get that." Then I said, "Bill must have really loved Estelle deep down, don't you think?" The robot, by now clearly suspicious, said, "Sorry, I didn't get that." I said, "Sorry, I didn't get that." The robot said, "Sorry, I didn't get that."

I said, "Samuel Beckett lives." The robot said, "Sorry, I didn't get that." I said, "Sorry, I didn't get that" and hung up.

Sunny and hot once again. I waited all morning for Sean to call, and he didn't, so I took a long walk through the neighborhood. Cars were huddled around a house on one perfect street, and Father Tanner came walking out the front door toward his car, and he spied me and waved, smiling.

"Someone's died," I said.

"Cam Carriker," he nodded. "An airline pilot, a pioneer, really. He was ninety-six years old. He died like a slow summer sunset, Lucy. Had time for all the children, grandchildren, and great-grandchildren to come and say goodbye. He was never in pain and was lucid until the end. Had his favorite music and food there. Last night, he told me stories of flying cross-country with Lindbergh. He snuggled down peacefully into his passing. Not many of us get such a good death."

"It's hard for me to think about a good death," I admitted. He put his hand on my shoulder, and I felt revelation come close and then pass me by, a phantom in mid-day.

"You should try to imagine it," he said. "Try to imagine everything, Lucy."

And so I did as I walked. I tried to imagine myself without jealousy toward any woman who ever touched or spoke to Sean Crayton. I tried to imagine Pratt whole once more and striding confidently down college halls, toward that podium for his Pulitzer, up the fairway toward a green on which his chip shot lies like an unhatched egg. I tried to imagine my mother going to the hospital and gathering up the unwanted child in her arms and looking down and seeing beyond betrayal. So, after dinner, after wine, after quiet conversation with Pratt, who seems even more improved than two days ago—is this a miracle?—I called my mother.

"Hey, Pumpkin," she said. "Victor called earlier and left a message that Dad is doing much better. It's a hard disease to understand. It appears to ebb and flow, but of course, in the end …."

"Mom?"

"...it always wins, as such things do. I've been talking to Dan Kamchitz, he's at the Turner Center here, and he thinks that ...."

"Mom?"

"What, Pumpkin?

"Pratt told me. He told me about me. I can't believe it's been this deep, dark secret all these years. I'm thirty-five years old, and you never told me. That I'm not really yours." Long pause at the other end.

"Of course you're mine," she said softly. "Oh, Lucy. I know we should have told you. But we didn't, and then I couldn't, and he couldn't. And we didn't. I didn't know a thing about his affair or about the baby until you were born. It was like being hit by a bus. I was going to leave him. And then I went to the hospital and saw you through the window with all the babies, there alone in your little bed? And I started crying."

By then, I was crying and so was she, but she kept talking.

"And I couldn't bear the thought of you going to someone else. So we made the arrangements. And you were ours. We had our careers, and we had you. That's no way to make a family. I've wondered a thousand times if you might have been better off adopted by someone else. But I had to have you."

"You've got me," I said.

"I love you so much," she said. "So does your father. You do know that, don't you, Lucy McKay?"

"I know it," I wept. "It's just that he's improved since his confession, and I'm falling apart. How can we learn to love what we have and not try to love what we create in our dreams? James wanted to be Faulkner, and when he couldn't, it killed him. I want to be here, but I have to be in Oxford. I can't find the right place to be, Mom."

"You will, Luce. I know you. You're the strongest of all of us. Maybe that's why I went to the hospital. Did you ever think of that? Maybe I went not so we could save you, but so you could save us."

The epiphany exploded in my heart and mind. I could see the falls across the valley through the French doors. I thought of a happy woman flying across the country, watching America beneath her, feeling joy in the lift of air and the blessed forgiveness of everyday things.

❧

Late now, late. My cell phone begins to hum to itself on the bed. Should I answer it? I will not. I will.

July 17

Mist hovers through the valley this early morning, the fog of pioneers and pre-contact Cherokees. I surf the net on my laptop, scan the news of idiot politicians. Yet this summer I have been as disconnected from that larger world as the Earth can be from sky when this white layer descends. It's the inner landscape I have traveled. Now I am like a child's top that's giving up to inertia, wobbling before the inevitable collapse. I didn't realize until I awoke this morning that I didn't even ask my mother if she knew my birth mother's name. I can't see myself as one of those women in a talk-show sobfest, manufacturing a narrative from imagination and chance.

I knew Sean would be on the phone last night. I heard his voice in my head. I felt his work-roughened hands on my back. I tasted him. He would say the authorities were handling his ex-wife's arrest—word, sentence, clause, paragraph, page, and book. It was my teacher friend Laurie Teagarten, and I have never felt more deeply sorrowful to hear from someone I like. Laurie: five-four, one-fifty, chubby cheeks, and a pageboy, her husband a bloated glad-hander who coaches Little League, sells cars, and deacons at their church. (Can't *deacon* be a verb?) I've never seen Laurie unhappy. She never questions anything she learned as a little girl. She is placid, at peace. In my cruel moments I might think her bovine, but I envy that placid joy and the fearlessness her faith provides. I did not want her to call. I wanted Sean.

121

"…there's this…on it…my God…finished." She was talking so fast I couldn't make sense, but she never used the name "God" in that way, so I tried to slow her down, but it was hard. She bounces when she talks.

"Laurie, what are you talking about?"

"Whew, I'm flustered. Girl, listen to me. You didn't go to your old house when you were here for the funeral, did you?"

"No. It's not my house anymore, Laurie."

"…was talking to Lou Marsh, you know Lou, his daddy was sheriff in the seventies but had a stroke and had to go to that home in Tupelo? Anyway, Lou's a deputy, and he said, he said, they go to secure your place after James's death, routine, and there's this this this *altar*, sort of, and on it there's a *manuscript*. Big big big thick manuscript!"

"Really." I try to maintain my distance.

"Well, what if he *was* another Faulkner after all? You could be rich!"

"Goddamnit, leave me alone!" I cried. A deathly silence came over the air. "Oh, Christ, not you, Laurie. Not you. I meant *James*. I was talking to James."

"He's dead, honey."

"I know that. I—Jesus."

"I wish you'd quit using the Lord's name like that, hon."

So now what do I have: a second *Confederacy of Dunces* or a three-hundred-page screed against my lack of constancy? I don't want either.

It's mid-morning now, another blank hot day in the mountains of North Carolina, and I took breakfast with my father, and he's oddly uncommunicative today, and I let Victor help feed him, and I feel the long slide of autumn shadows gathering around me. If I were Mr. Sludge, the Medium, I could summon our past ghosts and bid them speak. We would know who we have been and who we are to become. Right after breakfast, I took a long walk in this cage of a neighborhood, and the cars had all gone from the dead man's house. He's changed into memory. Leathery Ella Seitz was out plucking the *Asheville Citizen* from its tube, and she hailed me, and I walked over, not wanting company.

"Looks like it's going to be hot for the rest of our lives," I said.

"...of our lives. Well. *Well*. Nobody loves the sun more than I do. But enough of it is enough of it, as they say." No, Ella, I don't think anyone's ever said that in the history of the world. I drifted off, smiling blankly, as if she were interrupting my workout, but I don't work out.

I feel wrong, someone else's child. If Pratt brought me to this mountain for his summer confessions, what is *my* confession, and to whom must I make it? I walked the sharp slopes of the streets and found myself hating these wealthy and their gate and their golf course. And yet I never felt this safe walking in New York. Once, a robber confronted James and me when we had about twelve dollars between us in the world, all in a sock beneath our mattress. When the thug had searched us and found nothing, he gave us two dollars, and we chatted for a while about Thomas Pynchon!

So, of course, that's when Sean came around the corner in his mud-crusted pickup and stopped, his face blankly unhappy.

"Can you get in and ride with me?" he begged. "I've been looking all over for you. You don't have your cell phone on."

I climbed into his landscaper's truck, which smelled of dirt and conifers, and he drove slowly through the perfect streets, past weed-less lawns. He gripped and ungripped the steering wheel and drove out through the gate, giving the security guard a finger wave before turning on to the highway and gearing up. I said nothing, and he stared straight ahead. I wanted to touch him worse than I wanted breath, but he was distant, almost broken, and I could not reach him, not with love or money.

He drove to his house, and he got out, and I followed him inside, and he fell on to the leather sofa. He all but writhed, agony in his eyes.

"Can you at least tell me?" I asked. "I need to call my father. Victor will think I've been kidnapped. I think he's sweet on me."

"My ex had some kind of breakdown, withdrawal, something. She's under arrest but in a charity ward in Seattle."

"I understand," I said, touching his arm. "Don't you know I understand?"

"No, you don't," he said.

"You have to go, go. I'm not a child, Sean. Summer camp ends. I know that. Always does."

"That's not it. She's pregnant."

I started to laugh, but the agony in his eyes stopped me. The narrative made no sense. This was out of sequence, as Faulknerian as anything that had happened during this strange summer.

"How could it be yours? You were just there. And you didn't have sex, did you?"

"I was out there three months ago trying to reconcile. I didn't ask if she was on the pill. I didn't do anything. I just took what I wanted." He laughed bitterly and flexed his hands into fists. I knew he was thinking of his father.

"But it could be anyone's, Sean. That doesn't mean it's yours."

"It doesn't mean it isn't."

"I see."

"What have I done?" he cried. He stood and walked around the den, which now looked so different to me—like a museum of my failed life. "I knew it. I *knew* it was going to happen. I came here and I hid out, and it goddamn *followed* me, like a mad dog breathing down my neck."

"What are you talking about?" I wanted out of there, and stood and began backing toward the door.

"What happened to *him*. Payback for what *I* made happen to *him*." I suddenly felt sick enough to throw up, and I fled outside, but he was close behind he, calling my name, grabbing at my arm. I didn't even know I was half running down his driveway until he grabbed me hard enough to raise bruises on my arm.

"That hurts!"

"Lucy! Lucy! I wanted to ask if you'd go with me to Seattle. That's why I was coming to see you." He was a broken man, begging and utterly different from the smart-talking wiseacre of a few weeks back. I could not believe that I'd wound up yet again with a man who would bring me nothing but unhappiness.

"Get a DNA test, for God's sake," I said, turning on him.

"I can't even afford to get my teeth cleaned," he said. "The Prius belongs to a friend. Everything else is in hock to my eyeballs. I don't know what in the hell to do except I don't want to ruin things with you."

"Let's see. Getting your ex-wife pregnant and having a nervous breakdown in your own front yard isn't the best way to start a relationship, Sean." My voice was ice, and I was the Princess from the Poles, frozen with cruel intent. I was no longer the friable ruin I'd been at James's grave. I was dust, summer dust. His anguish vanished as if it had gone east in a mistral. His blue eyes turned inward, cold as memory.

"I'll take you back. Get in."

"Fine."

We have the capacity to destroy what we love. We can gut our darlings as fast as we adore them. At that moment, in the high cab of his landscaper's truck, I felt the pulse of rage. Why had he asked me to go to Seattle with him? I couldn't imagine, but the idea of it was wrong, almost sickening. I watched the mountain greenery, the deep gorges, the distant vistas as he drove me silently home. I'd never see him again. I knew that much.

I didn't look at him as we skimmed the surface of the Great Smoky Mountains. I tried not to remember how we'd met and loved. I tried to close my mind against James's secret manuscript, but I knew it had to be a great disaster, because alcoholics don't write masterpieces. I said nothing as we pulled into Cedar Acres, through its guarded gate. I said nothing as we passed Betty and Hunt Bearden out adjusting a bird feeder and laughing, heads together, at a private joke. I said nothing when I saw the car of Mary Lou Wadely, handsome home health nurse, in front of Pratt's house. Finally, in the driveway, I looked back toward Sean, and a different man sat there.

This Sean was small and broken, much as my father was when I first came to this mountain in June. Confessions are not enough sometimes. Through the large windows on the front of the house, I could see Nurse Wadely laughing as she watched Pratt walk on his own. She threw up her hands in amazement: a miracle.

"I don't know when I'll be back," Sean said. "Not that it...." His voice trailed off like a small animal rushing from danger in the woods.

Then it hit me. Now, in the night, it feels disingenuous to say I hadn't thought of the pregnancy and my own situation, but it never rose among my thoughts until I sat there in the loud-idling cab of Sean's truck in my father's driveway. What would happen to the child if she had it? Was it Sean's? What should I do? Sickness rose in me, literal nausea, and I had to grip the door handle to keep my balance.

"I'll be here for two more weeks," I said. "Not that it...." My whole body was trembling. "Shit." I opened the truck door.

"Lucy?"

I turned, and he was reaching for me, and I felt a tide of revulsion, for him, for myself, for this false town, for these lethal streets— for the buoyant emptiness of my life.

"Sean, just fuck off." I still can't believe I delivered myself of that line. I got out and slammed the door, and he backed up and was gone. I walked around Pratt's house and sat, still trembling, on the broad deck, for a very long time.

Now, on a clear, hot night, I feel the keel of my life breaking, and I am thinking of moving back to New York. I still have contacts in the book business, and I might be able to get an assistant editor's position and a one-room flat in Queens. My old friend Anne Hallerman, who started out with me, is now executive editor of Chelmsford Books, an imprint of Random House. She might be able to help.

I am lost to my life. Perhaps I always was.

July 18

My journal's turning into something by Tolstoy. No more. This morning, I decided to take a long drive, and I spent an hour with Pratt and Victor, and then drove alone into the high mountains, puttering slowly on the most remote back roads I could find.

I longed for balm, and I found it. Coves and colors, greens and slate grays. (James always said, in his cups, that you could tell rookie writers when they used the British spelling *grey* because it looks more literary. That was one of the few things about which he was probably right.)

Came to a turnoff with a brown woods sign: Woodcock Creek Falls, 3 mi. Why not? I turned in, drove through the emerald cave of close trees, windows down, Eagles CD on. I sang out loud, banishing men and orphans from my life. There were four turns to the falls in that three miles, and each road was worse, until the last was dirt and crumbling, but I made it to a barely maintained parking pad. Lovely and silent and just me.

"Slow, Luce, slow," I said out loud. I walked at the speed of garden statuary. There was a trail through an old-growth forest, a fine woodchip trail as it turned out, broad and shady. Another sign: Falls: 300 yds. I touched the leaves of beech and oak. A wind came, and it was lovely—probably twenty degrees cooler than stifling Oxford. I came to a bench, and I sat on it, and I knew I would not go back to my school. That there would be no more gentle Timothy Sains for me. That I had one trip left back there, to close the house and get James's manuscript. I would stay here until I knew. I now owned the house outright, and it would bring probably a hundred thousand, maybe more. Plenty to take a year off, longer. (We bought it as a wreck, and Pratt had helped us pay for it outright. The sweat equity in it was beyond calculation. James was going to buy my half, but he would have had to sell the whole thing to pay me.)

The world released me from its mortal grip. But I had to get out of Cedar Acres. I will find a cabin for the summer and into the fall and *then* think about New York. Close enough to visit Pratt, far enough away to know my own heart.

I walked on, and the falls were barely five feet wide but fell two hundred feet, a dazzling plunge, and I adored them, cream on cream as they fell into a lacy pool. I stood in the cool mist and held out my arms like a little girl.

Father, forgive me. I wanted to laugh at the phrase, which entered my mind there, me the lapsed Episcopalian who has only seen Catholic confessional booths in movies, usually ones about the Mafia. And yet the elemental power of that phrase shattered me, and I saw the child in its bassinet, behind a hospital window, lost already, accepted already into a home filled with anger and despair.

Memory takes me back to their last doctoral days, the couple sinking wildly in debt and still giving parties with cold kegs and sipped joints. I threaded through that world like a kitten, petted and passed along. Always, they demanded and got a double deal at universities, assistant professors at Princeton, associates at Johns Hopkins, and full professors at Harvard. By then, I was off to college myself, and they lasted in Cambridge for only three years before the chairs came, he at Chapel Hill, and she at Duke. The marriage, held together by time and convenience, fell apart then. I knew nothing but academia and so was determined to avoid it.

My dreams of being a book editor, like all dreams, crashed not on the shore of the publishing industry, which I liked, but on my weak resolve. I could bear the business but not the authors, most of whom spent their waking hours in hand-wringing paranoia and next-book anguish. It seemed a crazy way to live. So I got a job substitute teaching in Brooklyn and found out, to my utter shock, that I loved it. We came back South to Athens, where I got my master's in education, then to Oxford.

Now what? Not Oxford. Not a thousand American children for the two sensitive ones who understand Quentin Compson's anguished lie all too well. What must I do? *Father, forgive me.*

In this reverie, the purpose went out of me. I let go of the phone call to my boss. I let go of Sean Crayton and the mess of his own making. I let go of my dead ex-husband. I let go of my father and his mellowing rage against the dying of the light.

"Peace, be still," I said. At first, I barely knew where the words came from, and then I did. I almost expected the waterfall to stop and the pool to lie flat beneath it, but of course no such thing happened. What *did* happen was that a deep calming peace entered me, and I knew that I *couldn't* return to the high school and that I would be here until the end of the year or until the end of my father's narrative. I had not yet entered into his story as I should. I had turned the summer into the cache of my own sorrow, the barrow of wounds.

I would change my life before it was too late. Shafts of gorgeous creamy light buttered the waterfall, and I was alone there for an hour. The air filled with mourning doves, and they settled in the grass near the falling water, six of them, three pairs.

July 19

Called my school's acting principal Nan Bright and resigned my job, and she was quiet for a moment and then sighed heavily.

"Lucy, don't do this to me," she said. "The whole school's in an uproar because of Richards, and I've got to replace Heather, too, as I'm sure you know."

"I heard. I'm sorry, Nan. Sorry to put this on you. But everything's changed for me."

"I'm so sorry about James. And your father. I can't imagine what you've gone through this summer, Luce. But don't you think you'd be better with your students? Don't you think they need you? Don't you think Oxford needs you?"

"No, no, and no, I'm sorry to say, Nan, though I dearly love Oxford. And it's not about James or my father, not directly. I'm not who I thought I was."

"Who is?"

I called a Realtor friend in Oxford and told him to put James's house on the market, that I'd be down in the next two weeks to clean it out. He said it would probably bring $150,000, and that it would sell, which shocked me. I also have the account my parents set up for me years ago—plenty. I need to find a house up here to rent. Maybe something isolated and far away from possible amorous entanglements.

Hee. Can't believe I wrote that sentence.

July 20

I told Pratt that I was driving him to Kindleman's Cove Overlook today, and he said all right, and Victor immediately said no. I told V. I needed to see him on the deck, and he came after me, walking as if land wasn't his native environment. Rather, he seemed boneless or arthropodal, shoulders small and round, like a little boy caught and about to be punished.

"Pushing him too far," said Victor. His skin color is bad.

"Let me make something clear for the last time," I said. "I don't need to ask you permission to do anything with my father. Period. Do you understand?"

"I don't want anything to happen to him," he said. Then, quickly, "That was stupid. I know you don't. Lucy, can I tell you something? The new book? That he's narrating, the reason I'm here? He's not doing the new book. He's mostly talking about his life and narrating into his tape recorder at night."

The depth of my stupidity shocked me. Six weeks of speaking at night in his room, and all this time I thought he was seeing ghosts or exercising his vocal cords.

"Narrating *what* into his tape recorder at night? I hear him through the wall. I had no idea. I thought he was talking to himself or praying."

"I really don't know. He won't tell me. Lucy?"

"What, Victor?"

"Do you like me at all? I mean?"

So there it was. Another opportunity for cruelty, presented to me on a silver salver. Victor, the failed academic, in the sad train with James the failed novelist and Sean the failed landscaper and lover. And my father, the great success, failed by his own body. And now Lucy McKay, who has failed her students and has become unmoored from the rocks of her life. My heart, my mind, my eye, my nose, my body all told me what Victor must have already known, and I pitied both of us, available and unable to leap the vast human gap between solitude and genetic incompatibility.

"If I could, I would," I said, touching his arm. "I mean it. But no, I don't feel anything, and I'm sorry."

"Well, it makes sense, you're fucking the landscaper," he said, pushing himself off the deck rail. It felt like a physical gut punch. He blushed deep crimson, and I could see his shame and deep rage. I thought I'd hit him when he passed me on the way back inside or cuss him out or simply scream; I did nothing.

"Not anymore," I whispered.

I got Pratt in his car—a monstrous Cadillac Escalade that I could barely wrestle in the road. I turned his XM radio on to the Forties station, and Frank Sinatra's glorious voice melted through the whisper-cool cab. Dad's thrashing seemed mild, medically symmetrical.

"You pissed off Victor mightily."

"He hit on me. I hit back." Pratt laughed softly and shook his head. "Pratt?"

"Mmm?"

"I have no idea what to do with my life. At first, when you told me about Rachel Motes and Mom and what happened, I just thought it was one of those things. But I can't stop thinking about it. I feel like I came in in the middle of a movie. It feels like I don't know where I'm going anymore."

"We all get that way, honey."

"Not you."

"We pretend it's a straight line. Isn't. Never was. You know what a seismograph looks like? It's like that. A tracing back and forth for your whole life with earthquakes sometimes that go off the scale. James dying, that's the earthquake. Me dying, that's not the story you need right now."

"You're not dying, Pratt."

"Lucy."

"So you're saying the little zigs and zags are how we move forward?"

"We're not moving forward. We've just moving. We just *think* its forward because we can't imagine it any other way. Sun rises one more time, and we fill the day up, and we say we're accomplishing something. It's a narrative, honey. Then people come along and kick the seismograph across a canyon. Martin Luther King. But they can't do it without strong winds at their backs."

"The women of the Civil Rights movement. Your life's work."

"Smart girl."

Kindleman's Cove Overlook might be the place where Satan took Jesus and showed him the world and offered it to him for homage. It's at nearly five thousand feet, and three cars were parked there, and my ears, confused by the air pressure, waffled and hummed. I got Pratt's lightweight wheelchair from the trunk and helped him in to it and rolled him on to the long observation deck built by WPA boys in the Thirties, still rock-solid, cantilevered out over the green heaven of the Smokies. God, I love these mountains, their old breath rising in thermals on which rapturous hawks rise and fall. I pushed my father to the rail, and I could see by the joy in his eyes that he could die here, die now, and yet there was a melancholy tilt to his head, a passing glance between regret and sorrow.

"Luce, I did love Rachel. I don't know how it came to that. I have thought about it my whole life, and for years I believed I was morally corrupt, a bad man. Betrayal of one you love is the greatest

sin. I will never outlive the shame of it. But you need to know something. Your mother hated me, but she *never* hated you. She loved you
from the minute we brought you home. Adored you. She made
clothes for you."

"*Mom?* Mom made baby clothes?" I laughed so hard a madly-in-
love young couple a hundred feet away turned, both smiling.

"Nothing in my life means anything but being worthy of your
love," he whispered hoarsely, and I didn't like how I felt. I wanted his
affection, of course, his close attention, his ability to accept my care. I
wasn't a creature built for adoration.

"Pratt, that's ridiculous," I said. "You just be you, and I'll be me.
We're friends, aren't we?"

He was quiet for a long time.

"That's what your mother always said. To stop expecting more
from her. That she could be my friend but nothing more. Can you be
nothing more, Lucy?"

Shattering. I felt myself disassemble into dry bones, brittle emotions. That was James's eternal lament, that I could not give him love
and that he needed a lot of love. I'd tell him to get a dog. Now, I'd
ruined the day for both of us. I stared at the sea of green earth before
us, and I tried to give more, to say something that would ease the
sting of my inability to reach for him, and nothing came. I was a dry
well, and my aridity desiccated the South and broke it apart, broke it
down.

July 21

Miserable. Pratt having a bad day, and Victor back to being a distant
bastard. I called Sean's cell phone and hung up while it was ringing.
For no reason I called Luna Marcovic, Eastern European haircutter
who lives in my apartment complex in Oxford.

"Oh, hon, I'm in the middle of perm on Miz Faulkner," she said.
"Say hi, Miz Faulkner." Luna held up the phone, and the lady called a

cheery *hi*, and I missed Oxford and didn't even think of asking if she was related; lots of Faulkners around that town. "So, my hands is both of them busy, Lucy. You be back soon, yes?"

Yes, but not for long.

I looked at my face in the mirror for minutes. Do I look like her? Like Rachel? Does she awaken in the night and wonder what happened to me? She must.

Drove to Dogear Books and tried to talk with Olaf Knussen, the owner, but he was happily reading and smoking his pipe in the deeply stratified office, not caring if he sold one broken-back copy of *The Carpetbaggers*. That is the way to manage a career: Give me money if you wish, leave if you wish.

"Oh, Miss," he said, waving his meerschaum in circles as I was about to leave, "did you hear about that good Mr. Howard Reuther? The one with the Jaguar?"

"No."

"Died." He nodded, raised one eyebrow as if he'd just finished narrating *The Odyssey*, and went back to reading his book. I remembered Howard with his ascot and his offer for a ride, his claim to being a liar, his need for human contact.

I can't live like this. I must let love find me. I must give in.

☙

This was always the day James had a birthday party for Hemingway and Hart Crane, reading "Big Two-Hearted River" and parts of *The Bridge* while slurrily drunk.

Call this morning from Nan Bright begging me to stay as a teacher, and for a moment, flattered and unsure of everything, I wobbled, but it passed, like the threat of violence in the parking lot after a high school dance. No, I will not come back. She, tapping her teeth with the ferrule of her pencil, a ghastly sound.

Got the local papers and real estate magazines and found several interesting places for rent, especially this one:

"Unromantic cottage near crest of Bluebell Mountain, six large rooms, silty well, varmints, and rough road. No neighbors close enough in case of emergency. Cell phone service spotty at best. Furnishings are Early Lodge Provincial. Huge fireplace that drafts well sometimes. Reasonably livable in spring, summer, and fall. A challenge in winter. Not for amateurs. Also, the most beautiful place on Earth."

∽

Wild storms that wreck the neighborhood, bringing down a number of perfect trees and generally spreading Poor Taste to Cedar Acres. After it was over, I took a long walk and wanted to feel superior, but they were just humans, sorrowful at the disorder that had come into their lives.

July 23

Went to the real estate office and was taken by a white-haired man named Norris Euler to the house-for-rent. Euler drove his Jeep Cherokee, and he told me the story of the property's owner.

"Name of Jared Minter, lives in D.C., and won't sell and won't fix the place up and expects us to rent it for him. Last person lived there for three weeks and woke up—how squeamish are you?"

"Not very," I said, said, laughing.

"Woke up with a black snake in bed with him. Fella came here to write a novel. Is there anybody *not* writing a novel is what I want to know. *I'm* not writing a novel. Like a disease, like that Ebola. Woke up with a black snake curled up to get warm. Well, a black snake's not poison, for heaven's sake, and they keep the bad snakes *away*, in fact. Like he had the Loch Ness Monster in the house. Said it ruined his novel. I told him he ought to use the snake story in his novel, and he said Thomas Wolfe didn't have to live this way. I said Thomas Wolfe probably didn't even have indoor plumbing growing up and had this man ever seen what lived in an *outhouse?*"

Before we even reached the place I loved it, and I wasn't sure if Norris Euler was shrewd in knowing me as a potential customer or if he was just being friendly. It *was* rough. The ad didn't lie—and if it wasn't the most beautiful place on Earth, it was damned close. Just breathtaking, with a view, a spring, a cascade one hundred yards into the woods, and forty acres of privacy. The road to it *is* horrible, and cleaning the house will take days.

I *have* days. I told him I'd take it.

"I had a feeling about you," said Norris Euler.

"Wish I did," I said. He nodded.

"A feeling we all have."

July 24

He called finally. I was drinking a homemade cappuccino and trying to finish the Julia Glass novel when my cell phone began playing the opening of the Adagietto from Mahler's Fifth Symphony, an admittedly odd ringtone I re-load sometimes.

"Hi," I said, seeing his number, knowing who it was. Was my voice cold, functional? Did I betray how hungry I was for his voice?

"I'm coming home tomorrow, Lucy," he said. "It's been rough. Rough going. Tough time. Kay's sick, real sick."

"Sorry."

"I should have called, but my hands have been full. I've been on the phone all day trying to keep my business going and dealing out here with the law and with doctors. She almost died twice."

"Sorry." I hated myself but I couldn't say more.

"Lucy?" I exhaled and thought about hanging up.

"What is it, Sean?"

"She lost the baby. She almost bled to death. She had to have nine pints of blood. She looks like she's sixty years old. You wouldn't wish this on your worst enemy, believe me."

I began to sob. It wasn't for his ex-wife, a woman I've never met and already despise anyway but for myself, for being a bastard and an orphan, for being a rescue project, for my father's betrayal and my mother's salvation. All my life I'd seen them backward, and now I can't stop and suddenly reverse their roles. Sean, of course, misunderstood, and I wanted to hang up on him.

"Stop," I said. "Just stop."

"What?"

"It's complicated," I managed, getting under control. Then I thought: Oh *God*, Lucy, what in the hell are you doing? Have you completely lost your mind? Will pride ravage what is left of your heart? Can you get out of this summer alive, after all? Your father sick, your mother estranged, and your lover's heartbroken ten ways from Sunday. And you, with your dead James and your profession in the past—who are you now? I felt as if I were the lost child in the bassinet again, scrambled genetics scaring off all but the saintly.

"Okay." His voice had grown berg-cold. Kind men die young, marry the wrong women, wreck their lives, and writhe in agonies of the sensitive. I'd seen James break down a dozen times, wishing to be someone else. A pipefitter, a shrimper, a farmer, a dull survivor. In full Faulknerian flush, he went deer hunting once in Oxford, and though he didn't shoot anything, his friend did, and James came home with crusted coat cuffs. He went into the bathroom and vomited and then got drunk and gave me a bitter speech about rednecks and Bambi. Not his finest hour. I realized that the same thing I loved early in James I loved late in Sean—the sufficiency of quiet words, the poetry of light, and an inability to stake out the wide territory of ambition. God help me, I wanted a gentle man who would not judge me quickly, who might, in fact, not judge me at all. And for that need, I would be cruel and malignant. I would walk out of my late husband's life and let him tread water and then sink. I had it in me to abandon love as love had abandoned me.

"God, I'm sorry," I said, squeezing out each word as if it had some kind of unimagined specific gravity. "Sean, can you come home?"

"In a couple of days. I'll be coming home in two days. Her mother has flown out here. They've been estranged since she was a little girl. But she's here. They're going to give her probation, and her mom's going to live with her until she's back on her feet, try to keep her clean."

"I'm sorry about the baby," I whispered hoarsely.

"That's the only good thing that's come out of this nightmare," he said.

I hung up on him, enraged. I could not breathe. I knew who he was abandoning, even though he didn't even mean it. I dialed my principal to beg for my job back, and then stopped. Sean called right back, and I didn't answer. Mahler played and played.

I looked at myself in the mirror: Why did they bother bringing you home at all, Lucy? Better to have taken your chances with the next person who walked through the door claiming to need a child.

July 25

Nightmares, a terrible sleep, and I awoke in twisted covers, soaked to the skin. Sean had called three times and left three messages, and my bitchiness was a tower from which I could see the world. Perfect time for terrible menstrual cramps and one of my heavy periods. I sat on the toilet and bled and trembled with chills and waited to be sick, and after I threw up and took a long hot shower, I felt better.

It's still early now, not yet seven, and I looked in on Pratt, and he's sleeping on his side, a bare bump beneath the covers, and he looked so alone—one man in a huge king-sized bed. I try not to go maudlin, for I know he's brought female grad students here and lived his life fully. He's had plenty of lovers and three wives, and so I should feel nothing for his solitary slumber, but I still ache for him.

And I feel sick about how I acted with Sean. I know what I need here. I need Sean. I need my new cabin (into which I'll move on August 1), and I need a girlfriend to whom I can talk. And I need, finally, to sit down with Pratt and work through the mysteries of our lives that we have not yet approached this summer. His confession isn't all. There must be more.

❧

Victor: I was an asshole. I had no right to say what I said, Lucy. It's just that you're a beautiful woman, and you're here, and I forced myself to say what I never say. I've gone through my life falling in love with girls and then women, and I never tell them. I stand around and watch as other men pick them off one by one. I live in the past so I don't have to deal with who I am in the present.

Me: It's okay. I was flattered. And I'm not beautiful, but thanks for saying that.

Victor: You're beautiful. And I promise I'm not hitting on you again. I'm just saying that as an objective fact.

Me: Victor.

Victor: You know, I guess I thought that if I hung around your father long enough, it would rub off on me. The talent and the ambition. That way of seeing the world whole. He's published four books, all of them superb, but he's published one indelible masterpiece, the book he was born to write, and it won the Pulitzer. But that's not how it works for love or for talent. Nothing rubs off.

Me: You sound like you're about to leave. Don't. He needs you. Maybe he's lost his focus since he's sick, but does he have a better friend? Do you? (The shades go up on Victor's eyes, and a new light illuminates him.) Don't get the wrong idea from this. But it's how much I want you to stay here with Pratt. (I take two steps to him and kiss him—light smack—on the lips. He holds his emotions and his place, and we know the distance between us. All feels well.)

ℒ

By ten, seven his time, I can't bear it anymore and call Sean's cell phone, and he answers it on the first ring.

"I don't know how you can stand me," I say. "I'm a witch when I get my period, but that's no excuse. I want you home. I've rented a cabin. I've got to go back to Oxford to close up James's house. But I'm not going back to teach. I'm staying here, at least for a while, until I can find my way and settle things more clearly with my father."

"It's not that I couldn't be a good father," he says. "But I wasn't taught very well. When you have to start anything from scratch, you start at the bottom. With landscaping, I started by growing peas in a cut-off Dixie cup in my third-grade class. I couldn't get over the idea of roots and shoots, of water and sun and light and how it all works. With fatherhood, I'm at the pea-in-a-cup stage. I'm not ready. I've already told you that I'm scared I'll turn into my father. It scares me even more to think I'd do that if I had a child I was responsible for." I can't say anything. "That you're staying makes me happier than waking up in the Garden of Eden."

I try out snappy comebacks in my mind, trash them all. He speaks like a man who has been through utter hell and once again stands outside, stunned to see the stars. I've taken a Percocet, and maybe it's the med, and maybe it's me. I don't care.

"Come home to me this minute, Sean Crayton," I say dreamily.

"I am," he says. Then he veers off in a direction I could not have predicted. "I want to find out about my father, Lucy. Who he was before what happened happened." A shock of recognition makes me shudder. "Before I made it happen." *What?*

"And I want to find out about my real mother, who she was and what happened to her," I say. America—and a quiet resolution—lies between us, cell-phone air. I want to say I love him, but is it true? I want him to say he loves me, but I fear it. I begin to wonder if I can live through a breakup if it comes. Or perhaps I fear what I will find about fathers and daughters, mothers and daughters, or women and their lovers. I know nothing, and that absence of knowledge has always terrified me, and I must not let it tear me apart now. I must not claw my future apart.

He will return on July 28.

He did not say he loved me. I did not say I loved him. But all day long I have felt nothing less, and I have felt nothing else.

July 26

I thought Pratt would be delighted to know that I am moving to these ancient mountains, but when I told him, his shoulders sagged, and he began to thrash mildly in his chair. He'd been reading a book about Custer—he's obsessed with Little Big Horn—and it fell to the floor from his lap with a slap.

"Just because you won't have to work doesn't mean you shouldn't," he said, wounding me. His confessional ease of a few days past seems to be fading. I sense that his narrative of our summer is breached. He wanted to confess, be forgiven, and then have me leave for Mississippi, safely away from his disease and any chance we might know each other better. I feel betrayal in his anguish.

"I'm going to try and find out about my mother," I said softly.

"Oh, Lucy," he whispered. "I understand. I do. I don't know what to tell you or what to do. But isn't that history?"

"I thought you were a *professor* of history," I shot back bitterly. "Maybe you can give me some tips." It was a bitter thing to say.

"I apologized and told you how wrong it was, how wrong it all was. It was my fault. I was young and stupid and had no idea of the chain of events that would get set off."

"Yeah, well, women get pregnant sometimes when they fuck, Pratt. Now you know."

"Lucy." His voice was like a wizard's in an animated film, an acute rendering from some well-paid character actor. "I've told you I'm sorry. I've spent my whole life trying to get up the nerve to tell you how monstrous I am. I've begged your forgiveness. You're a teacher. For God's sake, go back to Oxford. Go back to *Brittany* and *Jason* and trying to cram their heads with nouns and verbs and whatever else you teach them."

Now he was the Pratt I recognized from childhood, a champion archer with his quiver-full of pain, ready to aim straight for my heart at the least provocation. Oddly, I felt almost nothing, and he knew it. Power poured through me. When I was little, he would trot me out at parties and get me to perform poems he'd trained me to recite. Once, when I was eleven, I did "The Cremation of Sam Magee" in French, Italian, and Hungarian, the stoned grad students going wild when I finished the last version with its mouthful of garbled consonants and vowels. I cried that night in bed, feeling like a freak, a glittery shard of my parents' vanity. No more.

"No, Pratt. I'm selling James's house in Oxford, and I have my account from you and Mom. I'm taking a year. I'll watch over you. From a distance, if you like. But I'll be here."

"His father was a suicide," said Pratt, hissing out the last word like a genetic code of which I was unaware. "An embezzler and a suicide. I wouldn't forget that."

"Pratt, you're so full of shit that sometimes you're a work of art," I said cheerily. I smiled and petted him on the cheek like a little boy, and he writhed. His arms throbbed in all directions like an octopus with tentacular disease.

"This is wrong," he managed. "I didn't mean for you to stay."

"Well, maybe Mom will feel the same way, and we can all celebrate," I said. "I have to go do some cleaning on my cabin. I'll be back by mid-afternoon."

"What will you do?"

"Maybe I'll write a novel."

My victory was short-lived, and by the time I arrived at the cabin I felt a sick and hollow horror that he did not want me—yet again—and that I was disobeying him once more.

July 27

S. back tomorrow. Talked to him for a long time last night. K. stable and filled with regret for her life. I didn't say welcome to the club, but I felt it.

Walked to Betty and Hunt Bearden's house, and they were inside listening to the Brahms Violin Concerto and reading. They welcomed me like a daughter come home from a college far away. I asked him to tell me about being the chief historian of the Gettysburg Battlefield.

"Lucy, it wasn't a job," he said in his lecturer's practiced consonants. "It was an honor. Sounds like a cliché, I know, but it was. Many times I'd take retired military men on special tours of the battlefield, and we'd be at Little Round Top or the Wheat Field, and I'd be talking and pointing—it was a set speech after all."

"The most beautiful thing this side of heaven," said Betty. "I could cry just thinking of it." She teared up, and he took her hand.

"...be talking and pointing, and these hardened men would see it for the first time, see those thousands and thousands of boys walking straight into their deaths, and you'd hear a soft gasp or a catch in an old man's voice. Sometimes they'd go so silent you could hear a car horn honk back in town. We're not who we are without Gettysburg."

"Best people in the world, so nice to us while we lived there," said Betty.

"Every July, on the anniversary of the battle, this sort of holy feeling came. Hard to explain. I'd take Jimmy, our son, every year, and oh, how he loved it. I think he might have wanted to work as a Park Service historian if he'd lived."

"We've both always thought that," nodded Betty. "Tea?"

Loss comes in different shades. If I was lost to my birth mother, lost to the proper context of love, Jimmy was lost to everything but memory. Yet Hunt and Betty go on, loving the son who died, a casualty not of war but genetic misfortune. I wanted to feel *taught*, to know that I have not earned the grief I seemed destined to bear. Most of all, I wanted to sit between them and pull them close and tell them if Jimmy walks only in memory I walk in life, and they can cling to me if they will let me love them. Hunt can teach me the cautionary lessons of Gettysburg, and Betty can take me shopping, mother and daughter, do things that Mom never did with me.

Of course, I nodded when she mentioned tea, and we chatted amiably, and I asked for nothing from them, as I have forever asked for nothing. If I am broken, I have always reasoned, it is because I deserve it. Can I knit my bones in the mountains? Is there an answer to make me whole?

July 28

Sean's plane doesn't get to Asheville until two, and his truck is at the airport, and he won't get back here until late afternoon, and this morning I find this delay intolerable. Last night, Pratt shouted into his tape recorder, and I wanted to go stop him, but I didn't dare. Instead, I drove to a bar called Hook and Horns, a dark place filled with fishing and hunting trophies.

Stupid thing to do, but I had to get out of the house. I sat at a corner booth and ordered a beer and a grilled cheese sandwich, and I hadn't been there five minutes before a tall man, with the old pocks of acne scars came booting up to me, nodding once, as if he thought he was handsome. Maybe it was a Masonic signal—dunno. I started laughing.

"I couldn't help but notice you were by yourself," he said.

"You couldn't," I said. I knew that locution would trip him, and it did.

"I—couldn't what?"

"What?"

"You were by yourself."

"Why couldn't you help it? Did you try?" He canted his head in clear confusion, at first thinking that maybe he just wasn't getting it. Slowly though, over about ten agonizing seconds, he understood that I was mocking him, and a cold hardness came into his eyes, and a sneer shriveled his face.

"You having a good time? Sitting there like you own the god-damn world."

"I'm the stupidest person in my family, actually," I said. "My father won the Pulitzer Prize, and my mother has an endowed chair at Duke."

"Yeah, right," he said, not believing a word. "And what is it *you* do?"

"I'm independently poor," I said, nodding. He glanced around to see if anyone had been watching. He scratched his ass and shook his head.

"Shit," he said. He walked off, befuddled by rhetoric. I doubt William Faulkner could have done better in the tangled bank of his thorniest paragraph. My beer came, and I toasted: "Happy days."

Now, it's mid-morning, awful, and I want my Sean. I want to stand before an aging woman and look into her face and say to her, "You always knew one day I'd come home, didn't you? It's me, your little girl."

ℒ

Quiet conference with Victor in Pratt's library while he, my father, takes his early afternoon nap. In the soft light of that book-lined space, that expanse of expense and rare volumes, I could see how sadly unattractive Victor really is. Have I said he wears glasses with black frames? Have I spoken of his hair? Thinning and splayed with oily ringlets? Have I told how he wears his watch inside out—dial to the inside—on the wrong arm? (He's right-handed and wears it on his right arm.) Have I said his face is not clean and that he shaves poorly and leaves neck rubble, like a badly edged driveway? Poor Victor, one of the Academically Unaware, living his life in books and in ideas. He teaches a hideously heavily load and has for years—the department's in no hurry for him to graduate because of it. And yet in his discomfort I sense a decent man, one who never even learned vanity.

"Lucy, he's not going to be able to go back to Chapel Hill after the summer," he says, sitting in a leather chair and folding invisible origami with his hands. I'm stunned and sit on the matching sofa across the coffee table from him.

"But he seems so much better," I said. "He's even back to being a bastard with me. I grew up with him treating me like an idiot stepchild." I don't know what he's told Victor about my birth mother, and my own words stun me, trap me. It's true. I'm like the heroine of *A Little Princess*—never sure who I am or who I was.

"He can do that," sighed Victor. "But for long stretches when he's narrating, he loses sense."

"Loses sense? What do you mean?"

"I'd say it's like free-form association or improvisatory jazz, except I'm absolutely sure he's not aware of it, Lucy. I really think something organic is happening to his brain with the disease. I believe we're going to have to get someone to take care of him. I don't see how he's going to get back to Chapel Hill at all."

"What?"

"I mean full-time medical and social help. I'm lost enough without quitting the last little grip on reality I have at school. I've thrown away any semblance of a career because I felt safe as a permanent doctoral student. Fall semester is about to start. He's not teaching anyway this fall, so it won't matter, but I am—four miserable classes. You're going to have to do something here."

"Christ, I hadn't even thought of this. I've been so involved with myself...."

"Well, you should have been. Listen, I talked to Mary Lou Wadely, his home health nurse? She's interested. She isn't happy with the company she works for. She's not quite sixty and in good health, strong, stable. She's got a college degree. She lives in an apartment. She said she'd move in here. Have you ever talked to her? She's nice."

"Not really. Maybe that's what we should do. Pratt's rich, isn't he? I really don't know."

"Like an oil baron," said Victor. "I saw his statements from T. Rowe Price earlier this summer, and he has nearly four million there, and I think he has accounts with Vanguard, too. Money won't be an issue. You'll have to get Dr. Retherston in Asheville to say it's necessary, though. It's probably the only way Pratt will agree to it."

I've never heard him address my father familiarly, and it moves me.

"All right, then." The effort of telling me this has exhausted Victor, and he looks sweaty, even clammy. He sits back and nods. "Victor, I want you to come here on weekends. Pratt will still want to work when he can, and you're the only one who can help him do that. Your room will be here. Promise me."

I go to him and kneel before him, and he sits up straight, head tilting with heartbreak and awkward unfulfillable desire. I take his hands together between mine and hold them, and our four palms appear to pray in unison.

"I will. Thank you for that." Then he does something unexpected that almost frightens me. He leans forward and kisses me on the forehead and then stands and leaves the room, me still on my knees. I am shocked to be suddenly aroused and deeply confused and not knowing what has just happened or why.

I write because I cannot dream. Because Sean has called and has landed safely and is on his way home.

"I'll swing by and pick you up," he said. His voice was raspy and emotionless. "I'll get some steaks and potatoes and a bottle of wine. I'm taking you back to my house and locking you up and throwing away the key. How's your father?"

"Not the same, unfortunately."

"Huh?"

"Never mind. He's well enough for me to be swept away and ravished." He could hear the smile in my voice. I made sure of it.

"You may have to do half the ravishing. I've never been so tired in my life, Lucy. We can talk about your father. I want to help. I *should* help. I never really knew my own father. I'm sure of that. Maybe I can know yours."

"He's not worth meeting at the moment. Ravish me now, and let's talk later."

So I sit here and wait for my lover. An hour ago, I had a massive attack of regret about my students in Oxford, and I remembered how much I love the first day of school each August. The air conditioners are always broken, the kids are fractious, and the superintendent usually comes to give the teachers a lecture about how worthless they are in the grand scheme of things compared to him. But I always looked for that one student in each class with bright eyes, the one to whom I could teach Faulkner or Hemingway or maybe (out of season, as it were, a bit of Marvell or Keats). I remembered how it was when we first moved there, how I'd come home, and James would glow with perspiration and a day's hard work on his book. He'd bring me pages to read, cat-scratch messes of edits and overstrikes. And I always said his work glowed, that it approached some kind of transcendence. In other words, I lied. And poor James never knew it, or perhaps he always did. Two or three nights a week, he'd go out drinking and smoking with the local writers or go meet the touring authors at Square Books and try to get addresses of agents and editors—the next step on the ladder. He would tell them of his time in the City and how he'd once been repped by a fine agency, that his first manuscript was read and admired at Viking and Random House and other places.

I'd sit home and grade papers while James went out howling and came home late, snuggling into bed and telling me stories I had no interest in hearing.

But even before my regret had time to ferment, I wanted only Sean Crayton and this holy mountain chain. I wanted to uncover the secrets of fathers and daughters and mothers and daughters. I wanted to make love with a damaged son whose recent ex-wife had gone through her own hell on another coast.

I write to keep from being alone.

July 29

It's early afternoon, and I'm sitting on Sean's porch, well-loved, with my second cup of coffee at hand, listening to *Daphnis and Chloe* on Sean's sound system while he still sleeps. Making love three times in seven hours isn't for amateurs. Oh, my God, I can't believe I just wrote that in my journal. But I'm drowsy and happy, mostly melted and deflowered, about as post-coital as a girl can get.

Except I'm thirty-five years old, and a girl doesn't look back at me in the mirror. I'm six years older than Sean, something I've tried to ignore. Well, I'll ignore it today anyway.

His appearance was shocking. He's lost nearly ten pounds, and his eyes are unpolished marbles, his arms wraith-like. When he got out of the truck, I wanted to run and leap into his arms, but I was so stunned by his fragile state I simply let myself fit into his arms, and he clutched me, kissed me, and told me I had no idea what it felt like to be back home and with me.

We got back to his house with plans to grill and sup, and he was bone-weary, but he could sense the urgency of my angles and curves, and he did as I did not ask, took me to bed and loved me well. After the first time, when I lay snuggling and happy, my face on his chest and crickets out-singing tree frogs in the vast forest around his house, I wanted to ask him his story. But men do not adore their confessions as women do. If anything, it's the opposite. We want to open our wounds to the wind; men hide theirs from anyone's knowing.

"I know you don't want to hear this," he said, surprising me. "But she told me something."

"Of course I want to hear." I caressed my lover.

"When she was a child, she got left overnight while her parents went out drinking. They just thought she'd be all right. It destroyed her. That one night. She never got over it. She nailed her bedroom door shut, and the next morning, they had to break in with a crowbar, her screaming the whole time. She was so scared she gave herself a funeral. She was seven years old."

"Oh, my God, Sean."

"She never told me one word about that when we were dating or when we were married, not one word. Her therapist asked me if I knew about it. Actually, it just kind of came up, as if we both knew about it. Her therapist didn't want to tell me, and I made her. Unprofessional, I know. I nearly died when I heard. And that's one of the nicer things that adults do to children in the world, I guess. Every minute of every day, some fucking adult is destroying some child's life with something equally stupid or worse. It's amazing anyone grows up happy at all."

"It's okay."

It was not okay. Worse came from him, wrenched up with writhing horror.

"She was three months pregnant and took a massive dose of morning-after pills and vodka, and it nearly killed her. That's what aborted the baby. She was several months pregnant. I don't think it was mine. But. Oh, Christ. I can't think of it. I know she was thinking of that little girl alone in her room giving herself a funeral."

We both cried then and made love a second time, and now it was more urgent, as if we were each trying to climb into the other's skin. I hated his ex-wife and wanted to hold her, salve her wounds, and whisper that love can find us. We do not need to die in our dreams.

Now, I feel cleansed and surer than I have in months. If my childhood as Pratt's grad-party toy was somewhat shameful, I was *not* unloved, and until this summer I had no idea that I arrived in a womb other than my mother's. Does that matter? Only by holding our lives up to others can we see what gives us joy and light and what breaks up down and apart.

I do not know where I will go from here. I want to know my father before he passes. I want to believe that I can understand myself and find some kind of life with Sean Crayton. I must confront my mother. But all that will unfold in time. For now, it is enough to sit here summering on this porch with Sean inside.

Pratt, do you hide other secrets from me? And what must I do to break through to who I am?

July 30

All day shopping for Pratt and helping V. get ready to leave for Chapel Hill and his classes. He (V.) moping and looking at me with tenderness and regret, and me wishing I felt anything for him, the perpetual nerd who will never find love until he does. Please let him find love or let it find him.

Sean, way behind, working dawn to dusk today on landscaping jobs scattered in small towns from here to Asheville. Day of my taking the cabin is August 1.

Pratt cloudy and glum, and I think it's because I'm not leaving the mountains for Oxford. But I am. Tomorrow, in fact. I've put it off as long as I can, and I'll fly to Memphis and drive down and go through James's house and clean out what I can, sell the rest, save his manuscript. The dread I feel is worse than death. I fear I'll drive by the high school and fall apart and just stay.

I want to tell all this to my father. I cannot.

July 31

I'm sitting in the terminal in Asheville waiting for my flight to be called to Memphis, trying to reconstruct how my life has changed since I came here in June. In every way. I can't stop thinking of that abandoned child nailing her door shut and giving herself a funeral. How strange to be heading back to Oxford, for that is too Faulkneri-an to be half-believed. James would have gone wild at hearing such a story.

James. I've thought of him driving here this morning, my dead lover lying in his narrow room a few hundred yards from his hero. When we met he was gorgeous with his long brown hair and pale blue eyes, his swan's neck, and too-sensitive gaze. For almost a year, I thought it was real but slowly I began to understand that most of his posture was posed, even his distant gaze out Midtown windows when we partied hard after midnights with a few friends he'd met in the book biz—rising editors and associate publishers who hadn't yet crossed him off the list. They casually courted him, hoping he might yet fix what remained palpably wrong with his manuscript. He posed for them all, early James Taylor, morbidly sensitive, too good for this world, standing over the City with a straight Scotch, not brooding but beautifully connecting.

My flight's delayed forty minutes. Shit.

In those days, I was part of his act. When some young editor on the make saw him gnawing curtains and staring toward the Met with Great Moment, I'd take the editor by the elbow and steer her away.

"Not now," I'd whisper. "You shouldn't interrupt him when he gets like that. He'll come back over in a bit. Give him time. He's inside his book. Inside the characters."

The editor would lap her lips lustfully and nod, moving away. But I'm being a bitch, and this is all wrong anyway. The editors were the ones in the right, the ones who loved words and the Word. They *did* care and still do, I'm sure. They got paid nothing and worked a hundred hours a week. I know. I was one of them. It was James who, by then, was running his Sensitivity Scam, as I called it in one of our fights. He didn't live in his characters. And he wasn't rewriting his manuscript. By then he was mostly Making Speeches.

When he lost his hope, he began to lose his looks, too. Girls would see it at parties—the bitterness, his tendency to drink too much and too fast. He began to sleep around, too, and I paid him back in kind. It was sordid, and it had to end. So we left Manhattan and moved south where my family lived so I could get the master's in education. But the Dream never left James alone. And so I fear what I will find on this "altar," this manuscript surely left for me in a house I do not even want to see.

ℒ

Why do people say they love to fly? They *must* be lying. Now, on my brief flight across the Old South, I write to keep from screaming. A light load this morning, and I try to exult in the joy of an open seat next to me. The flight attendant, a chubby girl named Kelsie, knows I'm afraid, and when she comes by she puts her palm on my forearm and smiles at me. I want to leap out of my seat and hug her.

This morning before I left, I told Pratt I was scared to be going home to Oxford one last time, and that when I came back I'd get my things and move straight to my new cabin higher up in the mountains.

"Good," he said. He shuffled papers.

"Pratt, you don't have to be such a bastard," I said.

"What if I do?" he said, turning sharply to me. I thought he would begin to cry. Mary Lou Wadely is already moving her things into a large spare bedroom, happy as light in summer. "Wait. Lucy. There's more. I've blown this. There's more."

"What?" I needed to leave. For a hundred reasons I needed to leave.

"The story about you and Rachel. It's not right. My life has been this great slowly unfolding disaster. I've been trying to repair it for decades." He was quiet for a moment. "Pray for me." I was stunned.

"Pratt, I'm a lapsed Episcopalian. You could do better in-house here behind the gates on the streets of gold. Call Father Tanner."

"I can't get out of hell," he said.

"Never knew hell was a gated community," I said bitterly. "I guess I should have guessed." It was a stupid and adolescent thing to say, and it lacerated him, but by then we were too far apart for apologies or more talk. I found Mary Lou in the kitchen.

"I don't think that helped," she said. She has a musical voice and moves with a grace I hadn't noticed before. "But it can't be easy." I wanted to explode, but I took a deep breath and managed not to ruin everything.

"No. Nothing seems to be easy these days. Do they get easier?" She's in her late fifties at least, and there's a placid acceptance in her eyes that I envy.

"Everybody's broken, like a little China doll," she said. "But we gather up our pieces and at night when it's quiet, and we're alone, we glue ourselves back together and go on. And we pretend the cracks don't show and that we're not broken, but we are. We're all just doing the best we can until we're gone. That's just the place to start, though. From there, you can imagine any life at all."

I stood looking at her, realizing I didn't know her at all, had no idea who was about to live with and care for my sick and probably dying father.

❧

But no more of this! I want a day of mystery, possibly of Romance. Regrets, be gone. Sorrow, throttle yourself. Wheels touch, wheels touch, wheels touch.

Now.

4. Pratt

July 1

Lucy, you took me for a walk tonight on these summer-quiet streets. You do not yet know, but I have resolved to defeat this disease. And more. I have resolved to give you my confession. It may come in stages. And I will speak more clearly. Which is why I speak so slowly here on my voice-operated recorder.

You took my arm tonight, and we walked alone down the still street as we never did when you were a little girl. I know you feared my falling. Feared I would break apart and be bed-ridden, carried away by aneurysm or double-grief. I told you that my disease came on so quickly that I did not have time to believe in it. I ignored the early symptoms, as humans do.

We must believe in our disorders. We must know our Brother Disease and Sister Sorrow to gather them unto us. Lucy, I have secrets. I will try to set them in order. I am trying with all deliberation to move toward grace.

July 2

You were gone today, out looking for bookstores, your passion as always. When we went on vacations—before your mother and I began to take them apart—to conferences in Nice, to seminars in London— we would visit the nearest beach, but you would start fidgeting for a bookstore as soon as we arrived. And we'd set off to find one.

In the early days, we had so little money that we saved for months so you could buy what we called beach books. Did you ever know that? I remember coming upon you at home when you were fourteen years old in your room, softly sobbing, sitting with your cat Bobby in your arms. It frightened me until I saw that you'd taken the bookmark out of *Les Misérables*, which you'd been reading all summer and started at the beach. Meaning you had finished that great story of sacrifice and redemption, that you had become part of those lives as we all do. So I knew. You were crying from the misery and joy of having finished a long book.

Whenever I wonder what makes life worth living as I struggle against this terrible force, I think of that little girl, so deeply moved, so shaken to leave a story in which she had become a character. Is that what we are doing here, now, as this summer unwinds, and we thrash toward what has happened before and what will happen after?

July 3

You're hanging out with Sean Crayton, the landscaper, and I want to approve, but I'm wracked with the seven jealousies. I invited you here this summer for a specific purpose which I have not yet been able to reveal. Now, though, I am trying to fight against the disease, and it is fighting back.

What is my obsession with the Civil Rights Movement, a white man of a certain age, honored for telling a story that should have been others' to tell? On some days I feel shame in it.

Victor wants to become what he thinks I am but am not. He has slipped straight from adolescence into senility, and I want to shoo him away, and yet a part of me sees him as a father might a son. Not that I have needed a son. I have never needed more than you, my fine-spirited daughter. But I begin to see at this late date the permanent glory of family and how my generation has wrecked it.

Father Tanner came late in the day to pray with me, and I begged God to step down from his Presumed Cloud and show me his Goddamned Face. Lightning? Should I be the Lightning Rod of Cedar Acres? God, if She exists, knows I jest. I have never wanted that

Old Time Religion, that foot-stomping certainty and blessed assurance. In fact, I want perpetual and blessed *doubt*. I want the goad of explication.

Give me footnotes, Father. Give me narrative. If anything, I'm a Narrative Pantheist who craves balm. Tell me a story to see me through this night. Tell me your tale for a thousand (and one) Arabian nights. The same plot over and over with slightly different details and a delayed ending—my survival, against odds. Make me imperishable.

July 4

Independence Day but not for me. I shall be increasingly dependent, and I must learn not to hate it. I must learn to peel one layer off suffering to see if a small joy lives there, sleeping like a cat on a sunny sill.

Early this morning, when I was still trying to wrestle my way out of this tangled bed, you and Victor had some kind of long conversation in the kitchen. I could hear the rising and falling tide of your voices down the hall. Later, before you went out with Sean Crayton for dinner and fireworks (of all kinds, I hope, dearest) and before Victor settled down to read me from a history of D-Day, I thought to ask each of you about that conversation but didn't, of course. (I am also reading about Custer!)

I have always imagined this world with me in it, and now I begin to imagine it with my absence. It feels odd, Luce, cold. I see you stopping at a traffic light and beginning to forget my face and the sound of my voice. Ambition ruined me. Or perhaps it began long before that. I betrayed all that I valued when I was a young married man. Oh, dear God, how can I tell you. And *can* I tell you?

Suffering is a wild and sacred country. Don't ever go there if you can avoid it. I pray that the genetic misfortune that led me to this disease will pass you by. Paint blood over your lintel, Lucy McKay, so that it shall pass you by.

July 5

Nooooooooo! God *damn* the day! I know that to drink while taking this medicine is suicidal. Can you understand the words? Do my sentences scan? Now you're gone back to Oxford, James dead from booze and pills in the woods behind Faulkner's house—good God what do we become?

What do we become? *Dolce.* I will try to calm myself through will alone. I have not been drunk since the disease came on, but I have unleashed the long-stashed crock. I want to say I never liked James, but that's a lie. He was my only son but just for a time. Ambition ruined him, too. It destroys us. He had ambition before he had talent, which is so American, isn't it? And now you've gone to bury him and clean up his mess.

Your heart must be torn apart, my beloved girl. And I cannot be at your side, and it destroys me to be here alone, a broken-down old man in his cups. Did they bring you in to see the body? Did you pick a suit for his burial and tend to details? You drove to Asheville and flew to Memphis almost immediately, gone by midmorning. That's Lucy, always on time, always taking care of business, a woman in love with schedules and who can command a classroom as I never could.

How can I tell you my terrible secrets now? How can I add to your suffering the mistakes I haven't been able to reveal yet this summer? These efforts and this liquor both exhaust me. I can't talk more. I wish I could tell how…I wish I could just…when I was your age and despair came over me, I….

July 6

You called and found me in terrible shape, and I couldn't confess that I was hungover, so I confess it now. You were not shattered on the phone; in fact, you sounded disgusted and angry, provoked.

"He'd been talking about suicide since the first week I met him, but it was like a villanelle or a sonnet," you said, "a form of speaking or writing, something he never intended. But he meant it this time. He ate forty sleeping pills and drank, apparently, a pint of vodka. Just enough to knock him out but not enough to make him throw it all up. He was within sight of Faulkner's House. I know he sat there leaning against the trunk of a tree in this god-awful heat dreaming of Faulkner sitting in there tapping out masterpieces. Pratt, I haven't gone in James's house, *our* old house. They want me to, but I won't. I told them I'm his *ex*-wife. I'm waiting. I don't know what to do. I want to strangle him."

Grief breaks us. James's grief was over knowing that his ambition exceeded his talent. Yours is over being unable to make a marriage work or knowing exactly where you fit in this working world. And, I know, over your failed family, over your father, whose grief could move mountains.

I must tell you what I brought you here to tell you, Lucy, all of it. But not now, not yet. James died for himself. I want to die for you.

July 7

Can we turn human pity into joy, rage into gestation? I want to believe in the sanctuary of benevolent ghosts, Lucy. I want to know that the dead and the damned do not hold grudges.

My own father, about whom I told you in early June, was prematurely sour, bitterly political, and filled with festering fury. He was a wanderer, but he came home near the end of his life, howling into his grave against his imagined enemies, against his wife, my mother, against immigrants, against imagined and invented enemies of all kinds. History was my refuge as a boy, my sinecure, the bell tower where I hid from his razor strop. You could not have known.

Forgive my struggling voice. Somehow I loved the man, and he loved me, and yet we shared the agony of broken communion. We never made it right. I hated him, and he hated me. How could both be true? They were. He was a wanderer his whole life, uneducated, suspicious as a peat farmer in some Twelfth Century Irish bog.

I did not find the records until he was long dead, but as a boy he was kidnapped and lost for almost a year and then brought home, mute and brutalized. I wept when I found out, for it whispered to me of his rage. We do not tell why we are who we are. And so do not judge James too harshly for his lost ambition, Lucy. Another man may have lurked inside him, one broken down and begging for light.

July 8

You back, and worn out. Me here, and worn out. Victor in the morning says he has a new angle on his dissertation, and his eyes glow. But by night, the fire's out, and I can tell he no longer believes in it, no longer believes in himself.

July 9

Horror of a day and a furious fight with Victor, whose failed belief in his own ideas led him to provoke me over this book on which we supposedly write. But Lucy, how can we believe in God once we have been to Hell?

"If you want to quit, just quit, and I'll pack up and go back to Chapel Hill," said Victor, rider of the purple rage. "I've dedicated my life to helping you, and this is the fucking thanks I get?"

"Fuck rhetorical questions," I said. "Speak to *me*, you miserable shit."

Oh, God, why did I say that? He went for the heart.

"I came here to keep you working and to keep you company until you shriveled up and died, you goddamn miserable torturing asshole!" he screamed. He was wild, waving, crimson.

"I will fucking finish nothing because I fucking said I won't!" I cried back, though I can't imagine what sound came out with my foam. Then you came in Lucy, eyes beautiful and wide to see us wildly fighting.

"Stop it, both of you!" you cried. Victor grabbed a fistful of typed notes and wadded them triumphantly into his perpetual grad student fist.

"Burn it!" he shouted. "Burn the whole goddamn thing!" You, Lucy, then did something utterly shocking: You came to him and slapped him on the cheek as hard as you could, and that smack resounded in the cool, quiet room. Utter silence followed, the grave, the awful tomb. Victor held the wound and his eyes filled with tears, and he sat beside me on the sofa and gasped once in shame.

I said something—I don't know what. Victor may have said something. I was watching you, beloved daughter, standing there in the tower of your righteous vindication. You fled outside. Victor and I sat there for a time. He wept into the cup of his hands.

"I don't want to quit," I said hoarsely. "My *body* does. I'm fighting it."

Lucy, will this summer end in despair? Is my recording filled with my confession for you? I have filled it with folly. I wanted to end the fight with forgiveness, but I could not speak. He left me. I lay twitching on the sofa. I realized classical music played in the background. It was something beautiful, soft, glowing with hope I would never have again.

July 10

Just as yesterday was evil and dark, today, this evening, was memorable and loving, the kind of evening a father and his daughter should have shared so many times before. You made a lovely dinner. I ate better than I have in days. I took my medicine. Is some kind of reprieve coming into my muscles? Will love undo this disease? Will my confession save me?

We decided to read aloud, and I read "Mr. Sludge, 'The Medium',", a narrative poem by Browning that a classmate read aloud at a party in graduate school a thousand years ago. I did not tell you that each word seemed to be swimming on the page, around and through its fellow nouns and verbs, and my eyes had to trap it and fix it as one might small game. So I read slowly and poorly, which made it even more amusing. I made it seem part of the joke, and you and Victor howled.

And then I had to ruin it by losing my mind and my temper over something one of you said—no idea what it was. I apologized just before the evening was wrecked, and Victor read, to my horror, from my book, and then you, Lucy, picked up a children's book from which to read. But when you opened it, you burst into tears. You fell apart. Perhaps it had something to do with James or your own childhood or your growing friendship with Sean the landscaper—we did not know. I stood, and Victor put his arm beneath my shoulder and guided me to you, and we fell into each other's arms. The reading party broke up then, and Victor helped me to my room so you could clean up.

Why did you cry, Cricket? What in that child's volume could have touched you so much? If we have a good childhood, we always try to swim back toward it like salmon going home to spawn. If we have a bad one, we try to swim back to change the narrative, to invent a happy beginning so we might find a happy ending.

And I have not yet told you of your beginnings. And I must before I reach my own end.

July 11

To the doctor in Asheville today. I knew on the way there that I am dying. I knew in the waiting room that I am dying. I knew as he examined me, knew as I dressed, knew as we drove slowly home.

And yet I cannot believe it. And I cannot believe *in* it. I believe I will live forever, Lucy. Too tired to talk more.

July 12

High midsummer and the last warm season of my life, and I have blundered Lucy. You are out right now with your friend Sean, or is he becoming more than your friend? It isn't just that you do not know me, and I do not know you. In many ways, we do not know ourselves. We hide from the truth all our lives.

My lies have caught up with me. You will know *some*. Perhaps you will know *all*. Victor assists the idea of Pratt McKay, the historian, not the man. The man is a phantom, illusion of honor, pretender to grace.

When I began to write my famous book I felt as if I commanded the Earth. I was the pilot of it, Lucy, and every sentence came crafted in its full perfection, sprung full-born from my brain and hands like Minerva from the temple of Zeus. I could not bear to let go of the adrenalin which makes morphine like some lily-pad balm, a child's sleep aid. Why was that book and that time given to me? I have never known. Time and knowledge conspired. My sins were forgiven me for the four years I spent bathing in that text.

Those women of the Civil Rights Movement made me weep for joy. I was not their equal and knew it. But I was their Moses, the one who could bear their words down from the mountain and give it to the People. And then, God help me, God forgive me, I loved the fame. I *became* it. I churned into its monster and bully boy. I would sweep into meetings with unforgivable élan, metaphorical ascot in place.

What am I talking about, Lucy? I don't know. It's summer. I'm a sick old man. I want to be a boy again.

What is that—my God, it's Sean out there with a sparkler! And what are you doing out there...you're...wait...I'm coming to the window...courting, I see. I'm backing away now, back to the bed, back to the recorder, back here.

Maybe the world *will* end in fire, as Frost says. I want to take Crayton by the shoulders and shake him and say, "This is my beloved daughter. You treat her well or do not come to this place again."

July 13

Lucy, today was the time of my confession. All summer I have built toward this, and I awoke strong and wanted to walk on the deck, and my therapist Ginger helped me, and I found that I was less disabled than I thought. Are we all? Then I sent Victor, poor befuddled Victor, to the store for groceries, and I asked you to sit with me for the story.

And it came out of me—not all of it but some—the story of Rachel Motes and our love affair and the baby that we created, the child that was you. The baby that your mother saw through the nursery window at the hospital and said we had to adopt. I told you everything I could, but now, here in the night, can I tell you more?

Sean came and got you late this afternoon, and Victor has gone back to Chapel Hill just for the night, and I—getting better, am I?—sit here alone with this recorder in my bedroom, speaking out my life.

I remember how I felt as we stood looking at you. I was the monster in Beowulf, the Beast of Betrayal, and yet I loved your mother *and* Rachel, and dear *God* I loved you. Also I hated Rachel, I hated your mother, and I utterly *loathed* myself. I had lost so much weight I looked skeletal. Passion destroyed me. But it was the passion of infidelity and betrayal. I knew then that I was a man of no character, that I would always be weak, and that my moral center would always be suspect. I also knew that your mother, in that act of adoption did two things: She committed an act of utter love and self-denial, and she also found a way to control me for the rest of our lives.

I love being alone for now though I know it cannot last. Is this my last night alone? Victor will be back first thing in the morning. Will you? I hope you are doing what we humans must—taking what love we find when we find it.

I need to tell you more. You may think this is the whole the story. It's barely started. Oh, Lucy, love of my life, how can I tell you the rest? And how can I make our story come out right?

July 14

Victor back, and it's still early, and I'm up and it's raining. Am I dreaming this, or is my body getting stronger? Do miracles still exist? You did not come home last night, Lucy, and I awoke feeling gratitude for it. I know you must lie there well-loved.

Lovely all-day summer rain, and you came home, cloudy-eyed in the early afternoon, and I feared a lovers' quarrel or something else gone wrong. I had been napping, and when I awoke I saw you sitting in the den, doing nothing.

"Everything all right, Luce?" I asked, oblique by necessity.

"Fine, Pratt," you said, and your words came out hard, but then you changed the shape of your face to show me that I was not the problem.

No, dear girl, grown woman, I *am* the problem. I have been the man of no woman's dreams, and I know it. With shame, I tell you I have slept with graduate students, sometimes even undergraduate women, sharp girls who see sex as recreation, like shooting pool or bowling. Maybe it's to buff a grade or just for an evening's adventure, but it's *nothing* to them. Afterward, they raid the fridge, smoke a joint, call girlfriends (even *boyfriends*), watch TV, prowl the library. And I lie in bed thinking of how wonderful it was and that what we substitute for love sometimes creeps close to the real thing.

Is that what you are doing with Sean Crayton? I hope not. I hope there's love or at least a deeper affection. Not that the mere physical is worthless to us as humans. But it can curse, and it can wound. And it gave me you, my heart's darling. You told me one time that Faulkner used that phrase—I forget who he was describing. But I've never forgotten it, because that's who you are to me. My heart's darling.

Do you remember your favorite expression when you were a little girl, "right as rain"? Do you know why you started saying that? You were five, too young to know what was going on, but your mother had left me—she did it several times, as you know, but she always came back until she didn't anymore—and you and I were on the porch, and it thundered very loudly, and you ran and jumped into my lap, crying.

"Don't let it get me!" you said.

"Why Lucy McKay, that's the Sky Lion saying everything is right as rain!" I said. Then I told you a story about the Sky Lion and how he guarded the Earth against Bad Things, and you calmed down and began to relax in my lap, and I stroked your hair, and you began to say, like a mantra, over and over, *right as rain, right as rain, right as rain.*

And you fell asleep against me. And when you awoke the storm was gone, and the sun had come back out, and your mother was pulling back into the driveway. And you said "Right as rain" and you *danced* out to the car to welcome her home.

Did you know that? Do you remember? Then I told you that everyone was safe and loved when they lived in the shape of rain. Remember? But why did I tell you that then or now? Was it salve to a wound? Have I offered you healing at all? All we have to do is live in the shape of rain, and we shall be loved always.

July 15

It is *not* my imagination. I *am* getting better. But how is this possible? I do not want to sit on my bed and talk into this voice-activated recorder. I want to go hiking. I want to believe that in misdiagnoses, that soon I will be back in my classroom, that some visiting professor will look at me and let me invite her out for drinks and that halfway through talking about Selma I'll find her hand on my thigh.

Is this making you sick, Lucy? Are men incorrigible, even old sick ones? Probably. It seems to me that you and Victor have concluded some kind of separate peace.

Summer has settled in my bones. It is my favorite season. I do not want winter to come again. I have always thought that I will die in winter. I could not die in summer.

Yet even as I sit here, my left arm begins to go haywire on me, a reminder that this disease will ebb and flow, but, even if slowly, it *will* always flow. It will bear me onward, tide on tide, until I am history myself.

What are you thinking, Lucy? Have you begun to forgive me? Do you even think about me in the web of your complicated life? I already miss you, and I think about you driving back to Oxford and listening to these tapes. Have they made you know me better? Love me at all?

July 16

I can talk into this goddamn thing but have trouble feeding myself anymore. Goddamn this disease to hell.

Lucy, I.

July 17

It's midafternoon nap time. Nice morning visit with you and Victor, and I tried to see from your eyes if you forgive me or if hate boils just beneath what I see. I wonder if you have begun to guess the next level of my secret, which is *so* near and yet far from my lips.

Victor spends hours googling MS and reads to me the latest scientific papers and advances. He would be the Merchant of Hope, the Good Son. But he speaks of something abstract, not of the prison in his bones. I feel in my body the same betrayal I gave to my young wife, and the justice of it rings like freedom's bell.

When I get this way, I make Victor play the soundtrack to *The Deer Hunter*, and then I sit here and cry. Maudlin man that I am, but that simple guitar theme tears my heart from its anchor of veins and arteries. I think of those friends shattered by that film's evil war—Vietnam—and of the evil men who kept it going in this country. Especially now I think of the man wheelchair bound, half-man, memories of himself as a young lover intact, his body smashed and destroyed along with his ideals.

You were gone all day. I do not know what you are thinking or where you are. I thought you would be with me this summer, Lucy, and you have found a friend to help you bear burdens—or is it the other way around?

I miss who we could have become when you were young, and I was younger—father and daughter, sitting by sandcastles on sunny beaches. I wish my act had not created the world in which I have made too many crawl.

July 18

Glory. Can you understand a word of what I am saying? I rush it out like a dying man crying aloud for water in his usual desert. I haven't played back any of what I've recorded for you, but I am certain my voice gets less and less understandable.

You took me to Kindleman's Cove Overlook, driving me there in my own car, that ghastly living room of a Cadillac Escalade I bought with a royalty check last fall. Like climbing a mountain to get me in. And you, arguing with Victor about even taking me. Apparently, Victor made a pass at you, and who could blame him? You, beautiful and desirable and present. Poor man. Alone with his narratives—the story that a homely man can become attractive through his words and actions alone. Beauty and the Beast. But there is no Beauty and the Dullard. Poor Victor.

You said you do not know what to do with your life, and I sensed you are considering not going back. I felt flushed and unsure of what to say. I do not want you to quit. Have you not seen what quitting has done to us all? I told you that we are not moving forward, that we think it's forward, because we can't imagine our lives any other way.

I told you that I did love Rachel Motes, and I loved your mother. I told you about Mom making you baby clothes, and you didn't believe me, since you couldn't imagine it—to be honest, I can no longer imagine it, either, but she did it.

Lucy, I asked you here this summer to become worthy of your love, and I have told you less than half of the truth. The truth is *much* closer than you can imagine, and yet I do not have the courage to show it to you. And what if you have talked yourself into quitting your job and leaving Oxford because of James's death? What then must I do?

I see distant lightning tonight. I want to live, my beautiful daughter. I want so badly to live and to set things right. Will I have that grace? And can I tell you the rest of my secret?

July 22

I have been sick with some virus in addition to the MS, and for three days I had given myself up for dead. I dreamed of Gericault's painting *The Raft of the Medusa*, and I was the wretch falling into the sea. Now, as I'm sure you can hear, thunder and lightning illuminate this audio manuscript I am creating for you, Lucy. The wind howls, and we see nothing through storms that could sink ships.

This storm reminds me of that day in Philadelphia, Mississippi, when I went to visit the family of a black man murdered for trying to vote. This had happened before Goodman, Cheney, and Schwerner, and the sharecroppers' small house shuddered with the thunder and lightning and, it seemed, the memories of those days of violence from thirty years past (thirty years at the time of the interviews).

The boy slain, Vernon Bunning, was only twenty, and his mother sat in a rocker near a window closed against the storm. The room was airless. They'd stapled newspaper insulation on the walls. My guilt could have filled the Gulf of Mexico brim-full. Her name was Delores Bunning. She was a laundress. She was tiny as a bug, and she spoke in a hoarse whisper and kept looking at the rain-smeared window as if she thought Satan might leap through and snatch her out.

I asked her what Vernon was like.

"He was a kind, gentle boy," she said. "He read to the younger children and said to them they should go on with they education. He graduated high school and was working to the funeral parlor with Mr. Hightower. Would of been a funeral man directly he'd lived, but they kilt him, Mr. McKay."

"I know. I'm so sorry. I can't begin to tell you how sorry I am."

"He loved a storm like this and he'd sit with me 'cause I was scairt like I am right this minute. He'd read me the Bible and soothe me. Ain't nobody left to soothe me. That's what growing old do to you, Mr. McKay. Nobody left to soothe you."

But I do not want to be soothed, Lucy. I have the need to soothe. In this storm—God, that one was close!—I have the need to touch you and help make you whole. And yet I have lied and cheated my way through life. I've been the sun and let my family and friends be the moon and the stars. (And some, like Victor, be faint tracery from unnamed pinpoint galaxy.)

Too tired to go on.

July 23

Victor took me to ride to see the storm damage. My God. Trees down, limbs scattered, trunks uprooted and splayed. Out on the highway, that gorgeous red barn overlooking the scenic pond—that calendar icon—had wall planks spread redly all over a cornfield.

You? Where were you today, fragrant daughter of mine?

Each morning I awaken and wonder what my body will do to me this day. I believe less and less that I can ever get back to Chapel Hill and my office or classroom. I do not see myself as one of those men whistling his way down the hall in a wheelchair with a mobility-straw or writing books with the blink of an eyelid.

"I've been looking into getting a ramp built on your house in Chapel Hill," said Victor as he drove me through the debris. "It will help until you're walking better again. And, of course, as I've read you, the course of the disease is unpredictable, and you may sometimes need a permanent wheelchair. Or not."

"I know what must happen next," I said. He glanced at me, not knowing. Of course he doesn't know. No one knows but me. That is the reason you are here, Lucy, not just my confession. There is much more. Am I dying to tell you or am I just dying? Is there a difference?

July 24

A slow-motion late life. You so miserable, but Sean finally called you from Seattle where he has gone to deal with his crazy wife—or is it his ex-wife? Have you once again entangled yourself with the wrong man? We marry the wrong men and the wrong women. But we *can* make things right. We can resurrect the ancient ghosts that have haunted us for all our days, and we can say to them that we never meant them harm, and that love once found us, and that it was real, and that grief can be toxic and tonic.

All the nightmares I created began accidentally. That's how tragedy begins—one misplaced turn, one unraveling thread. I thought I could love your mother and Rachel at the same time and have two women adore me. I thought somehow that I deserved it. I deserved *nothing*. I earned *nothing*. It is easy to say that it was one small domestic dalliance, the kind that wrecks lives the world over every day. But it's more than that: It becomes tragedy when left alone too long. Have I let our love turn into tragedy? Have I saved anything by telling you half the truth?

We solve nothing. I brought you here to resolve it all, and you fall in love with my landscaper, and your ex-husband kills himself. I love you more than my coming death wants my body and my bones.

July 25

I heard you open the door early this morning and stand there for a long time and look at me before Victor was up, before anything else stirred. I lay like a mummy, a memorial historian, already entombed, controlling my disease with all willpower ever given a human so that you would believe I slept.

You are changing, something is changing. You have quarreled with the absent Sean Crayton, but you also seem to be a ship moving away from your past, and how I can blame you or not understand? When you were about seven, you suddenly began to look exactly like Rachel, and I said nothing nor did Mom, but her coldness became glacial, her grandeur Napoleonic.

You may remember me "working late" or being gone to "conferences," but it was tawdrier than that. I do not even remember their names—married colleagues at meetings, socialites adding a Pulitzer-winner to the cupboard, or a failing grad student who hated me before we did it and hated me after. I lived in self-loathing. The only respite I had was two minutes of forgetfulness just before and during. Right after, in the quietness of memory—knowing that you were at home with homework and false ideas, I would ball my fists and writhe. Most of them would shrug me off—an hour's impersonal relief and on to the day's next appointment. After a while, thank God, the allure of the Pulitzer began to fade, and the younger ones recoiled from my touch. Only those left alone, the desiccated and the unlucky, took me down, and often they offered me salve or comfort—not love or sex. They petted me as one pets an old man or an old dog.

I had gotten what I deserved, and I knew it. Now I lie alone and pretend to sleep when my daughter looks in on me so she will not fret more. I pretend that no one is at home, that no one is suffering, that I am content with my life, the one I wrecked from the beginning and still cannot save.

Victor reading me about Little Big Horn. I took the book to bed with me but just dropped it on the floor and can't get it back. You can't get some things back, not ever.

July 26

So it has been coming to this, Lucy, your own summer decision, and yet when it came I was not ready.

"You should work, even though you don't have to," I said. That wounded you, and perhaps I meant to. I felt like your drill instructor, your goad. Then your own confession came, and I should have known I had uncorked the genie, but the wound still sprang blood: You want to find out about Rachel. I made a terrible blunder and told you, with the face of a traitor and wretch that it was old history now. Oh, dear God, what a fool I am.

"I thought you were a professor of history!" you shouted. What a moment of triumph, Lucy—your lance, your hammer and nail. And God, did I ever deserve it. For me to dissemble now is madness. But I did. I tried to apologize again, and, of course, it got worse. It always gets worse. I am not an eloquent man, that one book to the contrary.

I lost my mind. I became the monster I can be and insulted you, made fun of your job teaching high school English, knowing full well in my heart and soul that one day of it is more important that my entire career. We all know it. That wasn't it at all.

You being here reminds me of how I ruined our lives. You see, I had this plan—one you cannot know. I had a plan that might resolve things in the end so I can die in some kind of peace, but now it, too, is falling apart. Instead, you are going to stay here, and you will *not* be listening to this recording as you drive back to Oxford, this ridiculous recording, this failed confession. I even insulted your friend Sean— the worst thing I could have done. And I said I did not mean for you to stay.

I became the monster you see. When you left, I pushed Victor away and thrashed my way down the hall to this bedroom where you can hear me now, hear me crying, a sick and stupid old man who loves you more than his own last breath and still cannot quite see how to make it right.

Oh, God, forgive me, Lucy. Forgive your fallen father.

July 27

You went to the Beardens' house today and talked with Hunt about his work at Gettysburg. You came home and wanted to find some way to link Civil War to Civil Rights, but I pretended to be sleepy.

I wasn't. I was being a bastard. Now that you are not leaving, what is the purpose of all this? When will you hear it, if ever? But there's more, Lucy, a decision I have made about which I cannot yet explain. Will it become clear? Will you look in the mirror and see what I see now? Will the truth be revealed unto you?

I do not want to be old. I want to be young again and in love. If she comes to me, will love come again? Do you know what I am talking about? You cannot. I want to open up before I am broken down, but with your staying I do not know what to do. I do not.

July 28

What I have done to Victor is beyond forgiveness. All summer, when you are safely out of earshot, I have begun to narrate and then gone mad. Did you know I was theatrical in my youth? I was in many plays—I once essayed Iago—and when I lecture I can become Alec Guinness or Laurence Olivier. I have done this with malice afore-thought like Hamlet. I know where it will lead. I know where I am leading it.

You will see it soon enough and know. Perhaps then it will be made clear what I meant to do this summer and have done so badly, sweet girl. I have not made things right as rain.

Your Sean is back from his nightmare, and, of course, you are gone to him. You will love him all night in his nightmare. But will he salve *your* nightmare, Lucy? Victor would be shocked at the clarity of these words for he has heard an old man in his raving all summer. I would begin a disquisition on Klan organization and end with a fillip on bears, somehow leaping from Klavern to cavern, from sheet to meat. I could see the sorrow in his eyes. He would stop typing down what I wrote and look out the window and let me rave. I have done to him what I have done to everyone who has ever loved me: betrayal and manipulation.

I will make it up to him. I will make up all things to you.

July 29

And so you were gone last night and gone all day today, not bothering to call, not needing to, and I found myself sitting on the hot deck looking at the waterfall across the valley and filling with joy and hope for you, Cricket. I needed Victor to help me out, and we talked.

"I've got to get back for my classes," he said. "I'm not sure that you're going to be able to...."

"I'm not teaching this fall, but it's over for me," I said. "I've called the department. It's time for me to let them hire a young assistant professor." Weeks before, I had suggested he think about asking Mary Lou Wadely, my home health nurse, if she wanted to come live with me. It was so long past he probably believes it was his idea now. Already today we've talked about her.

"Are you sure?"

"Old men are more sure than young men can ever be," I said. "Call it good fortune or a curse. Maybe she can help me work. She is smart enough."

He left me alone after a time, Lucy.

Later, and you have called from your lover's home, and you are sorry for leaving me, and I tell you that I love you and want you to be happy. And your voice spills with his suffering and perhaps your own. You tell me you will be going back to Oxford to close up the house, that you will be moving into your new cabin here in a couple of days, and I tell you that I love you, too.

I tell you I've agreed for the nurse to live with me, and you sound relieved. What will you find when you go back to Mississippi? Ghosts? The pull of history? Plots and characters? Students whose eyes haunt you? Too many rhetorical questions, but I am the professor, and it is my calling to ask them.

July 30

A strange sorrowful day. You went out with my credit card and shopped half the day for me. Mary Lou Wadely moves in tomorrow. Poor Victor crept around in the death pall of his regret, not knowing how long I can survive but realizing my days of teaching and writing are gone, blown by.

I tried to be cheerful for you Lucy, but it was no good. With Victor leaving and you headed to Oxford to face your sorrowful past, and me not going back to Chapel Hill, I feel a molt coming. I am turning into a frozen thing, a caterpillar that will not, in spring, sprout colorful wings.

You come home with my car full of groceries and supplies and look like a woman under a death sentence. I want to tell you why joy enters me today, too, but I dare not.

July 31

So you've gone back to Oxford, and Victor has returned to Chapel Hill, and I am alone here with Mary Lou, not alone at all, bound by a narrative that I cannot yet untangle for myself or for others.

I wanted to be kind and gentle before you left, Lucy, but I fear I ruined it in my rage of uselessness and fear. She looks after me and at me, with kindness and a good heart. Can I pass that caring on to you when you come back?

We talked this morning before you left, and you said that when you returned you'd be gathering your things and moving to the cabin you have rented. I thought you sounded relieved, and I blistered you.

"Good," I said.

"Pratt, you don't have to be such a bastard," you replied. Then I tried to apologize, to explain, and I even asked you to pray for me, which shocked you. You told me to call Father Tanner, and I told you I was in hell.

You went into the kitchen and talked to Mary Lou Wadely—she told me later in the day. I wanted to die for ruining your departure. Now Victor has gone back to Chapel Hill, and I am here on the slow slope of this disease, secrets still held, unable to reveal to you what I must before I die.

I was a good man to begin with, Cricket. Then I broke apart on my own human weakness and I brought down the world with me. Can I save you now, and in doing so, save myself?

5. Lucy

My God. I would never in this life have believed what has happened to "our" house here in Oxford. It's late morning, and I'm taking a break to write in my journal and center myself. The heat inside is suffocating, the filth beyond description. James had clearly begun to lose it months before, and in these walls is his madhouse. I want to hate him, but all I feel is a shattered grief.

The power is off. I opened all the doors and windows and went to the Kroger and bought huge boxes of 30-gal. string-tie trash bags. I've carted out eighteen bags-full of garbage and trash so far, and I'm sitting here at the kitchen table with a bottle of water in the warm cross-breeze from our blue-check curtains. I've mounded all his dirty clothes in a corner on the bedroom floor, cleaned out the stinking fridge, which made me gag. I have incense burning in almost every room, and it barely helps.

The front porch lay buried in a mound of mail. It lies heaped before me on the table, spilling out, bills to a dead man. The yard is feet deep in weeds.

And there, in his study, is the altar as I was told, a ghastly table with bled-out candles and a neat red velvet covering, and on it, his manuscript. I have not touched or looked at it. The scene's power is ghastly, its message a whisper from the nightmare.

I found the bedsheets blotted with pools of stain, none of them from me—the sad residue of his unclean couplings over God knows how long. I pulled the sheets off and found the stains penetrated to the mattress, and I screamed in rage and disgust. Who were they? I don't want to know.

I had taken out probably ten bags by eleven when there was a small knock on the front door, and I found Carrie Johnson, who's lived next door for years, standing there peering in. When she saw me, she started to cry, and I hugged her. She's retired now, another high school teacher, mid-fifties, great shape, and holding two Diet Cokes. I came outside.

"You don't want to go in there," I warned her. She led me to her cozy patio, and we sat in her white wicker furniture. She put her hand on my arm and held it there for a long time, and I let her.

"It was such a shock," she said. "I never saw James much after you divorced. Sometimes he didn't come out but maybe once a week, and then he'd maybe go to the store and come right back. People visited him sometimes."

"Women."

"Sometimes."

"We'd quit talking. I hadn't spoken to him much in the past couple of months, much less come by here, even though we lived in the same town. We were still haggling over ownership of the house. I'd stupidly let him put it in his name. Lots of problems that caused. And then he left everything to me in his will."

"To die like that. Alone in the woods out behind the Faulkner house. He always wanted to be something he just wasn't, I guess."

"Don't we all." She looked puzzled as she sipped her drink.

"This is all I ever wanted to be. A teacher and married to Bobby and living right here in Oxford and watching my kids grow up and going to church and loving football and so forth. I never wanted anything more than that."

"Then I envy you, Carrie," I said.

"They said you'd quit at the high school. That couldn't be true."

I told her it was and that I was moving to be with my father, which was only partly true. She stared at me as if I had lost my mind like James. I promised that I'd get the lot and house completely cleaned in a few days so the house could be put on the market.

"You've suffered," she whispered. "I'm so sad that you've suffered. You're due some peace."

How could I tell her about Pratt and Rachel Motes? How could I explain that I was now a woman who did not know her own family?

I'm sweating on the paper of this journal. Several doors down, someone is cutting the grass.

August 2

I called Pratt last night around seven, and Mary Lou Wadely, wearing her sweet soft voice, answered and said my father was napping and doing just fine.

"I can't tell you how much it puts my mind at ease knowing you're there," I said. "We need to sit down and talk when I get back. I'm sorry we hired you without even having a chance for a long conversation."

"It's all right, Lucy. There's time. It's just going to be a long, slow sunset for him. There are worse ways. He's had a rich life. My job is to keep him as healthy as I can and to make sure he does not suffer."

"But he suffers in his mind," I said. "Shouldn't we get him some counseling or something, too?"

"I'm pretty good with my patients. Let's see how I do."

"I didn't mean it that way. Of course you'll help. Tell him I love him, and I'll be home in just a few days. I have a lot to deal with here."

"I know you do, honey," she said.

I'm taking a break—it's noon—and the house starts to look clean and to smell better. The power is back on, and the AC cools down the smell, the heavy moldy aroma of disease. I've turned the mattress, vacuumed, dusted, and emptied, scrubbed the ghastly bathrooms. Last night, Carrie's husband, Gary, came over with his riding mower and cut the grass neatly and even bagged the clippings. They want to scrub the stain as much as I do.

I've turned over all James's bills to my lawyer friend who's probating the estate. At midmorning, when I was up to my elbows in cleaning out from under the kitchen sink, my cell phone rang.

"I miss you," Sean said. "Come home right now, or I'm sending a private investigator out to see what you're up to out there in Yoknapatawpha County. If you have another suitor, I'll challenge him to duel at 20 paces with copies of *The Sound and the Fury*."

"I miss you, too. No suitor but you, if that's what you are."

"I wake up every day wondering if I suit her," he said in his best Groucho impersonation.

"You suit her," I said, laughing. "Oh, Sean, it's horrible. You let a little chaos into your life, and it takes over. Like losing control of a car. You can't imagine what his house was like. Just a nightmare. Except the altar for his novel. It looks like it might be a finished manuscript. It's thick enough. I can't bear to read more than the title page. He called it *Right As Rain*."

"You say that a lot."

"I know. It's from my childhood. Another cliché to work around. I'm scared to look at it because I know it can't be good. Some days I think it killed him when I stopped believing in him."

"Didn't kill God when Nietzsche said He was dead, did it?"

"Very funny. I'm serious."

"Being serious doesn't suit her," he said. "I liked her better as my straight man."

"I'm not a man."

"Woo hoo did I ever notice that already. Now get home, or I'll have to send one of my associates to fetch you.

"Forget it, Jake," I said. "It's Chinatown."

His laughter was deep and unspooling, the most beautiful music I've heard since spring, and I wanted to be in his house, in his arms, and in his bed.

Back to work.

It's late. I'm in my apartment, in the familiar but slight clutter of my stuff, feeling odd and lost that school is starting, and I will not be there in the halls to stop spitball battles or see a love of literature in that one special student's eyes. Dinner tonight with Laurie Teagarten, and she was filled with lively school gossip, Oxford stories, of writers coming to Square Books this fall, prospects for the Ole Miss football team (bad), and sorrow at my decision.

"Will you ever come back?" she asked.

"The movers are coming in the morning," I said. "I'm not leaving anything, Laurie. James wasn't my husband anymore. I don't feel anything for that house. An apartment's an apartment. I'll miss the people there, Luna and Rico and Dwight."

"Dwight is a woman, right?"

"Right."

"But you *have* to come tend James's grave," she said, twirling her spaghetti. "The widow always tends her husband's grave."

"He wasn't my husband. I'm not a widow. Not technically."

"But it feels like it, doesn't it?"

"I don't know what I feel like. More like getting divorced again. I just feel sick with guilt about so many things."

"*He* abandoned *you*, hon, not the other way around."

"He abandoned himself. I wish we didn't have memory. I wish we could have it erased like they do in science fiction movies. I keep thinking of him in New York when he believed in himself and anything seemed possible. He was so close to succeeding, Laurie. If he had just published that one book I think he might have made it. But he spent years making that same manuscript worse and worse. It was the best it would ever get right when I met him, and neither of us knew it. Oddly enough, so were we. I thought we'd be this famous literary couple. But the best he could be was this faint echo of William Faulkner."

"Lots of people come here to be that," she said. "No shame in it."

"But I loved him, Laurie. And I abandoned him. I know I had to. He was impossible for the past two years, drinking and taking drugs like Pez. I was terrified he'd die in bed next to me. A lot of nights, he didn't even come home, and I didn't know where he was. I wasn't perfect, either, and that stuff started back in New York. But I changed when I became a teacher. I did. He never grew up."

"You needed someone to love you," she said. I nearly died. I thought of the baby in the hospital, her birth mother letting her go, my father's writhing grief. Yes, I needed someone to love me, and in the past year that need has grown, but I have not yet been able to include the man from whom I need it most. Nor have I managed to move closer to my mother the art historian. The hope of finding my birth mother is not hopeful at all. It's hopeless. I have no strength for detectives and obsessive Google searches. And yet I know I must know more of her as Sean must understand what led his father to theft and self-slaughter.

"Well, we all do," I said, conversational coward. I changed the mood and the words instantly, unable to bear them more.

Now, in the late summer ticking of my last Mississippi night, with my late beloved boy buried and insecure in his vault, I want to shatter all alarm. I want the dead to bury the dead. I want to know peace.

August 3

On the plane back to Asheville and home. On a flight this short, no peanuts, no coffee, not even any warm hand on my trembling arm. My white knuckles grip the pen as I write.

The movers came early this morning, and I gave them instructions, settled the bill, and mapped out their route. A fortune this is costing, but strange to me, I have a fortune, and it will swell when the house sells. I said my goodbyes to the ones who were there: Luna Marcovic, heading off to her shift at the beauty parlor. We shared cheek kisses and a singled pearled tear. Rico, just coming home from the poultry plant, stinking and clearly exhausted, kissed me on the lips and called me babycakes, which made me laugh and then tear-up. Dwight Peale was already gone on her rural mail route, but she left me a Post-It note on my storm door that said:

Careful in the mountains
girl come see us some
times. – Love, D.P.

The lack of punctuation touched my heart. I was just about to get in my rental car and drive to Memphis when a young man pulled up in the parking lot forty yards from me and got out, his hand up waving as if he were catching fire. I had to fight my emotions.

"I heard all that happened, that you were back, and that you were leaving," he said. "I just wanted to come say hail and farewell or something. I'm a senior at Ole Miss."

"Timothy Sain," I said. "You were always my favorite student."

"And you were my favorite teacher, Miss McKay."

"Lucy."

"Never mind. What are you majoring in?" I expected him to say English literature of course. I did not expect him to say physics, which he did. In truth, I didn't believe him and said so.

"I got interested in how things work listening to you talk about the plot in *Absalom! Absalom!*" he said. "From there it went from one thing to another and ended up with an obsession with string theory. And I found out I'm great at theoretical physics. I should have stayed in touch. I've never forgotten that class with you."

"I remembered you too, Timothy."

"It's Tim. I go by Tim now."

I hugged him, and it was awkward for both of us, two people who seemed familiar to each other, who each bear deep debts and who no longer bear familiar names.

❧

I'm in my cabin now, and already it feels more like home than anything in Oxford. It's fifteen degrees—or more—cooler here. Delicious. I'm leaving in a few minutes to go see Pratt and Mary Lou Wadely, and then it's over to Sean's for the night.

My late-blooming adolescence won't release me. I'm all hormones and slick need. I want to have a long talk with Pratt, but I want my body pressed against Sean's far worse. It's all I can think about. I'll look like a slut, but I can't help it. When I see him, I'll jump his bones.

Right as Rain sits on my kitchen table. I can't turn a page. I am frozen with fear. This journal is my story—is that book his?

August 4

First day of school back in Oxford, and I'm sitting here alone in my softie flannel PJs on Sean's sofa with coffee, without a thought of makeup or even doing my hair. I want to write in this confessional space that my homecoming to his arms was perfect and perfectly beautiful, and it almost was, but he still bears his grief like a visible scar, and it burns him. I'm afraid I attacked the man. I love the way his body smells, the texture of his hair, the taste of his kisses. I like to run my hands along his biceps, hard from landscape work, or to work my way up the territory of his back with my fingers. I tried not to moan and groan, but then I gave up—need trumps decorum every time. Right now I am a chasm, and the need feels eternal.

Pratt last night looked settled and well-tended, unwell but calmer in his eyes, as if a plan were unfolding. Nurse Wadely, happy, I suppose, for the relief, left us alone and went out for several hours, and she didn't say where.

"Is she taking care of you, Pratt?" I asked.

"She's good company and a good nurse," he said. "It hurts to be so helpless sometimes. She has to do…personal things for me. She snaps on rubber gloves like she's delivering a calf. Efficient." He cut his eyes as if avoiding something he wanted to say.

"Well."

"Cricket, I'm sorry you had to go back and close up the house. It must have been full of ghosts. I guess we all have our ghosts, but I couldn't stop thinking about how hard it was for you. Are you okay?" Then he did something he had never done in my life: He stroked my hair. He did it only twice, but I wanted to run away or fall into his arms, with the need of nations or the fear of a little girl. Of course, I did nothing.

"I'm okay, Pratt. I brought back James's manuscript, which I now own, and I suppose I have an obligation to do something with it. He didn't leave a suicide note or an instruction letter or anything. At least not one I found, and I went through every piece of paper in the house. But I can't bring myself to do more than read the title. I'm good at beginning things. Not so good at ending them. I guess James wasn't, either."

"You can get better at ending things right," he said softly. "It takes a long time to figure it out. And it's slow. But you can make it happen. Takes serendipity and planning and lot of humility, but you can make it happen." I had no idea what he was talking about and so changed the subject.

"I'm not going to just be sitting up here doing nothing. I want you to know that. I want to see if I can find where I went wrong and go back there in my mind and get started over. Maybe metaphorically or something."

"You do teach English."

"Did."

"It's a lifetime's work, becoming who we are."

"Right," I said, deeply moved and, of course, not showing it. "And there's my journal. I'm serious about it. I guess you're sort of doing the same thing with your audio journal, aren't you?"

"Mmmm." Non-committal, drowsy, nodding, the disease writhing him slightly.

"What's winter like up here?" I ask.

"I've never spent a whole winter here. Usually I'm in Chapel Hill or traveling. I've always traveled a lot. You know that. But the times I have been here, it's wonderful. When it's 40 in Chapel Hill, we have four inches of snow here. There's still enough child in me to love the snow. Lucy?"

"Mmmm?"

"Turn your journal into art. Be hard on yourself. Make each sentence hard and clean and beautiful. Be even harder on me. *Savage* me. And remember how much we love you."

I hugged him, but now, half a well-loved day later, I wish I had asked him to clarify that *we*. I haven't heard him speak of himself and my mother as *we* in years, and now I worry that he feels the cold hand of Death creeping up to him.

And *can* I make art of my journal? Can I give it my pure and true confession? I am webbed by this triangle of men, Sean, Pratt, and James—one dead, one dying, and one damaged by his own father. And I realize yet again what I need as I move here: a new girlfriend. But where do I find one. And how?

It comes to me just now as I write: Olaf Knussen's Dogear Bookstore. Now it's time to finish my coffee and go to my new house. That picture on his desk: his daughter? Here? But later. Now I must settle and shop, to await the coming of the moving van tomorrow, bringing belongings from the house I shared with James and from my apartment, everything from my floral sofa to my fourth-grade notebooks, each one with a flower for a new day of the week.

August 5

Working at my new home all day, no time to write. The world is still and warm, thick with possibilities. I dust and rearrange, shop and store. Late morning, I watched a ruby-throated anole doing mating-ritual pushups on the porch rail, not knowing someone new lived inside, not caring.

August 6

My possessions arrive in a groan of diesel smoke, the truck grumbling against angle and altitude, and the two men remarking on the beauty of my rental house. They're tired and parched, and when I offer them a beer before unloading they say they can't.

"Against company rules," says the smaller of the two men, though both are broad-backed bows of muscle and leverage.

"*I'm* the company in these parts," I say, imitating a Western heroine. They laugh, and I hand then each a dripping Sam Adams. After that, they glide through the afternoon, putting everything right where I want it, eager to please, stopping sometimes to remark on the low humidity or the sound of birdsong that seeps from the forest.

Late day, and Sean drives up in his big truck, and I show him around, take him through the pieces of my life, telling him stories. Halfway along, he puts his big hand on my shoulder as a buddy might in grade school, and I love it.

"I don't know what I'm doing here," I admit. "I should be teaching. I miss my students." When I say the last word I burst into tears, something so utterly unlike me I almost have an out-of-body experience. His touch is no longer like a buddy's, and I grab him to keep from sinking, but I miss even the worst of my students as if I'd lost a limb. Slowly, though, it fades. Fades and fades but doesn't dissolve. I look around, and it feels as if I've landed in someone else's home and am just pretending it is mine.

Worse, I find myself pretending Sean is mine. That I will blink, and he will be gone, that this house will be gone, and that I will be more alone in this world than a woman could bear.

August 7

Thought I'd go to Sean's house, or he'd spend the night with me, and neither happened, and I slept alone, and I felt the hurt viscerally. So I awoke this morning and called Pratt, but he was showering so I talked to Mary Lou.

"Does he ever mention me when I'm not there?" I asked. I couldn't believe I asked it, fishing, pathetic.

"He talks about you endlessly, Lucy," she said, her voice like a lovely lacquer on a teak box. "You know, when you first said you were going to stay, he wasn't sure what to do. He'd planned his life so that you'd have this kind of sweet, dramatic parting, and he'd tell you all his secrets, I think."

"He told me his big secret," I said. "About my birth mother. Has he told you any of this? You're there with him all day?"

"I know some of it. He talks in bits and pieces. It's the equivalent of a kaleidoscope. His words are like those little pieces of glass. They sparkle and make patterns, but sometimes they don't fit." That tone— not quite right. And why?

"Victor told me about that. I haven't really seen it yet."

"I don't mean he's not making sense. I just mean he trickles it out. But men are like that. The thing I do know is that he loves you more than anything. He just feels like he's ruined and wasted his life, and he's trying to make things right. It takes a while."

"I know how he feels. Maybe we could talk sometime. I'd like to know you better."

"I'd love that, Lucy." A pause moved between us. "I'll listen to your dad and see if he says anything you might want to know."

I drove to Dogear, dallying, enjoying the hot day, knowing from the Web that it's fourteen degrees cooler here than in Oxford. No doubt, the AC is broken in my former classroom as it is at the beginning of every school year. Dogear was empty, and, as before, Olaf Knussen didn't seem to notice, much less care. He sat smoking his pipe in his office and reading a huge thick dusty book. He raised an eyebrow and marked his place with his finger and wordless asked if he could help me when I stepped inside the office.

"I was wondering if there might be somebody else like me, a woman my age, who shops here? I've been in here several times. Maybe you remember me. I'm new to the area, and I'm looking for a friend, and I thought I'd start with book-lovers. Crazy question, I know."

"Jan Trask," he said, poking each syllable with the stem of his pipe. He went back to smoking and reading. I felt absolutely merry.

"Mr. Knussen, I need more than that. You're a scamp, you know that?"

"So I've been told. My daughter. Lives with me. That's her divorced name."

"Her *divorced* name? I've heard of married names." He showed absolutely no emotion and was clearly having a fine time. "That must be her in that picture. I've been looking at it all summer."

"She works part-time at the *Herald-Spyglass*. The *Herald* bought the *Spyglass*. Should of chosen one name or the other. That's the problem with the world. People won't make choices."

"I had no idea you were so chatty, Mr. Knussen."

"Only with people who really annoy me," he said, and I knew from his eyes that he remembered me, that he liked me, and that he wanted me to be his daughter's friend. I could have hugged the man. He is older than Pratt, gray and with the odd habit of pursing his lips every few seconds as if he's about to kiss something. "Here." He wrote a phone number on a small business card in elegant script, lines through two seven's in the European style. "She has the boy to take care of, Jared. He's eight and a coming polymath. Ask him to multiply or recite Emily Dickinson."

"*Jared*? That doesn't sound like a Scandinavian name," I teased.

"It's from the Norwegian Diaspora," he said gruffly. "Which, of course, you know nothing about." He didn't crack a smile, but I was shaking with laughter.

"I'll call her tonight."

"If you like."

"You shouldn't smoke. It causes cancer. You don't want Jan and Jared to suffer."

"Sunlight causes cancer. Where's your hat?" he cried, pointing at my head with the stem of his pipe. My laughter filled his office, and I had to admit—though only to myself—that the smell of his pipesmoke was lovely and calming.

"Touché."

"En garde." I thought he'd smile then, but he didn't. He went back to his book, and I looked at him with what I felt: warmth and gratitude.

So I did, I called her around eight, introduced myself, and said I'd been prowling her father's bookshop all summer, that I'd moved here, and that I had no girlfriends, and I was wondering if we might meet just for coffee or something? I felt stupid, thinking halfway through my nervous little speech that she'd bray some Religious Right passcode or burst into bad grammar. I loved the sound of her voice from the beginning.

"Oh, hi, Lucy. He said you'd call," she said, as familiarly as if we were cousins. "He said you liked him, though I can't imagine why. He loves to tease people."

"I *do* like him."

"Well, he didn't say you told him, but I could tell. The corner of his mouth twitched when he talked about you. He said you weren't entirely stupid, which I knew meant you were extremely intelligent. Jared, get away from that right now? That boy's like a ship's dynamo. He's on full blast all day, and then he goes off at bed time. You moved here from Oxford, right?"

"How'd you know that?"

"Oh, God, I work for the paper. I hear everything. Not a real reporter, just your usual English major without a job. I might as well go ahead and admit that what I know about Faulkner you could put in a corn cob pipe. I've been obsessed with Thomas Mann for the last five years, go figure."

"You'll *love* Faulkner," I said.

"Oh, I've read all the books, except for *Pylon*, I think," she said. "But I mean I just don't *know* him. You know? Jared!"

"In the Biblical sense?" Her laughter was suddenly fruity and slightly too loud.

"Something like that. How'd you find Dogear?"

"My Dad. He lives over in Cedar Acres—I don't know if you've heard of him, Pratt McKay, he's...."

"...I know who he is, and I know who you are. Small place. I've read his book, the one that won the Pulitzer. Masterful." That she flattered Pratt was far less important than that she used a word like *masterful*. The whole conversation was a revelation—almost literally, for I felt as if I'd met her before, as if we'd been cut from the same material and sewn into separate bodies.

We made plans to meet.

Have I become my journal? Am I turning from woman into words? There is a pattern here that I seem to feel and can't yet see or imagine. Yet I'm glimpsing it, understanding that I'm here for a reason. What is it? Tell me. Someone please tell me.

August 8

Worked in the yard. Hacked weeds, freed wildflowers from the shadows of debris, felt the rain promise to come and then break its promise. I picked up the phone three times to call Pratt and put it down three times, unwilling to face his suffering.

I'm hiding here from the world. James's miserable ghost lilted through the landscape today, telling me to read his manuscript, saying the Great Mystery was within it. No, James. You are a dead man, dissolute, gone to memory.

I have had enough of sorrow.

August 9

Finally had my long conversation with Mary Lou Wadely today, and I can't remember a kinder woman or one who seems more attuned to me. She listens like a tuning fork hums.

I'd gone over to see Pratt, but he was tired and wanted to take a nap. She and I talked for half an hour about his estate, about Victor, who will be coming for the weekend, and about my house, which he and Mary Lou will come visit this weekend if he's well enough. He freezes in poses, struggles for words, and looks at his hands as if they are just-uncovered fossils of rare provenance. And yet there is a slow kindness about his eyes that wasn't there before, an acceptance or a settling—a shaft of light bearing peace.

"You're doing this for him," I told Mary Lou when she'd settled him in bed and come back in the living room. She sat with her feet underneath her on the sofa, sipping sweet tea and looking years younger than I know she is.

"He's doing it for himself," she said. "Letting go of the body is harder for men, Lucy. Their brains keep telling them to reproduce. It's not entirely their fault." I started laughing, but she put her finger to her lips and shushed me. "I'm absolutely serious, dear. I've seen it before as a home health nurse. Old men who will reach out and hold my boob when I lean over. You're supposed to take their hand away and chastise them like a child and write it in your report."

"But you never did."

"It seems like a small enough gift for a dying old man. But the point I'm making is that your father is letting go of one thing on his way to becoming something else, and it's harder for him than you can imagine."

"I can't imagine it at all. Not yet."

"He's a good man, Lucy. He suffers for his mistakes. He suffers every day. Bad men don't do that. He wants so desperately to know you better, but he just doesn't know how. Give him time."

"What if he doesn't have time?" I said. "My ex-husband ran out of time, and I still can't believe it or deal with it, Mary Lou."

"The world shocks us," she said. "And we try to go on. We make terrible, terrible mistakes. We spend our lives trying to find ways to make them right. And maybe there's no chance. Or maybe one day there's a perfect solution, and things begin to fall in place like all the doors in a castle opening at once."

"Please tell me you're not planning to leave anytime soon," I said. I suddenly felt desperate, and she knew it.

"Now why would I do that?" she asked. "I have everything I've ever wanted right here."

I know so little about her I didn't ask more, but I'm sure she's gone from job to job for many years, giving the best of herself each time. Her presence comforts me.

August 10

Heavy, dark rain—mountain rain. The whole world seemed to be draining down the slopes, and I stayed inside drinking tea and thinking about Sean. He came over last night, and we talked for an hour—politics and environmentalism—and did not make love, which left me crabby and empty. Later, drowsy in bed, I thought of him and took care of myself, and it was a pleasant enough substitute for about three minutes.

Almost cool enough for a fire. I made a mug of Earl Grey and got James's *Right as Rain* and sat at the dining room table and looked at the bulk of its pages, and I flipped through them, feeling nauseous and bringing him back to me. I read a few detached sentences and then several paragraphs, and the more I read, the more despairing I felt. The writing was sub-first draft, the dialog filled with exclamation points and *ah-ha*, mustache-twisting epiphanies. In places, sense utterly evaporated, and I knew that was when he'd been too drunk to make sense—I'd seen it before in sequential drafts of his New York novel. This book, the one he'd left as his legacy on an altar before killing himself with booze and pills in the woods behind William Faulkner's house, was no masterpiece. It was what I feared: an inchoate mess, a rambling disaster resembling in many details the man who wrote it. It was James revealed, and perhaps that was his legacy to me—to show what my lack of love and support had turned him into.

And yet I felt there was some mystery at the heart of it all, some message to disentangle from the syntax. I knew I needed to read it from the start. Only then, perhaps, would it become clear. Perhaps that was how I'd missed the meaning of my own life so far—I'd misread its context, failed to follow clues in full view.

Went out shopping, to, my God, Kmart, and I slogged down the aisles with the damned, and I wound up buying cashew nuts, detergent, and tampons. A redneck next to me in line, bearing a huge ghastly belly as if it were a Nobel Prize, stared at the tampons and grinned. He was saying, *I know where those go and what you touch when you use them.* Sickening.

August 11

Dear diary—how strange to write that, just as I did when I was twelve! But dear diary, I have a new friend, and, I think, a good one: Jan Trask. She's lithe as a stick, somewhat plain like me, but with eyes that glisten as she speaks. She gestures, hands crafting rainbows. She is small and taut, a runner's build, dark blonde hair just touching her shoulders, as if it were toes testing the water. She has beautiful green eyes and jingles with a dozen bracelets on each thin arm. There is more than an ounce of like-me about her; still, she's as natural as sunrise, as unaffected as a child. She doesn't guard genuine laughter or shade a frown when it passes through her. Twice she upended her salad fork, waved it in tiny circles, shrugged her shoulders, and said *comme-çi, comme-ça.*

"Where'd you go to school?" I asked.

"Oh, my God," she said. "School. Well. *Well.* Yale, actually."

"What's so *actually* about that?" I asked, laughing.

"Well, you know, *went to Yale* and here I am a part-time reporter for the *Herald-Spyglass* and a single mother, living with my *father*, who's profession is reading and selling an occasional book. Good thing *his* father owned Scandinavia's largest shipping firm."

"So you're rich?"

"Jared asked me that very question a couple of weeks ago. I told him we were rich in a family's love. He said he'd rather be rich in money."

Which, I was left to gather from her laugh, they are. But if they are, she's utterly unaffected by it, and she told me charming stories of her late mother, of growing up in Connecticut, of Jared's funny ways, and of her father's iconoclastic and downright peculiar ideas of business. She tried to work with him when she and Jared moved here after her divorce a year back, but he drove her crazy, and she abandoned that ship.

"But he's the best father you can imagine," she said. "Always was, even though he never knows what to do or how to do it. He will be gruff to me before dinner, and when it's time to eat he'll be standing there with a bouquet of wildflowers he picked himself, and he will tell me why each petal is like my face. Once when he'd hurt my feelings, he closed the shop and drove over to the Cowee Valley ruby mines and stayed there a solid week until he found a gorgeous white topaz that had cut into a heart pendant for me. He brought it back and said, 'I'm as sorry as the Earth is old.' How could you not love a man who could do that?"

Tears filled my eyes. I noticed a middle-aged man watching me, and I liked it rather too much.

"Why do you love Mann?" I asked, desperately changing the subject.

"Mostly *The Magic Mountain*," she said. "I'm addicted to it. All those sick people at that sanitarium in the Alps doing absolutely nothing but talking and getting sicker and watching each other slowly die. Something about it comforts me, Lucy. Am I insane? They don't have any responsibilities. Every need is taken care of. It's hopeless, even desperate, and yet every day is just achingly alive. And there are bright people and dull ones, the manipulators and the downright malicious ones. The doctors don't want the sick to get well, and most of the sick don't want to go back to their old lives, either."

"Sounds like what my father's life has become. I only read it once years ago, and it didn't take. I'll have to try it again."

"You teach me why I don't get *The Sound and the Fury*, and I'll teach you the static beauties of *The Magic Mountain?*"

"Deal."

She is so *familiar* to me. Her love of literature is mine. She only spoke of her ex once—he is (I'm not making this up) a vascular surgeon in New York City. She said the only book he remembered reading that wasn't assigned was in the seventh grade and called *Touchdown for Tommy*.

I laughed brightly, and she waved her fork gaily, a small victory pirouette.

August 13

To Sean's for dinner last night and wound up spending the night with him, and from the moment we went to bed, our lovemaking was all wrong, leg bones and angles. Whenever he reached one way I did the same so that we seemed to be fighting rather than loving. At first, we laughed about it, with *sorries* and *oopses*, but after a while, we just did it, like an old married couple at their perfunctory time, and when we finished, he rolled away and I stared, dumfounded, at the ceiling fan.

I lay there thinking about Jan's father driving to the Cowee Valley to look for that white topaz so he could find forgiveness.

"What was that about?" I asked finally.

"What are you talking about?" he said. His tone. Unconvincing. I wanted to know if he loves me. I wanted to know if I loved him. If he doesn't love me, then what am I doing here? Then I thought: Fool, this is supposed to be about your father, not about Sean. I felt wretched, confused.

"Sean. It was like Kabuki Theater. Like we were miming sex. Like you weren't there. Like I wasn't there. I want us both to be there when we make love."

"Well, I've got work to worry about," he said. A knife in the heart, his rough sandpaper voice.

"And I don't." He sighed and rolled away from me.

"My business is in trouble. You don't want to know about it. I've spent eight thousand dollars dealing with Seattle. The competition for work is brutal. I'm great with plants and terrible with money. It's a family tradition."

"Sean, don't."

"*You* don't have to worry. There's nothing for me to embezzle from unless you're worried I'll rifle your purse."

"This isn't your father's fault. It's not yours, either. I can lend you some money." I rubbed his shoulders, half afraid he'd leap from the bed with testosterone rage over my offer of cash. Instead, he rolled back to me and sighed.

"I'm scared," he whispered. "I don't want to be a failure, Luce. I've never been so fucking scared in my life. I wish my father hadn't done what he did. I need to ask him what to do. I wish that baby hadn't died. I could have taken it in. I would have. I wish a lot of things."

I felt his sweet breath on my face. I stroked his cheek, and he let me. I could not imagine what his confession cost him.

"Could—could I help you, then? Setting up your schedule? Your appointments? I could keep books. I'm good with numbers, believe it or not. James never wrote a check in his life. I always handled the bills. I could make a budget."

At that moment, half of me warned me off of it, and half of me prayed he would let me. We began to move back together, and our choreographed arms moved, arc to arc. His gentleness was beyond

199

description. His rough fingertips on the side of my breast, slow as a season. The palm of his foot gliding with glacial slowness up my thigh. My hand growing down the fur of his chest and over his flat hard stomach. Each movement matched another and was right. We became ballet partners, ice dancers. The kiss was slower than geology.

Our partnership unfolded in my mind. What I had said was perfect. This was his long unfolding *yes*. James's fears were all theatrical and had to do with losing his "talent" before he was "discovered," tragic man, but Sean's sorrow was deep and genuine. He radiated love. It felt like his landscaping, created with a subtle eye, generated with slow fire.

Each *give* created a perfect *take*. I shifted under him, and he weighed nothing over me. The kisses were not hard but soft, not urgent but withheld. My body filled with blessings from him and for him. I came from every pore every second, but it was a *whispered* orgasm, an ancient story, the beginning of the Earth and its races.

This morning, after loving once again, he said, "I can do better than I've been doing. Let me see what I can do before I ask you to help, Lucy. I've been licking my wounds too long. I need to be a man. Advice I couldn't have gotten from my father."

"I'll be a man, too, then," I said, smiling.

"Like hell you will," he said, the kiss starting on *hell* and taking me completely on *will*.

August 14

Web research all day on the day I was born—date, place, hospitals, the name Rachel Motes, *Moates*, anything, anything. I did find Rachel Motes, and she was a woman who lived in nineteenth century San Francisco and was accused of kissing a "Chinaman" on the sidewalk. A jury found her guilty, and while awaiting sentencing, she was found dead in her room near the docks. She was in a blue silk kimono, sitting before an incense burner, a long dagger in her chest.

"The chief of police instantly ruled it a lover's suicide, but poor Mr. Wong, the man she kissed on the street, wailed that such suicide is Japanese and is not done with a knife in the heart. He was dismissed and led away. Large crowds of pigtailed Chinamen watched the confrontation, sad-faced men and women knowing that love's tragedy had once again played its final notes. Small Chinese children played on, unaware that anything was amiss."

I wanted to call James and tell him the story—he would have seen the possibilities for fiction immediately. He would have spent days drawing up character lists and reading vast numbers of period histories. He'd be telling me I could get a job teaching in San Francisco! He could do his research right there! Imagine!

Now, I sit and redraft the story for my own needs. It is the *girl* who was Chinese and the boy who was American.

The girl's name was Shun Wing, and next to the man, David Furness, she most loved her father, a quiet gentle man who worked on the railroads in the day and with his gnarled and broken hands painted calligraphic images of home by night. Always, on his rice paper, the geese were flying. She adored her father, and though she could not remember China, he would tell her stories of it—the mists in the river valleys, the vast rivers, the rich dark earth. He would withhold the starvation and the wars, the sorrow and the dank, slow-rocking boat ride to America. When she was a little girl, he would walk with her along the wharves and show her the incoming boats and tell her fantastic tales of the world beyond, of the great East and its fragrant incense and rich tea. He would, in great detail, explain how silk cloth is made. There would be stories of Genghis Khan and Marco Polo, of palaces higher than a bird could fly. And he would speak of an inner peace that one could summon even in savagery. If anyone could have saved the girl it would have been her father, but she loved David too much.

Madama Butterfly—the story has been told before or parts of it, but I want her to live and grow old with her father. I want them to return to China when she is sixty, and he is eighty. In my version they will walk that gorgeous countryside arm in arm, and she will ask him to reveal the secrets of great age, and he will. He will ask her to tell him what it feels like to be young and in love, and she will remind him of that.

And in each other's stories, they will be whole once again.

August 15

Worked in the yard all day. Exhausted.

August 16

Can't stop thinking of my China story. Dropped by to see Jan at the *Herald-Spyglass* and found her listening to a woman begging the paper to leave her husband's arrest on domestic abuse charges against her out of the paper.

"But he didn't mean it is what I'm saying!" the woman said frantically. "You can't put it in the paper if he didn't *mean* it!"

"Ma'am, it's a public record," soothed Jan. "We *have* to print it. We can't pick and choose. Are you in danger? Should you tell the sheriff or someone? Get a restraining order?"

"For what? What are you implying? I'm telling you he didn't mean it! It was my fault!"

Jan raised one eyebrow at me, and I walked into the lobby to wait. I heard them through the open door. The *Herald-Spyglass* is a strip-mall storefront, undistinguished, though a mildly good newspaper. After a time, the woman came out. Two or three other employees swept through, paying no attention at all to the contretemps.

"She always calls 9-1-1 and reports him whanging on her and then recants when push comes to shove," sighed Jan when the woman left. "This time, there were two witnesses at the house next door, and it's not domestic abuse. It's assault and battery. He's in the county jail. Spouse abuse is sickening. How's your day going?"

"Better, I see, than yours. I've been killing myself working in the yard and trying to find out anything about my birth mother, and I realized I needed to get out in the world."

"So you came to the *Herald-Spyglass*? This is your idea of the world?" The front door opened, and first I saw unsmiling Olaf Knussen, and below him, with enough energy to light a small neighborhood, was Jared, Jan's sweet-faced son.

"Papa's reading me a book about a gamekeeper!" Jared, eight, shouted, summer tanned, his sneakers half-laced and flapping. "Lady Chatterbox!"

"You're reading him *Lady Chatterley's Lover*?" cried Jan.

"Just the good parts," said her father, taking the unlit pipe from between his teeth. I was laughing so hard I couldn't catch my breath. Jared leaped, loving, in his mother's arms, and from two feet away, I smelled lovely little boy—peanut butter, dirt, perspiration, and the utter joy of a summer morning. "A mind is a terrible thing to waste."

"It's better than that *Magic Mountain*," Jared said, falling back and seeming to float in her lap. "Nobody's done a *bit* of magic yet."

"You're reading him Thomas *Mann*?" I said. She nuzzled him, kissing his neck and making secret smacking sounds, and I suddenly felt a plummeting sorrow, terrible self-pity. It couldn't stay.

"This is Lucy," said Jan. "I've told you all about her, Jared. She's my new friend." He sat up in her lap, far too big a boy for such play. He climbed off her and came to me and extended his hand formally.

"Hi, Lucy," he said. "Mama said you were smart and pretty. I don't know about the first one yet. She was right about the second one."

"Are you flirting with me, young man?" I asked, laughing and shaking his hand.

"I am," he said brazenly. "Is it working?"

"You're sweeping me off my feet,"

"Taught him everything he knows," said Olaf Knussen blandly.

Unexpectedly cool day, and Mary Lou Wadely set us up on the huge back deck of Pratt's house with its view of the falls across the valley. She brings us hot Oolong tea, and I sip it and remember James making us crockery mugs of Darjeeling during a New York blizzard. The small apartment we rented was so cold we stayed in bed all day reading, making love, and inventing futures that would never happen. He'd gotten a book called *An Anthology of New York Poets*, and he read me these gorgeous, casual, funny, warm poems, and I thought I had a future as a muse.

Pratt thrashes worse now, and sometimes he seems to have frozen—he turns into a statue, and his words sound like the Tin Woodman's before Dorothy finishes with the oilcan. There is something almost translucent about the skin on his face, as if a Death's Head were stretching to break through. He is also calm in a way that I have never seen before, as if he has finally accepted it all. I have read of men in combat with mortal wounds who fight against death for hours like wild tigers and finally give in to its inevitability, welcoming it, like Whitman, as a soothing friend. Pratt is now letting it whisper sweet nothings to him.

"I know now that I will never write anything else," he says. "I have come to terms with it. For a long time, that's all that kept me alive, Luce. I had this idea that if I were in the middle of a project I couldn't die."

"You could do something smaller," I say. "Write your memoirs. I could help you. We need a project together."

"I'm too sick now," he says in his raspy voice, now that of an old, old man. "But it's all right. Even ruining everything from the start, I'm managing to make something of it in the end. And another book isn't part of it."

"And what are you making of it, young man?" I tease.

"Forgiveness. Sanctity. Father Tanner was over here today, and I told him the whole story, and he agreed that it was my masterpiece."

"Huh?"

"I'm slow, Lucy. I've grown slow in my sick old age. Now that you live here I have time. I'm still dictating my life into the machine or trying to. Nurse Wadely is there to help me now if I need something. I thought getting a home health nurse would be the end of me. Like admitting defeat. It was admitting something, all right."

"What?"

"I can't tell you yet."

"I'm getting teased a lot these days. When are you going to come clean, Pratt?"

"When I can. When I see the story aright."

"You look different," I say. "You look as if you've solved some problem that's been occupying you for a very long time. Like Einstein did when he imagined himself riding on a beam of light and wondering what he could see as he passed by."

"I didn't solve it," he says softly. "It solved me."

So what can he mean, my sick, ailing father? Will he take me to the "Old Country" now and show me the gorgeous landscape of his youth and how it created both of us? What is his secret? What is our story and where does it end?

August 19

Two days without an urge to write in my journal. I am just living these slow long summer days. Estelle Faulkner once said to her husband as they sat outside their house in Oxford, "You know, Bill, there's something different about the light in August." He whispered, "That's it," and ran inside and wrote it down, the title of the novel on which he worked. The August mountain light is different from that in the Delta. It shimmers here and presages. It hints of unmasked chlorophyll and riot colors—the season of change.

I can't shake the biology of Sean. When I think of him, I want sex. When I see him, I want sex. When I hear the timbres of his voice, feel the touch of his hand, see the grace of his muscles stride, I want his sex. I find this shaming and human. I should want more—Great Ideas, long love, a framework for the slow burning affection of lifelong friendship.

How do those couples like Betty and Hunt Bearden do it? Those men and women who live their entire lives together, vaulting over nightmares like the loss of a child to stay aimed toward a single future? How do they stay side by side for forty, fifty, sixty years? My parents were never together from the beginning—they were there simply as a structure to protect the foundling in their care. My father early in his life fell in love twice, and it broke two women's lives and saved mine.

Is this, now, the price he has paid for that impulsive act of youth? This disease when he should be at the peak of his power? I don't believe it, of course, but a sick man well could. Did James die for the failure of his dream? Was his suicide an homage to Faulkner or a shriek against him?

Mary Lou called this morning and said, "Next time you come over, ask your father about Rachel Motes, honey. I think he may be thinking about telling you more. He's been hinting at some things with me lately. It may take a while. Just sweet talk him."

"That's the only way I'll find out anything, Mary Lou, because I've done web research almost every day and found nothing," I said. "I'll give it a try."

And so I sit here, supposedly thinking of my father and yet thinking of Sean, and, in thinking of Sean, thinking of his bed and my hormones, still boiling and wild to roam at this almost-late date.

August 21

Luna Marcovic, Eastern European hairdresser from my old apartment building in Oxford, called with the sad news that our female rural mail carrier friend Dwight Peale was killed yesterday in a wreck.

"It looks like she must have went to fiddle with the mail, looking down in her pouch or something, and just ran off the road and right into a culprit," she said, sniffing. I felt caught between deep sorrow and a fit of giggles and had no idea how to arrange my emotions. I began to say *culvert* and then stopped.

"Oh, Luna, that's terrible," I said finally, trying hard not to laugh or break into tears.

"She had no relatives at all, this sister in like Vermont or something, so I volunteer to be her next of kin," said Luna. "The steering wheel it hit her chest, and it broke her heart, Lucy."

After I hung up I laughed for a moment and then fell apart sobbing. I want to tell everyone I love: *Do not live alone so that you will not die alone.*

August 22

Sean over last night, and something is terribly wrong with him, an unspoken confession fighting like hell to erupt.

"Baby, what is happening?" I asked, sick that I'd spoken out loud an endearment that I didn't quite feel and that sounded phony from the moment I spoke it.

"I just—I don't know how long I can, I mean...." Then he shook his head and smiled and asked if I wanted to go waterfall watching, and I did, and we drove to Castle Creek Falls, a droughty-looking spit that drops three hundred feet into a room-sized puddle. He paced and gave me a natural history lecture filled with Linnaean nomenclature that bored me.

We got back to my house, and I thought that I should just let him go home, that a man with that much on his mind needed space. Instead, I all but clubbed and dragged him to the bed, and in return his lovemaking was within one hard nibble of assault. It shocked and excited me beyond anything I could imagine, and when he was gone, I felt so nauseous that I wanted to bolt the doors or move.

What is wrong with Sean? What is wrong with me?

August 25

Jan Trask and her flirty Jared over for dinner. I cooked tuna steaks on the grill and had made fresh green beans and a huge salad with balsam vinaigrette dressing lightly insinuated through it. My fresh yeast rolls with homemade butter.

"I'm going to marry her," said Jared after taking a bite of everything. He jutted his thumb at me. "She's a great little cook."

"Jared Trask! What kind of talk is that?" cried Jan, horrified. "You know better than that! And besides, you're only eight."

"I'm going to wait until I am *twelve*," he said, speaking to her patiently and slowly, as one does to a moron. "I plan to graduate from Harvard by the time I'm fifteen. Then it's on to grad school."

"Really," I said, laughing. "And what will you study, future husband of mine?"

"I want to be either a doctor or a mercenary," he said, waving his salad fork exactly like Jan does. He munched his lettuce. "Maybe both. If not one of those, then an astronaut. And, oh, I'll write my books, of course. The Hundred."

"Oh, God, not The Hundred," said his mother.

"I'll bite," I said.

"I'm going to write a hundred novels about one small town," he said. "Critics will call it The Hundred. I'll be famous."

"This is crazy," I said. "Are you really eight, Jared, or are you forty and a dwarf?"

"Technically, I'd be a midget," he said. "As my proportions are proper, etcetera." He ate a cherry tomato and smiled beautifully, marking a period to his sentence and the thought with the tines of his fork while his mother shook her head and shrugged at the same time.

"I do," I said. "I'll marry you."

"We have to get engaged first," he said. "I forgot to say explorer. I might want to be an explorer, too. I'll learn the languages to make it easier."

"Which languages?" I asked.

"All of them," he nodded.

"This is what I live with," said Jan, eyes open wide, as if to say: Now do you see what the price is for being different? Do you understand what Jared faces every day and what he will face as he gets older? And do you understand my part and my father's part in making him this way?

All that in a glance, but I read it, her Rosetta Stone, *her* confession.

August 26

I drove to Pratt's this morning, this hot, blank-slate morning, without announcement, without calling ahead, and he was propped in a recliner that Mary Lou had moved into the breakfast nook, replacing the table so that Pratt has a lovely view across the valley. He can't see the falls from here, but he can see the scope of this green world. The table is against the wall across the room and looks fine there. He was covered in a soft blanket and listening to Rachmaninoff. The banking fire in his eyes lit when he saw me. His hand crept from beneath the covers and beckoned for me, like something not attached to his body.

Mary Lou came soundlessly into the room wiping her hands.

"It was his idea, not mine," she said. "But I rather like it."

"From here, I can see a world without men," he said. "I want to imagine myself into that pre-human Earth, the one before we arrived to ruin things."

"We've done some good things. Emily Dickinson. Martin Luther King. Faulkner and Mother Teresa. We've done some good things, Pratt."

"I know, Cricket. I guess I lived with the evil side of human nature so long in writing about the women of the Civil Rights movement that I've become something of a rabid old crank. It's hard to look into the darkness that long and remember where the light is."

"Well put."

"Oh, hell, it's a chestnut, a cliché. Pull up a sofa."

"Would you like anything, Lucy?" asked Mary Lou. She stayed back—almost out of the room, and I knew she was leaving it to us, father and daughter. I told her no, and she nodded and was gone. I pulled up a chair from the table and sat next to my father, who looked strong and frail at the same time.

"She shaved me," he said, touching his face with an unsteady hand. "Shaved me. I can't imagine shaving someone's face without butchering it. Not a nick. She went at it like Michelangelo carving the *Pietà*, with a kind of timeless effort. I wish I could go back and slow down every minute of every day of my life. I want to start over and do things right. I don't get to do that, do I?"

"None of us does, Pratt. Sorry."

"Sorry. Well."

"I've been thinking about Rachel Motes," I said. "I know there's more to tell. More you can reveal to me. Is today the day?" He turned and looked out over the valley, over the green enduring world in which he cannot last for many more months. He opened his mouth and then closed it. He did it once again and then stopped. Finally, he said:

"When I was a boy, there was a black funeral home a couple of blocks from our house, run by a man named A.J. Copeland. Every time a white person saw him, they'd say the same thing to him: `How's business, A.J.?' And he'd make this look of delight and surprise and say, 'Oh, it's dead! It's *deeaad*!' I know he must have gotten tired of it—but he always did it. Then one day, *he* died. And his partner, who was a man named Johnson, was walking down the street, and I stupidly asked him how business was, and he looked at me and he said, `I can hardly forbear to speak of it.' I've never forgotten that.

He wasn't angry with me. He was just so broken and sad. I've been trying to tell you this story for my whole life, and it keeps trying to come out, and then I can hardly forbear to speak to it."

"It's all right," I said. "If somebody asked me to tell the story of my life with James, I'd hardly know where to start. I have this new friend, Jan Trask? Her father owns that bookstore, Dogear? And she has a story, too, and it's complicated, and I don't understand it. I want to know Mary Lou's story—I don't know much about her, either. I can't wait."

"Olaf's a good man," said Pratt.

"Did you say you knew him? I didn't remember that you knew him or had been to his shop. Wait—you're the one who told me about it, aren't you. I forgot."

"I know him very well. Luce, do you believe in symmetry?"

"Symmetry? I'm not sure what it is anymore. A pattern in which everything fits and makes sense? I want to, I guess. I've been trying to find one since I came here in June, but there's not one. We get sick, we get divorced, people live, people die. It's the world. We just have to live as we go along."

"No. It's more than that, Cricket. Maybe I'm going slowly because I'm afraid something will end if you know the whole story. I don't want it to end."

"Pratt, what are you talking about?"

"About us, Luce."

But what about us? I left feeling intrigued and exhausted and frustrated and sorry that Mary Lou was wrong—he wasn't any readier to talk about Rachel Motes than he's ever been. Perhaps there isn't more to tell.

Rachmaninoff in my head all afternoon.

August 27

Midmorning, and I was scrubbing mold off my back porch when my cell phone rang and a British voice greeted me. Leonora Shingler, Pratt's second wife, musicologist, and scourer of Bavarian castles for manuscripts.

"Lucy, darling, how is he?" she asked, each word wrapped in its own British bow and tied neatly, packaged with concern that might be true or false—I couldn't tell.

"He's not well, Leonora. The MS is progressing, and he's been in some kind of remission for a while, but they say it's the kind that gets steadily worse until, well."

"Oh, dear. Such a vital man. I can't imagine Pratt as an invalid, Lucy, just can't. He was always like a force of nature. I mean, all right, I was away too much. I know that. *You* know that."

"Actually, I was in college most of the time you were married to him. And if I remember, he was away from you as much as you were away from him."

"Professional obligations and all that, certainly. Darling, do you know what? I've discovered a set of dance suites that I am *certain* is by Wilhelm Friedeman Bach! A lesser son, to be sure, but a Bach! I was so excited I almost wet my pants! Can you imagine?"

I didn't know if she were asking me to imagine the dance suites or her wetting her pants, but one was boring and the other disgusting, so I got her off the phone as quickly as possible.

Ghosts. They won't leave us alone. They keep floating back and back, filling us with their irrelevant adventures, reminding us of lives we no longer lead.

August 28

Sean over. We watched my DVD of *Jean de Florette*, and he sat, bored and beery, eyes glazed with something too deep for tears.

August 29

This strange summer nearly at its finale, and I've never been so happy to see a season end. In June, I had a job, an apartment, a home town, and an ex-husband. Now I have none of the above.

I staked off a plot for a winter garden, for cabbages and lettuce, but it will be a long time before planting. Some mornings, there seems a wisp of autumn in the air, but I know I'm just dreaming that change.

I've spent dozens of hours looking and looking for Rachel Motes online, but so far I've found virtually nothing. Is the whole story fabricated? From where does the word *fabricated* come? As in to sew or create whole cloth? Who is Sean Crayton? Some nights he is funny and filled with endless passion and others he seems poised to plunge off the edge of the Earth, bearing with him the darkest secret known to Man.

I want the world to unburden itself to me. I want to know the Whole Truth and nothing but the Truth, so help me God.

August 30

Have I substituted a journal for religion? Is this my confessional? I hope not. Here, I speak only to myself. I need to speak outside myself. And yet I am certain I would have gone mad without it this summer, without the ability to speak out my pain and sorrow and anger.

And fear. I want to say that I can bear nature taking its course with Pratt, that I know he will settle down and die. But nothing about it salves me. Too many problems lie unresolved. Too many movements in a minor key.

And still I cannot read this manuscript left to me. It lies on the kitchen table in its well-thumbed mockery. (I realize that I haven't mentioned in here that I copied the entire chaotic contents of James's hard drive on one thin sliver of a CD and threw the computer away. Dozens and dozens of new novels—started and stopped after a chapter or two.)

I have this profound and overpowering sense that some kind of answer lies around me and that I can't see it. Will I? And can my father and I find our way through this thick forest of old fables to one loving day before he is gone?

August 31

Dropped by to see Pratt on my way to Sean's, and I talked to Mary Lou briefly in the kitchen, and for a moment—one bare moment—there was something odd and telling in her glance, as if Pratt had revealed all to her, and now she knew. If so, she wasn't telling. I like her more and more, and I can't quite believe that I found her out of all the people on Earth to take care of him. While I was there the phone rang, and it was Victor, calling from Chapel Hill.

"Hey, it's Lucy, how's it going? Just over visiting?"

"Wanted to see how he's doing. And he's hanging in there. How are you, Victor?"

"One of my students wrote on a test that the Whiskey Rebellion happened last year at Myrtle Beach. That's how I'm doing." I laughed in commiseration.

"Well, give him half credit for creativity."

"I gave him no credit because he's stupid. Sure wish I could see you all." The silence between us hummed with tension, because I knew he meant *me*, and the back of my neck felt itchy. Poor Victor. Poor everybody. Sean doesn't completely want me. I don't want Victor. And yet we go on and we go on, marrying our British musicologists and withering down to dust. None of us knows a thing, and we go on.

Will September change that? Can anything?

6. Pratt

August 1

You have gone to Oxford to close up or close down the house you once shared with James, now dead from his own hand. Oh, Lucy, what grief you must feel. The silence of the house is the silence of years, but not yet the silence of the grave.

She is here. I cannot quite believe that she has come to me, this Mary Lou Wadely. That she has come to save me now that I cannot save myself.

She stands there in the doorway now, watching me, arms folded over her chest, waiting for me to say I need her, that I need anything in the world.

You called me a little while ago, and she answered the phone and told you I was doing fine. I was asleep in my chair. She was right not to awaken me because I sleep badly, and when I do, dreams come in assault waves. She can tell when the sweet sleep comes, when I am in my untroubled world. Then, she leaves me alone, keeps the world far and farther away. But I was not asleep, and she knew it.

August 2

Harder and harder to read. So I sit and watch television. Hours go by. What have I seen? Movies pass by me. Our lives pass by us. I don't see one, we don't see the other.

August 3

You're back but you don't come by here—just call on your way to Sean's, needing what I cannot give you, the intimacy of a warm body, the reassurance of memory. Did you burn James out of your memory, Cricket? Did you go by the cemetery and sit in the August heat and listen to the sounds of summer by his grave?

We suffer even for those we no longer love. And I imagine you feel some anger, too, for I know you must suspect that James's death came coded with a message for you, one of abandonment and a lack of support, neither of which was true. If anything, you stayed too long, let him drain you to the marrow before you escaped just in time.

All along, he planned his own tragedy, but he was wrong. Not tragedy. Comedy, and a pathetic one at that. Not even enough weight for farce. Let him go, Lucy.

Breathe again.

I'm wrong. Just as I'm sitting here speaking into this machine, I hear you in the other room, talking to her, to Mary Lou.

August 4

You asked if Mary Lou was taking good care of me. How could you know? I said of course she is. I told you about the personal things she must do to help me. You looked ill and turned away.

"Houses like that are full of ghosts," I said. I asked if you are all right.

You said you are, that you brought back James's manuscript and that you felt obliged to do something with it, though I wonder why. You seemed worried that you didn't have a job now, and said that your journal was becoming a serious passion. I said you were a teacher—we're a breed, you know. I told you to turn your journal into art, but did I mean that? I guess I meant the art of true confession. I don't know what I meant. I've always lectured–meaning been full of hot air.

Today, I've thought of that conversation, and I dream of you as a little girl, how I used to sit at my desk and wonder who you would look like when you were grown. Now that I know, can't you see it? Can't you see it at all?

August 7

Haven't felt well enough to speak into this thing for a couple of days, but I have not let Mary Lou call you, and I won't. You must get on with your life, Cricket. She came to me and sat next to me on the bed and let me tell my long life's story and she held my hand and nodded. Is this the job of a nurse?

Father Tanner came by late this afternoon.

"Did you ever consider converting to Catholicism?" I asked him.

"Constantly," he said, looking like a boy caught with his hand in a cookie jar.

August 9

You came by today, and I pretended I was tired and that I wanted to take a nap, but it was a ruse, Lucy. I wasn't tired. In fact, I haven't felt better in some days, and so I retreated to my bedroom to continue reading my latest favorite book, *Masters of the Air*, a history of the Eighth Air Force.

Why the ruse? So you could talk to her in the quietness of this house, just a little. So you could see what she is doing, what she has done.

The weather is about to change—I can feel it. Remember that I always knew when it was about to rain? When you were a little girl and you had some kind event coming up, you'd come to me and ask if it was going to rain. You never believed the weatherman on TV—you wanted to know what *I* said. Only when I had spoken did you feel at ease. It wasn't really a father's fond ruse. I do have some kind of kinship with rain. It comes to me with intimations beforehand, like death does to men going into battle.

Tomorrow, rain. Today, you and Mary Lou, speaking quietly in the other room, each learning the sound of the other's voice.

August 10

Glorious heavy, enclosing rain. I come alive on a day like this. Mary Lou has gone shopping—I sent her out so I could be alone with my book and with Mahler. With my walker I made it to the bedroom and this tape recorder. Can you hear the downpour through the open window? Listen.

A cool strong northeast wind. And my first-rate sound system aching with Mahler through every room in the house. It's a writerly kind of day, and one that makes me want to keep on living.

But I am no longer a writer, Lucy, and I feel a kind of wild freedom from my life's obsession. If I were not speaking this story for you, I would have run out of narrative entirely. And it has not been what I planned—not my life's story or yours and not ours together. I have botched it with hints and hinterlands.

And yet some part of me remains in this world, something to summon that will bring grace to us, Cricket. It's an explanation that I'm working slowly toward but that I cannot yet quite make.

Hear the music behind me? That glorious extravagant suffering? Do you love Mahler? Have I ever asked you that in my life? I want to ask you a thousand things I've never asked you before. God grant me time. God grant me grace.

August 11

Steam and sorrow. Rain gone, steam out, and I feel the deep heaviness of regret today, Lucy.

How did I meet Rachel? It wasn't in the halls of Vanderbilt where we were in school, as you might guess, but in a Nashville Laundromat where your mother and I took our clothes. Our small apartment didn't have a washer or dryer, and I'd go there and study—I loved the white noise of washers and dryers, the combination of moist and dry heat at the same time, especially in winter, which was when I met Rachel.

We were the only ones in the place, and she was striking, quite beautiful, and I had not seen her before. But her beauty was unlike any I'd seen before. Her hair was off-red and her features pale, fraught with a galaxy of the finest freckles. She looked wild, as if she'd just stumbled from the bush—her eyes had a lack of guile you could almost call innocence.

"That's my life," she said, pointing at the dryer, through whose window we could see her clothes dancing. "Around in circles, trying to stay warm but going nowhere." Then she laughed, and, oh, my God, that sound—like music not meant for human ears—and I fell. I was *gone*. It was over just that fast. I introduced myself, and everything she said was slightly off-kilter.

"They say the snow's coming back Thursday," I said. "I'm a Ph.D. student and teach classes, and one wishes it would snow enough to cancel classes, but it takes a blizzard to do that."

"It takes a blizzard to trump a flurry," she said. "I mean, if they were hands in a game of cards kind of thing." I was entranced.

"Oh, like, don't count your money yet: You may have a flake but I have a whiteout?"

"A flake trumps a whiteout, you idiot," she said. "You'd better not get into a strip poker game knowing the rules so poorly, or you'll be wandering down Sutter Street in the altogether, and frozen things will start falling off."

She said it with odd stops and starts, near-cadences, with music. She was quixotic, alien, *exotic*, and I'd never seen another human like her. We swapped names, and I told her about your mother, and she nodded. Turns out she knew her slightly from school.

"I was engaged one time, but then he took my mother's silver and moved to a distant land," she said. I laughed, but her eyes said to stop, she wasn't kidding. "You're serious?"

"Well, it seemed like a distant land when I was eighteen. Nebraska." I tried not to laugh, and so she did. "It's one of the middle ones, Pratt. With cows and sheep and snow. I bought a bus ticket to Cheyenne and was almost on the bus before I found out it was in Wyoming."

No one else came in. We were alone in the Laundromat, and though she was strangely beautiful, I hardly knew what to make of her. The next thing she said flayed me, though, brought me down.

"People get lost all the time," I said. "It's nothing to be ashamed of."

"Being lost is the only way you ever really find anything," she said. "When I was a little girl and visiting my Grandma Mary in New Hampshire, I got lost in the woods behind her house, and I was afraid, and I came to clearing, and there were rocks, and the sun seemed to be preparing a place for me to rest, and so I did. It was like a throne. And I sat there, and hawks came, and they bowed down to me, and they spoke my name—it *sounded* like my name. And I felt as if my whole life had been planned for that moment, that everyone else on this Earth was lost but me. That I was the only one who knew where she was supposed to be. And I saw how everything worked, and I understood it, and a great secret was ready for me when I heard Grandpa Oliver call my name, and the spell was broken. He didn't mean to break the spell, but he did. So when I look into something like that dryer there, I always wonder if I'll see what I saw when I was lost and found at the same time and in so many ways."

Lucy, do you wonder that I can say that long speech after so many years? It's indelible—it's engraved like DNA in my marrow. If I had been attracted to her before that, I was wild after it—wild to know her more. So I began to ask about her and found that she worked in a boutique around the corner when she wasn't in class, that she lived alone, and that all who knew her felt the same strange wildness I did—that Rachel Motes was a spirit from a distant land herself.

That is how it began. She did not want to fall in love with me, and if I had not hunted her down, she would never have come into my arms. But I wanted to know her secret. And my *God* she was beautiful, Lucy, with a steady hand and a need to touch others that you cannot even imagine. She would stop to console beggars and without giving them a nickel (which she didn't have), they would *change*, visibly, before our eyes. She saved fallen birds and lost kittens. An old lady next door had cancer, and Rachel went over and read to her every night for the last four months of her life, read her *A Little Princess* as if she were a small child. She was reading it when the old lady, who had no family, fell asleep for the last time.

I was sick with guilt, but to call Rachel an addiction does not begin to describe her magic. She deserved more than me. I stole her future from her. I have suffered all my life from it.

I am exhausted, too tired to go on.

August 13

The news no longer interests me. I live in archives and memory. Mary Lou took me for a drive today, insisted on it, and I told her no, fought her, and she fought right back.

"You will just wither up and die in here, and you need to be out in the world," she said. "Lift up your legs."

So she dressed me like an invalid child. She handles my body as if she was moving delicate furniture around, does not distinguish private body parts from public ones. I cannot live unless I let her.

She wrestled my convulsive body into the Escalade and drove us slowly through the mountains, which are heavy and green, not considering a change of season. Does autumn come as a shock to deciduous trees or a delightful relief? She put on music from the Sixties and sang along in her pure, vibrato-less soprano, a gorgeous sound.

We dallied at an overlook, got ice cream at a touristy parlor, though the tourists are gone—school's back in session now. I felt green and glowing, alive and not transient. I did not feel lost.

August 15

Nothing gold can stay.

August 16

They say a cold front is coming through tomorrow, a "dry front," a change in temperature without a change in precipitation. Odd this time of year to have a front at all. Old men—is that what I am now?—become obsessed with the weather because they're like it— heading toward somewhere with no real destination.

What are you doing, beloved? Days go past when you do not call, not that you should. You should live your life as I am trying to live what is left of mine.

She makes me exercise. She tells me stories of her life away from mine. She never leaves me alone and listens for me in the night.

August 17

You came over today—did you intuit my grief from my "entry" yesterday in the oral journal? We talked. What did we say, beloved?

"I can't write again," I admitted. "I'm too old and sick now, and maybe I never really needed to write anyway."

"Write a *little* book," you said. "Do your memoirs, and I could help you. We need a project together."

"I can't—too sick. But I've learned it's not how you start things, it's how you end them that counts."

Did I really say that?!! You must think I'm as addled as a Hallmark card! I did talk about sanctity and forgiveness, I think, but you can't know all of it, not yet. I tried to give you hints, as autumn gives us bare hints of herself this long summer. I told you I'd come clean when I could see the story aright, but that's not really true, Lucy. I see it clear now; I just can't tell it that way. But I will, and in high fall. When the world is red and gold.

Only then will you see who you are and what this has been about.

August 20

Terribly sick for three days but not telling you. Nothing to do with the MS—flu. What godforsaken misery. I remember health like I remember the Eiffel Tower—an artifact of another age.

This morning, finally well enough to "take the air," I had Mary Lou roll me on to the deck in my wheelchair. She sat with me. Apparently last night, in my penultimate sick-bed ravings I told her to call you and say that I wanted to talk about Rachel Motes, but I can't—not quite. And yet almost.

August 21

A sick person learns to live inside his disease as if it were a tent in the Himalayas. You huddle up in here, wrapped in disbelief and weakness, remembering yourself striding through the world like a colossus, lecturing like God, accepting praise, waiting for the MacArthur or the Guggenheim. But now you are the eternal camper. You watch the new ones take your place, and yet you have not yet gone.

For the first months it was utter agony, Lucy. I planned suicide. You can know only because I was strong enough not to. After the diagnosis, I got a prescription for a powerful sleeping aid—it took nothing to get it—and I planned to take the whole bottle, lie down on my bed here in the mountain house, and simply go to sleep. I'd leave the most eloquent note in history. They'd print it in *The New York Times*. They'd *teach* it, for God's sake.

Then the phone rang. Deus ex machina—I know. You'd chastise me for faulty plotting, but it happened. God strike me dead, it happened. I knew the voice on the other end, and I was saved. I was not James.

Great beauty does live with us in this world. Sometimes we have to look hard to find it, but it's there, Lucy. It's there.

August 26

I was sitting in the recliner that Mary Lou moved into the breakfast nook when you came this morning, just showed up. Your face would heal me if anything could. It had occurred to me to put the chair here just yesterday, and though Nurse Wadely grumbled, she did it beautifully, and isn't it a fine view?

I told you that I now had a view without people in it, and of course, you, being still among the living, took up for your own kind. You talked of Emily Dickinson, Martin Luther King, Faulkner, I think. I lectured to you—thank you, darling, for giving me the opening to do it.

You asked me about Rachel, and for a moment—for a sharp second—I was going to tell you, and then I wandered away on that nutty story of the black funeral home director and his "dead" business. Then you told me about Jan Trask, and dear God. Dear God. Can't you see, Lucy? Can't you see what is right before your eyes? The amends I've tried to make?

I asked if you believed in symmetry, and you wondered if I'd lost my mind, I'm sure, but I haven't, not yet.

August 31

No longer every day. I mean, dear Lucy, that I no longer live every day. Some days the disease has me. We are dueling to the death, and on days I cannot speak into this machine, we are wrestling with each other, and it is mortal.

I loved that old locution—that a wound was *mortal*. Not *fatal* but *mortal*. There was something kinder about it, more personal. Most wounds are neither. Most wounds are hidden away for our lives, surfacing to torment us and others in equal measure.

Will it surprise you to know that right here, right now, I am happier than I have ever been in my life? That right now I am more content than I ever was in Chapel Hill, than I was on any gilded dais?

Love has found me. My heart is finally full.

7. Lucy

September 1

Took a deep breath and sat down again with *Right as Rain* and began to read more closely, trying to go as slowly and fairly as I did when I was the slush pile reader in New York. It's third person, set in Oxford, and the protagonist is a young man exactly like James—a failed novelist from the North who has moved to Mississippi to try and discover the secrets that "created" William Faulkner. His name is Harold Grenelle, and he's poor but proud, and his early work has shown much promise—James left out the beginnings of his collapse in New York. He left me out, too. Harold is single, and by page 10 he's met Lila Swift, a sensational southern belle who introduces him to meth and many pages of the worst sex scenes in the history of literature.

There is no evidence of any editing. The pages are filled with typos, dangling modifiers, and simple mistakes. On page seven he calls a nearby town Potterville, and two pages later, it's Pottersville. By page twelve it's Pittsfield. Worse, Harold is the most wretched image of James writ large—as if my ex took a hard look at himself, decided his vices were his virtues, and skimmed off all the scum to praise. I read with a knot of nausea. Lila is an undemanding sex machine. She reads James's pages and proclaims him the Southern Shakespeare. And the reader is given to believe it may be true. Harold broods by the Tallahatchie River and Acts Poetic on the town square, where people are in awe of him for reasons that remain obscure.

He makes friends instantly with Larry Green, another writer, embarrassingly based on Larry Brown. Green, a former policeman, reads one chapter of Harold's novel-in-progress and says, "I might as well damn quit if there's somebody like you in town." I'm not making this up.

I turned page nineteen over and found, to my surprise, a hand-written note instead of the next typed sheet. Here is what is said:

Lucy,

I knew before I started this. I think I knew by the time I finished the first manuscript when we still lived in New York. I knew all along that I just had one book, one story in me. That was it. I couldn't believe it, but it was true.

I'm drunk, forgive me. This place is a mess, I can't keep up with things since you have gone. Knowing what you are doesn't mean you can do anything about it. <u>Pretending</u> *to be a writer is better than* <u>really</u> *being a realtor.*

You are a teacher. You will always be teacher. If I had that, it would be no need to pretend that I am what I am not never have been.

Sorry a man drink's he tells the truth. So you see I didn't throw it all away I never had it to begin with there's a difference. There is.

Love,

James

I fell apart. I sobbed hysterically for half an hour and then just wept, praying the phone wouldn't ring and that no one would come to the door. That was James, typos and all, poor James, the man I once loved, whose bright weakness was his virtue, whose glowing hope was addictive.

I took a long walk and tried to call Sean on his cell phone, but he didn't answer, and I gave it up. James could never be what he dreamed, and it killed him. Pratt was all he hoped, and that almost killed *him*. And Sean? And me?

September 2

There is a full-length mirror in the bathroom, and I stood before it naked after my shower this morning trying to know her. For thirty-five, she is trim (and untrimmed—I can't wear a bikini) and has visible tan lines on her arms and legs; her muscle tone is adequate, no more; her boobs still point out but look like they're slightly *sighing*, releasing themselves for the Fall; her eyes give her age away. And twenty years from now? Will everything be headed for the basement? And will she still be alone?

And yet I think she looks rather nice, too. Her hips still have a nice curve, and her waist is narrow enough, though more womanly than girlish. I hate her toes—they have always been hideous, even in the mirror, like something from a witch, claws or warts. The mole under her left breast is still there where it has been as long as she can remember—the one that has always fascinated men the morning after. They touch it, name it, draw invisible line from pubis to mole and back.

"Do you look like your mother?" I asked her. There she stood, naked as the day she wrestled her way out of an unmarried womb. "Does she look like you? And what did she think when she handed you over?"

I tried to think of having a baby and giving it away, and I don't think I could. But we do anything, don't we? What would I do if I got pregnant with Sean's baby? The pill isn't one hundred percent—they always warn you. Would I have it, or would I rush to have those early cells scraped away?

I don't know. Something is wrong with him, and he won't tell me. Now I fear that woman in the mirror is making the same mistake all over again, falling in love with another James, a broken heart without the strength or tools to mend itself. Or *am* I falling in love?

I want autumn to come. I want this godforsaken summer to end, not with the calendar but with the heat and its colors. I want the high mountain light to shift and all the leaves to change into ravishing colors and fall down around me.

September 3

Labor Day, the supposed end of summer, and Sean takes me to a secret place on the Camhatchie River to fish for trout. He's back in
high good humor, bright as a new penny, and I step in the swift water
with sloshing ecstasy.

"Watch," he says, and he paints the air with his fly line, back and
forth, back and forth, back and forth. He is all muscle and grace, and
I think *oh my God* and just watch the absence of his sorrow and regret.
"It's got rainbows and brookies, hatchery bred and released, some two
pounds or better. On a day like this? Pretty close to heaven, Lucy."

"You said being in the sack with me was heaven," I mock-huff.
"You sure have a lot of heavens for a humble landscaper."

"Well, there *are* a lot of heavens if you know where to find them.
But that's the problem. Nobody gets too much heaven no more." He
sings the last sentence in a perfect Bee-Gee falsetto, and I laugh, surprised and thrilled to have back the man who so strongly attracted me
back in June. He casts and recasts, and his fly lands far away in the
water, and no trout comes up to it, and he does not mind.

He does not mind anything. He catches three and throws them
back. I catch a bush and spend twenty minutes untangling my fly.
After, we sit on the bank and have a picnic, and he looks out over the
water with flat-calm eyes.

"How on Earth did you find this place?" I ask. "Why aren't there
a million people here? It's gorgeous."

"It's the last piece of land from the fabled Crayton holdings," he
says. "Or was. It's getting sold to a conglomerate in Raleigh. They're
going to build condos here. Nobody knows it yet. They have plans to
fuck up this heaven as far as the eye can see. So take a long last look."

"Oh, shit."

"Aptly put. My dad used to bring me here when I was a boy.
We'd camp here and fish. Back when we owned the whole fucking
thing, a thousand acres. He always said someday this would be mine."

"Sean, I'm so sorry."

"It wasn't his fault."

"I'm sure."

"No," he says, turning to me and putting his suddenly heavy hand on my arm. "*It wasn't his fault.*" His face grows almost crimson, and I'm stunned, but he realizes what he's doing and he smiles through the emotion and tries to become a blithe spirit. "But enough of history. Want to *see* some history?"

"Uh—*huh?*"

He leads me, holding hands to a low and lost Indian mound on a slight rise above the river in the forest, and he gives me a learned lecture about Woodland culture, leans down to pluck a patterned potsherd from the ground, says its illegal, and then puts it back.

"You're lucky we live now instead of a thousand years ago, or I'd be doing nothing on the side of the river, and I'd have you making lunch for the both of us," he says.

"That about sums it up, cowboy," I say.

"Busted," he says, and then he sweeps me into his arms (and off my feet). Like either would have taken much or anything at all.

September 5

Jan called this morning, asking if I could get Jared after school because she had to take her father to the doctor in Asheville.

"Is it just a checkup?" I asked.

"I hope so," she said, edgy.

Jared's school is small and smug, a private academy with (from looking at it) a zillion-dollar endowment. I remember: shipping-money. He had a note from Jan, but the headmaster, a reed-thin man who looks, in the face, like the young Albert Finney, still wanted to query me, and when he found out I was THE Pratt McKay's daughter, he melted, seeing a potential speaker and donor.

"Do you know the word *unctuous*?" asked Jared when he got in my Honda and clicked his seatbelt. I told him I did. "Headmaster is unctuous. My friend Sanjay Khan and I made a Wikipedia entry saying his name was Humbert Unctuous, but it only stayed up for a couple of minutes. Tangelo?" He held up a small orange orb.

At my house, he dutifully did his homework (a ridiculous amount for third grade—since when does third grade even *give* homework?) and then played outside, being brilliant at amusing himself alone as all only-children can. After a time, I called him inside and we made brownies, and I played him some Robert Johnson, which he hadn't heard before and loved.

I told him the story of Johnson supposedly selling his soul to the devil, and he said it was a good story, like Jonah and the fish, and he gave me to understand that he didn't believe either.

It was almost six when Jan returned, and the love in the eyes of mother and son could create world peace if magnified a million times. She told him to go on out, that she'd be right there, and I knew immediately that the news was not good.

"He has a mass in his left lung, a large one," she said. "The doctor said we'd need an MRI to be sure but that we should hope for the best and expect the worst. Of course, that set my father off, laughing and slapping his knee. He asked the doctor for another cliché, and it so unnerved the poor man that he just left. The MRI is Saturday. It looks bad. He said he doesn't mind except that he hasn't read Proust yet."

She began to cry, and I hugged her to me, and she instantly threw the tears away—she didn't have time for them. She said she'd call me.

"I love you," I said. We haven't known each other that long, but she turned there amid the dark chocolate smell of brownies and reached back for me.

"I love you, too," she said.

"Any time you need me, just call."

We must share our sorrows—another cliché. Santayana had it wrong—we're condemned to repeat our consoling clichés, not history. Without them, we would dry up, and we would blow away.

September 6

I drive to Dogear, and there's Olaf Knussen, oblivious, still smoking his pipe, and I march into his books-high glass office.

"What in the hell are you doing?" I ask. "Jan told me. And here you are, back smoking again? Do you really want to die?" He puffs the pipe thoughtfully, as if considering the question.

"When I was eleven, my brother Michael drowned. I had been sent to watch him, and I didn't. Oh, I wasn't being bad, hadn't left him or anything. He was actually a year older than I was but had a withered leg. Polio. I was daydreaming, and he just went out too far and slipped under. He never once made a sound. Or if he did, the sound didn't reach shore. I looked up, and he was gone. I was blamed, of course. As I should have been. Michael Knussen, the boy with the withered leg, whose body was never found. He simply disappeared from our eyes one summer day and never came home. Since then, I've watched a dozen people I love die in utter agony. And I cannot decide, Ms. McKay, who had the better life or the better death. Would you like to tell me?"

I am lecture-ready but can't speak. My voice drowns. I think of Pratt's coming death struggle and my own death—how will I go when I go? What of sweet Jared? Will he be spared for ninety years or will some calamity claim him, some Dresden firebombing we can't now foresee?

"I don't want to die," he says hoarsely. "But I will. I knew there was a good chance it would recur. We don't live forever."

I don't realize until later in the day that he said *recur*, and I try to remember again who first suggested that I visit Dogear. I know somehow—know it like my own blood and sinew—that some force is

233

at work in my life, that facts are piling up on me that will soon make glorious sense.

September 8

Victor came over from Chapel Hill last night for a flying visit, and Mary Lou made a grand meal—shrimp casserole, a huge salad with basil vinaigrette, baked potatoes, fresh green beans.

"My third period's pretty good," he said. "There's one boy in there, Pomley, unusual name, who writes amazingly well, a sophomore English major. I'm trying to talk him into changing to history. He's mostly interested in Iceland of all things. Everybody in sixth period is an idiot, certifiable. One girl thought the Magna Carta was one of the three main documents in U.S. history, along with the Declaration of Independence and the Gettysburg Address. I'd despair if I cared."

"I'd always scream and wave my arms and then seduce them," said Pratt. "That was the part I loved, the seduction of pedagogy. Maybe I was a pedagogist."

"Sounds like something you could get arrested for," I said. Mary Lou tenderly wiped Pratt's chin. She ate with us.

"A serial pedagogist, too," said my father. We all laughed, but Victor wasn't through, and he launched himself on a fifteen-minute-long declamation about how even bright students—the kind who can get into Chapel Hill—can't find Bolivia on a map and don't know whose side Italy was on in World War II. He finally trailed away, realizing the rest of us had gone silent.

"I miss the idiots," said my father. "Like I'd miss air."

Victor immediately realized the depth and breadth of his gaffe and blushed, his agony spreading as the evening unfolded. A while later, as Mary Lou took Pratt to the bathroom, Victor and I went to the deck. Days are getting shorter, and the luminous waterfall shimmered like meaning across the valley.

"You should have just shot me in there," he said miserably. "I just wanted to see him, to be around him. And I've ruined it. I *know* he must miss teaching. It was his life." He paused a moment. "Jesus Christ. You must miss it, too. What in God's name was I doing in there? You should have thrown your wine in my face."

"It's all right. I enjoyed the stories, Victor. I did. I had a student once who thought whoever wrote the Bible got the story of Absalom from Faulkner. I'm not making that up. So."

"So." We looked at the waterfalls. "He looks frail, Lucy. But changed. Something's changed. Like he's getting calm deep down inside. Like he's come to terms. I hope that doesn't mean he's stopped fighting."

"It doesn't. In fact, he's happier now than I've ever seen him in my life, and I don't know why."

"I do. He has you close by. I'd be delirious." He drained his wine in a long gulp and raised one defeated eyebrow.

"Victor, don't."

"I think I just did."

"Okay, then, how do *I* look? Do I look calm deep down inside?" He waited too long, and I knew anyway, so when Mary Lou came rolling my father out in his wheelchair, I fled to them, leaving Victor's eyes on my back and—God help me—I hoped on my back*side*, too. I would not let the man touch me, but I wanted him to want me. Humans revolt me sometimes, especially the one in the mirror.

September 10

Jan and I go to lunch, and she gives me the preliminary verdict with resignation and what seems almost like relief.

"The biopsy was positive, and it's in his left kidney and his pancreas. The doctor kept asking if he wasn't in any pain. Like that: `And you aren't in any pain, Mr. Knussen? None *whatever*?' And my father just sat there and shrugged. He doesn't believe in pain. He told

235

me that over and over when I was growing up. If I had a headache, I had to count to a hundred and then push hard on my temples."

"Do you still do that?"

"Now I count to three and take a Percocet," she said. I laughed too loud and fell silent. "They want to remove the lung. It's the only thing they can do. He said he thought he'd keep it."

"Why?"

"A souvenir. He said he wanted it as a souvenir. You can't reason with a man who says something like that to an oncologist."

"Maybe he's happy the way things are. My father is sick, too, and he has this unearthly calm about him. I'm afraid it means he's about to die. But maybe it means he's about to live. I don't know. James always looked like he was about to die—he smoked and drank—but I never thought he actually would die. At least in the last few years he looked that way."

"Did you finish reading his manuscript?"

"Nothing past the letter. I just froze at that point. Oh, God, Jan, I just want something to happen. I just want fall to get here. I want my father to rise and walk again. I want whatever is bothering Sean to come out into the open. I want to know why I'm here."

"Those people in the sanitarium in *The Magic Mountain* thought they could understand things by talking about them. I guess I always believed that, too. But they found out it wasn't true, not in the end. They just died anyway, like all of Europe died in World War I. Nothing we do changes that."

"Does Jared know?"

"Of course. I don't hide things from him. He's mad at me."

"Why?"

"For not telling him that Dad had it before and that this is a recurrence. He said if he had known he could have done some web research before it got this far."

"It must be wonderful to have that much faith in yourself. I'm not sure I ever did. Or if I did, I lost it long ago. Maybe Jared can give it back to me."

236

"Well, I live with him, and I'm an English major who works for the *Herald-Spyglass*, so he's grown accustomed to failure."

The miracle of finding Jan—how has this happened? There is more here than a domestic drama but I simply can't unknot it.

September 12

A cold front swoops through these North Carolina mountains, and today is windy and cool though still green as summer, and I want to know autumn. This bedside-waiting is more than I can bear.

Sean dropped by after work last night and one thing, as they say, led to another. After, when the rain was still coming down, and he lay snoring quietly beside me, I felt more lost than I ever have in my life.

September 14

Today I finally read past James's letter, and for twenty pages, it was the same story, terribly cast, amateurishly written, but then it stopped in the middle of a sentence, and when I turned the page there was a blank and then another. Then this:

He never believed in himself as much as she did. That spring, the rain came too often and the Park was shaggy as the halo of an old man's hair. He'd go there as the days lengthened after work, cheap spiral notebook in his left hand and the scraps of a story in his right. As he walked, he gestured words and shaped syllables, but since it was New York in the spring, no one noticed, or if they did, they didn't care.

"What in the hell is *this*?" I said out loud. This wasn't anything I'd read before, and it sounded like nothing I'd read from James before. The writing was assured if not especially original, and I knew immediately who the characters would be, and my heart shifted rhythms inside me. Suddenly, I was pumping out trochees like an

Elizabethan poet, and my hand was damp before I could turn the page.

I knew what the story would be. Anyone reading that first sentence would: young love, before corruption sets in, before the world breaks us down into our sad parts. It was the narrative before sorrow, with Central Park as the Garden, James as Adam, and me as Eve. But the middle of the second page I was crying, and I had to make tea to settle myself to read more.

The boy's name was James and the girl was Lucy—he wasn't even going to bother with the polite pretenses of fiction. The writing got better from paragraph to paragraph, gorgeous prose, strong ideas, and silver days. He didn't send them straight to bed. They found each other off and on for several months before they had an actual date, and even then their innate awkwardness kept them wary but gentle. There were no *bon mots*, and the conversation was nothing like the Nick and Nora Charles banter he usually tried to write. They simply spoke. This was a manuscript without an eye out for an editor. It was utterly free, and it roamed and wandered.

"James" would go to the Met and walk slowly through the armor displays on a rainy Saturday and find himself thinking about "Lucy." He would draw elaborate analogies about his own armor, how he kept others away with silence or the shape of his eyebrows. He would think about how all his love affairs had ended badly and how he had wanted to be a writer since high school and yet had been too afraid to try. That fear was his paralysis, the trunk in which he had hidden himself. And here was "Lucy" with the key—the symbolism all wrong, he laughed, on the male-female front.

I read forty pages, and the more I read the slower I went. I went back and started over, feeling in my heart some kind of disbelief that he could have done it. But it was filled with my life—what no one else could have known.

So it is this: James *could* write, but in all the earlier pages he had simply been *telling the wrong story*. The idea staggered me. I felt as if an elevator shaft as deep as a galaxy had opened beneath me. Is that what dooms us? To tell the wrong story our whole lives, only to discover the correct one too late or never at all?

I put on an overshirt and walked in the woods, for miles it seemed. The country up here is still wild enough to get lost in, so I marked my way with visual delights—a cedar tree whose aroma vibrated in the clean air, a spring gurgling up out of the cooling Earth.

What is my story? I asked it aloud as I walked, mantra to mantises, words to worms. If each of us is given her own tale to speak, what is mine? I saw a thousand secret doors open before me, and behind each was a treasure, a trail, and a book. How could I have missed this?

I got lost coming home, and for a while I didn't care, and then fear lifted me out of the reverie just as I saw, downslope, my rented cabin's corner. Oh, James, I am sorry I didn't know then what I still don't completely understand now.

September 16

Drove to Sean's after work last night without calling to tell him about my discovery, and I found him in the blackest mood possible, pacing and literally wringing his hands. He had just shaved off his beard, and the change was so disorienting I wanted to run—a man I didn't know walked wildly in his den, a man with whom I had been making love for weeks.

"You shouldn't have come over, Lucy," he said. "Or you should call first."

"I'll leave. I'm sorry."

"Don't leave! Wait." He came and hugged me fiercely to him, and I stood there with my arms limply at my side, not knowing what to do. Every muscle in my body cringed.

"Sean, please just tell me what's wrong?" I backed away and literally fell into his red leather sofa. He put his face in his hands and sat at the other end of the couch and groaned like an Old Testament prophet. When he looked up, I no longer knew him. I would have left forever if he hadn't told me then what tore my heart apart.

"My father gave me everything," he said hoarsely. "He always said he worked to build for me what he never had as a young man. I was an only child. The thing is, he never stopped saying it. Maybe he was saying it to himself. When I was fifteen, I started drinking, and when I was sixteen I started taking drugs. When I was seventeen, I started gambling."

"I see." He stood up and paced, and he began to fall apart, every word a nightmare of self-recrimination and vast pain.

"Cards, then anything. Any fucking thing. Basketball games. Football games. The goddamn weather. I couldn't stop. I stopped taking drugs. I didn't need them anymore. Even my drinking was only to keep a slight buzz. I was never drunk. I *gambled*. It started in high school, and by the time I was in college, I was in the big leagues." He stopped and pressed his forehead to the mantle. "I lost ten thousand dollars in one night on a free throw in a Tar Heels game, God help me. I managed to get hold of my trust fund—my father didn't even know how I did it. I drained it. I started selling stuff from the house—expensive things from Europe.

"Finally, I owed more than three hundred thousand dollars to serious professional gamblers, and they were going to kill me. I don't mean that as a metaphor. I had a golden retriever, and they killed her and put her in the seat of my car to warn me. It was like the goddamn *Godfather*."

He gasped, and I would have risen to flee if I could, but I was frozen with the ghastly realization that once again I'd picked the wrong man. I felt myself falling down into the sofa.

"I told my father. He *cried*. It was the only time in my life I saw him cry."

"That's why he embezzled the money," I said, not really speaking to Sean but completing the tale.

"*Yes*," he almost shouted, falling back into the sofa and closing his eyes. "He was going to try and find a way to pay it back, but the bank examiners found out about it."

"He could have told them the truth," I said.

"What truth? He killed himself and took the blame to get me off the goddamn hook, Lucy. The gamblers got their money, and my father's son got his life back. But my father had to die and lose his reputation to save me. Since then, I haven't done one thing wrong, but I can't keep the business going. You said you'd help me, and we haven't gotten around to it yet because I knew that sooner or later you'd have to know the truth about me. Sooner or later you'd never want to see me again."

"My God."

"God gave up on me a long time ago. The only thing I've had is plants. It's where I started. Growing beans in a Dixie cup. I thought they could save me. I was wrong."

I tried to say something, anything, to offer him the consolation he seemed to be seeking, but I was too shocked to offer it. He was a stranger to me in too many ways. And yet I felt a sick certainty that if I walked away it would be like James all over again. Would Sean take his own miserable life, too? I felt sick rot to my core.

"What will you do?" I heard myself say.

"Now? I'll go on without you."

I was home before I knew I had even risen from his sofa. I went straight to the bathroom and threw up. There was no wind, and in the evening, the world seemed to pause, utterly still, as if waiting for a command.

September 19

Three days and I cannot call him. Three days, and no one has risen from the dead. Three days that I have not spoken to Pratt or tried to understand, like, James, where my own story went off the rails.

I imagine him dead over there, lying in a bathtub filled with horror-house blood, one arm draped out like Marat. If he does not leave a note, I alone will be left to tell thee. I have eaten almost nothing. Once I made a box of instant rice, and after four forkfuls I nearly got sick.

What am I doing here? What am I doing anywhere? I never should have left Oxford. Even if it was not home it was a familiar anchor—not familiar through my own life in the end but through literature, which for me is how life is most familiar. I realize that through this disaster there is one person I do want to see, one face that can calm me: Mary Lou Wadely.

But that is her profession. What is mine? Do I have one? Or have I come to the country of rhetorical questions? I can't even lift the phone to call Jan or ask how her father fares.

I begin to see how people become fatally stuck in their lives and never escape—loveless marriages, hated jobs, streets that go nowhere. They daydream affairs they will never have, watch "Globe Trekker" and see themselves in some obscure Nepalese camp, or write books in which they can slip on others' lives like an overcoat on a cold, damp day. They begin to make the best of what they have and one day they realize that's all they have ever done.

But if everyone is a Lost Soul, what then? Just stopping by woods on a snowy evening? Is this Jared's inheritance? Does he know? Should we tell him?

This cannot be all. There must be a way out, the thread of Theseus. I can't believe we're bits of kaleidoscope glass, shifting into new patterns at the world's whim. Or rather *we* can't believe it. So we craft religion, politics, family, books, universities, landscapes, bookstores, high school classrooms, and small-town newspapers. We work to stave off our inevitable spin toward Black Holes and nada.

I want that. I want joy, the clear knowledge of some possible pattern, some story that can save me. But who will come whisper it in my ear?

September 20

Mary Lou calls me early and says I should come over soon and see my father.

"What's up?" I ask, trying to sound chipper and sounding half-mad.

"He's beginning to lose some of his muscle tone, and we're going to have think of a better place for him some time in the next few months, Lucy," she says. Her voice is like aloe on a burn, like sun on a bud. "He's been trying to talk to you all summer, and I think he's getting closer, but you need to spend some time with him. Maybe just sit and hold his hand."

I feel sick and realize my hand is shaking on the phone, and I say nothing so she does.

"What are you thinking, sweetheart?" The way she says it makes me want to bawl.

"I'm just so scared," I manage. "I feel like I'm about to lose everything I have left. I'm so scared I don't know what to do."

"Don't be afraid, sweetie" she says. Her love fills me like a flood in a dry sponge. "It takes a long time to come home sometimes. Some people never make it."

"But I don't know if I know *how* to come home," I said, my tone small, almost the sound of anguished girl-talk.

"I wasn't talking about you," she said. "I was talking about your father."

The idea goes off like a small internal explosion. How can she be so intuitive? Clearly, he has been talking to her, confiding in a way he never has with me. I gather myself, remembering how I could manage the rowdiest classroom.

"I'll come over tomorrow. You're right. I'm taking too long between visits. I'll try not to be afraid, and we can talk about the alternatives. I know you know all about that, it being your job and all. I don't know what I'd do without you there."

"I don't know what *I'd* do without me here," she laughs.

Calmer, I call Jan, and she says her father will begin chemo in a week and that he's asking her to quit the newspaper and take over Dogear.

"It's what he's always wanted, which is why I never wanted to," she admits. "When I was a teenager, I listened to every word he said and did the exact opposite. I guess I'm still doing it. Why do we treat our fathers like this? Men seem to have an easier time of it with their fathers."

"They don't," I whisper. "It's hard to be tied to something and apart from it at the same time." I laughed.

"What?"

"I started to say I'd pray for you. I have no idea where that came from. I haven't been in a church since I was a teenager. I don't know that I believe in anything."

"Pray for me anyway," she says. "Jared, please don't. That's not a book for children." Faintly, in the background, a small voice says, "So who's a child?"

September 21

I was half asleep and in bed this morning when I realized someone was on the front porch. I don't own a gun, and for the first time in my life I wanted one. I couldn't even remember if the door was locked. I slipped into my jeans and crept into the kitchen and got my serrated cutting knife, the one with which I've shivved myself as much as I've sliced ham or turkey. I could not breathe. My hand trembled so badly that I doubt I could have stabbed a serial killer. Fortunately, I saw Sean's face looking through one of the porch windows into the den.

"Jesus Christ," I allowed, and I let him in. His beard had begun to grow back, and he has begun at least to *resemble* the man I met last summer.

"Sorry. Didn't mean to scare you. I just have two jobs going that will take me all day, and I had to see you." I wanted to scold him for frightening me, but instead I managed to offer him coffee, and we went into my cozy kitchen, and I put the kettle on.

"I need to get a shotgun," I said.

"I've got an extra one you can borrow," he said. "Do you know how to shoot one?"

"No."

"You don't need a shotgun then."

"No." I took a deep breath. "Are you all right? I've been so scared for you I haven't been able to sleep or eat." I realized he was looking me up and down, and I knew he saw how thin I am becoming.

"Oh, Lucy, I'm sorry. Jesus. I'm so sorry."

"I thought you might hurt yourself," I said, and I gasped once, and he came to me, folding me up against him, and I clung like a frightened child, face buried in the sweet space between his clavicle and chest.

"What I have to tell myself, what I have to believe, is that he didn't mind dying for me," he said. "Somehow, that was what his life was all about, even to the point of throwing away his reputation. In the end, he must have finally snapped, but he must have seen from the beginning that he could save himself, or he could save me. I have always thought I wasn't worth saving. But now I don't know. Maybe I am."

I had the word *love* on the tip of my tongue, but I did not speak it. Nor did we do what we would have done for most of the time we had known each other. We did not make love. It went deeper than that. Too deep for tears.

September 22

The first strong cold front of the fall came through in the night, and this morning, a sharp blue sky filled with lint clouds filled in the space left by storms. As I drove to Pratt's house, I could see what I had only imagined—the first hints of color in the hardwoods, lemon yellows, apple crimsons. I will need to get some firewood. I must get on with planting my winter garden.

He is changed. Sitting in his recliner in the breakfast nook, he is changed. And yet it is not the dark night of dissolution that awaits him. Though his body is failing him now, his mind is gloriously sharp, and his happiness is like burnished fruit. He speaks slowly but clearly.

"I never really stopped to think about why I wrote that book about the women of the Civil Rights movement," he said. Mary Lou left us alone and baked fragrant bread in the kitchen. "But maybe it was a longing to understand how they made a home under the worst of circumstances. I was a disaster at making a home, Lucy."

"Oh, come on, Pratt. It wasn't that bad. Everybody has her childhood disasters. You and Mom shouldn't have turned me into a dancing bear cub at grad parties, you know. That was pretty lame."

"I know, Cricket. The sick thing about people who make their children perform is that it's mean to make the *parents* look smart," he said, exuding apology with every syllable. "*Aren't we great parents? Haven't we taught our child a lot?* It was unforgivable."

"Oh, God, don't overrate your sins," I laughed. "No hair shirts and self-flagellations in this family, puh-lease. The truth is I loved the attention and the praise. Sometimes, I think that was when I was most on top of my game, as it were. I knew exactly what the game was, Pratt. I wasn't naïve, even then. I got passed around among them like a joint. Those students just adored me. At first I may have learned that stuff for you, but later it was for me. I remember memorizing 'Oh Captain, My Captain' in my room one winter when it was snowing outside. I was eight, I think, and I wanted to *become* Jo March. I thought the poem was about a shipwreck."

Pratt's eyes went merry, and he laughed soundlessly.

"The first Saturday in October," he whispered. "Then."

"Then what?"

"All, as they say, shall be revealed. Sorry to be so mysterious. I have been on a longer journey this summer and autumn than you can imagine. I've been trying to prove to myself that life moves in circles. It does, Cricket. Now, music for the season. Mary Lou?"

I didn't think she could hear us in the kitchen and was about to tell that to my father when she appeared at his side, hands sweetly white with flour from baking. She smiled at him beautifully to ask what he wanted.

"The Strauss. The jewel box is on top of the CD player."

"Oh, that Strauss," she said with wonder. I knew, had known it since girlhood, my father's totemic composition but one whose meaning had changed as he grew sick and old. Now it would be almost too exquisite to bear, and that made it lovelier than a meadow of roses.

He always made me say the title in German, *Vier letzte Lieder,* but in my head they are always *Four Last Songs.* Strauss composed them at age 84, four incandescent, transcendent songs for solo soprano and orchestra. Each one is emotionally shattering, but the third, "Beim Schlafengehen," is unearthly, almost unbearable in its slow majesty.

> *Now I am wearied of the day;*
> *all my ardent desires shall*
> *gladly succumb to the starry night*
> *like a sleepy child.*

I sat beside him on the arm of his chair and watched his face, and he entered a sick man's trance of ecstasy, into a deep glade of grace, into the place where joy lives and shines alone. Our hands found each other. His face did not betray regret or sorrow. His lips parted slighted. A perfect tear escaped each eye like a fugitive opal.

I memorized him for the days when he is memory alone.

September 23

I called Jan at the *Herald-Spyglass* this morning just to hear her voice, and a woman with a smoker's basso said she no longer worked there.

"Excuse me? Since when?" The woman turned her head slightly aside and hacked horribly.

"Her father passed away late yesterday afternoon. She called and said she wouldn't be coming back. She was only part time. Good writer. We will miss having her. She knew a verb and a noun."

I managed to hang up and staggered to the bathroom and sat on the closed toilet and wept. I did not know my period was about to start until I felt the weeping between my legs, and I managed to get the lid open and my pants down, and I sat there and leaked tears and blood. Then an odd, settling peace came over me. I was alive, still a fertile woman, here in a lovely house in the mountains with fall coming on quickly. I could be strong. I could be stronger.

I cleaned myself and dressed and drove to the small house where Jan lived with Jared and her father, and through the window I could see her, handing something to Jared and nodding. For a moment, I wondered if the woman at the newspaper had it all wrong. No, I knew. That's the one place they know what is happening. She saw me through the window and came on to the sunny porch.

"Jan…?"

She nodded, and we came together, hugging tightly, and I shocked myself by kissing her on the cheek and smoothing her hair. She led me inside.

"What happened?" I managed.

"He didn't go to the bookshop yesterday morning," she said. "He was tired. He lay down for a nap on the bed and never woke up. You know how they say someone slipped away? That's what he did. He slipped away." She fought against tears and won. Jared, ashen and holding a sheet of paper in one hand and a pen in the other came into the room.

"Hey, Lucy," he said. "I guess you heard. It makes my heart hurt."

"Oh, dear Jared." I hugged him, and he stepped back to clarify things.

"I don't mean my literal heart, if you were thinking that. I was meaning the heart as in poetry and the seat of grief. As in 'my heart leaps up when I behold a rainbow in the sky.'" I laughed—too familiar, all of this. He patted my hand as if I were a crazy aunt then left the room, still pale and moving like a small ghost.

"He didn't want a service of any kind. He was an atheist. I'm having him cremated."

"What are you?" She looked puzzled. "I mean religion-wise."

"I don't know what I am. What are you?"

"I don't know what I am, either."

"Well, we don't have to know, one way or the other. Do we?"

"I don't know, Jan. I'm thinking I ought to try and find out. At least try. They said you quit at the paper."

"Someone has to run Dogear," she said. She tried to smile, but it could not stay. "He was a good man, Lucy. Such a good man. I've only recently found out...."

"What?" Just then, to my shock, Mary Lou Wadely pulled up out front and got out with a large Tupperware container and came to the door. Jan let her in.

"Do you two *know* each other?" I asked.

"I've brought you bread, dear," Mary Lou said to Jan. "It's fresh, made it myself." They spoke for a moment, and Mary Lou hugged me. I felt completely confused.

"She helped Dad the first time he had cancer," said Jan after she left. "This was almost two years ago. She'd just gotten here. I...." I knew I had to leave, and so I did, but the world swirled around me with infinite possibilities as I drove home—narratives that not even James could create in his deepest plunge into a bourbon bottle.

Leaves are changing. Now, I am sure of it.

September 24

Sean comes over after work, and he wonders how he will get through the winter, with jobs falling away as cold comes in.

"We will figure something out," I say. "Now build us a fire. It's cold in here."

He does, and I watch him as I sip my wine. He is tall and strong and unsure and nearly ruined with guilt and shame. And yet he has broken through the wall of his nightmare and can at least see beyond it. We sit on the couch and hold hands, and he speaks of it as naturally as a confidant-cousin would.

"I've been thinking that maybe I could find a way to rebuild his reputation that doesn't involve me destroying mine," he says. "I can't say out loud what happened. The people I was messed up with, the gamblers, they're not just small-town crooks. The only way I survived was to keep my mouth closed. But maybe my father saved me for a reason. Maybe he died so that I could do this thing. Will you help me find out what it is?"

"That takes some people their whole lives," I say.

"I don't have any immediate plans," he says.

This time we do kiss, and soon enough, but not too soon, we blanket my sofa, build up the fire, and turn Adam and Eve, without expectations or fear. To love so slowly is a gift, and each of us gives it, with hope, to the other.

Now, he sleeps, and I have covered him, and I, still naked in the very warm room, sit before the fire and write my life out. I have this deep feeling that I am meant to be here. I sense that all is planned, but I do not see how I could have planned this. If didn't, who did?

Pratt? Sean? God?

September 26

I live in the Garden of Eden. Each step I take is deep in the mysteries of faith and narrative. I walk in the woods and keep finding incandescent glens, sylvan seats filled with the gold shafts of coming autumn.

This morning I took a long hike and found myself in a cove where a sparkling spring bubbled happily (or so I can pretend) from the rich Earth. I sat by it and saw, to my amazement, a large potsherd, with the familiar check-stamp that Sean had shown me on our Labor Day picnic. I did not pick it up. Instead, I dreamed of the woman who built that vessel, and I knew that I had a vocation, one that James and my journal, that this summer and my father's illness, have been leading me toward.

I looked up, and the green world seemed mine to command.

"I am a writer," I said out loud. All my life has been aimed, without my knowing it, toward this revelation and moment. My young years as an assistant editor in New York City. My life as proto-Muse to poor James. The knowledge of life and suffering that I kept traveling to avoid but that finally drew me in. There is an arc in this life, a psalm, a deeper breath, and a candle. Dogear is part of it, and so is Jan. I am so sure of it that without them the mystery is incomplete.

And yet there is one great shower of understanding that I have missed. It is what my father will tell me on October 1. I have been afraid to think of what it might be. And yet somehow I know. If you live long enough, all stories come true in your own life. The terrible ones rub us raw, but if we do not stop, we can move, like Goethe, toward more light.

September 28

I drop by Dogear, and Jan is there, with the burnished urn bearing her father's ashes on the newly cleaned desk. She does not have to tell me that she is still in mourning. The entire office looks more businesslike, and the female touch already commands the dusted shelves and the new order she is bringing to the old man's comfortable world. There are two windows in the office, and both are open to let in the gorgeous cool mountain day and its lovely light.

"It'll take six months just to get the smell of pipesmoke out of here," she said. A few customers browsed idly, sliding books from the stacks and peering at them with deep delight. "One minute the idea makes perfect sense, and the next I feel like I'm abandoning him."

"Jan, let me ask you something," I said. "Did you talk to him? Did you tell him you loved him?"

"Oh, Lucy. I've told him I loved him almost every day of my life. I never stopped telling him I loved him. When I was far away and married, I'd call him a couple of times a week just to tell him that and hear his voice. After Mother died, I called him more. And yet it only seemed real in the past few weeks. Before, it was like saying the Mass. You get used to the words, and they give you comfort, but you can stop listening. You can lose the meaning. Saying it every day doesn't mean more than showing it every day and never saying it. I'm not making sense."

"You're making more sense than anyone I've ever known," I said, and I was coming to her, and she stood, and our eyes were damp, and we held each other past knowing, somewhere deep in the sisterhood of daughters.

September 29

I have not done what I planned. I have not become the detective of my own life. Let it go. We have lives to live, and the past is sometimes beyond retrieving.

Another cold front last night with a brief gust of rain. Today, it is autumn in these glorious mountains, and a sharp cerulean sky arches over me, and the leaves are in riotous flame. Sean came by after work, covered with dust from head to toe and smiling, his beard now growing strongly back in. He begins to look like himself. He's gotten a huge job, a landscaper's delight.

"It's a hideous new subdivision called Oak Amble," he laughed. He shook his head.

"What?"

"Say it out loud." I did, and it came out *O, gamble.* I put my hand over my mouth, and he rubbed my arm as if to say: *This world is filled with such dark jokes, and we might as well laugh. We might as well just go on singing.* "I've got the job to plant all the trees in this place, and it's huge."

"How in God's name did you get it? There must have been a dozen companies who bid on it. And how can you handle it?"

"I'm hiring, starting tomorrow. Which means I need a bookkeeper, one I can pay. Part time. Maybe fifteen hours a week. I've rented a space for an office. It's a run-down little cabin of a house off the road not far from here. It needs some loving. It's a huge contract. A secretary."

"You still haven't told me how you got it."

"My presentation was from the point of view of a grandson of one of the new owners, coming back after forty years and sitting beneath one of the red maples I planted in the back yard. This grandson has been out in the world, has been to Paris, done things. But it's this tree that says *home.* He says it must have been planted by someone who loved it and cared for by someone who loved it more. And the grandfather says the man who planted all these trees is gone now, but *this* was his crowning glory. This is what goes on from family to family. And the young man and his grandfather sit in the shade and realize that if you look around, you would never know that this wasn't a true forest, one planted by nature instead of man."

"So you made them feel these trees would be your legacy."

"I wasn't kidding, Lucy. Or being sentimental. I meant it. It's the green world I can give to rest my father's soul."

And before me, he changed in the way my father has changed. Out of that deep grief has come a new whisper of hope, just as it has for me with writing. I was going to say it all aloud, to make it make sense, but the best I could do was kiss him and imagine seedlings as they grow, inch by inch, through the new narratives of our lives.

September 30

So it is tomorrow that Pratt will give me his last confession. The weather has joined in his lovely conspiracy—a high of seventy-four. I fear that I am making too much of this. Maybe it's some family souvenir or story. I pray God it is not about his estate. Pray *God?*

I called my teacher friend Lona Belle in Oxford last night, and she was delighted to hear my voice. She told me this year's class is the worst yet, that they are unruly to the point of utter wildness.

"This boy Randy Wilkins rode a mule down the hall Tuesday, the whole time yelling out the call from the last Kentucky Derby, which he had memorized. It was amazing. He's been suspended for ten days. I wish we had more like him."

"Faulkner could have made a great story with that."

"He's dead, honey. *You* use it."

"I might."

Mary Lou called to tell me she had taken Pratt to see Dr. Retherston in Asheville and that Pratt was no worse. Not quite remission and not quite relentlessly progressive. A new path, it seems, one science doesn't quite recognize.

I parked on a side street in Cedar Acres at some distance from Pratt's house, and I took a slow walk through the lovely day. Betty and Hunt Bearden were out and gloved, raking up the thirty or forty leaves that have fallen so far.

"You should see Gettysburg in the fall," he said, waving me over. "Lincoln didn't give his address until November, and it's cold by then. But this time of year, the first of October? Gorgeous."

"Jimmy loved the fall," said Betty, remembering their long-dead son. "How that child loved football."

"He did," nodded Hunt with a smile that showed no grief or anger. "He was a boy in love with fall."

Ella Seitz stood in her front yard looking half lost.

"Ella, I'm sorry I haven't been around the neighborhood much since I moved. How are you doing?"

"...are you doing? Watching the light leave. I was thinking of getting a tanning bed. What do you think of those?" She's like old cowhide, leathery and sun-ruined.

"They're bad for you, and I don't want you to get one."

"...want you to get one," she nodded.

Earlier this evening, in a mood to reminisce, I called Victor in Chapel Hill, and he was startled to hear from me but clearly glad. And yet he seemed to be guarding every word.

"Victor, I'm interrupting. Is someone there?"

"Virginia Whelton, an assistant professor of geology. She's a little older than I am. Divorced." He was whispering. "We've been seeing each other for a while. She works with fumaroles and hot springs. Bacterial mats and the like. Ginny. She's called, or rather I call her, Ginny."

"Victor, you sound like a schoolboy," I said.

"God, I know it!" he said, and then he giggled.

I built my own fire tonight, and I'm sitting here, journal on my lap, cup of tea at my right hand, and I do not know if I can breathe, much less sleep. My Father, into your hands I commit my spirit.

8. Pratt

September 1

Memory, that lovely and treacherous battlefield, is the canvas of my life now. Mostly, I try to remember health. Eighteen months ago, I was still striding the world, flying to conferences in Europe, declining invitations to Berkeley, talking with "my" publishers, sitting dully but dutifully on university committees. Suddenly now I am an old man whose body is wrecked by disease, whose days are, at best, uncomfortable.

But Lucy, I feel as if I have come out of a long, deep tunnel into the sunlight of some English pastoral scene. I am Dante just up from Hell in time to see the stars. I cannot quite believe that I shall be allowed to die in such peace. Shall I?

Every missed chance in my life was my own fault. Each time I was crowned, I howled inside for more. All the time, I was lost and mapless, fleeing what I had to set right. Now, I believe I am doing that, and the lift and shine of it dazzles me.

I did not think I could do this. All summer, I planned for you to leave untold. I would give you this long audio confession, and on the drive home you would or would not listen. Only when your once-dear James died did I see it clear.

I wish you could be here right now to smell the chicken that Mary Lou is cooking for our lunch. This is what a home smells like.

September 3

When I was a boy, I got lost once in a small wood near our house. No matter how many times I tried to walk out, I kept coming back to the same cluster of stones. Finally, I realized that my footsteps had slowed and that I was not afraid. It was summer and warm, with that long slow light, and so I sat on the rocks to think.

Birds came to me as they supposedly did to St. Francis. I had two cookies in my shirt pocket, and I crumbled them and threw the rubble into the sand, and the birds came unto me. Blue, red, black, white, and pale brown. I was a churchgoer then, and I stood on the stones with my arms out to my side as I'd seen Charlton Heston do when parting the Red Sea in *The Ten Commandments*. The forest swelled with the songs of all the nations of winged creatures, Lucy.

I felt an ecstasy I'd never known before. I sat down on the sun-warmed rocks and was still sitting there near dusk when my father found me, desperate and miserable, thinking surely I had been kidnapped and killed. I tried to tell him about the birds and that I was meant to become lost, and he exploded, his own fear for me becoming fraught with all his own fears. He made me cry. Then he apologized and kissed my face—something he had never done before in my memory.

It is no sin to be lost, daughter. There is no crime in taking the wrong road home. I have been given this suffering as a great gift. It tells me that my worldly life, now fading like that sun, is gone and is nothing to cry for. All I must do now is to tell you the final truth of things. And at that I am slow because it is so hard.

Do not try to become unlost too quickly, my darling girl.

September 4

I was going

Ah, Lucy. Trying to talk into this goddamn thing but today I feel

My medicines fog me. I'm a boat that can't find its harbor.

September 6

Mary Lou just played me back the entry from two days ago so I could see where I was, and we both laughed. There is nothing comic about pain, but I sounded like a running-down wind-up toy. Now she has found a way to balance my medicines better, and I sound more human.

Dearest, we heard about Olaf Knussen's tests yesterday. Things like that travel fast in the mountains, believe it or not, in these several small towns crowded together here, now nearly ruined by the wealthy and yet, in some unjust way, saved, too. When the scars heal, life will reclaim its niche.

Mary Lou knows him, of course, and she knows of your friendship with his daughter. I know much more than that and will tell you in time. Did you know Olaf was one of the major contributors to the chair I hold at Chapel Hill? He did it anonymously, and by even speaking these words, I am breaking some kind of legal covenant. But since he now knows you, he would not mind.

He knows more than any other man I've ever met. The world is in his head. If he does not live to pass it directly to Jared, at least he has given it to Jan. That is our mission—to pass on the stories of the world and the stories of our lives. I always hoped you would have a child, but even if you do not, there are thousands of children that you taught who already know many of the facts and the sweet secrets embedded in them.

Always be blessed, Cricket, and bless others. The great lesson at which I failed. You can be a virtuoso.

September 7

Ginger Dumont came by today, my perky freckled physical therapist, and she is ripe with all life, and I envy her, so I told her that.

"Oh, my God, don't do that," she said, laughing. "My boyfriend won't ask me to marry him, my car sounds like it has asthma, and something large and slow is creeping around in my attic. It has scratchy feet." She made monster claws and then dug them into my back.

"You forget what being well is like once you get sick for good," I said. "I'm close enough to the beginning of my illness to remember. And you make me remember. Don't take that the wrong way. It's just that I thought that dying old men must be bitter about losing it all and that they must be jealous of the young and healthy. But it's not that way for me. I just like being near that strong life in you."

"Dr. McKay, that's about the nicest thing one of my clients ever said to me," she said softly.

"Love being well and being alive," I said.

"I will," she said, but her voice was so soft I could scarcely hear it.

September 9

Too tired to speak into this thing last night after Victor's visit, and I'm still weary from the long meal and conversation.

I wonder: Are we telling the same stories through different lenses? You've told me of your deepening need for your journal, and the path—which you can't yet see—on which it may be leading you.

Do you remember me saying that I seduced my students? I hope you understood that I meant that asexually, that the art of seduction can be the art of teaching, too. But I suspect you have known that for a long time. I suspect that you are a better teacher than I ever was because of it.

I said I missed my students like I miss air. Do you not, too?

Victor has been going through the motions for years, and if we did not need intro-history teachers so badly, he would have been kicked out of the department years ago. But he clings to keep from drowning, and we all pretend he is part of the department, though at best he is like an old sofa cushion you can't bear to throw out.

But he is so much more, Lucy. He is a genuinely fine teacher. Did you know that? He has won our graduate teaching award three times and would have won it more if the committee hadn't finally (with his encouragement) ruled him ineligible to win again.

I saw you hug Mary Lou in the kitchen to thank her for taking care of me and for cooking such a wonderful meal. I saw your arms around each other, as if you stood in a Vermeer painting, washed with all light.

September 12

Very sick for three days, but I have asked Mary Lou not to call and bother you. The house shivers and shudders today with a new air mass come down from Canada, an early hint of autumn.

She tells me that Olaf is extremely ill and that the prognosis is not good. I called him at Dogear, and we talked for a while, but I would not subject him to my strange pauses and near-absences from the conversation, and he would not share his regrets or fear in a phone call.

September 13

The time is coming, and it is very soon, Lucy. Ever the professor and bookman, I have been writing and rewriting it in my mind for weeks—the way I will tell you, the manner in which you might take it.

I told Father Tanner I would just blurt it out the next time you are over, and he said I couldn't do that.

"It has to be special, Pratt," he said. "A special time and a special place. Epiphanies aren't for the living room. They should be for all time and with the beauty of the ages."

"Not to put pressure on me or anything, Jack," I said. He laughed at me.

"That's my *job*, Pratt."

So it is. And mine? To do what I have only partly done so far: to bring you home.

September 15

The president of the university called me last night and said everyone was waiting for me to come back to my office and my home in Chapel Hill. I told him I appreciated it but that I would be retiring immediately.

"Why, Pratt, that would be one of the saddest events in school history," he said. He is a good man, and it would be small of me to believe that losing a Pulitzer winner would put a dent in fundraising. I am not that valuable. No one is.

"I'm too sick to return, and I'm set up fine here," I said. "Sometimes we just have to let go of what we love best."

"But it hurts," he said. I don't press it, knowing he lost his son to a car accident a few years back.

"It hurts," I said.

But Lucy, it only hurts if you haven't grabbed on to something else.

September 16

Your mother called me last night from Duke, and I told her what has happened, and she was quiet for a moment.

"It's almost perfect, isn't it, Pratt?" she said softly. "The way things worked out? With her there? It's almost perfect?"

"Almost. It's probably more than I deserve considering the way I lived my life. For how I betrayed you when we were young and just married. It's funny, but when I married you, I thought I was going to be one of the greatest husbands in the history of the world." She laughed.

"I know you did. You waited on me like I was a queen and told me every day how beautiful I was. But even then it wasn't right. Even before you found Rachel it wasn't right. And it wasn't just you. I never went to bed with anyone else until you told me about her, but I wasn't really faithful, either. Kissing and fondling at graduate parties, half-naked beneath the coats in some professor's guest room with a boy I barely knew."

"At least my philandering was monogamous." We both laughed.

"And Lucy? How's my sweet girl? I talk to her but I'm not sure. I always say the wrong things."

"She's finding her way. Losing James, even though they were divorced, seemed to hit her hard. You need to come see her soon. Make the time. Your job isn't everything. Others can handle the lectures for a couple of days."

"I will. She hasn't known what to say to me since you told her the truth. To be honest, I haven't quite known what to say to her. Pratt?"

"Mmmm?"

"You sound *so* old." She burst into tears, and I had to comfort her—an odd role for me at this point in our lives.

I must believe you have talked to her before you are hearing this, Lucy. If not, call her and invite her to your new home. Tell her the sweet distractions that have changed your heart.

Honey? It's Mary Lou. Your dad's asleep in his breakfast-nook recliner, and I wanted to sneak in here in make an entry in his audio journal. He won't know because he never rewinds it—his life only moves forward now.

If you knew how hard he has worked to straighten out his life as his body has failed him, you'd be so proud. So proud. I have never seen a man who is more set on making a miracle happen. Being with him has been such a joy for me, because he awakens every day with a desire to stay alive and to stave off death.

He tells me now that he sees that he lost you a long time ago and wants to mend things before he is gone if he can. Everything he has done has been for that. And darling, you don't yet know half of what he has done. He plans to tell you soon, and I keep hoping the right moment will come, but I worry he will keep putting it off.

Should I call you and somehow prompt you to call him? If I do, will you forgive me?

I wonder if you *can* forgive me. Forgiveness is a hard stone, dear, among the hardest on this Earth, but it can be a gemstone, you know. My own apologies would take years and even then be left unfinished.

You let days go by without calling him. Come to him and let him pour out his truth, darling. If you want to ease his passing, give him that. I should not be in here! He's calling my name!

September 20

Mary Lou came out on the warm sunny deck this afternoon and said she'd called you just to talk.

"To talk about what?"

"Girl talk. You wouldn't be interested." Ah, so we are in the land of euphemism! I've been here often. But she is right. I should not wait for you to call me. It is just that I fear worrying and interrupting you. I remember the mighty irritation of a ringing phone when I was in bed with an unexpected conquest—hers or mine I never knew. Sometimes, God help me, I answered it, telling her it might be from my publisher or from some bigwig who owed me a call. The last thing I want you to hear when making love is your father's voice.

"I *would* be interested," I said.

"Then it's a secret," she said. "Mind your own beeswax, professor."

October first. The beginning of my favorite month, and yours, too—or at least it always was. The day on which our story will change.

September 22

A tremendous storm last night, and as the thunder roared, I cried aloud, and Mary Lou came from her book in the den and lay beside me in my bed and held me close and hushed me—I was half-asleep and fearful as a child. I came to my senses in her arms, and she rubbed my legs alive with alcohol and said she had the weather on and that the storms were strong but not severe.

After that comfort, I slept for twelve hours and awoke for your visit today in good spirits and almost ready for what must come. I was in my recliner when you arrived, and I could tell from your eyes that the calmness in my heart surprised you.

Mary Lou went to bake bread, and you and I talked, and I began by trying to connect what she was doing in the kitchen with my "famous" book. You weren't buying it. I managed to apologize for making you perform at grad parties when you were a little girl, and you said "don't overrate your sins," which was absolutely priceless. Then I said it:

"The first Saturday in October. *Then*."

"Then *what?*" you asked.

"All will be revealed," I said. I got Mary Lou to put on the Strauss *Four Last Songs* then, a sentimental twist to things, I know, but, oh dear God, how perfect it felt. And so I did, for once, exactly what I had to do: I bathed in joy.

September 23

I am an insufferable mess of tics and tangles, Lucy, and tonight the weakness washes over me in huge waves, as the sea does to us when we are small and staying close to shore. And yet I am still alive in this body as Olaf Knussen no longer is in his.

I imagine his body's favor in lowering him to the grave while asleep and before the real suffering began. Or was it God? We have never spoken much of God, that topic being in perpetual bad taste among us intellectuals. I have never thought of God as some male stand-in, some human-cloaked deity dabbling in Earthly matters. To me God is the sum of the best of us and the place where our ideas of the universe must necessarily begin. Social historians never get back that far, but I know the Civil Rights movement was never far from the church, at least not until the Black Power days. All those men were ministers, and like many ministers, they were strong and weak at the same time.

How do we know if God guides us? If there is a God of pity, I believe he must have leaned down to touch Olaf and bring him into eternal rest. I have thought much lately about that phrase "eternal rest," and it seems beautiful and plaintive to me. It originated when life was short and suffering was long. People did not look ahead to supposed glory or a long, healthy retirement as most people in Cedar Acres have. They looked forward only to eternal rest. They worked themselves into the grave, and in the end, they were put to bed forever. No more work. No more pain. No more suffering for themselves or those they love.

I will not have minded suffering if I have suffered for you, Cricket. Eternal rest will come soon enough. In my prayers for Jan and Jared and even for Olaf's "eternal soul," if there is such a thing, I find room to pray also for you, my beloved.

September 24

Quick call from you: have I heard? I have heard. Cremation, no service, a simple end to a good life. To me, he still sits in the glass office of that old house he turned into Dogear, chewing on his pipe and reading.

He is part of our story, too. Did you know? Have you begun to understand yet?

September 25

Mary Lou took me for a long ride today through the increasingly autumnal mountains, and we spoke of our long separate lives and how we remembered the key moments in them—births, deaths, and the shattering world events.

"The hardest thing is remembering that we can't take what happens out in the world personally," she said. "Like it's happening just to us. But we do, don't we? Like our country's latest mindless war is directed at me alone, created to enrage me. But we are not the world, are we? We're not even small cogs in a big machine. We're letters in words on pages in a book that has no end."

"How can a home health nurse get this smart?" I asked, laughing.

"I'm a reader, Pratt," she said. "My mother said I was born with a book in my hand. When I was a little girl, my father told me that I'd probably read as many books as there were freckles on my face.

Well, the freckles faded away, but the books didn't. I've even read *your* miserable books."

"Then you've known boredom."

"You're adequate on your best days," she said. I roared.

She took me to familiar roadside overlooks, from which a man can see the world below. At the Brushy Mountain overlook, we could see all of eastern North Carolina. She unfolded my wheelchair and help me out and rolled me to the edge—God what a view.

"I'll buy you this if you want it," I said, trying to extend my arms in a suitably god-like attitude.

"I already own it," she said, and I knew instantly what she meant. We both owned it at that instant, and I rose with hawks on the day's thermals and became part of the story of that one spot for one moment, one day. This one small life, well-enough told.

September 28

So Mary Lou is now repenting for taking me out, since it took me two days to recover. She is sorry to have pushed me so hard, but I absolve her.

I was reading Stephen Ambrose around mid-day when the doorbell rang, and she answered it, and your friend Sean Crayton came in, smelling like the soil in which he digs. He looked different, and then I realized he had cut off the beard and was now letting it grow back.

He came over and knelt by my chair.

"It's about to storm, and I thought I'd drop by and see how you are," he said.

"Quite well, in fact. I presume from the visit that you are still seeing Lucy? She doesn't tell me much about that kind of thing."

"Seeing her? As long as she will let me. I've had a bad summer. Lots of things in my life...well, I guess you know about some of them."

"Some. Not much, really. Are you all right?"

"Things are getting…clarity. That's an odd way to say it. But it's right. I'm starting to understand things. I was wondering if that's true as we grow older…I mean, in general, has it been your experience…."

"Do we get wiser as we age?" I knew he was asking me for fatherly advice, and I desperately wanted to say the right thing, Lucy. "No. Or if we do, that's grace. If we keep our eyes and our minds open, though, we get more charitable about ourselves and others. We learn that if there is a holiness in life it must begin with forgiveness and end with love."

He simply nodded. I stopped myself before I could lecture, before I could begin to spin homilies and ruin the sentiment. Let it go right there, I thought. Wrap it up and let it go. Then he did something shocking. He had been squatting by my chair, and he reached out and put his hand on my arm and squeezed it, and when he stood fully, he leaned down and kissed me on the forehead.

As he walked out, I saw Mary Lou standing in the doorway to the kitchen, silent, arms folded over her chest, and tears streaming down her cheeks.

September 29

A strong cold front just after seven last evening and with it a new world, a new mass of air, sharp and fresh—a new season and a time for every purpose under heaven.

September 30

A nearly all-day visit to Dr. Retherston in Asheville, Lucy, and this time I did not sit in his waiting room as if part of the Damned awaiting sentence. I know my sentence well enough and have accepted it.

What I fear is our meeting tomorrow and my confession. Not "fear"—that is the wrong word, for I totter on the knife-edge of ecstasy in thinking about it. But I am anxious to tell you properly. The weather, Mary Lou says, will be gorgeous. You do not know it yet but I have arranged to take you to a place you know already—that stretch of the Camhatchie River that Sean still owns, where you picnicked with him.

Dr. Retherston put his hand on my shoulder and told me that I was no worse and that it was possible—he heavily stressed the word *possible*—that the progress of the MS may have slowed a bit.

"It certainly isn't getting any worse any faster," he said. "She's taking good care of you, isn't she?"

"I couldn't begin to explain," I said.

"My advice is to love every day that you feel well and don't be angry on days when you feel bad. My sense of it is that we have more to live for than we think we do."

"What do you do besides being a doctor?"

"I carve duck decoys and paint them," he said, laughing. "You're the first person who has ever asked me that question. And I don't even hunt. And I refuse to give them to hunters. They take my mind off everything. We need that, don't we?"

We do, Lucy. I have a sense, too, what it is you need, and I pray that you will forgive what I have done. Just say no to him if you're not interested. But I'm guessing you will feel that gravitational tug and say yes.

I need to rest now and gather my strength for tomorrow. Do you know how much I love you? How much I have always loved you?

9. Lucy

Is the truth always before us, calm and waiting as we slowly open our eyes? Now that the day is gone, now that midnight is only a few ticks away, I sit with my journal by the fireplace embers I will not quite let die. I am afraid that if I close my eyes the beauty will slip away.

I must tell this slowly now, write with the deliberation of lineage, even if I am awake until dawn. I believe what happened today and do not; its perfection dazzles me, and yet I feel myself filling with bittersweet wonder. Surely there must be some graceful way to say my life began today, that all before this is unsettled prelude. Can I feel this great change without lapsing into greeting card sentimentality? I must try. I will write, and *then* I will weep. Yet again.

I awoke to a day of the most wondrous glory—pastel blue morning, a fleece of golden, mythic clouds hanging low, and a promise of revelation. All I knew was that I was to arrive at Pratt's house at noon and that we would be driving out for a picnic.

"Driving out where?" I asked two nights ago on the phone.

"Some place without wild animals or humans," he said. "A beautiful place, I promise. I won't get you chigger-bit or gnawed up by mosquitoes."

I had five hours between awakening and the picnic, so how would I fill my nervous hours? Sean helped, walking into the bathroom unannounced, having not spent the night here, while I was showering and scaring me half to death.

"Jesus, I thought you were a serial killer," I cried, sticking my head out and holding the curtain over me like a Wagnerian shield.

"Nah, serial killers come in with cutlery, not with flowers," he said. His large body filled my eyes and the cramped bathroom, but his smile seemed even wider. He held a single yellow rose, my favorite blossom. "Just wanted to tell you to break a leg or whatever is appropriate."

"That's the best thing you can say to a naked lady?" I asked. My hair was soaked and stringy. I would not have been happier to see God Himself, and Sean knew it.

"How do I know you're naked? You're holding a groundcover over you." He came close and kissed me on the lips.

"Very funny, you." I thought he might climb in. I relaxed my death grip on the curtain and when it still covered me, I gently pulled it back, desperate for his eyes on my body. He roamed me, loving what he saw, lips slightly parted but knowing it could wait. We no longer needed to hurry. We have time. So he handed me the rose, kissed my lips, kissed my clavicle, kissed my hot wet right nipple, raised one eyebrow, and was gone. I pulled the curtain back and stood in the warm rain with the rose, feeling vaguely unhappy that he hadn't said he loved me. But he does. I raised the flower into the flow, and it seemed to exult.

I refused to listen to or watch the news. I didn't even turn on NPR, instead racking up five CDS in my player—Freedy Johnson, Ravel, ZZ Top, Nickel Creek, and finally the Eagles. Halfway through "Pavane for a Dead Princess," the phone rang, and I hit pause and answered it, praying it was not Mary Lou telling me my father was too ill for the picnic.

"Ms. McKay?" I said it was and pivoted to set my empty cup in the sink. I walked the phone on to my sunny deck. Spangles burnished the strongly turning hardwoods. "This is Robert Newfeld, and I'm principal of Haycombe County High School here?"

"Oh. Right." Immediately I thought of Jared, but he goes to a private school. Instantly I knew: I was being suspended, and he was telling me before he told my father. I giggled into the receiver and then had to explain. He laughed in a relaxed and appealing way. "I still find myself walking up and down the hall wondering what I'm doing here. And I'm fifty-eight. You'd think after forty years you'd forget being in high school. But we never do."

"If I'm not being suspended, how can I help you, Mr. Newfeld?"

"I was hoping I might talk you into helping me. We have a senior English teacher named Kelly Cartwright who's going on pregnancy leave after Christmas. This is her second child, and she had so much trouble with the first that she's going to be on bed rest even though the baby's not due until April."

"I see." No, I thought: *Don't ask it.* Then: *God, please ask me, please please ask me.*

"I'm a social friend of your father's. We have been looking for someone to fill in for Kelly for the second half of the year, and he somehow heard about it. He said you probably wouldn't be interested since you'd just left your job down in Oxford. I called your principal. Well, she's the acting principal right now. I understand there's been some problem." I tried not to laugh, but I found myself smiling wickedly. "Anyway, she said you were the most respected teacher in the school. That losing you was, in her words, a nightmare. That's the word she used. A 'nightmare.' So I'm here hat in hand, offering you a half-year teaching job. Your accreditation is fine, and your experience speaks for itself. I won't try to snow you. A lot of these are kids from rural families where education isn't the first priority. Staying alive is. But there's one student, Mary June Andrews, who is a junior this year and wants to be a writer. She makes straight A's, and Ms. Cartwright says she writes like an angel. I'm not quite sure what that means. I was the football coach."

The apology and irony in his voice charmed me, and I found myself ready to say no thank you, but instead I imagined Mary June, saw her standing before my desk on a spring morning with something she had written. She would be thin, with messy hair, and the eyes of a minor zealot, begging me for one word of approval.

"I'm taking a year off," I said slowly, "but this comes as a....What did my father say about me? Can I ask that?"

"Well, to be honest, he said you were beautiful. He was talking about the whole person, I took it. As a person and a teacher. He said you are beautiful. I have two girls myself. I knew what he meant. He didn't have to explain it."

I would never be unprofessional but one soft sigh escaped—one easy gasp of sweet surrender. Was Mr. Newfeld *this* smart? I leaned against the porch rail.

"Tell you what. I wouldn't say I'm interested, but I have to think about it. Could I have a couple of days?"

"Of course, Ms. McKay. Let me give you my home and cell numbers."

I stood on the deck after the call was over, thrilled to be wanted and still knowing what it would mean—committees, idiotic paperwork, sleeping slackers, petulant mothers, and a steady stream of minor scandals. I twirled my rose, careful not to let the thorns cut me.

I never took the CD player off "pause." After a while in the pregnant silence, I turned it off. A thousand narratives flitted around me like monarch's wings. When the phone rang again, I jumped and pressed a palm against my chest to keep the heart from leaping out.

It was Lona Belle, teacher friend, calling from her desk during planning period back in Oxford.

"Craziest thing," she said after we had shared news. "Some of the younger writers are sort of turning your James into guitar hero kind of thing."

"*Excuse* me?"

"I mean, as a writer, hon. A lot of them knew him, the younger ones. He'd lived in New York, knew a lot of people, and had a literary agent. That's a big thing, I hear, to have an agent. There's talk of having a conference in his honor. I heard things about the grave and went out there after school yesterday, and it's half covered with pennies and pencils. People are coming by and leaving pencils and pens!"

"Jesus, Lona Belle. James is getting famous, and he never published a word? Oh, my God. That's America."

"Whatever that means. And I hear by a birdie that you're going to back in the classroom come January."

"What?! I just got off the phone with the principal here an hour ago. How in the hell do you know that? Wait. Never mind. I know how. He said he called the school."

"I thought I was pregnant again for a couple of days. I sat in the bedroom and cried and wouldn't come out and called Bobby Joe every name in the book. False alarm." She sang the last two words.

Before heading to Pratt's I drove to Dogear and found Jan helping a customer who was looking over an old copy of *Leaves of Grass*. Three or four people wandered around, and the shop was brighter—she'd brought in new lighting—and Bach played on the sound system. The customer started nodding, *kept* nodding, and then cradled the book, and I knew it was sold. Jan cocked a delighted eyebrow, and I followed her into the office.

"Do you like it? I mean being here every day with the books and the people?"

"I love it," she said, eyes aglow. "I have no idea why I wasn't here before. It worried me for awhile, but then I decided to forget it. Life doesn't make sense. It's a waste of time to pretend it does." I told her about the offer to teach. "What do you think?"

"Do you know anything about the high school? You were a reporter here."

"It actually has a good reputation. Not the best. You could see why Jared wouldn't fit there. He barely fits anywhere. But it's solid. That's the word I think I'd use. Shitty football team. Great band. Pretty bad literary magazine and a school paper that's won some awards, I think. Newfeld is a good man. He was a helicopter pilot in the Gulf War, I think. His wife is a home health nurse."

"Well, shit."

"What?"

"Never mind," I said. I was laughing, and it would have taken too long to unravel all the associations with my new best friend. "I've got to go."

"How's Sean?" She smiled hopefully, wanting details.

"He brought me a yellow rose this morning while I was still in the shower."

"Oh, my God that's romantic. That doesn't sound like me does it? Well, there you have it. I'm a closet romantic. You tell anybody I said that I'll pull your hair out." She only kissed my cheek, though.

❧

My heart was beating rapid iambs as I pulled into Pratt's driveway and parked to one side on the concrete pad. All morning I had been too distracted to think much of what my father's revelation might bring me. I had a sick feeling that he would be handing me a huge check or giving me his house. Surely he had more to give me than that.

Mary Lou met me at the door, bright eyed, tall and lithe as a girl.

"How is he?" I whispered. "It is worse?"

"He's nervous," she said brightly. "You know how men are. They will lead a thousand soldiers into machine gun fire, but they can't say how they feel. It's one of life's great mysteries."

"I can say how I feel, but I'd be running away if there was a fight. I mean, a serial killer came into the bathroom while I was taking a shower this morning, and I almost had a heart attack." She nodded, waiting. "He didn't have a knife. He had a rose."

"Sean."

"Am I *that* predictable?"

"You seem like the kind of girl who wants one lover at a time," she said, cupping my cheek with her warm palm. Her eyes narrowed

276

as if she were telling me something, and she was, though I was too dense to know it.

Pratt, who all summer had worn flannel pajama bottoms was in the den, standing by himself and dressed for the classroom—khakis and a crisp blue Oxford shirt, black penny loafers, and dandy's cane on which he leaned, grinning.

"I hope you're hungry, young woman," he said. "You look malnourished. Nurse, doesn't this young woman look malnourished?"

"No, she looks fine," said Mary Lou. "Come on, you two." She went to my father, and he tenderly took her arm, and she helped him to the Escalade while I got the two heavy picnic baskets from the kitchen and put them in the back. The vehicle was massive, and I wanted to unburden myself about its wasteful size, but Pratt needed the room. Mary Lou drove and I sat in the back.

"I picked the music," said Pratt, turning. He nodded to Mary Lou, who stuck a mix-CD in, and Bob Dylan came on, followed by Frank Sinatra, Eric Clapton, and the Jefferson Airplane.

"Where exactly is this place you're taking me?" I asked. My father said something but I couldn't understand, so I leaned over the seat and asked again.

"You'll see," repeated Mary Lou.

Soon enough, I knew, though I didn't understand: Sean's secret trout stream. I wanted to ask, wanted to unravel the DNA strands of the day's story, but by the time we got there I was so nervous I could not speak. Pratt was worse, his face a ruin of need, and his nurse helped him to a huge flat rock near the stream, where she laid out a blanket and we set down the baskets. I smiled and tried to think of something to say to my father, presuming small talk was best. Surely Mary Lou would leave us at the right time—stroll down the riverside in the autumn sunlight. But nothing happens as one dreams it must.

Instead, she sat close to my father and took his hand, and they looked at me together and for the first time I knew: They had fallen in love. He would marry her. It wasn't enough for me, and I cocked my head and nodded and then held my palms up to invite revelation.

"I was going to wait until we had eaten lunch, but I can't," Pratt said. His words were rough as droughty farmland. "It has taken me all my life to come back to the place where I stepped off the trail as a young man. It's scary to think most of us never get that chance."

"Pratt, what are you trying to tell me? Any chance you could just cut to the chase instead of giving me one of the patented McKay lectures? I've been a wreck wondering what is going on here."

Shockingly, Mary Lou Wadely came and sat right against me, hip to hip, her face an inch from mine. I looked from her to my father and then back, and in that length of time, I knew. In her cheeks and eyes, I saw mirror shards—pieces of my own image.

"Oh, my *God*," I managed. "Is this what I think it is?"

Pratt was up by then, struggling but walking, and he got to us and fell hard to his knees in front of me. Wind blew lovely leaves on the stream's currents, red on yellow, red on yellow.

"I am so sorry," she said. "I was young and scared, and I didn't know what to do. And then our lives went separate directions. Pratt raised you—that's all I knew. All my life I suffered knowing what I had done. It was a long journey here, a long journey back, and a long story. But I do love you. I have always loved you."

I couldn't breathe.

"I am so sorry I could not tell you before now," said Pratt, his voice a husk. His color was gone, and I felt afraid for him. "I was going to tell you on that tape. I had this idea that you would find out on the drive back to Oxford and then you'd have time to let the idea sink in. Then things changed."

"*You're* Rachel?" She held back, waiting. She nodded, eyes like lovely flames. I do not remember moving nor do I recall that she moved toward me. I tried to choke some kind of thought, but I realized that she and I were locked in a fierce sobbing embrace and that Pratt was close, then closer, then with us.

The shape of it shattered me. My *mother*. The first time I had hugged my own mother. And yet I had a mother I loved already. How should I feel now? And how could this change my feelings toward Pratt? It would all have to wait. We stayed like that for a long time, a very long time. She stroked my hair and kissed my cheeks. Pratt, exhausted, sat beside me and then leaned against Mary Lou. I grasped their hands and put my head against her neck.

"Honey? There's one more thing you need to know?" she whispered. I sat up, laughing. "Really, there's more?"

"I came here when my first cousin got sick. His wife had died some years ago, and he had cancer, but he went into long-term remission. I got divorced myself, oh God, a lifetime ago, so I came back east. He had a grown daughter."

I stood and walked away from them, wobbly with understanding, hand to my forehead, trying to put it together. The river flowed past me, and I remembered Sean standing in it, strong and sorrowful, saying how it would all soon be lost. Pratt must have asked Sean to name my favorite place. I knew who Mary Lou meant, but I couldn't believe it.

"Olaf," I said, turning. "He was your first cousin. My God, that means Jan and I are—what—*cousins* of some kind?"

"She doesn't even know, honey," said Mary Lou. "Don't blame her. I got erased from the family a long time ago. It would have been too much to explain, I thought. I was so wrong."

"Come here to me," said Pratt, and I obeyed him like a child. I sat with him, and he took my hands and looked me in the heart.

"We want to tell you the whole story of our lives, Lucy. How we came together, how we fell apart. How in the end we found each other again. It doesn't make any sense. I have spent my whole life away from you, but I want to spend whatever time I have left giving you the stories of your family. So you will know. Would that be all right?"

"That would be more than I ever dreamed," I said.

"We will go slowly, then," he said. "No need to learn everything in one day. I will live as long as I can. I have a good nurse."

"You changed your name?" I asked her after we began to eat the picnic.

"Yet another foolish mistake. As if changing a name can change who we are. We can't do that, Lucy. We're who we are born to be."

I had a thousand questions, and my stomach lay within me in a huge Gordian knot, but I told myself: *Don't hurry. Go slow. Let it take as long as a huge fresco, not a sketch.* And yet I had to hold my tongue to keep from peppering her with questions. Soon enough, Pratt looked too tired to stay, and she told me so with a glance, and I helped her bundle my sick father back in his car for the drive home.

I kissed him goodbye as he settled for a nap in his bed, and she walked me out to my car, and I turned sharply and grabbed her and held on and on and on. When I finally let her go, she kissed me softly and lightly on the lips, the way you kiss a frightened little girl to make the shadows go away.

I have not called Jan or told Sean. For the rest of this miraculous day I sat alone in the warm sun light and tried to make sense of my life and found that I couldn't. The clues were there before me all along, and I missed them. Each time I try to think about how I will manage this new life I cannot dream it. Twice I have gone to bed only to find myself unable to sleep.

Now, I have written myself out and am dreamily available for that newly rearranged world of night. I will never forget today, never. It will bless my bones. But to whom will I tell it? To whom will I pass it down?

April 18—Many Years Later

My God. Sean and I were cleaning the attic today, and I found this journal crammed behind a stack of ledgers. Four years have passed since that last entry—four indelible years of loss and joy, of new narratives and sweet sorrows.

How does one even begin to add words to such a story? Shall I try?

I still have Pratt's legacy tapes, so I will try to finish this journal for you, Casey, beloved daughter. You never knew your grandfather so perhaps you will, at the right age, read this journal and understand. I will tell you about the arc of love and how some are saved and some are not. Only then will you know why I hold you so fiercely. Only then will you understand who you are.

୬

My beloved father died of pneumonia the following May when the spring wildflowers had come full along the mountain ridges once more. By then he was bedridden with the MS. Rachel—by then she had legally changed her name back—had brought in a hospital bed and managed to squeeze it into the breakfast nook where his recliner had been.

It was a good death, Casey, slow and dignified. You know the hurricane lamps we keep for light when the power goes out? He passed away like turning one of those down as slowly as daylight goes out. Rachel and I took turns reading to him. In the last month or so, he was beyond us, but that March, while he could still speak a little, a great snow came, and school was canceled. I managed to get to his house, and he asked me to read to him by the fireplace.

"I want you to read me Milton," he said. I laughed.

"Milton?" (Honey, I'm going to pretend you are reading this at twenty-five and know what I am talking about. Otherwise, I could spend the rest of my life explaining.)

"I want to hear `Lycidas,'" he said, and I didn't quite remember why until I got to the part that framed his own dying days:

Weep no more, woeful shepherds, weep no more,
For Lycidas, your sorrow, is not dead,
Sunk though he be beneath the watery floor;

So sinks the day-star in the ocean-bed,
And yet anon repairs his drooping head
And tricks his beams, and with his new-spangled ore
Flames in the forehead of the morning sky:
So Lycidas sunk low, but mounted high
Through the dear might of Him that walk'd the waves;
Where, other groves and streams along
With nectar pure his oozy locks he laves,
And hears the unexpressive nuptial song
In the blest kingdoms meek of joy and love.
There entertain him all the saints above
In solemn troops, and sweet societies,
That sing, and singing, in their glory move,
And wipe the tears for ever from his eyes.
Now, Lycidas, the shepherds weep no more;
Henceforth though art the Genius of the shore
In thy large recompense, and shalt be good
To all that wander in that perilous flood.

I just wrote that from memory, Casey—how could I forget? It isn't the last verse of the poem, but it was the last one I could read before I wept—before my own flood. What a gorgeous and lovely moment it was. I lay my head on his chest by the firelight, and we could hear the sound of wind and snow and Rachel in the kitchen making tea for us.

"I love you," he said in his fading voice, and with his stricken hand he stroked my hair.

"I love you," I said.

Pure grace—no other words describe it. To have had that moment made the hours of his passing somehow calmer and sweeter. He simply slept away.

You know him simply as a famous ancestor—the grandfather who won the Pulitzer Prize but who died before you came along. But to me he was an emblem of atonement, a man who suffered to right his youthful wrongs, something very few of us do. That takes courage. So please know that your grandfather Pratt McKay was a courageous man, Casey.

If ambition almost destroyed him, love saved him in the end as it always does the lucky ones among us.

By the time he died, your father's business had gone from modestly prosperous to ungovernably successful. I kept his books for a while after school each day, but he began to hire more and more people. Within a year, he had the largest landscaping business in western North Carolina. In three years, the franchise covered the South. His first stores in the West and Northeast will open this fall. If you are grown as you read this, you know more than I do! After all, you are only three years old now!

✍

Who am I? I am a wife—Sean asked me to marry him a few weeks after my father died, and of course I said I would. We were married in a civil ceremony at the riverside in what is now the James H. Crayton Wildlife Sanctuary—a thousand acres set aside in memory of his father. Also, with my inheritance and Sean's success, we have endowed two chairs at UNC—one in MS research and another in Civil Rights history.

It was a lovely wedding ceremony—the Earth provided her own landscaping, and Sean brought me a single yellow rose. We lived in his modest house for a year, but as his business prospered, we designed and built this house you know so well, this "green" and sprawling home high on a mountainside, invisible from land or air. As you know, he carves wood to keep the quieter pleasures close.

I am a mother. You, Casey Pratt Crayton, are our darling girl, with a birthday of July 21—the same as Hemingway and Hart Crane. You have your father's chin dimple and my eyes, his hands and my toes. You began to talk a little late and then began to babble in recognizable polysyllables—clearly your mother's daughter. You are blonde and have green eyes and love amateur theatricals and nature walks. My fellow teachers adore you and pass you around like a stuffed animal, spoiling you with small gifts and sweets. You are afraid of thunder and leap suddenly into bed between your father and me without warning. (If we hear thunder, we stop whatever we are doing to get ready for your arrival—you will understand later, or now, if you really are reading this as an adult!)

I am a cousin. Of course I had cousins before, but Jan was my surprise cousin. I know you call her Auntie Jan, and Jared, her brainy boy, makes valentines and "books" for you. You spent many rainy afternoons crawling around on the floor of Dogear while I ran an errand, and Jan looked after you. Jared stayed with us for a month when Jan went to Europe with her boyfriend (and now husband) Liam. We became family.

I am a teacher. The woman I replaced decided not to return, and they hired me full-time, and I understood how badly I missed "my" students and how much I needed the sinecure of classroom and hallways. This is not my *job*; it is the shape of my days, Casey, the meaning in me. I thought I was going to be a writer—I even "told my diary" that I would be a writer. But I was wrong. I am a teacher, and my father knew that as surely as he knew that waterfall across his valley would continue to fall.

I am a friend. Victor Ullman, Pratt's assistant from Chapel Hill, married his scientist friend Ginny Whelton, and they got jobs at Southern Mississippi—tenure-track assistant professorships. Better late, he writes, than never. The Oxford crowd is unchanged—Lona Bell and Laurie Teagarten, my best teacher friends; Luna Marcovic, hairdresser of vague Eastern European origin; Rico, the Cuban who dresses well and works in a poultry plant; and Bobby Vunal, still idly poor. Timothy Sain sends us a Christmas card from San Francisco. I do not know what he does now, but he is not a physicist. Hunt Bearden died last year, and his Betty moved back to Pennsylvania, Ella Seitz is in a rest home near Raleigh, no doubt still lost in echolalia. Father Tanner is still at St. Michael's and still comforts the comfortable, as he says.

I am a daughter. Things are better with the Thomas and Morene Schantz Professor of Art History at Duke, though I suspect we will never be close again. She calls me to check, and I call her. She comes to visit you, Casey, but not so often. Not as often as she should. I wish this part of the story had turned out better, but so far, it hasn't. Rachel lives in the house we bought her half a mile away, a comfortable and small place, but she has no intention of retiring soon and works all day as a home health nurse. She dotes on you, Casey, and she gives me what she never did for all those decades she was out of my life.

I am a memory-keeper, too. James's novel, in the end, was like his life—good stretches and terrible ones, no real coherence and no epiphany. The friends who sought to turn him into a hero moved on, and now he is forgotten except for the small stone I bought to mark his grave in Oxford.

&

We are consumed by what we fear most. I wrote that back at the beginning of this journal, and it is still true, sweetheart. I came to the mountains that summer because I had lost the meaning of fathers and daughters and wanted to know him as I never properly had. Neither of us could have known how it would turn out.

Years from now, if someone asks how you came to be a mountain girl, say it was because of a father's love and let it go at that. It will be twice true—for my father and for yours. My life and Sean's changed at the same time and in much the same way. We have always believed that we were "meant" to find each other, that sometimes in the webs of life where we lie trapped, a sibling spirit arrives—that brother/sister/lover who can salve our suffering like no other; who can make us laugh in the hard, dark times; and who can with a kiss unbreak the world's broken boundaries. In the same way, I believe that my father knew what might happen when he invited me up that summer. Healing is a slow art but a great and necessary one, Casey.

The other night when Rachel was headed home, she kissed you, and your face frowned for a moment, a sweet darkening.

"Be back soon?" you asked, in your just-learning-to-talk voice. She touched your nose with the tip of her finger.

"Right as rain," she whispered.

You waved as she drove off, smiling again, leaning, like our family's history, against my grateful heart.

The Author

Philip Lee Williams is the much-honored author of numerous volumes of fiction, poetry, and creative non-fiction. He won the 2004 Michael Shaara Award for the best Civil War novel published in the U. S. He has also been named Georgia Author of the Year four times in three different categories, and won a Georgia Governor's Award in the Humanities. In addition, he was also awarded the Townsend Prize for Fiction, and is a member of the Georgia Writers Hall of Fame. *Far Beyond the Gates* is his twentieth published book and his thirteenth novel. He lives in the country in north central Georgia with his wife, Linda.